Praise for
Crystal Lies

"Raw, real, and provocative, *Crystal Lies* thrusts us into a world inhabited by more people than we may realize on the surface. This account of one mother's struggle for the healing of her drug-addicted son speaks to all who have ever loved anyone else. Melody Carlson never fails to drag us out of our Christian easy chairs and right into the coals of the confusing culture in which we find ourselves. She never fails to reveal that place of compassion within each of us. Excellent."

> —LISA SAMSON, author of *The Church Ladies* and *Tiger Lillie*

"As an addiction specialist, I was moved by *Crystal Lies*. With great confidence, I can say that Melody Carlson's story will enlighten, encourage, and empower you. Read this book; walk through its pages toward healthy, God-directed relationships."

> —GREGORY L. JANTZ, PH.D., founder and executive director
> of The Center for Counseling & Health Resources, Inc.

"An honest, doesn't-pull-any-punches look at the reality of addiction and codependency in Christian families. Told in Carlson's adept style, this novel will lead readers into the light of a powerful God, who stands firm and loves beyond all measure and who delights in meeting his children inside the world's most impenetrable, convoluted issues. I found myself praying Carlson's prayers over my own children as I lay in bed. Read, enjoy, and—most important—pass this along to everyone you know who is struggling with addiction."

> —DEBORAH BEDFORD, author of *If I Had You, Just Between Us*
> and *When You Believe*

"*Crystal Lies* creates a permanent image of a family in pain and the various ways they choose to sugarcoat their lives rather than face it. We are this family, whether touched by methamphetamine use, alcohol addiction, super-perfection and adultery or not. We are this family because we avoid, separate, pretend blindness, live inside fogs of drugs or denial because to face the pain alone is just too great. What Melody reveals through her crisp yet tender words is that we are not alone even when we separate ourselves. God has chosen to bring each of us closer. We are given the gift of hope and God's love to take us through the lies, pain, and disappointment into a steadied peace. Melody's *Crystal Lies* is *brilliant.* Her best."

—JANE KIRKPATRICK, award-winning author of The Tender Ties series

"Melody Carlson knows addiction is an issue that affects not only addicts but their families, their friends, their associates. And she shows that when the addict is a believer, addiction affects the body of Christ. *Crystal Lies* is a wonderful lesson, taught the way Jesus taught—in story. I recommend it especially to those of us who have believed we were being charitable when we looked at those marginalized by addiction and thought, 'There but for the grace of God go I.' Carlson's highly personable prose puts that viewpoint on its ear and teaches us to see it as, 'Here we are together, in need of God's grace.' *Crystal Lies* is clearly truth—revealed in fiction."

—TOM MORRISEY, author of *Yucatan Deep* and *Turn Four*

"*Crystal Lies* pulls no punches about the emotional devastation caused by addictions, and yet it offers beautiful, accessible hope. Having been through the turmoil of addictive behavior in my own family, I wept with both the agony and the joy of what I read. Don't miss this book!"

—JANELLE BURNHAM SCHNEIDER, author of "From Carriage to Marriage" in the *Brides for a Bit* anthology and "A Distant Love" in the *Christmas Duty* anthology

Crystal lies

Other Books by Carlson

NOVELS
Finding Alice
Armando's Treasure
Looking for Cassandra Jane
Angels in the Snow
The Gift of Christmas Present

TEEN NOVELS
Diary of a Teenage Girl series, 1-12
TrueColors series, 1-9

NONFICTION
Lost Boys and the Moms Who Love Them
Take Time
Women Are Sisters at Heart
Letters from God

CHILDREN'S BOOKS
The Easterville Miracle
When the Creepy Things Come Out
'Twas the Night
Bitsy's Harvest Party

Crystal Lies

A NOVEL BY

MELODY CARLSON

WATERBROOK
PRESS

CRYSTAL LIES
PUBLISHED BY WATERBROOK PRESS
2375 Telstar Drive, Suite 160
Colorado Springs, Colorado 80920
A division of Random House, Inc.

ISBN 1-57856-840-4

Library of Congress Cataloging-in-Publication Data
Carlson, Melody.
  Crystal lies / Melody Carlson.— 1st ed.
      p. cm.
  1. Married women—Fiction. 2. Mothers and sons—Fiction. 3. Ice (Drug)—Fiction.
4. Drug abuse—Fiction. 5. Adultery—Fiction. I. Title.
  PS3553.A73257C795 2004
  813'.54—dc22

                                                        2004011320

Printed in the United States of America
2004—First Edition

10 9 8 7 6 5 4 3 2 1

To Lucas Andrew

Your strength is inspiring!
Thank you for sharing your life and experience with me.

Addiction messes with your mind. And I don't mean just the addict's mind. Unfortunately, an addict's life affects everyone around him, mostly the ones who really love him. As the mother of a son who has gone through, has been treated for, and is recovering from addiction, I understand from a closeup perspective how devastating addiction can be. When I wrote the first draft of *Crystal Lies,* I tossed out the chronological time line, and like a Ping-Pong ball, I jumped back and forth between seasons and events—one chapter was summer, the next was winter. I did this purposely to show how life doesn't travel in a neat, smooth line for the family of an addict. Sometimes you go down the same road over and over, and other times you feel as if you're going in circles. And too often you wind up on a dead-end street.

Of course, my wise editor quickly realized that this style of writing, although it might artistically portray the frustration and confusion of a codependent parent, would probably just bewilder the reader. And so I straightened it out. Well, mostly. I still allow the story to hop around in a couple of places, but I hope and pray that you'll bear with me and that you'll try to get inside the skin of another person—a person whose life has been turned upside down and inside out by drug addiction, codependency, and recovery.

Acknowledgments

I want to thank all of my publishing friends at WaterBrook Press. You guys are such pros! I really appreciate the quality of attention that each of you gives, and I always know I'm in good hands through every step of the process. Thanks so much!

Chapter 1

Late fall

I haven't seen my son in nearly a week now. Always a bad sign. But I'm trying not to think about that at the moment. Unfortunately, that's a bit like trying not to think about purple elephants—as soon as you tell yourself not to, it's all you can imagine. The mind is funny that way.

I saw a public-service ad on TV this morning. "Parents, the antidrug," is the theme, and it shows a tough-love mom grounding her teenage son after she discovers him smoking pot. This woman is quite impressive, solid as a rock, and almost believable. But what the ad fails to show is what happens later. What does she do when her son totally ignores his "grounding" and sneaks out after everyone's asleep? What then?

Really, I'd like to know what in life prepares a parent for something as invasive as drugs? Where is the *How to Prevent Your Son from Becoming an Addict* handbook when you need it? Or is this simply the kind of thing you must sort out after the fact? Is this just one of those painful lessons that just goes on and on?

And some days, like today, I don't even have the energy to consider these questions. All I can do is put one foot in front of the other and try to remember how to breathe. I honestly don't know where I'll go from here. Maybe I don't even care. Or maybe it makes no difference.

When I think of what my life used to be—all that's been lost this past year—I feel as if I've been filleted with a dull and rusty knife and my insides are now spilled out across the dirty pier for curious onlookers to view and to judge. But my therapist says I must face all this if I want to get better. In order to recover, I must allow myself to grieve. And in order to grieve, I must acknowledge what's been lost. It feels like a vicious cycle of pain to me, a spiraling hopelessness without end. But I promised her I'd try.

I've only seen Dr. Abrams for a couple of months now, but she appears to be a sensible person, reasonable and caring, and I *want* to trust her. But it's been my trusting nature that's betrayed me in the past. Or so it seems. Although I have learned at least one thing through all this, and it has become my number-one rule in dealing with my son, Jacob, especially lately, and that is to never trust an addict. It felt harsh and unloving at first, especially since I'm talking about my only son, but I have come to believe it is necessary and, more important, true. Because the fact is, drugs are liars. They convince the user that their chemical highs will make him happy, but all they do is destroy him. Even so, the user falls for it again and again. Oh sure, he may end up facedown in the gutter, locked up in jail, or even nearly dead from an overdose, but he still believes the drugs. Jacob's drug of choice, crystal meth, is one of the worst liars. And I'm sure that's what's occupying my son right now, but as usual, I am digressing. My goal is to focus on my own life today. Why is that so difficult?

My promise to Dr. Abrams was to ask myself how I got to this place. I know she wasn't referring to this physical place, but as I sit here in this shabby, two-bedroom apartment that still smells faintly of pets I have never owned, I have to wonder. Day after day I look out at the busy street below and watch others. I study those people who have places to go and people to see as I make a feeble attempt to chart the series of events that have dragged me to what seems an almost certain dead end. Still I am determined to try to make some sense of what feels completely absurd and almost random at times. Or perhaps I will simply follow my best friend's lead and take up smoking to cope with the losses in life.

It's hard to believe that less than three years ago I was actually living out the American dream. A spacious and beautiful home on the hill, in-ground pool in the backyard, a Porsche and a Range Rover in the garage, a dog and a cat, and neighbors who not only knew our first names but had celebrated birthdays, anniversaries, and various milestone events with us over the years. It seemed so, well, perfect. There's no other word for it really, and that's what makes it all so ironic.

During our last year of "normal," Jacob was sixteen and quite hand-some. My brown-eyed, blond boy, a reflection of his father, lived and breathed basketball, soccer, and baseball. Academics were another thing, but that had more to do with his lack of motivation than IQ—or so the academic counselor assured us. Sarah, on the other hand, had just been named valedictorian of her senior class and consequently was offered sev-eral impressive scholarships. My husband, Geoffrey, was a senior partner in his law firm. And life was oh so good. Or so I made myself believe by skating on the thin surface of it all.

How quickly things change when you're not looking. How easily we can be blindsided just when everything seems to be going well. And the harsh reality trickles down into every decision I make. Now when I set down my pen and go back for another cup of coffee, it's the kind that comes in a tin can and smells vaguely like tuna fish. I can no longer afford the good stuff. I never realized that grinding whole beans costs about five times as much as this generic brand in the big blue can. So many impor-tant things I've been learning lately. Still, I assure myself that I will forget those little luxuries in time. I *will* move on.

I sip the acidic coffee and absently glance out the window to see two young children playing on the sidewalk next to the busy street. I know their names now, but I still remember the first time I saw them down there, a girl about four and her little brother, who's still in diapers. It was shortly after Jacob and I moved into this place, about three months ago.

Naturally, I went dashing down the cement stairs like a maniac, afraid that the small children had slipped out of their apartment unnoticed and would now wander into the street and be hit by a passing car. I'm sure I thought I was going to save their little necks. But when I got down there, breathless and on what felt like the verge of a heart attack, I noticed a young woman with bleached-out hair just sitting on the steps and complacently painting her toenails an iridescent shade of electric blue.

"Are those your children?" I gasped as I clung to the wobbly metal stair railing, attempting to steady my shaking knees.

"Uh-huh," she muttered without even looking up.

"Aren't you worried about all that—that traffic?" I pointed to the busy thoroughfare, four lanes of nonstop vehicles moving at forty-five miles per hour. "What if your children go out into the street?"

Then she squinted up at me and scowled, and I could tell that she wanted to tell me to mind my own stinking business, but she simply shrugged and said, "Yeah, well, they know better than that."

"But how can you be so—"

"Look, lady, are you from children's services or something?" She stood up now. Narrowing her eyes, she twisted the lid on her bottle of fingernail polish, then stuffed it into the back pocket of her low-cut and tight-fitting jeans as she peered at me accusingly.

"No, I'm just a neighbor who—"

"Then, *butt out.*" She glanced over at her children, who I felt were playing precariously close to the street just then. "Avery! Warren!" she screeched. "You two get over here right this minute!" Then tossing an angry look my way, she grabbed her children by their scrawny little arms and yanked them, crying and complaining, back into the apartment just below mine.

As I trudged back upstairs, I felt as much like a spoiler as a busybody.

And I had to ask myself, just who am I to tell another mother how to raise her children?

But I suppose I relate to this arrogant young mom in some ways. I remember when I thought I knew it all too, back when I was about her age or slightly older. After all, I'd taught kindergarten for five years before I decided to take time off to start our own family. I felt certain I knew everything there was to know about raising *good* kids, and what I didn't know I figured I could easily learn from one of the many parenting books that were already beginning to stack up on my bedside table. Naturally, Geoffrey, pleasantly distracted with his still fledgling law practice, wholeheartedly agreed with me on this. After all, we were intelligent and educated people. We were Christians. How hard could raising children be?

And certainly we'd fare better than our parents. Geoffrey's biological father had been an abusive alcoholic, abandoning his wife and child while Geoffrey was quite young. Not that Geoffrey ever spoke about this era of his life. What little I knew about it had been learned from his grandmother. And even she rarely spoke of such things. "Some stones are better left unturned," was her polite way of changing the subject. To be honest, I didn't really care back then. I suppose I thought what we didn't know would never hurt us. And I wasn't particularly proud of my own family, although my parents had managed to keep their marriage intact until I was grown. I later discovered this was mostly "for the sake of the children and church friends," but by the time the last of us left the nest, my dad, tired of the charade and experiencing what I'm sure must've been a midlife crisis, called it quits. My mother, a very religious and somewhat oblivious woman, still tries to act as if this never happened. I suppose it helped her case that my dad died shortly thereafter. I think she considers herself more of a widow than anything. But we don't talk about that. I suppose both Geoffrey and I come from a long line of denial. We were both experts at concealing anything that made us uncomfortable. As a result we displayed this lovely veneer of comfort and ease while underneath it all we were slowly dying.

Wouldn't Dr. Abrams be proud of me, I think as I jot down these profound thoughts and observations. I am making real progress. Then the phone rings, and I come completely unglued. It must be Jacob, I think as I strain to listen for the second ring so I can hopefully locate where it is coming from. Like most things in my life, the phone is not where it should be at the moment. I finally realize that the cordless receiver is in my bedroom. I had it with me last night, just hoping my son would call.

I trip over a running shoe that's in the doorway as I dive onto the bed and grab for the phone. I'm sure my heart rate and blood pressure have risen again.

"Hello?" I say breathlessly, hearing the desperation in my own voice. How I long to hear the voice of my son, to be reassured, once again, that he is still alive.

"Mom?"

"Jacob, is that you? Where are you?"

"Mom, I need some...some help." His voice chokes.

"What's wrong?"

"Can you come get me? Right now?"

"Sure, honey. Where are you?"

"Just outside of the city."

"But where exactly?" I demand. Of course I imagine some of the worst areas outside of Seattle. Trailer parks. Crackhouses. One of those places I would never have seen if not for my son.

"I'll meet you at Ambrose Park," he says, "in the west parking lot."

"Okay," I tell him in a firm voice although my hands are shaking. "I'll be right there."

And, of course, I feel relieved. Just to hear his voice on the phone reassures me that he's not lying dead in a Dumpster somewhere, the result of an overdose or a disgruntled drug supplier who hasn't been paid on time. Despite my departure from what used to be my life, I still read the paper and watch the news, and I know for a fact that these things *do* happen. And while I realize I should be thankful this isn't the case with Jacob right now, times like today always unnerve me. I never quite know what to think or do. I wish I had someone like Geoffrey to lean on right now. But that, too, is over. And I need to move on, to stand on my own two feet.

The problem is, I'm always second-guessing myself when it comes to Jacob. I'm never sure whether I'm doing the right thing. As I hang up the phone where it belongs by the breakfast bar, words like *codependent* or *enabler* or just *plain fool* roll through my brain like those metal balls in a pinball machine that go around and around but never find a place to rest.

And so I dash like a madwoman down the stairs, fumbling through my purse with shaking hands as I search for my keys. The adrenaline is already racing through my veins as I climb into my decrepit Ford Taurus, and I am praying that, despite the freezing temperature, it will start. I've long since quit missing the silver Range Rover I used to drive around this town. I am attempting to forget its luxurious heated leather seats and eight-slot CD player as well as all the other amenities. Really, it seems nothing more than a faded memory now or perhaps something I've imagined altogether. If only I can get this temperamental engine to cooperate with me today.

The Taurus finally turns over, and I am driving down the street with a cloud of black smoke trailing me. And now I begin to run all the possible scenarios through my head. Has Jacob been mugged and beaten by one of his "friends"? Or perhaps he has overdosed again and needs medical attention. Has he reached the end of his rope and attempted suicide? Who wouldn't in his situation? Or maybe he's simply in trouble with the law.

Finally I settle on the most positive possibility. Maybe my son is at last willing to get help. Maybe today is the big day—the big turnaround I've been hoping and praying for, for nearly a year now. But, like I said, drugs are deceptive, and the users aren't the only ones who get taken for a ride.

Chapter 2

Six months earlier

"I will *not* go to Al-Anon," Geoffrey informed me in no uncertain terms.

Jacob had been missing for several days by then, and racked with worry, I had desperately phoned an anonymous help line and sobbed out my greatest fears. Unfortunately, the phone counselor had been trained to give support to actual drug addicts, not distressed and slightly hysterical mothers.

"I'm sorry, ma'am," said a young female voice. "But maybe you should try going to Al-Anon."

"Al-Anon?" I echoed. "But I'm not an alcoholic."

"It's not for alcoholics," the girl assured me. "It's a support group for loved ones. Like people who are related to addicts or alcoholics, you know?"

"I know," I said, although I really had no idea. Then she gave me the local phone number, and still feeling frantic and no longer caring who knew, I gave the number a call. Although I did manage to sound a bit more controlled on the second phone call.

"We meet at St. John's Presbyterian Church on Thursdays at seven," the man informed me.

"And this is for parents of teenagers who struggle with, uh…" I still had difficulty using the word *addict* back then. Addicts were criminals or homeless people or second-rate actors in a movie of the week. "Drug problems?" I finally finished.

"Yes. It's basically a support group for family and friends. But we also have special guests who come and enlighten us regarding some of the problems that come with addiction."

"Thursday at seven?"

"Yes. And if you're married, I encourage you to bring your husband along as well."

"Oh, I don't know…" Suddenly I was thankful I hadn't given him my name yet. Stafford is a relatively small town. Oh, not so small that you couldn't hide, but a lot of people knew the name of Geoffrey Harmon, city attorney.

"It can be very helpful for the afflicted person to have the full support of the entire family," the man told me.

"I'm sure that's true, but my husband's a busy man."

"And you probably know that parenting a child with an addiction problem can be quite stressful on marriage relationships."

"Yes, I know."

"We also encourage siblings to attend. They have their own set of problems, you know."

"Yes, I'm sure that's true." I felt like I was reciting the same line again and again, and all I wanted was to get off the phone. What if these people had caller ID? I thanked the kind man and hung up. My heart was racing, and I was breathing hard. Still, I felt he was probably right. Perhaps it would be better if the whole family showed their support for Jacob and his recovery by going to Al-Anon. Except I had no idea how I could possibly talk my husband into attending. And even though I waited until after dinner and after I felt certain he was feeling somewhat relaxed, it still blew up in my face.

"But the man I spoke with said it would help Jacob to have us both attend," I tried after my first attempt failed. "He said Jacob needs the support of his entire family."

"Jacob had the support of his entire family when he decided to become a junkie. It didn't make a difference then, and it won't make a difference now."

"How can you know that?"

"Because, Glennis,"—he was using his placating tone with me now—"I know that the only one who can change an addict is the addict himself."

"But that's not what the Al-Anon man said."

"Look, if you feel the need to go to a meeting like that, then just go. But don't think you need to drag me into it with you."

"But what if it could help—"

"Jacob needs to help himself." Geoffrey picked up a folder of papers, his sign that this conversation was over.

So I went alone. And I must admit to feeling a bit foolish and self-conscious as I perched on a metal folding chair along with a bunch of complete strangers. Most of them turned out to be spouses or significant others. And most were there because of drinking problems, although one woman was there because her boyfriend was a cocaine addict. Even so, I did derive a small sense of comfort from hearing their hard-luck stories. But when my turn to share came up, I froze. Suddenly I was eight years old and being called upon to spell the word *rhinoceros*. I just couldn't do it.

That's when I realized I had no desire to spill my sorrows in front of total strangers, or anyone for that matter. And as I looked around at the faces that were watching me, intently waiting for me to say something, I knew that Geoffrey would call these people "losers." And, despite my attempt to remain nonjudgmental, I suppose that was how I saw them too. I ended up saying very little and leaving early. Then, as if to spite my efforts at getting some much-needed help, I came home to discover Jacob sitting on the sofa in the family room, eating a bowl of Rocky Road ice cream and watching a rerun of *The Simpsons*. His hair was wet, from either a shower or a swim, and he looked tan and healthy and was just sitting there laughing at Homer Simpson's stupidity and acting as if every-thing were perfectly normal. I suppose it was, for him.

"Where have you been?" I demanded as I threw my purse onto a chair.

"Sorry, Mom." Jacob tossed me that old smile, the one that used to work when he wanted something simple like cookies hot from the oven or "just one more" video game before dinner.

"Do you know how worried I've been?"

"Yeah, Dad filled me in." He rolled his eyes.

"You've already talked to Dad?"

He scowled. "No, as usual Dad talked to *me*. Like you could call it that. It was more of a sermon or lecture. We all know that he never listens to anyone."

"Well, he was worried too."

Jacob laughed in a cynical way. "Yeah, you bet, Mom. Believe what-ever you like."

I sat down in the chair across from him now. "He *is* worried, Jake. We're both worried. We know you have a…a problem. We know you need help."

"I'm *fine*." His eyes narrowed now. "I just need people to be a little more understanding is all. I'm going through some stuff. And I'm trying to sort it all out. I needed some time and space to just think about it."

"But you've been gone since Friday." I shook my head, forcing myself to remember exactly what had happened, even wondering why I'd been so upset and worried. One thing I knew by then was how my son had become an expert at changing the subject or throwing up smoke screens. "I've called your friends—"

"Who did you call?" he demanded.

I listed off a few kids who had been good friends before Jacob had started to change.

"They aren't my friends," Jacob said quickly.

"Well, those were the only numbers I knew to call." I sighed. "You won't even say who your friends are anymore. You hardly talk to us at all."

"Because you're always putting me through this kind of crap. It's either a lecture or the Spanish Inquisition." Then he cursed.

"Please, don't use those kinds of words in this house." I gave him my automatic response to his occasional use of unacceptable language.

"It's just a stupid word, Mom."

I took in a deep breath and closed my eyes. What had we just been talking about? Oh, yes, my missing son. "But this is the deal, Jacob. You've been gone since Friday." I used my fingers to count. "That's four days. And since today is Monday and you obviously missed school—"

"I did *not* miss school," he roared back.

I blinked. "You went to school today?"

"Yeah. I knew I'd better not get another unexcused absence if I want to graduate this spring."

Well, that was something, I told myself. At least he still cared about graduating. Although it was hard to understand exactly why he cared since he'd given up sports last year and had begun attending an alternative school during his senior year. That was only after the school counselor convinced all of us that Jacob might "perform better away from the restrictions of the more traditional campus." Whatever was that supposed to mean? Was it simply their way of getting him out of their hair? Was it a mistake for us to agree to it? After all, everyone in town knew what the alternative school was all about.

I could still remember the day I ran into Margie Smyth at the grocery store. Or rather got cornered by her in the produce section. I'd already noticed her getting some carrots, and I'd tried to appear consumed in my search for the best-looking cucumbers.

"Oh, Glennis," she'd called out. I greeted her and attempted to make small talk as I selected another lovely cucumber.

"Todd told me that Jacob's not playing basketball this year," she said in a troubled voice. "I hope nothing's wrong."

I just shrugged as I reached for another cucumber. I already had far more than I needed. "He was tired of sports," I told her, which was exactly what he had told us. "And then he took up the guitar." I attempted to make a move back toward my cart. "He actually seems to be quite musical."

She nodded. "Well, that's understandable. Basketball is fine while you're a teenager, but music is something you can take with you throughout your lifetime." She smiled now. "Then I guess it's not true that he's going to that *alternative* school." She lowered her voice and glanced over her shoulder. "Todd says that's for 'losers and users.'" She laughed as if she'd said something funny.

I wish I could say that I looked her straight in the eye and told her that Jacob was indeed going to the alternative school, but instead I told her I was in a hurry and went straight from the produce section to the checkout counter.

"Making pickles?" the cashier asked after I set my bag of cucumbers and nothing else before her.

"Yes," I snapped at the poor woman. "That's right."

But I'd eventually adjusted to the idea of alternative school and had even been fairly impressed with their curriculum. "Well, I'm glad you went to school today, Jacob," I said, trying to start all over again. "But that still doesn't take care of everything. Your dad and I both suspect you've been using drugs again."

He took in a deep breath then and just held it as if he was waiting for me to finish. But his eyes were still on the TV.

"Okay, we're not even sure what kind of drugs, or maybe it's alcohol, but we know you're doing *something*. Maybe it's pot, but that's still a serious—"

"Pot?" He laughed. "Is that what you guys called it back in your day?"

"Well, marijuana, grass, weed…" I shook my head. "I don't know what the popular term is right now. But we're concerned—"

"I've already had the lecture, Mom."

"I'm not lecturing you, Jacob. I'm worried that you might have an, well, an addiction problem, and your father and I would like to see you get some—"

"Mom!" He exploded now. "You just don't get it. I am *not* an addict." He stood up and began pacing, pounding his fist into his palm as if he really wanted to hit something or perhaps even someone. "You people are all alike. You think *everything* is about drugs." He turned and glared at me. "Well, it's not. Some people just have problems, you know? But does any-one want to listen and help them out?" Then he began to stomp from the room.

"Wait, Jacob," I called after him. "I *want* to listen. Just give me a chance." But it was too late. He was already bolting up the stairs. The banging of his bedroom door still rang in my ears as I collapsed onto the sofa and stared at Marge Simpson's big blue hair. Where had I gone wrong? I wondered. Besides everywhere, that is.

"I see how that Al-Anon meeting of yours really helped you deal with your son." Geoffrey poked his head into the family room. "Makes me really wish I'd gone too."

I wanted to throw something at my husband right then, but instead I just shrugged. "One meeting isn't going to change anything," I replied.

"Obviously."

Just the same, I didn't go back after that. I decided it might be better to just play Geoffrey's game—pretending as if nothing were wrong. Well, most of the time anyway. But like a kettle that has been left on the stove too long, Geoffrey would also boil over on occasion. And his rages didn't help mat-ters. If anything, I think they gave Jacob another excuse to go out and get stoned, or high, or whatever the popular terminology of the day was.

Afterward Geoffrey would be sorry, and I know he felt guilty, although he never actually admitted as much. I remember the time I saw him looking at a photograph right after one of these blowups. He didn't see me watching him, but I could tell he was staring at Jacob's soccer picture from seventh grade. It was the year Geoffrey had helped coach, and their team had gone all the way to the finals. But I'm sure I saw tears in his eyes that day. I almost said something to him, but I knew it would've embarrassed him and made him uncomfortable.

Geoffrey had always made it clear to me that he felt it was a sign of weakness for men to show emotion. Early in our marriage I'd assumed this was simply because he was an attorney, but over the years I began to suspect it was more than that. I think he'd learned to shut down his feelings as a child. Maybe it was because of this suppression that he was prone to his little rages. Occasionally I'd worry that the neighbors would hear him ranting and call the authorities. And sometimes I even reminded him of this possibility, which was always a sure way to quiet him. There was no way he, the respected city attorney, wanted a police car showing up in *his* driveway.

But it was usually on one of those same nights that he would stomp out of the house, not to be seen again until the following day. Oh yes, we were quite the loving Christian family back then. Something to behold.

Chapter 3

I know I should've felt relieved when Jacob managed to graduate in June. But it hurt that he chose not to march with his class. He laughed off the cap-and-gown routine as "moronic stupidity" and refused to participate in any of the traditional senior activities.

"Don't you want to celebrate this with your friends?" I asked.

"They're not my friends now."

"But you've known them for years," I tried.

He would have nothing to do with my rationale, and I made a valiant attempt to conceal my feelings. But I felt cheated by his choice. After all, I had spent years being his room mother, PTA president, fund-raising chairman, booster club member. You name it, and I'd done it. I'd attended most of his sporting events despite the weather—all those cold mornings on the soccer field, all those stiff bleachers and weekend away-games— and now I was being denied the opportunity to watch my son march across the gym and receive his diploma.

Geoffrey was understandably angry, but he was also busy with a big lawsuit, and, as usual, we didn't discuss our feelings of disappointment, and I continued to keep my grief to myself. Why dribble gasoline on our already smoldering fire? As a consolation, I decided to throw a small, family dinner party to commemorate Jacob's graduation. Just Sarah—home from college—my sister and her family, and my mother, who happened to be visiting for the weekend. Unfortunately, the festivities fell slightly flat when the guest of honor never showed up. It turned out he'd been doing some celebrating of his own. Why should I have been surprised?

After he graduated, we hardly saw Jacob anymore. He became an expert at coming and going without being seen or heard. One time when I caught him slipping into the house at four in the morning, I suggested he might have a future in foreign espionage, although I wasn't sure such things existed anymore. I'm sure I was still trying to make myself believe that everything was going to be all right in the end. Besides, I told myself, Jacob was somehow managing to hold down a job washing dishes at a restaurant, and he'd assured me that he was preregistered for fall classes at SSCC, good old South Seattle Community College. Maybe it wasn't the impressive university that Geoffrey would've picked, but it was better than nothing. Or so I thought.

Fortunately or not, depending on how you look at it, Geoffrey was becoming more and more obsessed with a major lawsuit going on at city hall. It had to do with a multimillion-dollar contract for new sewer lines that hadn't been properly fulfilled, and if Geoffrey could win this case, he would become an instant hero in Stafford.

As a result, Jacob's somewhat errant behavior went fairly unnoticed by his father during most of the summer. That is, until Jacob was picked up by the police for underage drinking and being in possession of "less than an ounce" of marijuana. *Then* his father sat up and paid attention. Well, sort of.

I was the one who answered the phone that night. Always the light sleeper, and constantly consumed with worry over Jacob, I had a tendency to nearly jump out of my skin whenever the phone rang late at night. I must've caught it before the second ring, my heart pounding in my eardrums. I felt certain it was the emergency room informing me that my son had just died of an overdose or been run over by a truck.

"Mom?" His voice sounded like he'd been crying.

"Jacob, what's wrong?"

"I've been arrested."

"Oh no." I took the cordless phone into the bathroom and sat down on the tiled edge of the whirlpool tub. "What happened?"

"I'm really sorry, Mom." He was sobbing now. "I didn't mean for this to happen. My life is so screwed up. I know I'm a mess. I want help. I really do. This makes me see that I need it."

"Okay, okay." I tried to sound soothing. "Just tell me what happened."

"I was getting into my car, and I...I got stopped. I'd had a couple of beers with some guys from work," he told me. "And, well, I had a joint in my pocket. I didn't even know it was there, Mom. I mean I hadn't worn that shirt since last summer. I think someone else might've even put it there."

"So you're in jail?" I tried to imagine this, but all I could conjure up were images of iron bars and guys in zebra-striped suits, like in some cartoon from my childhood.

"I'm not in jail yet," he said. "I've been processed, and they'll put me in jail if someone doesn't come down and post a bond."

"Post a bond?"

"Pay for bail," he translated.

"Oh. Right."

"Do you mind, Mom? I'll pay you back. I mean it might take a while, but I will. Besides, the lady told me that you'll get your money back after my court date."

"Court?" I peeked out the bathroom door to see if Geoffrey was hearing any of this, but it seemed he was still asleep.

"Yeah, there's a lot of stuff I can tell you about later. But can you come *now*, Mom? Otherwise they're going to lock me up. And there's this guy in there who looks like a Satanist or something. I'm scared, Mom."

"How much is your bail?"

"Five hundred bucks." He sighed loudly. "And it has to be cash or a money order."

"But it's two in the morning, Jacob. I don't have cash like that—"

The bathroom door suddenly came open, and there stood Geoffrey rubbing his eyes. "What's wrong?" he demanded. "Who is it?"

"Mom," said Jacob. "I gotta go; my time is up. Please come and get me. I can't stand it here." And then the line went dead.

"It's Jacob," I told Geoffrey.

"What happened now?"

"He's in jail."

Geoffrey said a foul word. I blinked in surprise but didn't say anything.

"He needs us to bail him out," I said as I headed for my closet.

"Why?"

"So he doesn't have to stay in jail." I turned and looked at my husband of twenty-five years and wondered if this really was the man I had married and borne two children with.

"A night in jail might do him good," he said.

"How will it do him good?" I demanded as I pulled on my sweats.

"Teach him there are consequences for his choices."

"But you should've heard him, Geoffrey," I pleaded. "He was crying. He was sorry. He said he knew he'd messed up and he wanted to change. He wants help."

"I've heard that before."

"But he's never been this low before, Geoffrey. He needs us. He needs to know that we love him, that we forgive him. Isn't it what Jesus would do?"

Geoffrey rolled his eyes at me, then headed back to bed.

"Aren't you coming?" I asked as I shoved my foot into a clog.

"Nope."

"Geoffrey!" I went over to the bed now. "He's your only son. You're going to just let him rot in jail?"

"One night in jail won't kill him."

"How do you know?" I demanded. "I've heard stories about abuse... Or what about kids who get so depressed they kill themselves in jail?"

"They won't let him do that."

"How do you know?"

"Just go back to bed, Glennis."

But there was no way I could go back to bed with images of Jacob's lifeless body hanging by a sheet suspended from a light fixture in some creepy jail cell. And so I got my purse and climbed into the Range Rover and drove downtown to where our bank has an ATM. I had no idea how much money I could get from this machine, but I decided I would give it my best shot and take whatever I got over to city hall and beg them to release my son. Perhaps I could offer them my engagement ring as collateral.

After all, I assured myself as I drove down Main Street, his father is the city attorney. Surely that should carry some weight at city hall. But to my surprise I was able, after only two tries, to get four hundred and forty dollars, and I had enough cash in my purse to make up the difference. With a thick wad of twenties in my hand, I glanced nervously over my shoulder at the dark and deserted town as I quickly got back into my car and locked the door. I realized this probably wasn't the smartest thing I'd done, but then mothers will do almost anything when they feel their children are in danger.

I felt conspicuous beneath the glaring fluorescent lights in the receiving area of the city jail. I could hear strange sounds from down a hallway, but the only other person around was a young woman dressed in what appeared to be an "evening" outfit. She told me that the receptionist would be back shortly and that they were going to release her boyfriend.

As I stood there waiting my turn, it occurred to me that Geoffrey hadn't even inquired why Jacob was in jail. Did he even care?

I paid them my money, got my bond receipt, signed some legal papers, and then sat down to wait for my son. It was nearly four in the morning when he finally came out, looking blurry eyed and sleepy.

Naturally, I thought that Jacob would be glad to see me and be appreciative of my brave efforts to come down there alone, but instead he seemed moody and depressed. "I figured Dad wouldn't come," he said as we got into the car.

"He has an early morning," I said, which may or may not have been true.

"Don't lie for him, Mom." Jacob leaned back in the seat and exhaled loudly. "I'm not stupid, you know."

Well, I wasn't so sure about that, but I was unwilling to pick that fight just then. And so we drove home in silence.

But that night, I'd have to say, was the beginning of the end for my marriage. Geoffrey was furious with me the next morning when I admitted what I'd done.

"You went down there? After I told you not to?" he demanded as I handed him a cup of coffee. "I explicitly told you that it could wait until today."

"I didn't know what else to do."

"You know you're a part of the problem, Glennis. You're a real enabler when it comes to Jacob."

"Nice way to throw around the addiction lingo, Geoffrey. Enabler? *Please.* I'm his mother. What am I supposed to do?"

"You're supposed to respect your husband."

"I was bailing out your son, Geoffrey, so you wouldn't have to—"

"With absolutely no regard to how I feel."

"How *do* you feel?"

"Like you've taken his side, Glennis."

"*His* side?" I envisioned our family, divided and lined up against each other, stones in our hands ready to be thrown at the opposition. "But he's *our* son, Geoffrey. I thought we were all on the *same* side."

He didn't respond.

"Jacob *needs* help, Geoffrey," I continued, making my best plea. "He *needs* his family. He *needs* you."

"He needs to quit screwing up." His voice sent an actual shiver down my spine.

Then he set down his coffee mug with a thud and marched upstairs. I could tell by the sound of his footsteps that he was heading for Jacob's room. I followed him, certain this would not go well. But before I could say anything—not that I could've stopped him—he had burst into Jacob's room.

"Get up!" he yelled.

"Huh?" Jacob rolled over and looked up with sleepy eyes.

"Get out of bed!"

Jacob just groaned and crumpled into the fetal position.

"I said get up!" yelled Geoffrey. Then he reached over and jerked Jacob out of his bed.

"Geoffrey!" I cried.

"This is *my* house," said Geoffrey. "And if I say it's time to get up, you'd better get up."

Jacob cussed at his dad, and it quickly went from ugly to frightening as both of them began yelling and swinging fists. I ran for the phone and came back holding it like a weapon.

"Stop it!" I screamed. "Or I'm calling 911."

That managed to bring Geoffrey back to reality, and he released Jacob with a shove that threw him back onto his bed with a loud crash.

Jacob's nose was bleeding, but he didn't seem to notice as he let loose with a few more foul words, then finally said, "You're such a hypocrite, Dad. No wonder I'm such a freakin' mess. I hate your guts!"

"And you are no longer welcome in this house!" yelled Geoffrey. "Be out of here by the time I get home from work."

"Fine!" yelled Jacob. "This place makes me crazy anyway. I should've left a long time ago."

Geoffrey straightened his jacket and stormed out the door.

By noon, Jacob had heaped some of his belongings into his old Subaru wagon. I had tried to talk him out of leaving, but he insisted it was the only way.

"It's just going to get worse, Mom," he told me as we stood outside in the driveway.

"What do you mean?"

"This family," he said. "It's like we're all going down any minute."

"What are you saying?" I felt more confused than ever.

"There's stuff going on," he said. "Everyone's going to get hurt."

"Jacob." I looked into his eyes. "What exactly are you saying? Is this some kind of threat? Are you going to hurt us?"

He laughed and shook his head. "Not me, Mom. It's Dad. Watch out."

I frowned. "He's just upset, Jacob. He'll be fine."

He just shrugged. "Dad hates me, you know."

"He doesn't hate you, honey. He's frustrated by all this."

"No, Mom, he hates me. Can't you see I'm an embarrassment to him? Just like Grandma was. I gotta go." He hugged me so tight that it reminded me of his first day of school when I thought he'd never let go.

"Where will you stay?" I asked.

"I'll be okay, Mom. I'll call you once I get settled." And he got in his car and drove away.

As I followed the faded blue blur of the Subaru down our street and disappearing over the crest of the hill, I thought about what Jacob had said—"just like Grandma…"

Although she'd been gone a few years, I knew he meant Jeannette, Geoffrey's mother. She'd had what Geoffrey had loosely termed "mental problems." But never properly diagnosed, the poor woman had been shifted from one treatment center to the next until she'd finally ended up in a nursing home where she was sedated around the clock in the years before her death. Jeannette had never taken the role of a real mother in Geoffrey's life. It was her parents, the Madisons, who had raised Geoffrey after his father, whom they claimed was an alcoholic, had abandoned his crazy wife and infant son. Naturally, Geoffrey had nothing but praise for his maternal grandparents. Wealthy and educated, they'd made certain that Geoffrey had only the best of the best. Meanwhile, his poor mother was either locked up in her bedroom or in whatever institution they felt was most suitable at the time.

We'd only spoken of Jeannette a few times. But both of our children knew that their grandmother had never been "well." I think Sarah had been the first to mention the possible connection between her brother and grandmother.

She'd come home from college during last Christmas break. And, as usual, Jacob and Geoffrey had gotten into it when Jacob announced he was going to go "hang with friends" one evening.

"Maybe Jacob's like Dad's mom," she had teased as Jacob was pulling on his coat and Geoffrey was fuming. "What was wrong with her anyway, Dad?"

"She was unbalanced," Geoffrey had stated as if that explained everything.

"Yeah, maybe I *am* like her," Jacob had said flippantly. "Maybe I'm crazy too." Then he had stomped out the door.

But Sarah's less-than-thoughtful comment had started me thinking, and after the holidays, I questioned Geoffrey a bit more about his mother. Naturally, he was reluctant to talk.

"I don't *know* what was wrong with her," he finally said in irritation. "She was moody, okay? And she did bizarre things. And she'd take off in the middle of the night without telling anyone."

"But she was never diagnosed?"

"No. My grandmother always just said she was eccentric."

"Another word for *crazy?*"

"Maybe. I don't really know, Glennis. I was just a kid. And then she was institutionalized. That's all I remember. End of story."

Well, I wished it was the end of the story, but unfortunately the story just kept on going. And Jacob seemed destined to become the next chapter.

Chapter 4

It felt as if a giant pair of hands reached down and tore my life in half on the day that Jacob left home. It's not that I blame God exactly. Maybe it was my own undoing or just something inevitable. And I'm sure I was somewhat sleep deprived at the time—a little fuzzy from my previous evening of extracting bail money from the ATM and then waiting for Jacob to be released "into my custody" in the wee hours of the morning— but as I walked through my large, quiet home the following day, I began to wonder what my life was all about. I began to doubt everything about myself and to question everything about life in general. Even God.

In something of a daze, I went from perfect room to perfect room as if searching for clues. Something that would put it all back into perspective and cause my life to make sense again. I looked at the selection of family photos in their shining silver frames, gracefully arranged across the grand piano that Sarah used to play so beautifully. I picked up Sarah's graduation photo and studied the self-satisfied smile that played across her sweetly curved lips—as if she knew she had it all together. Her hair had still been long back then, gently floating around her shoulders as if she hadn't spent hours trying to get that tight natural curl to relax a bit. But there was a look in her eyes that didn't quite fit with the rest of the picture, or maybe it was my imagination, but she looked worried. Maybe she had still been fretting about her grades when the photo was taken. For a short time she'd been concerned that Amanda Frazier would beat her out for top honors at graduation. But that hadn't happened. Or maybe she'd been worried about something else. Something I had missed because I'd been focused on Jacob. A small stab of guilt punctured my mother's heart, and I set the photo down and reminded myself that Sarah's life was on track. She was excelling in college, making new friends, and seemed to be in complete charge of everything.

Not that I didn't regret how her visits quickly diminished as Jacob's troubles began to increase. But sometimes I thought that Jacob's problems were simply Sarah's excuses for doing something else—something that would further reinforce her independence.

"You seem to have your hands full with your son," she'd told me shortly before her last spring break. "I think I'll just go down to Grandma's or maybe hang with my friends." Naturally, I'd expressed my disappointment, but I didn't encourage her to change her mind since it seemed our family life only grew more stressful when she did come home. Sarah wasn't unlike her father, with her lectures about how Jacob needed to shape up and how I was a hopeless enabler. And her platitudes only seemed to make matters worse. As much as I loved my daughter, I knew she could be a royal pain at times. As it turned out, more and more Sarah had opted to visit her grandmother in Arizona during holidays.

My mother had moved down there less than a year after Sarah had started college and Jacob had started to become a handful. It was a double whammy for me—losing the support of the two females I'd been closest to—and I felt it contributed to Jacob's problems as well. I felt he missed the attention of his only living grandparent, but then my mother had never been much of an expert at timing. Like when she'd divorced my dad shortly before he died. Of course, we all knew he'd been having an affair, but we didn't know he was about to have a fatal heart attack. The ink on the divorce papers was barely dry before he keeled over in the arms of the "other woman." Fortunately for my mother and us, their life insurance policies hadn't been changed yet. That was a bit of luck that we all still shake our heads over. Even so, we kids were devastated to lose our dad. But it was maddening, too, because even in our grief we were all still angry at him for cheating on Mom. As a result, it was a very strange funeral, and I sometimes wonder if I've ever really completed the grieving process for him.

I peered at the old-fashioned black-and-white picture of my parents, taken on their wedding day just after World War II had ended. My dad had on his army uniform, and my mom wore a white satin gown she had sewn herself. They looked so incredibly young and naive and happy, with absolutely no idea their lives would take such a sad twist in the end. Who ever knows how things will end up?

Then I picked up the silver-framed photo of our family. We'd had it taken shortly before Sarah graduated from high school, when Jacob was just a sophomore and doing okay. Oh, life had been relatively easy and full of promise back then. I'm just not sure we ever knew or quite appreciated it. It's like they say: you don't miss something until it's gone. Back then, Geoffrey constantly pressured the kids to do and be their best. Not that I didn't agree with this, mind you. Everyone should be the best he can be. I'd just never been sure that anyone could determine exactly what that meant for someone else.

I studied Jacob's chocolate brown eyes, his straight nose, sweet smile, and sandy-blond curls. I looked and I looked at his face, trying to determine if something had been hidden in there that I'd missed. Storm clouds gathering that I'd never noticed. But all I could see was a happy family.

I picked up Sarah's senior prom photo and, despite myself, smiled. She had looked so beautiful that night. Her auburn hair, the same shade that mine had once been, had been piled high on her head, and her green eyes had sparkled with youth and excitement. It was as if she'd finally come into her own around then. Like me, she'd been a late bloomer. Always the academic and model child, she'd been on the sidelines socially.

But something had happened in her senior year, and she'd just blossomed. The next thing we knew we were packing her off to college, where she'd continued to blossom. Even now she was off touring Europe for the entire summer with several college friends. I had balked at the idea at first, worried that it was too expensive or that something could go wrong or that Sarah might get hurt. But Geoffrey took Sarah's side, saying that she of all people deserved this kind of treat. Meaning that compared to her younger brother, Sarah was a dream child. Of course, she was also Daddy's little princess. Always had been, and unless she did something terribly regrettable—something that would shame her father—she probably always would remain on his pedestal.

But as Sarah's life got better and better, her younger brother's life went steadily downhill. It felt as if the scales had suddenly been tipped—Sarah was up and Jacob was down. But was that how it really worked? Was that how life balanced out the blessings and the curses? "Why, God?" I asked for the umpteenth time. Why was this happening to us? But God loomed as silent as my big empty house. And stifled by the heavy stillness that made it difficult to breathe or even think, I finally went outside in search of relief.

I'd always loved to garden, but that last summer was different. Oh, I'd planted as usual in the spring. Slightly bolstered by the possibility that Jacob might even make it through to graduation, I'd planted starts of tomatoes, peas, zucchini—all kinds of things. Then distracted and possibly depressed during the following summer months, mostly by Jacob's unexplained absences from home and my growing suspicions that drugs were still involved, I had neglected, among other things, my garden. Oh, I'd left the automatic sprinkler system on, and I'd figured our landscaping people would maintain it, but I hadn't actually gone out there myself during the past several weeks.

But on this day I decided to go see it, hoping that my faithful flowers would boost my spirits when I needed it most. As usual, I first walked out into the manicured backyard, which the lawn guys kept to Geoffrey's high standards of perfection, and then past the pool, which, thanks to the pool man, shone like a polished piece of turquoise. Another one of Geoffrey's indulgences, since it seemed he was the only one to use the pool much anymore. I continued on around, back to the concealed area I'd been allowed to keep. This "out of sight" area was one of the few spots in our home that Geoffrey didn't really care about. It was my personal little paradise.

My sagging spirits began to lift as I heard the birds chirping in the tall trees, and I think I actually began to relax a bit as I followed the curving flagstone path that Jacob had helped me to put down when he was about thirteen and eager to show off his muscles. I breathed in the fresh air, looking forward to the peaceful comfort I would find in the happy faces of my colorful flowers and hearty vegetables and lush green foliage. But when I came around the tall boxwood hedge that sheltered my garden, I was greeted with only weeds and grief.

Something had obviously gone wrong in my automatic watering system this year, most likely the battery in the timer, I figured, as I surveyed the devastation. As a result, everything—I mean everything—in my sweet little garden was dead. I walked around and around in a daze, just staring at my perennials and annuals, all the vegetables. Even my everbearing strawberries were brown and dry and shriveled almost beyond recognition. It seemed that every single plant had been a victim of the summer heat. All had withered and wilted in the high August temperatures.

It reminded me of when I was a little girl. We'd had an elderly neighbor named Mrs. Peabody. The tiny, wrinkled woman had always kept a beautiful garden tucked neatly behind her white picket fence. But then she had died suddenly in early June, and with no one to tend or water her yard, it wasn't long before her garden succumbed as well. I can still remember the feeling of sadness that washed over me as I stood and peered over her fence. The garden of a dead woman.

And that was what I was looking at once again. Falling to my knees as if shot through the heart, I coiled into an almost fetal position, scooped up the hot dry soil, and clutched it in tight but shaking fists. "This is my life," I thought. "This is what I deserve." Dust and death and utter hopelessness.

I don't know how long I remained there, sobbing and crying over deceased columbine, daylilies, sweet william... Why, even the hardy lavender and sunflowers had perished. It was all gone. I stayed out there and wept for all that was lost and dead in my life, for all that was still dying. Then I stood and went back into my house, packed a couple of bags, and without even pausing to pet the dog or check on the cat, I left.

I don't even remember driving through Stafford that day, but I finally stopped when I saw a tattered sign that said Apartment for Rent. It was located in a run-down area on the other side of town. A weedy grass strip ran alongside the stark stucco apartment complex, but, like my garden, it was brown and dry. By four o'clock I had signed a six-month lease on a two-bedroom apartment and "moved" inside. I didn't have a bed or a chair or even a glass to get a drink of water. But I didn't care. Why should a dead woman care? I lay down on the matted, rust-colored carpet and, resting my throbbing head on my overnight bag, slept.

When I awoke, it was dark, and I felt disoriented but not frightened exactly. Perhaps I was too numb. But I did wonder where I was and why I was there. I fumbled around until I found a light switch, then felt stunned to remember what I had done. My surprise was quickly followed by dismay as I scrutinized my new habitat in the unforgiving light of a flickering fluorescent strip above the stained kitchen sink. There on the chipped Formica-topped counter was the lease I had signed. I looked at my watch to discover that it was nearly nine thirty. I knew Geoffrey would be worried, would probably suspect me of going out after Jacob again.

I paced back and forth in the limited space of the apartment. I guessed it was about an eighth the size of my previous home. And yet this did not disturb me. In fact, I think I found some comfort in the confinement. Maybe I imagined I had thrown myself into some sort of self-imposed prison. A place where bad mothers went to pay for their crimes. But what was my crime? Caring too much?

Even so, I did not look forward to the prospect of sleeping on that floor all night. Even prison inmates were offered the amenity of a bed. Besides, my back was already stiff and sore from my exhaustion-induced nap. So, knowing that the local Wal-Mart stayed open until all hours, I decided to set off in search of something to sleep on.

I felt a bit self-conscious and out of place as I parked my slightly conspicuous Range Rover in the nearly empty parking lot. I knew I must look frightening with my uncombed hair and rumpled clothes, but I felt the chances of running into anyone I knew at this place and at this time of night were quite unlikely. Even so, I remember how I held my head down and quickly passed through the entrance. I had no idea what I was looking for, but I remembered that the camping area was in the back of the store. I recalled taking Jacob there once, a long time ago, to get some items for his first year at summer camp.

To my surprise, I found everything I needed in that section. A dark blue sleeping bag, a foam mattress pad that rolled up neatly, a folding camp chair, and even a mess kit complete with a collapsible cup for water. I heaped these items into a nearby cart, then made my way back to the checkout.

"Going camping?" asked a freckle-faced young man behind the counter. He looked to be about the age of my son, and I wondered if perhaps I should know him.

"No," I lied. "It's for my son. He's going on a campout tomorrow."

"Lucky kid," said the guy as he totaled my purchase. I handed him my Visa card, then wondered how long I would have this little luxury of giving someone plastic and getting merchandise in return. And even as he ran the card through his machine, a chill ran down my spine. What if it didn't work? What if Geoffrey had already figured it out—that I had left him. What if he had canceled all my credit cards? Closed my checking and savings accounts?

"You okay, ma'am?" asked the kid.

I nodded. "Just tired," I told him. "So much to do."

"Yeah," he agreed, handing me my receipt to sign. "There's a lot of work involved in a campout."

I signed the paper and sighed. "That's the truth."

"Tell your son to have fun."

I made a pathetic attempt at a smile and assured him I would. Then, with my purchases heaped in the cart, I hurried out into the summer evening. I wondered where my son would be camping tonight. I knew he was probably better prepared than I, but still I worried. What if this final straw with his father was enough to push him right over the edge? What if Jacob used being kicked out of his home as an excuse to do something, well, something foolish? Or at least more foolish than what he'd already been doing? In the past I had prayed for Jacob during times like this, but more and more I felt that my prayers were like stones hurled toward heaven, but then gravity pulled those stones back down and heaped them upon me until I was buried alive in their rubble.

"Stock up while you can," I told myself as I drove through the quiet streets. "Once Geoffrey finds out you've left him, you will have nothing." And so I parked in front of the slightly sleazy all-night grocery store called More-4-Less. My cart limped with a jittery front wheel that made so much noise I was certain the whole store could hear me as I piled it high with staples. I couldn't imagine that I would ever actually cook or eat these things, but I proceeded to load my cart with cans of soup, boxes of pasta, and even several packages of rice pilaf. I suppose I felt the need to be prepared just in case Jacob should show up hungry and desperate. In a survivalist mode, I rattled down aisle after aisle until I was so exhausted it seemed I was walking through a dream, grasping at canned beans as if they were portals back to my old life.

To my relief, the bored-looking thirty-something woman at the checkout stand hardly glanced at me as she mechanically pushed item after item through the electronic eye, which worked only about half of the time, and the rest of the time she scanned it with a little hand-held thing. But like a zombie, I just stood there and stared at her, wondering how she managed to live like this, working in a smelly grocery store in the middle of the night. Her nametag said Sylvia, but nothing else. Did she, like me, have a crummy little apartment to go home to? Children? A husband? A dog?

"Did you know that this is self-service?" she asked me with frown creases carved into her pale forehead.

I blinked. "What do you mean?"

"I mean you have to bag your own stuff." Sylvia nodded toward the end of the counter.

With wide eyes I looked at the enormous pile of items and wondered where it had all come from and how it had accumulated into this giant mountain of *stuff*. "Oh," I muttered, as if this wasn't such a huge challenge. But the truth was, I wanted to bolt just then. I wanted to turn away from this rude woman, whose drab brown roots needed a serious touch-up to match her brassy blond bleach job, and I wanted to dash out of that run-down grocery store and leap into my car and drive far, far away. This was nothing like the organic gourmet grocery where Geoffrey preferred that we shop.

"The sacks are down there." She gave her thumb a downward jerk to point to some holders where piles of brown paper bags were nested.

I pulled out a bag and struggled to open it, shaking it and snapping it until it finally seemed ready to receive the contents. Then I looked for a place to set the sack, but the counter was full of groceries. Finally I went and got another cart, set the bag in it, and managed to begin filling it with groceries.

Sylvia called out the total to me, watching, I felt sure, to see if I flinched at the amount. But keeping my cool, I handed her my debit card and returned to the impossible task of bagging my stuff. I had managed to fill, and badly, only two bags before she handed me back my card and a receipt. Then she walked over and stood with her hands on her hips just watching me.

"Good grief," she said. "It looks like you've never even bagged groceries before."

I looked up at her, noticing that her blue eyes looked red and strained, then I shook my head. "You're right, I haven't."

"Well, look," she said, reaching for a bag and opening it in one graceful snap. "You gotta put the heavy stuff on the bottom." She grabbed several cans of soup in one hand, then planted them into the corners of the bag. "See?" Then she reached for some boxes and wedged those in between. And on she went until the bag was not only completely full, but it looked solid enough not to slump over like a tired rag doll, the way mine were doing.

"Thanks," I muttered, trying to follow her example.

"You new in town?" she asked as she helped me bag the rest of my groceries.

"Not exactly, but I'm moving into a new apartment today," I confessed.

She seemed to study me for a moment. "Divorce?"

I shrugged. "I'm not sure yet."

She nodded. "He cheat on you?"

I must've looked startled then. "Well, no. That's not really—"

She smiled then. "It's okay, honey. But just take it from me, it'll get better." Then she laughed. "Eventually, anyway. It'll probably get a whole lot worse first."

I thanked her as I filled the last grocery bag, then heaped it on the pile already threatening to spill from the cart. I hoped I wouldn't find too many broken items once I got home. *Home?* I thought as I wheeled the cart through the deserted parking lot toward my Range Rover. What a concept. Then moving more slowly and intentionally, as if I were beginning a marathon, I started to pace myself as I loaded, one by one, the bags into the back.

Driving toward the apartment complex, I peered up and down the mostly vacant streets, hoping I might spy Jacob's Subaru parked along a side street somewhere. I wondered if he'd be sleeping in the back tonight. Hopefully, he'd remembered to pack his sleeping bag, although it was still pretty warm outside. Or, more likely, he'd crashed at a "friend's" place. Most likely a friend with the kind of answers that helped Jacob to temporarily forget all his troubles. For the first time in my life, I think I actually longed for some sort of chemical escape myself. Something to take me away and end this pain. Then I remembered a story I'd read in the local newspaper. It was about a mother of teenagers who'd been arrested on drug charges. But it seemed to me she had introduced her children to the crud—not the other way around. I considered stopping for a bottle of wine as I passed by the liquor store but couldn't bring myself to face another clerk like Sylvia.

Chapter 5

I must've been up half the night unloading bag after bag of groceries from the car and carrying them up the flight of stairs. Then I opened all the cupboards, which weren't many, and searched for places to put all these various and sundry items I had felt so compelled to purchase. Of course, my new kitchen was about half the size of what had been my master bathroom. And naturally, there wasn't enough space.

So, like a crazy woman, I paced back and forth, trying to figure out where to put everything. It was like trying to work a giant jigsaw puzzle with too many pieces. Finally I gave up and decided to give the kitchen a thorough scrubdown with the new Super Orange cleaner and package of sponges that I found in the bottom of one of the paper sacks. I felt certain this apartment hadn't been cleaned in decades, and at least this was something I could do.

I think it was three in the morning when I finally stopped scrubbing. And then, without giving too much thought to order or organization, I simply stowed everything I could in whatever space I could find and left the remaining items sitting on the counter like orphans.

Then I sat down in my green canvas camp chair and began creating a list of other things I would need. I wrote this on the back of my grocery receipt, only listing the basic things, like clothes hangers and a laundry basket and maybe a few dishes and a pan or two. After all, I told myself as I got ready for bed and realized I had no towels or washcloths or even a shower curtain, I didn't really deserve anything more than the basics. Of course, I might do this thing differently if Jacob ever came to live here with me. I would at least want to have another chair or two. And maybe a coffee maker.

I finally unfurled my foam pad and navy blue sleeping bag and, wearing my T-shirt and old jogging shorts for pajamas, crawled into this makeshift bed and realized that I'd forgotten to get a pillow. I wondered if inmates were afforded the luxury of a pillow, and if so, it would probably not be one of goose down or even feathers. But perhaps tomorrow I could sneak back into my house—rather, Geoffrey's house—and retrieve my favorite pillow. There were just some things a person shouldn't have to do without.

I awoke to the sounds of loud voices and footsteps stomping overhead. It took me a moment to remember where I was as I crawled out of the twisted sleeping bag and rubbed my very stiff neck. My watch said it was six thirty, but I wasn't sure whether it was morning or night until I looked out the window and decided it must be morning. I shuffled into the kitchen and looked around. The plywood cabinets and plastic countertop looked bleaker than ever in the morning light. Among the leftover grocery items still sitting on the counter was a bag of coffee beans, Morning Blend. But, of course, I realized now that I had no grinder. Not only that, I had no coffee maker. I sat down in my camp chair with the bag of beans in my hands and began to cry. What had I done to deserve this?

Finally the tears subsided, and it suddenly occurred to me that I might be losing my mind. What if right now Geoffrey and Jacob were sitting at the breakfast table, enjoying a fresh brewed cup of coffee and discussing college plans for Jacob? What if Jacob had returned home last night, sorry for all he'd put us through, and what if he'd apologized to his father, and they had hugged each other and cried and said, "Let's start over again." What if? What if I was sitting here like a crazy woman, torturing myself for no good reason, and meanwhile all was well at home? Or even worse, what if all was well at home except for the fact that no one knew where I'd disappeared to, and what if I was now the source of stress in our lives. I dashed to my little bedroom and began haphazardly pulling on my clothes. Then I ran down to my car and quickly drove across town to apologize to my husband and son, to plead a sort of temporary insanity.

But when I got home, no one was there. And judging by the neatly made bed in our room, I knew no one had been there. I checked the message machine and found two messages. I pushed the button and waited.

"Hi, Glennis. This is Sherry, just checking to see how you're doing. You've been on my heart these past couple of days, and I'm praying for you. Give me a call. We should do lunch or something."

I thought about Sherry as I waited for the next message. Perhaps I should give her a call.

"This is Russ at the lumberyard, looking for Jacob this morning. If he doesn't show for work today, you can tell him he doesn't need to come back here at all." And, almost like an exclamation point, this was followed by a loud beep.

I erased both messages and looked around the kitchen, amazed at how huge it was compared to the tiny apartment. Two completely different worlds. I could hear Rufus whining at the back door. He probably hadn't been fed since yesterday. And the cat, Winnie, was nowhere to be seen. But that wasn't so unusual. I went out to the laundry room and refilled Rufus's water and food dishes as his tail beat happily against my leg.

"How're you doing, old boy?" I asked, leaning over to pet his scraggly coat. Rufus was a terrier mix mutt that Jacob had brought home about ten years ago. He'd found the abandoned puppy on the street, and, despite Geoffrey's allergies, there was no way I could deny my son this sad-eyed puppy. It had been agreed that Rufus's domain would become the laundry room, a place where Geoffrey never went anyway, and we would install a doggy door that led to the backyard. Jacob would be the primary caregiver, although that didn't last long. Soon I was tending to not only Rufus but also Winnie, the Blue Persian kitten that Sarah insisted she must have after our no-pet rules had been set aside for Rufus. The same restrictions applied to Sarah's cat, but after a while the pets seemed to come and go with more freedom, and Geoffrey's allergies seemed to magically disappear. I wondered now if he'd ever really had them at all. Perhaps it had just been a convenient excuse to exist in a pet-free world during the first fifteen years of our marriage. I refilled the cat's water and food dishes and went back into the house.

I walked into the sunlit family room and looked around. The room was so perfect that it looked like a page torn from a design catalog. Of course, this had more to do with Geoffrey than myself. His taste had always ruled in our home, even when we were first married and his grandparents had generously purchased our first home as a wedding gift for us. Certainly, it was a modest home, at least compared to this one, but at the time it had seemed like a small palace to me. It was a brand-new, one-story ranch with three bedrooms and two baths. Perhaps it wasn't exactly the sort of house I would've chosen, but then I hadn't been asked. Just the same, I remember feeling a bit like a princess as I walked from room to room admiring the squeaky-clean newness of it all. I had imagined picking out warm and cozy furnishings, perhaps in the country style that was becoming popular at the time. I told Geoffrey my ideas, but he just smiled in a knowing sort of way.

"No need to worry about that," he'd assured me. "My grandmother is doing a little redecorating, and she wants to give us most of her old furniture."

Now I'd been to his grandparents' expensive hilltop home several times, and while it was quite lovely and the furnishings were top of the line, they were definitely *not* my style. "But isn't everything blue?" I'd asked. "And dated?"

"Blue is my favorite color," he told me. "And the designs are classic."

I suppose it was my own fault that I never admitted blue was among my least favorite colors. I'd always felt it was cold and formal and nothing like the sort of interiors I'd have chosen. But I convinced myself it was kind of his grandparents, and Geoffrey had assured me this would allow us to save money for our next home as well as the new furnishings to go with it. Meanwhile, I'd put up with blue velvet couches and complementing chairs, formal dark wood pieces, Asian lamps, and those numerous Oriental carpets I actually learned to appreciate in time.

And, true to Geoffrey's promise, we eventually built this house and furnished it with new pieces. My plan, at that time, had been to select some attractive but comfortable neutral-tone furnishings, to bring in some informal antiques in golden oak tones, and then accent with warm and vibrant colors. But Geoffrey had seen it differently. After numerous long-winded discussions during which I was reminded that our home wasn't just for family enjoyment but also for entertaining clients, I finally succumbed to his design plan. And that was how our new home came to be furnished with two low-slung navy blue leather couches along with a number of other very contemporary pieces Geoffrey had found at a Scandinavian design store. He'd been assisted by a tall blond woman named Ingrid, who I suspected had made up the name as well as the accent to go along with the job. Naturally, I'd kept these thoughts to myself.

The only things I really liked about our interior design was the rich color of the oak floors and the old Oriental carpets that I had managed to convince Geoffrey to keep. "For sentimental purposes," I'd told him. Of course, I also liked the high vaulted ceilings and wide expanse of windows that looked down the hill to the city below. But those navy blue sofas always left me feeling chilled. And even in the summertime, I'd find myself reaching for the thick chenille blanket that I always kept handy. It was a bright cranberry color that Geoffrey said looked garish but I liked. I picked up the blanket now, holding it close to me.

"What are you doing?" I asked myself. My voice sounded hollow and empty, lost in all the space of the house. Then I wrapped the chenille throw around me and sat down on the leather sofa and attempted to think, trying to remember what exactly had brought me to this place of confusion and unrest. Surely it wasn't just the condition of my garden.

I knew that Geoffrey and I had argued yesterday. Nothing new about that, at least not lately, not since our son had begun pushing and pulling us in every imaginable direction. But then Geoffrey had engaged with Jacob, even to the point of getting physical, and then he'd told him in no uncertain terms to leave our home. He'd actually told our son he wasn't welcome here anymore. That was what had cut so deeply. But was that really why I'd left? I felt confused, unsure about almost everything. What was it that had really made me give up like this?

Of course I'd been devastated to discover the sorry state of my garden—not unlike the sorry state of my life. But that was no reason to leave my husband of twenty-five years. Only a crazy woman would do that. Really, I had to ask myself, what was going on here? Was this how people ended up in mental hospitals? I stood up and walked over to the door of Geoffrey's study. As always, everything was in its perfect place. I had usually avoided this room, had never felt comfortable or welcome there. But today I walked in and looked around. I sat down in the big leather chair at his desk and tried to imagine what it felt like to be Geoffrey Harmon. And for the first time in a long time I wondered if he was happy. He sure didn't seem happy. And more and more lately he seemed to be particularly unhappy with me. It was as if I could never quite measure up to his expectations. I absently pulled open the top drawer of his desk to find everything in its place. But a blank, white envelope caught my attention. I opened it to find several photographs that appeared to have been taken at city hall, apparently on Geoffrey's last birthday (his fiftieth) since he was the center of attention and standing in front of a big sheet cake. I flipped through the photos and started to replace the envelope when something stopped me. I took a second look at a photo where Geoffrey was standing with the city manager, Judith Ramsey. Several other city employees were in the picture as well, but something about the expressions on both Judith's and Geoffrey's faces stopped me. They both looked so happy. I couldn't remember the last time I'd seen Geoffrey looking that happy. Or maybe, like so many other things, I'd missed it.

I put the photos back in the envelope, replacing them in their exact spot in the desk, and in that same moment it occurred to me with the kind of clarity I hadn't experienced in some time that *Geoffrey didn't love me anymore.* Crazy as it seemed, I felt certain that was the truth. And I felt just as certain that it was time to go. The chenille blanket was still wrapped around my shoulders, and I realized that it really belonged to me and that I was going to take it with me. But why stop at the blanket? There were several items that Geoffrey would never want or need or even miss. Things I had picked out to comfort me and make this house more to my tastes, cozier.

And so I found a few boxes and laundry baskets, and I began to gather candles, pillows, linens, dishes—special things I had selected and Geoffrey had tolerated—and to take those things out to the Range Rover.

"Looks like you're moving," called my neighbor Elaine as she watered a pot of petunias in front of her house.

"Just clearing out a few things," I called back to her. I wasn't eager to have all of Stafford in on our personal business just yet. And everyone knew that Elaine Hodges was something of a gossip.

"You getting rid of those?" she called, coming closer, the hose hanging limply in her hand as she peered at the stack of jewel-toned pillows in my arms.

"Oh, they're for Sarah," I told her. "She needed some things for her dorm room this fall."

Elaine frowned. "Pretty nice threads for a dorm room, don't you think?"

I smiled. "Oh, you know how it goes, Elaine. Nothing's too good for your kids, right?"

She nodded but looked unconvinced, and I hurried back into the house and closed the door, my heart pounding in my ears as I leaned against it. I don't know why I felt like a thief, but I did. What was I taking really? Only the kinds of things Geoffrey would gladly toss out if given the opportunity. And, after all, I reminded myself, it was only yesterday that he'd tossed out his own son. I was only making it easier for him.

It wasn't long before the Range Rover was packed full and I was driving back across town, feeling like both a thief and a fugitive. But before I headed to the apartment, I decided to swing by the lumber yard to see if Jacob's Subaru was there. Unfortunately, it was not. I knew this meant that my son was jobless again. How was he supposed to survive on the streets without a job or money? What exactly was Geoffrey trying to accomplish with his little plan? Did he want Jacob to sell himself for money? To become a drug dealer? To wind up in prison or to die in a gutter somewhere?

"No," I told myself as I pulled into my parking spot, number thirty-six, "you are not a thief or a fugitive. You are simply a mother who loves her son and wants to make a place for him to come home to. It might not be much, but it's better than the streets or jail."

By noon I had hauled all my salvaged items into the apartment, which was beginning to look quite crowded despite the lack of actual furnishings. But that was mostly due to the fact that I had dumped everything onto the floor in what I must admit was a rather dysfunctional manner. But then I wondered why I should even care. Why should I expect anything about my life to be functional anymore?

I stood and stared at the colorful heaps piled around my ankles. It looked as if my other house had regurgitated all the items that my husband had never wanted, and somehow they had landed here in this shabby little place, along with me. But then I suspected my husband would be glad to be rid of me as well.

My plan was to take a quick shower and return to the house to pick up a few larger items that I hadn't been able fit into my first load. One was an old oak rocker that had belonged to my grandmother. Another was a small dresser I'd had as a child. And then there was the small pine table that had been from my father's side of the family.

I desperately hoped I wouldn't find Geoffrey at home. That would be out of character for him at this time of day, but then he hadn't gone home last night either. Nor had he left a message on either my cell phone or the home phone. That was out of character too. But I spied no sleek, black Porsche in the driveway and knew I was probably home free again since he rarely parked his car in the garage in the middle of the day.

Hoping to avoid the watchful eye of my neighbor, I opened the garage door and backed the Range Rover into it so I could quickly load my items and escape without further questions. Just as I was lugging the dresser through the kitchen, I heard the phone ringing. I paused long enough to listen to the answering machine pick it up, and then I heard Sherry's voice again.

"Sorry to bother you, Glennis," she was saying. "But I just keep thinking of—"

I snatched the phone and breathlessly said, "Hello."

"Oh, Glennis," she said, relief in her voice. "Am I catching you at a bad time?"

"Well, sort of." I glanced at the dresser in the middle of the kitchen.

"I'm sorry. Do you want me to call back later?"

"How about if I call you back on my cell in just a few minutes?"

"Great. I'll be waiting for you."

"Better yet,"—I felt a wave of hunger coming over me—"can you meet me for lunch at…" I was trying to think of a place away from downtown and city hall or anyplace where I might run into Geoffrey.

"How about Ziddies?" she suggested.

"Perfect," I said in relief since Ziddies was a new lunch spot near the mall, a place where Geoffrey would never think to go.

"Sure, I'd love to. When?"

I glanced at my watch. It was already one fifteen. "How about one thirty?"

"Great, I'll be there."

So I managed to get the dresser safely loaded onto the blanket that I'd spread out over the backseat of the Range Rover. I knew Geoffrey would be furious if I damaged the precious leather seats. At the same time, I wondered why I even cared. Habit, I guess. Geoffrey had picked out this Range Rover when both kids were still in high school. He said it was the "perfect family vehicle," although I had suspected he simply liked the idea of driving one of the most expensive rigs in town. For several years he was the primary driver of the Range Rover and parked it in prominent places at city hall as if to proclaim to anyone paying attention that Geoffrey Harmon had made it in this town…that the city attorney was a big success. But after a few years, he had grown tired of the Range Rover's size, or so he said, and that's when he urged me to trade in my old Mercedes for his new Porsche. Naturally, I became the driver of the slightly used Range Rover. At first I had balked at the size, but I soon grew accustomed to the luxury of this quality SUV and began to think of it as my own. How long would *that* continue, I wondered as I locked the back door to what used to be my house. Then I got in the Range Rover and left, without looking back even once.

Chapter 6

I spotted Sherry in a corner booth, already sipping a coffee. "Sorry to be late," I told her as I slid in across from her.

"No problem." She smiled. "It sounded like you were busy. What're you up to these days?"

I sighed. "It's a long story."

She nodded and handed me a menu. "I've got time."

I nervously glanced around the restaurant, not sure whom I expected to see, but thankful not to recognize any of the faces. Then I skimmed the menu and decided on the turkey-and-apple salad just as the waitress arrived to take our orders.

"Now, don't take this wrong," began Sherry after the waitress had left, "but you don't look so good."

"Yeah, I can imagine."

"I know you've been going through the wringer with Jacob this summer," she continued, "but you still need to take care of yourself."

Sherry was the only person I'd been able to confide in about Jacob. And then only partially. She had no idea that he was using drugs. She thought he was just going through a little rebellious period and partying like so many of the kids in our town seemed to do. The same way her own two sons had done not so many years ago. But now her boys were doing fine, and she would often tell me that, as if to reassure me that it would soon be the case with Jacob as well.

I weighed my options as I watched her stirring her coffee. I could spill my guts and risk shocking her so badly that I would lose her friendship entirely—if that was possible, and I wasn't even sure. Or I could skim the surface as I usually did and risk the chance that she'd find out about everything soon enough and be mad at me for not having come clean sooner. Although Sherry, more than anyone I knew, was not a person to hold a grudge. She was the most gracious friend I'd ever had, and now, perhaps more than ever, I needed that.

"Things have gotten worse," I told her.

She frowned. "I'm sorry."

"So am I."

"Is it Jacob?"

"It's Jacob and Geoffrey and me." I shook my head. "It's all of us, I suppose."

"What's going on, Glennis?"

"I've left Geoffrey."

Her blue eyes grew wide. "No, you're not serious? When? What happened?"

And so I began to tell her about Jacob's arrest and the fight over bailing him out and how Geoffrey had thrown his own son out. I paused as the waitress brought us our order.

"But, Glennis," said Sherry after the waitress left again, "you don't want to leave Geoffrey just because he threw Jacob out. Do you?"

"It's more than that," I told her in a tired voice. "It's like I couldn't breathe in that house anymore. It's like I never belonged there in the first place. I mean as long as everything was absolutely picture perfect, as long as we all stayed in our proper places and played our perfect little roles, well, then Geoffrey was happy. But one wrong step, one false move, and Geoffrey would be on us like—" I stopped speaking when I saw a familiar face coming into the restaurant.

"What's wrong?" asked Sherry.

"Oh, someone just came in…"

"Who?"

"Oh, it's just Judith Ramsey," I said in a hushed voice.

"The city manager?"

"Yes." I remembered the photo but told myself not to be ridiculous.

"Is she alone?"

"She's with a couple of women. I can't remember their names, but they look familiar. I'm sure they work at city hall too." I shifted where I was sitting so that the post behind Sherry managed to block me from their view.

"Didn't I hear that Judith got divorced recently?"

"Last year." I peeked around the post momentarily. "And, don't look now, but I could swear that woman's had some plastic surgery done."

Sherry giggled. "I'm afraid to ask where."

"Don't."

"Are you uncomfortable talking now?" asked Sherry in a gentle voice. "We could go somewhere else."

I glanced back over to where the three women had just sat down not far from the door and decided they couldn't hear us. Besides, I told myself, why should I care? "I doubt they'd even recognize me anyway." I sighed. "Looking like this I mean."

"Well, you don't really look like yourself today, Glennis." She patted my hand. "But now I can understand why."

"It all feels like a bad dream," I told her. "I keep thinking I'll wake up and everything will be like it was before."

"And that would be okay?"

"Well, maybe not. It wasn't so great before, either."

"But do you think you and Geoffrey would still be together if things hadn't gotten so, well, so out of hand with Jacob?"

I still hadn't told her about the drugs. I wasn't sure I even planned to. Or at least maybe not today. It seemed we had enough of the family's dirty laundry tossed onto the table for one day.

"I suppose it's possible, Sherry. I don't really know. Everything seems kind of hazy and blurry to me right now."

"I can imagine. So where are you staying? A hotel?"

I shook my head. "No, I can't quite believe I did it myself, but I signed a six-month lease on an apartment."

"You've got to be kidding." She looked at me in disbelief. "When did all this happen?"

"Yesterday."

"You left Geoffrey yesterday and signed a six-month lease the very same day?"

"I did."

"Oh my."

"Do you think I made a mistake?" I leaned forward and peered into her eyes, longing for some sort of confirmation or encouragement.

"I don't know what to think, Glennis. It's all so sudden. I'm sure your head must be spinning."

"It is. I literally feel a little dizzy."

She pointed at my untouched food. "Eat your salad."

I obliged her and considered my straits. Telling Sherry about all this made it more real somehow. What *had* I gotten myself into?

"What did Geoffrey say?"

"He doesn't know."

"Doesn't know? But you said you left yesterday. What did you tell him?"

"Nothing. As far as I can tell, he never came home last night either."

"Really? Do you think he's okay?"

"I'm sure he's perfectly fine. Probably just steamed at me for stepping over the line when I bailed out our son."

She frowned. "It would be hard to leave your son in jail, even for just one night."

"That's how I felt. But Geoffrey thought it would be good for him—those were his exact words. He was really angry at me yesterday morning. He probably thought it would shake me up when he didn't come home last night." Despite everything that had gone on during the last twenty-four hours, I couldn't help but giggle. "But then I never went home either."

"You two." She shook her head.

I sighed. "Too bad all this drama has just been going to waste."

"You should see a counselor, Glennis."

"*I* should see a counselor? What about Geoffrey? Or Jacob, for that matter?"

"Well, yes, of course. But you can't force them to get help."

"Tell me about it."

"But you can get help for yourself."

I studied her for a moment, so together in her off-white jacket and matching capri pants. Even the pale blue shell under her jacket seemed to bring out the color of her eyes. Her light brown hair styled neatly as usual and makeup just perfect, Sherry had it all together. I suspected that even her handbag and shoes matched. In some ways this was just the kind of woman that Geoffrey would appreciate. But she was devoted to her husband, a fine Christian man who had a reputation for being one of the only honest building contractors in town. I'd met Sherry at a women's Bible study. I'd been as impressed with her intelligent comments as I was with her coordinated wardrobe. I wasn't surprised to learn that she worked part-time as a very successful real-estate agent. It seemed that everything Sherry touched had a way of turning into gold. I suppose I'd hoped some of that would rub off onto me. Based on the recent events of my life, that had clearly not been the case.

"I know a woman," she continued, and suddenly I wondered if I'd missed something.

"What?"

"A counselor."

"Oh, right."

"She's wonderful. I know you'll love her. Her name is Lucy Abrams. I'll give you her number." Already Sherry had located a neat little notepad in her handbag and was writing down a name and number. She pushed it across the table to me. "It's not that I don't want to listen to you, Glennis. I do. But I just don't feel qualified to give you advice about, well, your marriage and everything. I'm afraid I might fall back on my old fundamentalist roots and start preaching at you about how divorce is the devil's domain." She made a face. "You know, stuff like that."

I nodded. I did know. She and I had both come from pretty conservative church backgrounds where words like *forgiveness, grace,* and *mercy* were seldom heard. But we'd found comfort in each other and in the understanding we had as a result of our upbringing.

"It's not that I think divorce is a good thing," she continued. "But I do believe there are some cases where marriages can't continue. For instance, abuse. I would never encourage a woman who's being abused to stay in her marriage."

"Well, Geoffrey never abused me. At least not physically."

The three women from city hall were getting up to leave. But I suspected that Judith had noticed me when her face suddenly changed from its otherwise placid expression to something akin to slight shock. I'm sure it was because I was looking so pathetic, like some unfortunate bag lady that Sherry had kindly picked up off the street and offered a meal. Even so, I managed to hold up my hand in a pitiful little wave and smile. To my relief, Judith smiled back and then simply exited. I would've been mortified if she'd come any closer or even greeted me in my current condition. And I couldn't imagine what she might possibly say to my husband the next time their paths crossed, and I felt sure they would. Perhaps she would ask him if his wife had been seriously ill.

"Did they go?" asked Sherry.

"Yes. But Judith recognized me."

"Well, you know it's only a matter of time before everyone starts hearing about this." Then she held up her hand as if in an oath. "But rest assured, Glennis, they won't be hearing it from me."

"Thanks."

"So what about Jacob? Does he know about this yet?"

"No. I've been looking all over town for him. I think he got fired from his job for not showing up today."

"That's too bad."

"Yeah, I'm afraid he's just about exhausted all the minimum-wage jobs in Stafford by now."

"He must have quite an interesting résumé."

I pushed my plate away. "I just hope I can find him, before, well, before anything bad happens."

"What do you think might happen?"

"Well, I can't imagine how he must feel, being kicked out of his home by his own father. Just before he left, he told me that he knew his dad hated him."

"That's too bad."

"I guess I'm worried that he might be depressed, you know, and possibly do something foolish." I didn't mention my biggest fear—that he might accidentally overdose.

"But Jacob wouldn't harm himself, would he?"

"It's hard to say." I wrapped the paper napkin around my finger like a tourniquet. "He was pretty down and discouraged when he left the house yesterday."

"Do you think he's staying with friends for a while?"

"I don't know. But even if he is, how long can that last when he doesn't have a job or anything to fall back on?" I wanted to say, how long can that last if he can't pay his so-called friends for their stupid drugs? But I didn't.

"Maybe he'll try to call you on your cell phone," she offered.

"Maybe. So far he hasn't. I just want him to know that I've moved out and that he can come stay with me. I want him to know he has a place. I plan to fix up the second bedroom for him. It's pretty small, but—"

"But it's a roof over his head." Sherry smiled. "And I'm sure he'll appreciate it."

"If he ever figures it out..."

"Did I tell you that Matthew is home for a couple of weeks before college starts again next month? How about if I ask him to keep an eye out for Jacob while he's here? He probably still knows a lot of the places where kids hang out these days."

I wasn't so sure about that. Matthew may have had his troubles a few years back, but he'd never sunk so low as my son. "Sure," I told her. "I'd appreciate that."

"Well, at least I know why I kept thinking of you lately," she said in a sad voice. "And I really have been praying for you, Glennis. Guess I'll have to pray even harder now."

I studied her. "Do you really think it makes a difference?"

She didn't seem surprised by my question. "I know what you mean. And I can remember feeling like that too. Especially when Matthew and Mark were going through their drinking and partying era. I swear that's the year when my hair went completely gray." She patted her head. "Of course, I don't have to tell the whole world about that." She smiled. "But

I can remember those sleepless nights when I felt certain I'd be called to the emergency room to identify one of my sons."

I nodded. "I've had those exact same thoughts."

"And I can remember praying the same things over and over again." She sighed. "It was always, 'Keep them safe, God. Just take care of them until they can take care of themselves.'"

"That's pretty much what my prayers sound like. That and 'Help!' I seem to be praying, 'Help me, help me,' more and more these days."

She sort of laughed. "Yes, I remember doing that too. But then I had a little breakthrough. I'm sure I've told you this before."

"What?" I asked, trying to recall whatever bits of wisdom she'd passed along to me in the past.

"Oh, you know, the letting-go thing."

I nodded but only vaguely remembered. "Yes, but maybe I need to hear it again."

"Well, it was one of those nights when Mark was away at college and not doing too well. And then Matthew had started partying at the end of his senior year."

"Right. I remember."

"And I just felt as if I was at the end of my rope. And I was praying for both of them one night when I couldn't sleep, and it suddenly occurred to me that if God had created both of my sons—you know, knit them in my womb as it says in that psalm—well, then it was like they were his sons too. And I just figured, well, if God is really God, then he should be perfectly capable of taking care of my boys, and much better than I could. And so I just told God, 'Hey, they are your boys, and I expect you to be taking care of them.' Then I thanked him and said 'amen.' And that became sort of a regular prayer for me. I called it my letting-go-and-letting-God prayer, and it really seemed to bring a sense of peace."

"I wish I could do that," I admitted. "But I get tied up in knots with worry. And I lie awake in bed just trying to come up with answers and solutions, ways to help Jacob get back on track."

"Maybe it's a timing thing."

"Timing?"

"Maybe God will put the letting-go prayer in your heart when you're really ready to let Jacob go."

"Let him go?" I tried to imagine such a thing.

"You know, and let God look after him."

"That sounds good, Sherry. But maybe you're right. Maybe it is a timing thing, because right now I feel like Jacob doesn't have anyone who loves him or cares about him anymore. Except for me."

"And God?"

"Yes, I suppose God cares about him too."

"But not Geoffrey?"

"I don't think so. I really felt like Geoffrey was completely washing his hands of Jacob. Like that was it. Finished, over and done with."

"Maybe just temporarily."

"Let's hope so." I unwound the napkin from my finger and set it aside.

"How about Sarah?"

I rolled my eyes.

"Still acting as if she doesn't care?"

"I don't think it's an act, Sherry. She really seems to dislike her brother."

"I'm sure she just dislikes how he's acting."

"Don't be so sure. Sarah is my daughter, and I love her dearly, but she can be a little narcissistic at times. She and her father react in a similar way when it comes to someone, even a member of their own family, inconveniencing them or making them look bad."

"Like the time she brought her college friend home, and Jacob came home plastered."

I wanted to say, "You mean stoned," but didn't. "Yeah, little things like that."

"Well, I'm sure she was embarrassed."

"Of course, we all were. But it's no reason to disown your brother."

"No, but she's still young. She'll probably grow out of it."

"You mean like her father has?" I could hear the trace of bitterness in my voice.

But Sherry didn't seem to notice. Or if she did, she didn't mention it. "Despite how perfectly miserable this looks and feels to you right now, Glennis, I know you're going to come out on top. You're going to be just fine."

"How do you *know* that?"

She smiled. "Let's just say it's a God thing."

"I hope you're right, Sherry. Because, to tell you the truth, I don't exactly feel like God is looking down and smiling on me right now."

Chapter 7

After three days in the apartment, I still hadn't heard from Geoffrey. I wasn't sure if this was good or bad or if I even cared. I seemed to be in survival mode, trying to get my life into some kind of order. As a result, I'd spent most of the day hunting down the items I felt I would require in order to continue living on my own like this.

After just two nights of sleeping on the floor, I had gotten up stiff and sore and with the full realization that I would need an actual bed to make it in my new habitat. So, armed with my plastic cards, which I hoped still worked, I'd set out shopping at the various discount stores, places where Geoffrey would never allow me to shop for home furnishings before. I was surprised at the bargains I unearthed, and by the end of the day, I'd not only purchased a full-sized bed but a futon as well, in case Jacob decided to make an appearance. I even purchased a few other pieces of inexpensive furniture that I figured I might as well get before Geoffrey canceled all my credit and bank cards, which I knew he would do eventually, maybe had already done. I'd brought some of the items home with me, and others would be delivered within the week. But I was exhausted by the effort.

By that evening Geoffrey finally called. As usual, I jumped when I heard my cell phone ring. Hoping it might be Jacob, I quickly answered only to discover it was Jacob's father, and he was angry.

"Where on earth are you?" he demanded. "Are you all right?"

I stammered for several moments but managed to explain that I'd left him.

"Because of Jacob?" he asked calmly.

"I don't know…" I struggled for an answer. "Because of everything."

"You're going to let Jacob destroy everything? All that we've built over the years?"

"You can't blame this all on Jacob," I said.

"Who then?"

"It's all of us. It's just not working."

"You're the one who left, Glennis." His voice became edgy.

"I couldn't stay any longer, Geoffrey…" I felt a tightening in my throat, hot tears burning behind my eyelids. I longed for him to say something comforting, something warm or loving—anything to make me want to come home again.

"Well, you've gone too far this time." It felt as if he'd just shut the door.

"Too far?" My voice sounded small and distant to me, but it was all I could do to get the words out.

"I'm warning you."

"What are you warning me about?" I asked, trying hard to keep calm.

"If you do this to me—if you walk out like this, Glennis—well, just don't plan on coming back."

I stood up and walked around the small, cluttered apartment. It felt reflective of my life. But as I walked, I considered his warning.

"I mean it," he continued, his voice growing sharper. "If you think you can pull something like this and then come waltzing back into my life, well, you just better think again."

For a split second I wasn't sure if he was talking to Jacob or to me. But I glanced around the messy living room and realized that Jacob wasn't even here. "Have you seen Jacob?" I asked.

He fired off an expletive, which I took as a negative. "Are you *listening* to me, Glennis?"

"I'm listening," I said, growing weary of him and the entire conversation.

"Do you understand what I'm saying, Glennis?" His tone softened, and I could imagine him willing himself to be composed. "If you leave me like this, it's over."

"I'm so sorry, Geoffrey," I told him in my most polite voice, the one I used for the opening day of kindergarten when I was meeting the anxious parents of my students for the first time. "But it was the only thing I knew how to do."

"Is he living with you now?"

"Well, no."

"So, Glennis. What's the point of your leaving? You're letting him rip our home apart, and it's not even doing him a bit of good."

"I'm just trying to make a place for him, something to come home to." I felt the tears in my voice. "He won't make it on the streets, Geoffrey. He's too—"

"It's his choice to live like that."

"Not really. He's in a trap, and he needs our—"

"He needs to make better choices," snapped Geoffrey. "And for that matter, so do you!"

"I'm making the only choice I know how to make at the moment." Tears were sliding down my cheeks now. "I'm just trying to help Jacob. I'm trying to just...just survive."

"So that's your answer?"

I grabbed a paper towel to wipe my face. "My answer?"

"Meaning, you are choosing *not* to return home?"

I looked around the shabby apartment, piled high with a bunch of cheap, junky pieces of furniture. "I think I *am* home."

"Fine!" And he hung up.

My heart felt as if someone had strapped a boulder to it and thrown it into the sea. I collapsed into my camp chair, leaned over with my head in my hands, and began to cry harder.

I think I sat there and cried for about three days. And then one morning Jacob called.

"Mom?"

"Jacob!"

"Where are you?" He sounded small and frightened, like when he'd been a little boy and awakened from a nightmare. "I keep calling the house, and you never answer. And the answering-machine message is different."

"Different?"

"Yeah, it's Dad saying to leave a message."

"Oh."

"Where are you, Mom?"

"I…uh…I moved out."

"Moved? Like out of the house?"

"That's right. I have an apartment now."

"You mean you've *left* Dad?"

I could tell he was completely stunned, but I wasn't sure how to soften the blow. "Well, sort of."

"What do you mean, 'sort of'? You've either left him or you haven't."

"Well, I had to get away for a while. I needed some time and space to think about things."

"Is this because of me?"

"Nooo…" I picked up a pillow from a pile of stuff on the floor and tossed it onto the homely brown couch that I'd gotten for cheap and had finally pushed into the only place a couch could fit in this miniature living room.

"It is, isn't it?"

"No, Jacob, it's not. Your dad and I have been growing apart for years

now. And it's not so much that I wanted to leave him, if you can understand that, but I needed to get away to kind of find myself. Does that
make sense?"

"Sort of. I guess I felt like that too."

I sighed. "It's so good to hear your voice again. I've been so worried
about you. I wish you would've called sooner. You know it's been almost
a week now."

"Really?"

"Yeah. Where have you been staying?"

"With friends a few nights and in my car."

"Are you…uh…*okay?*" Of course, what I really wanted to ask was,
are you doing drugs? But I didn't want to scare him off.

"Of course I'm okay."

"Did you lose your job?"

"Well, it's pretty hard to keep a job when you're homeless."

"You can come stay with me."

"Really?" He sounded hopeful. "Do you have room?"

I sort of laughed. "Well, it's a pretty small place, but I saved a bedroom for you, if you want it."

"Thanks, Mom."

I gave him the address, and he said he'd stop by later on and unload
some of his stuff. He didn't promise to move in with me, but at least I was
going to see him. Just hearing his voice was like medicine for me. I immediately went into high gear and started arranging the furniture pieces that
had simply been stacked and shoved here and there. I dug out the white
canvas slipcover I'd purchased for my dog-ugly couch, which actually had
"good bones," and I pulled and tugged until I finally got it on. To my surprise, it wasn't half-bad. And when I added the colorful pillows I'd confiscated from my previous home, it looked even better. It was a start.

I worked and worked. Moving and arranging and putting away. And finally it looked almost habitable and considerably bigger now that everything was in its place and out of the way. And then, feeling encouraged, I took a quick shower, and for the first time in days I put on something besides my gray sweats. As I ran a brush through my wet hair and noticed the strange woman looking back at me from the slightly steamed-up bathroom mirror, I winced at the tired image of my mother that I was becoming.

Oh, I knew that my once-auburn hair had gotten progressively grayer during the past year. In fact, it seemed almost colorless now. And I suspected I had more wrinkles than before, but the haggard old woman that stared back at me in the mirror was slightly frightening. And it became even worse as the fog from the mirror slowly evaporated and each line and wrinkle etched into my painfully pale face became more noticeable. I leaned forward and stared, touching my cheek with my hand to see if it was really me.

No wonder Sherry had accused me of letting myself go lately. Even so, I couldn't convince myself to apply any makeup or do more than just pull back my shoulder-length hair into my usual tortoiseshell clip. I didn't have time or inclination for primping today.

For one thing, I knew that despite my massive stock-up session at the grocery store nearly a week ago, I was currently out of the basics like bread and milk and eggs, and I knew from experience that when Jacob arrived, he would be hungry—probably ravenous. So I made a list, grabbed my purse, and left a note on the door.

As I was driving toward the discount grocery store, my cell phone rang. Even though I despise it when people talk on the phone while in traffic, I thought it might be Jacob again, and so I decided to answer.

"Mom?"

"Sarah!" I exclaimed, pulling over to a side street. "I've been trying to reach you all week. How are you, honey?"

"What's going on, Mom?" she demanded. "Dad told me I'd better talk to you."

"That's why I've been calling," I told her, trying to gather my thoughts as I turned off the ignition. "I wanted to explain everything. But, first, tell me how you're doing, Sarah. I've barely talked to you since you got home from Europe. Was it wonderful? I want to hear all about it."

"It was pretty good. But hot, really hot. They had record-breaking temperatures everywhere and no air conditioning. Leslie nearly had a heatstroke in Madrid the day before we were supposed to fly out, so we had to take her to the hospital and almost missed our flight."

"Oh my." I turned the key and let the windows down for some fresh air. "But she's okay?"

"Yeah, she's fine."

"And are you back on campus now?"

"Yeah, just getting settled into the dorm. But I really wish I could get an apartment. Leslie and Kara want to go in with me."

"Well, did you mention this to your dad?"

"Not yet. He seemed pretty upset about something. What's going on, Mom?"

I couldn't help but notice the somewhat accusatory tone of her voice and was reminded once again of how much she and Geoffrey were alike. "Well, it's been quite a week, honey. Jacob got into some trouble—"

"Wow, that's a big surprise."

I ignored her sarcasm. "Yes, I know. But your dad and I didn't agree about how to handle it."

"*No.* How shocking." More sarcasm.

"And I decided to help Jacob, and then your dad got mad, and I was so tired of all this—"

"All this?" She exhaled loudly. "You mean *all this crap* that Jacob has dragged into our lives?"

"Not just that, honey. Your dad and I have been having our problems too."

"What? You mean just because Daddy is trying to use tough love?"

"Tough love?" I echoed. "I'm not sure your father feels *any* love toward his son at the moment."

"Can you blame him?"

"I know Jacob has messed up, Sarah, but he's our son, your brother—"

"Don't remind me."

"Sarah!" I instantly regretted my scolding tone.

"You always take his side, Mom. That's probably why he's so screwed up."

"It's not a matter of sides," I said.

"Whatever." Now I could tell she was exasperated.

"I would do the same for you, Sarah. You know I would."

"But that's a moot point, Mom. You will *never* need to do the same for me. Jacob and I are two completely different people. I can't even believe we're related sometimes."

"Jake's just going through some hard things right now. But that could all change. I'm trying to get him to go into rehab and—"

"Good luck with that." Sarah sounded as though she was ready to end the conversation. "So tell me, Mom. Are you and Dad still together?"

"Well, not exactly."

"What *exactly* do you mean by that?"

"I've gotten an apartment."

"So you're separated then?"

"Well, sort of."

"Look, Mom, you moved out of the house, right? Well, that would mean you're separated."

"Okay. I suppose so."

"Mom, can't you see what's happening?"

"What do you mean?"

"I mean you're letting Jacob ruin your marriage. And that's wrong. Plain wrong. You and Dad have been happily married for twenty-five years, and just because Jacob's screwing up his life doesn't mean you have to throw away a perfectly good marriage."

"A perfectly good marriage?"

"Well, you guys seem pretty happy to me."

"You really think so?"

"Oh, I know it's not perfect. But whose marriage is?"

"There's a lot you don't know, honey."

"I know *this,* Mom. I know Dad doesn't deserve this kind of treatment. He has worked hard for his family. He's a great provider, respected in the community, and he doesn't deserve this kind of crap from you."

Her words slapped me despite the distance between us.

"And if you weren't so blind, you'd see it too," she continued. "Dad's exactly right about Jacob. He's made his own stupid choices, and there's nothing any of us can do about it. As much as I hate to admit that my little brother's a junkie, it's the truth, and the sooner we all accept it, the better it will be for everyone."

"Are you suggesting I simply turn my back on your brother?"

"I'm not saying you have to quit loving him, Mom." Her voice softened. "I mean as much as I hate him sometimes for all this crud, I do still love him. But I'm saying you have to let him do his thing and hope he doesn't kill himself doing it. In the meantime, I think you should focus your attention on saving your marriage."

"Saving my marriage?" I echoed.

"Yes. You and Dad are both Christians, and as I recall, you made a vow to God *and* to each other—you know the spiel, Mom—till death do us part. And you're not keeping it."

I swallowed hard. "A big part of me is already dead, Sarah."

She didn't say anything.

"I'm sorry, honey," I continued. "I know this is hard for you to hear. But like I told your dad, I just needed a break, a chance to regain myself and to think about everything that's going on right now. It's not as if I'm looking for a divorce. I'm certainly not. I just needed to catch my breath. Can you understand that?"

"Not really." She paused. "Oh, I think Leslie's here, and we were going to look at apartments this afternoon."

"Right."

"Think about what I said, Mom," she told me.

"Yes, of course I will."

"Good."

"I love you, honey."

"Love you too, Mom."

And that was it. I shook my head and looked around the interior of the Range Rover, trying to remember where I was and where I'd been going. Then, spying the short grocery list by my purse, I remembered. Oh yes, Jacob was coming home.

Chapter 8

I headed the Range Rover back to More-4-Less, not even sure why I was going there again, except that it was in the neighborhood, and perhaps I wanted to prove something to myself. I tried to push Sarah's words and accusations away from me as I walked across the blacktop parking lot. After all, my opinionated daughter was only twenty-one and still had a lot to learn about life and relationships. And, although I hated feeling like I was hurting her, I knew it was best for her to hear the truth, at least from me. Still, it seemed there was far too much hurt going around these days, and I wished there was some other way...something I could do to stop all the pain.

As I searched for a grocery cart without wobbly wheels or too much sticky grime, I wondered if Sylvia would be there at this time of day. For some reason, I wanted to see that woman again. I wanted to assure her I was doing much better now. Okay, perhaps "much better" was a huge overstatement, especially after that conversation with Sarah. But I was alive and moving—even if it was only two steps forward before I took one and a half back. At least those half steps were something.

Thinking of Jacob, I got a gallon of milk, some "no pulp" orange juice, a large carton of eggs, two loaves of bread (one white, one whole wheat), some sliced roast beef and smoked turkey, some leaf lettuce and tomatoes, a nice selection of fresh fruit. I even picked up some of the junk foods—cheese curls and powdered-sugar doughnuts—that I normally avoided but knew my son liked. Then, feeling like the prodigal's mother who was ready to slaughter the fatted calf, I even got a case of Dr Pepper, my son's beverage of choice. Well, at least in childhood. Who knows what he imbibes now? I also picked up a box of maple bars (another Jacob favorite) and a package of chocolate chips in case we felt like making cookies. Who knew? Then, feeling even more celebratory at my son's homecoming, I picked out one of those bunches of prearranged flowers, mostly carnations and chrysanthemums and only $5.99, before I headed to the checkout.

To my pleased surprise, Sylvia was there, and even though her line was slightly longer than the other two, I decided to get in it anyway. I absently flipped through a *Good Housekeeping* magazine as I waited my turn. After shopping at the discount furniture warehouses, I couldn't bear to look at magazines like *House Beautiful* or *Architectural Digest*, my usual preferences. I kept telling myself it was best not to look back. Just move forward.

When Sylvia began ringing up my purchases, I was ready for her. I expertly snapped open the brown paper bags and loaded my groceries almost as quickly as the moving belt funneled them at me. Sylvia didn't really look up at me until she announced the total, but I noticed a faint glimmer of recognition in her eyes.

"So you got it all figured out this time," she said as I handed her my debit card.

I nodded. "I'm figuring out a lot of things."

She nodded as she ran my card through the scanner on her register, but after a moment she frowned. "It's been rejected." She handed back my card.

I'm sure my face looked alarmed. "Rejected?" I asked in a mousy voice. "Really? Are you sure?"

"You want me to run it again?"

I glanced at the impatient customers waiting behind me, then fumbled through my billfold for cash. "No, no," I told her. "I've got it."

I felt a gnawing deep inside me as I handed her several twenties. It was already beginning.

"I'm sorry." Her eyes looked surprisingly kind as she handed me my change. "They usually stop the cards right away."

I sighed. "I guess I should've known it was coming."

She nodded to my bouquet still lying on the counter. "Don't forget those."

"Thanks." I picked it up and set it on top of a bag.

She smiled. "Well, hang in there."

Despite my sinking heart over the cancelled debit card, I felt like I'd accomplished something as I walked across the parking lot toward the Range Rover. Oh, I knew all I'd really done was bag my own groceries, but it was a start. Besides, I knew I still had my savings account, in my name only. I wasn't broke yet. And I didn't want to live off of Geoffrey anyway. Not if he wanted to be stingy. Somehow I would get through this. And, I told myself, Jacob was coming home!

Jacob's car was nowhere to be seen when I parked in space number thirty-six at the apartment. When I got upstairs, I noticed my note was exactly where I'd left it. So I began putting the groceries away, taking my time and rearranging a few things along the way. I felt pleased at how my little apartment was beginning to function like an actual, albeit rather tiny, home. In some ways it seemed like I was a little girl again, playing house. Not a bad feeling really. I even considered baking something, since I always thought the smell of baking made a place feel homier. But it was turning into another sweltering end-of-summer day, and without air conditioning I figured I'd better not add any heat to my second-floor dwelling.

After the food was put away and I'd snipped the bottoms of the flowers and temporarily stuck them into a juice pitcher, I fixed myself a late lunch and sat down at the narrow breakfast bar on a new pine barstool. (I'd purchased a pair of them for only $19.99 each.) There I quietly ate and watched out the window as cars zipped past on the busy street down below. I suspected that most of the minivans contained moms and kids doing their back-to-school shopping. I'd always loved doing that with Sarah and Jacob. Especially when the kids were smaller and we'd stock up on things like Crayola crayons, number-two pencils, bright plastic lunchboxes, and rain parkas. The older they got, the less fun and more expensive it became. But I still got a thrill seeing them with a new backpack or the latest thing in shoes. And whether they would admit it or not, I think they enjoyed it too. Well, except for Jacob in his last year at high school—I don't think he wanted anything last year. Another sign that he was becoming someone else.

I glanced at the kitchen clock—only $6.99, who knew?—and if my inexpensive clock was correct it was after four o'clock. My new bed had finally been delivered yesterday afternoon, and although I'd moved up from the floor to the futon in Jacob's room during the previous nights, I was still feeling sleep deprived and exhausted. So I decided to take a short nap, just until Jacob got here, which I felt would be any minute. I left my front door unlocked just in case I didn't hear him knocking, knowing that would be nearly impossible in such a small apartment. But I was taking no chances.

When I woke up, it was nearly eight thirty, and as far as I could tell, Jacob hadn't been there yet. Instead of turning on the lights, I decided to light some of the candles I'd confiscated from my previous home. Geoffrey had told me we shouldn't be lighting candles after he read an article on how the candle smoke can leave a thin coating of soot on the walls and furnishings, although I'd never seen that happen myself. Still, I continued to light candles when Geoffrey was working late or gone for a weekend conference. I guess it was my little rebellion. And tonight I was pleased by the effect of the candles in the apartment. It seemed to soften the edges, and somehow it made the spaces seem cozier and yet more spacious too.

Noticing my grocery store flowers still sitting in the juice pitcher in the sink, I remembered that I'd wanted to hunt down something to put them in. I knew I'd brought my crystal vase from home. It had been a gift from Geoffrey, something I'd almost left behind, but then, feeling sentimental, I'd decided to bring it along. Geoffrey had given this to me for our twenty-fifth anniversary last June. It was a lovely Waterford piece and had been filled with twenty-five perfect red roses—one for each year of our "perfect" marriage. One thing about Geoffrey: he always knew how to give perfect gifts, and he was never cheap about it, either.

He had also presented me with a brochure filled with glossy photos of sunny beaches and palm trees, promising me a trip to the Caribbean to commemorate our milestone. "Sorry, sweetheart. We'll have to wait until this case is over," he had explained over a lovely anniversary dinner at Sindalli's. "But we can have a belated celebration this fall. Maybe by late September." Naturally, I had agreed with him. When had I not agreed with him? Well, other than this thing with Jacob.

I rummaged around in the tiny linen closet right next to the bathroom and found the beautiful crystal vase. Looking out of place wedged between a package of toilet paper and some tile cleaner, the vase with all its cut-glass intricacies shimmered in the candlelight as I pulled it out and carried it into the living room. Although it was much too grand for this little apartment, still I put my grocery store flowers in it, then set the arrangement on the small secondhand coffee table in front of the couch. Such a lovely gift, a souvenir of a past that now seemed out of reach.

Had I been stupid to leave Geoffrey like that, to walk away from twenty-five years of marriage? Not that I'd meant to leave permanently. That had never been my actual goal. I think I had considered it to be more of a break, like a mental-health day, or week or month. I needed a time away from everything, a time for me to figure things out and to hopefully help Jacob. But what had I figured out, really? And how had I helped Jacob? The light from the candles grew blurry as my eyes suddenly filled with tears, and I questioned everything about myself. What had I done?

Did I think my absence would get Geoffrey's attention? Had I subconsciously thought that he'd miss me so much he'd jump into his Porsche and come flying over here, that he'd fall on his knees and beg me to forgive him? That he'd promise to be the father Jacob needed, and he'd take me into his arms and swear to me that everything would be different from here on out? My shining knight on a perfect white horse? Wasn't that how the fairy tales ended? Or at least those bachelor reality shows on TV?

I got a tissue and blew my nose. But I am forty-eight years old, I reminded myself, and old enough to know that the characters in fairy tales don't necessarily live happily ever after. Right? But maybe I'd been wrong. Maybe I was the one who should've gone running back. Maybe I should've gotten down on my knees and apologized to him. After all, I was the one who had left. My own daughter had even told me as much. I paced back and forth in my now somewhat livable apartment. Had I been wrong?

Suddenly I felt a real sense of urgency. I imagined Geoffrey sitting alone in that big house, weary from a hard week at work—it was almost time for the city's case to go to court, and he'd probably been working long, hard hours to get everything perfectly prepared. I envisioned him sitting by himself in the kitchen, which by now would be quite messy, eating a lukewarm microwave dinner and wearing a wrinkled shirt with a coffee stain on the front. Oh, I knew I was being overly dramatic, but I also knew better than anyone that Geoffrey was not the kind of man who could take care of himself. He didn't even know how to run the washing machine. And what about Winnie and Rufus? Did I really think that Geoffrey was going to take care of them? I would feel terrible if my absence had hurt those two innocent animals in any way.

I quickly blew out the candles and dashed off a note for Jacob, just in case he showed, then I jumped into the Range Rover and drove toward the house. Oh, what had I been thinking? I chastised myself. Had I even

been thinking at all? Surely Sarah had been right. Surely the most important thing for me to do right now was to save my marriage. Why was I
such a fool?

"God help me," I prayed aloud as I drove. "Help me not to blow this."

I must admit that the idea of being back in that spacious home and
sleeping on those four-hundred-thread-count Egyptian cotton sheets
(which I could no longer afford) and taking scented bubble baths in my
big whirlpool tub and looking out the front windows onto the city lights
below—well, it did have a certain appeal. Especially after being absent
from all that luxury for one long and exhausting week. Maybe *I* was the
one who needed to learn a lesson, I thought, as I drove up the winding
street that led to our house.

But when I got there, I noticed a car in the driveway. So instead of
pulling right in and bursting into the house with my now somewhat-
rehearsed apology, I drove on past and parked in front of the house next
door. I didn't recognize the car in the driveway, but that wasn't such a big
deal since I'd always been bad at recognizing cars. It was small and red and
sporty, and I suspected it belonged to one of his legal friends. Maybe John
Howard, since I'd heard he'd gone through a midlife crisis, and this looked
like a midlife crisis sort of vehicle to me.

Since the lights were on in the house, I knew I could easily slip up and
peer in without being noticed. I wasn't quite ready to interrupt what
might be an important business meeting, and I knew I could wait for
John or whomever to leave or even come back in the morning. But curious as to the condition of my poor, abandoned husband, I decided to take
a peek inside. I crept up behind the laurel hedge that lines the driveway
and then over to the window that looks into the dining room. I crouched
in the rhododendron bushes by the house for a couple of minutes. I think
I was even holding my breath until I got up the nerve to poke my nose
over the window sill and look inside.

My heart must've stopped when I saw them. Not that they were doing anything wrong, exactly. Even so, it looked *all wrong*. At least to my eyes. Because there, sitting at my dining room table, was my husband and Judith Ramsey. Even though I knew she was the city manager and this might've been an official business meeting, I somehow knew that it was *not*. Maybe it was the way they leaned in toward each other as they talked with animation. Or maybe it was the bottle of wine on the table— Geoffrey and I have never been drinkers. Or maybe it was my husband's face, the easy smile and sparkling eyes—an expression I hadn't witnessed in years. It was the same look he'd had in the photograph with Judith from his birthday party. The brightly burning candles offered more evidence that Geoffrey was no longer himself anymore than I was.

I sank down into the bushes and, pulling my knees toward my chest, buried my head and silently wept. I felt unable to breathe or even think, and I have no idea how long I stayed there in that crouched position. Finally, like a whipped and beaten animal, I slunk through the yard, across the driveway, and back to my car. Standing in the shadows, I dug through my purse to find my keys. Then I turned around for one last look, and something about seeing that sporty little red car parked in my driveway just flipped some crazy switch in my brain. Call it temporary insanity or whatever, but I ran back over there determined to let the air out of those perky little tires.

But when I got to her car, I took a deep breath and calmly ran my key along the entire length of the driver's side, digging a nice deep gouge of rage into the shiny red paint.

I was instantly embarrassed to catch myself doing something that immature, and I'll probably never admit those actions to any living human. But I just couldn't help myself. Then I drove home.

Chapter 9

I felt numb as I dragged myself up the stairs to my apartment. By now the realization was actually sinking in. My husband, the man I'd been married to for twenty-five years, was probably having an affair. It all seemed so unreal, so cliché even. Hadn't I seen this same movie on Lifetime last year? I felt trapped in someone else's nightmare, unable to even take it all in. I was so distracted by those emotions I didn't even notice that the note I'd left taped to the door was gone as I went inside.

"Mom," said Jacob with a smile.

I blinked into the light. "Jacob?"

"Are you all right?" He came closer now, putting his hand on my shoulder. To my surprise he didn't look too bad. His was clean and shaved and even looked sober.

"I…uh…I'm not sure."

"What's wrong?" He reached over and plucked a rhododendron leaf from my hair. "Where have you been anyway?"

I sank down onto the couch and just shook my head. Then before I had time to think or reconsider, I poured out my awful story.

Jacob gently put his arm around my shoulder and actually hugged me. "It's going to be okay, Mom," he said in a soothing and surprisingly mature voice.

I looked at him through my tears and somehow, despite my broken heart, I was able to smile. "I'm so glad you came home, Jake."

He nodded. "I'm sorry I'm so late, but I got a job."

I blinked. "You got a job?"

"Yeah, a friend of mine helped me get on at Mama Mia's Pizza." He made a face. "It's not much, but it's better than nothing, and I get free food."

I reached out and hugged him then. "Oh, Jacob, I'm so proud of you."

He frowned. "Well, I haven't done much to make you proud *yet*. And I'm really sorry that I've been such a total screwup, but that's all going to change now."

"Really?" I studied his face and was surprised at how bright and happy his countenance appeared. Almost as if he'd had some sort of revelation.

"Yeah. I had some time to think about everything—you know, my life and where it's heading and everything. And, to be totally honest, I wasn't making the greatest choices when I first left home. I did some stuff, well, some things I'm not too proud of. But I woke up a couple of days ago, and I just realized this has to stop."

I nodded eagerly. "Yes! You're right, Jacob. Oh, I'm so happy for you."

He smiled. "Yeah, I am too. And I made this really good friend. His name is Daniel, and he's a lot older than me, about thirty I think, but he's been through a lot of the same kind of stuff, and he really understands me. He's the one who helped get me on at Mama Mia's."

"That's great." I reached for a tissue to wipe the tears from my face.

"And I'm really sorry about that crap with you and Dad." He scowled. "I had a feeling that something like that was going on."

"Really?"

"Remember, I sort of tried to warn you that day I left home. I said we were all going to get hurt."

I nodded. "So that's what you meant."

"One time I went to Dad's office to see if he could loan me some gas money, just so I could get home, you know. Anyway, his secretary wasn't there, so I just walked in like normal. And I didn't exactly see anything for sure, but the way those two were acting, you know, the looks on their faces. I felt pretty sure I'd caught them at something. But the truth is, I was a little strung out at the time, so later on I wasn't sure if I'd imagined it or not. But I really don't think I did."

"Do you remember when that was?"

He frowned. "A pretty long time ago. Like last spring maybe. I think I was still in school."

"Oh."

He shook his head. "Man, I'm really sorry, Mom. It looks like the guys in your life have really let you down."

"No," I said firmly. "Your dad has let me down—hugely. But you're getting your life back on track now, Jacob. Honestly, I don't think anyone else could've helped me through this night the way that seeing you has done."

He smiled brightly now. "Cool." Then he nodded toward the kitchen. "I hope it's okay that I was fixing myself something to eat."

"Of course. Make yourself at home. *Mi casa es su casa.*" My attempt at lightness was as thin as cellophane, but Jacob didn't seem to notice.

"All right." He laughed as he went into the kitchen. "By the way, I really like what you've done with the place, Mom. When I first got here, I couldn't imagine you living in an apartment like this."

I attempted a laugh now. "Yeah, it was a pretty big change."

"But you've made it look really cool in here."

"Thanks."

I sat down on a barstool and watched as Jacob meticulously built himself a sandwich. Suppressing my churning emotions, I watched him layer on lettuce and tomatoes and cheese, carefully spreading mayonnaise and putting on a thick wad of roast beef. He really did look good, and healthy, too. And so, despite the blow I'd just suffered and the dull ache ricocheting inside, I told myself that perhaps my life wasn't going to end tonight after all. If my only purpose for being alive at this moment was to help Jacob, well, so be it. Wasn't that what a mother was supposed to do?

Nonetheless, I cried myself to sleep that night. But in the midst of my tears, I still paused to thank God for returning my son home safely to me. "Help us to pick up the pieces," I prayed—my first real prayer in months. "Show me where to go from here."

I called Sherry the next day and told her I needed to talk. We agreed to meet at my apartment as soon as Jacob went to work.

"This must be serious," she said when I opened the door and let her in. She glanced around with obvious curiosity. "Since it's the first time you've let me actually see your apartment."

I frowned. "Yeah, welcome to my humble abode." Then I collapsed on the couch and put my head in my hands.

"Talk to me," said Sherry, sitting down beside me. "What's wrong?"

I took a deep breath, attempting to steady myself. "It's Geoffrey," I told her, looking up. "I think he's having an affair."

Her eyes grew wide. "No way, Glennis. Not Geoffrey."

I nodded. "I really think so, Sherry." Then I told her about sneaking home the night before and seeing him there with Judith. About the candles, the wine—everything.

"You're kidding!"

"I wish I was." I shook my head. "And you know what's really stupid?" Fresh tears were filling my eyes again.

Sherry reached over and took my hand.

"I…I had gone over there to…to tell him that…I…*I* was sorry." Then I broke into sobs.

Sherry hugged me and assured me that everything was going to be okay. How she knew this was way beyond me, but I wanted to believe her.

Finally I managed to stop crying and attempted to compose myself as I told her the good news about Jacob.

"Well, at least that's something," she said with a bright smile.

"Yeah. It felt like a real lifeline last night."

"See," she said, "God *is* listening to your prayers."

I took in a jagged breath. "Maybe some of my prayers…"

"What are you going to do now?" she asked.

"I…uh…I don't know. What do you think I should do?"

She considered this. "Well, do you *really* believe he's having an affair?"

"I don't know for sure." Then last night's scene flashed through my mind again, and I nodded. "I really believe he is. If you'd seen the look on their faces, Sherry…" I covered my mouth with my hand, certain that I was about to be sick, or maybe I was going to scream.

"Oh, Glennis." She just shook her head.

"And even if they're not…not sleeping together…yet…" I bit into my lip as I thought about this possibility. "I know it's just a matter of time." Then I told her what Jacob had said about finding them in Geoffrey's office last spring.

"Well, you guys have both been under a lot of stress, Glennis. I suppose it's possible that Geoffrey used this as an excuse to, well, stray."

"An excuse?"

"Oh, you know what I mean." She sighed. "I'm sorry."

"But what do I do now?" I looked around my little apartment and realized that this might really turn into my permanent home now. "I…I don't know what to do."

Sherry grew thoughtful, and I waited. Finally she said. "I think you should confront him."

"Confront him?" Fear returned to my voice.

"Yes. Tell him what you suspect, and ask him if it's true."

"What if he lies?"

"Well, he might. Just do your best to discern whether he's lying or not."

I groaned. "I don't think I even know how to do that anymore. I feel like I can barely discern what's true for myself. How can I tell if someone else is lying?"

"Look at his eyes," she told me.

"But he's a lawyer," I reminded her. "I have a feeling he can tell lies without anyone knowing."

"But he's a Christian," she said.

"What makes you so sure anymore?" I asked.

"We can't judge him, Glennis."

I shook my head. "I'm so confused."

"Well, just pray about it," she told me. "Maybe God will give you some special insight."

I seriously doubted this but didn't say as much. "And what then? What if I *am* able to confront him, and believe me, that doesn't seem very likely. But even if I *am* able to do this, what happens next? I mean if he's…well, if he's really having an affair. What then?"

"Then you need to decide whether your marriage can be salvaged or not."

"Salvaged?" I imagined a pile of broken and worn furniture.

"Yes. Is it possible that you guys could get counseling?"

I forced a laugh. "Counseling? Are you serious? Geoffrey totally refused to go in for counseling when Jacob first started messing up. Do you think he'd go now?"

"You need to at least ask him, Glennis."

"Why?" I demanded, suddenly angry. "Why do *I* have to ask *him?* He should be the one asking me. Why am I the one who always has to do everything?"

Sherry patted my hand. "Just give it a try, Glennis."

"But I don't see why, Sherry. Why should I be the one to—"

"Because if you do everything you can possibly do to save your marriage, then you won't have so much garbage to deal with later."

"Later?"

Sherry nodded. "Yes, whether you believe it or not, there will be a later. Remember when my sister Marla got divorced a few years ago?"

"Sort of."

"Well, trust me, there's lots of *later*."

"Oh."

"But what if I confront him and suggest counseling, and he still refuses?" I asked her. "What do I do then?"

"Then…you get yourself a good lawyer."

Once again Sherry encouraged me to call her counselor friend. And finally I just gave in and sat there in my apartment, feeling like a six-year-old, as Sherry used her cell phone to call and make me an appointment for the following week.

"Do I need to come get you next Friday?" asked Sherry as she made her way to the door. "I don't mind taking you."

"No, I'm perfectly capable of getting myself to the shrink."

"She's not a shrink, Glennis. She's a counselor. And she's really great at marriage counseling."

"How do you know this for sure?"

Sherry winked. "I've been sworn to secrecy. If I told you, I'd have to kill you."

"Very funny."

"By the way," she said with one hand on the doorknob, "I like what you've done with the place."

I forced a laugh. "I'll bet."

"No, seriously. It's really nice. It seems more like you than your big house on the hill."

"I'm not sure how to take that," I told her. "Are you saying the real me is cheap and cheesy and—"

"No, not that part. I mean what you've done with the colors and everything. It's very cool and creative."

"Well, I'll take *that* as a compliment," I told her.

"You'd better." Then she studied me. "Have you ever considered doing something like this as a job?"

"Huh?"

"You know, decorating. You'd be great at it."

I frowned. "Yeah, sure. My degree is in education."

She waved her hand. "Oh, degrees are a dime a dozen. It's talent that's hard to come by."

I reached out and hugged her. "Thanks, Sherry," I said. "You are always an encouragement to me."

"I'm serious," she said. "You should consider it."

"Right," I told her. "I'll consider it…right in between helping my son to get his life straightened out, saving my marriage, and seeing your shrink."

"She's not a shrink."

"Yeah, yeah."

"And we're still on for lunch on Saturday?" she asked.

"If you're not embarrassed to be seen with me in public."

"Oh, Glennis." Then Sherry frowned as she surveyed my sorry-looking outfit of dirty sweatpants and a T-shirt. "But it wouldn't hurt to clean up your act a little. Maybe we should go shopping."

I sighed. "Whatever."

"I'll call."

"Thanks," I told her as I closed the door. And I meant it. What would a person do at times like this without a good friend? I couldn't even imag-ine. I knew she was right about confronting Geoffrey. But I just wasn't sure I was up to it. Perhaps it would be better to wait a few days until I cooled off a bit, had a little more control over my emotions. But what if it only became harder the more I put it off? My policy in all things had always been to take care of things immediately. If something needed to be done, just do it. Of course, that seldom had anything to do with matters of the heart.

I decided to take Sherry's advice about cleaning up my act. And after a long shower and a decent change of clothes, I felt slightly better. I was surprised though. I put on a pair of jeans that had been pretty snug just a month ago, and now the waist was a bit loose. It figures, I thought, as I combed my hair. It takes having your life fall completely apart to finally lose some of those unwanted pounds. Oh, I knew I'd put on some extra weight over the past few years. I figured it had to do with stress eating, and I was always well aware of my increasing size whenever I went shopping. Naturally, Geoffrey liked to remind me of this fact on a fairly regular basis too. It had started out in what seemed an innocent way when he'd generously given me a yearlong membership to a top-notch gym for a Christmas present a couple of years ago. I'd meant to go, I really had, but there always seemed some really good reason to put it off. Finally I'd just hidden the membership in a drawer, then thrown it away after I realized it had expired.

I suddenly remembered the day Sherry and I had seen Judith at Ziddies. I remembered how great Judith had looked, like she'd lost some weight and perhaps even gotten a facelift. Was that what had drawn my husband to her in the first place? Or had she tried to improve herself after getting involved with my husband? Would I ever know any of this for sure? And did it even matter?

But suddenly I knew for certain that Sherry was right. I did need to confront him, and the sooner the better. And if I lost control and acted like a complete idiot or said things I'd regret later, well, so be it.

Chapter 10

Before confronting Geoffrey, I planned to check on the welfare of Winnie and Rufus. I drove over to the house with a real sense of mission. Worried that they'd been neglected or perhaps even abused—who knew what kind of monster Geoffrey had turned into lately?—my plan was to rescue the family pets and get out of there. I just hoped he hadn't changed the locks on the house yet.

Fortunately my key still worked. I let myself in and set out in search of the animals. But there was no sign of them anywhere. Even their food dishes and water bowls had been removed. I called and called, but they didn't come. Feeling despair, I finally went outside and searched some more. I wouldn't have been surprised if Geoffrey had turned them both out. But there was no trace of them out there either. I called a few more times and was about to go back into the house when I heard a woman's voice.

"Mrs. Harmon?"

I turned to see old Mrs. Fieldstone standing on the other side of the gate between our houses. "Oh, hello," I called to her. "How are you?"

She smiled. "I'm fine, dear. Are you looking for your pets?"

"Well, I…uh…yes, I am."

She motioned for me to come over. "Winnie and Rufus have been visiting me."

"Visiting you?" I went over and stood on the other side of the gate.

"Yes. I noticed you were gone, dear. And your kitty began visiting me.

She seemed hungry, so naturally I fed her. Then I asked your husband about it, and he told me I could keep the cat."

"Keep her?"

She nodded. "Oh, I didn't mean to take her away, dear. But she seemed lonely and hungry and—"

"No, that's okay," I assured her. "I mean I wish I could keep her myself. But, well, my husband and I are having some difficulties, you know, and…"

"Come on over here," said Mrs. Fieldstone as she opened the gate. "I'll put on some tea, and we can talk."

Just then Rufus ran up and barked happily at me. I knelt down to pet the scruffy little guy, taking time to really scratch him behind the ears. Then I stood, and with Rufus running excitedly at my heels, I followed this small, white-haired woman into her house. I'd only been inside it a couple of times, but I had been quite impressed with its unique Frank Lloyd Wright–style of architecture. And everything in it was still original. Soon we were sitting at her kitchen table beside a window that overlooked the city and drinking tea.

"Yes, the next day your husband asked if I'd like to have the little dog as well," said Mrs. Fieldstone. "And I wasn't too sure at first, but then Rufus came over to visit me, and we've been getting along like a house on fire ever since. Both of your animals are very nice and well behaved."

Just then Winnie jumped into my lap and began purring happily. "Do you really want to keep them?" I asked, feeling somewhat dismayed at the idea that I wasn't only losing my home and my marriage but now it seemed my pets as well.

"Oh, I only want to keep them until you're ready to have them back, dear." She passed a china plate of wafer sandwich cookies my direction. "I just couldn't bear to see them taken to the pound."

"The pound?"

She nodded. "That's where Mr. Harmon said he was taking them."

I shook my head. "Well, I'm so glad you were kind enough to rescue them. Thank you so much."

"Not at all, dear."

"The problem is that I'm staying in a tiny apartment where pets aren't allowed," I explained. "And it's on such a busy street that I don't think they'd be safe there anyway. I signed a six-month lease." I shook my head. "And I'm already regretting it."

She nodded as she set her cup down. "Regretting the lease? Or leaving your husband?"

I shrugged. "Both, I guess."

"Are you two going to work things out?"

"I don't know for sure." I studied this sweet-looking little woman and wondered how much I should really divulge.

"It's hard making a marriage work," she said. "George and I were married for fifty-one years." She shook her head. "I wish I could say they were all happy years, but that wouldn't be completely truthful."

"You weren't happily married?" I was surprised, since I'd always assumed the Fieldstones were a perfectly happy family. I knew they had four children and lots of grandchildren, all who came to visit regularly.

"In my day you had to put up with a lot," she said.

"Oh."

"Yes, it's true. My generation of women were taught to just grin and bear it. If your husband cheated on you, you had to turn your head and pretend you didn't see. Or if you couldn't take it anymore, you threw a little fit and"—she held up a wrinkled hand to show me a very large diamond ring that hung loosely on her ring finger—"you earned yourself a little bauble. Something for your troubles." She laughed. "And in time it got a little better. Over the years George and I grew to be more compatible." She looked closely at me. "But the hurt never went completely away."

I nodded.

"And if I was a modern-day woman"—she smiled—"like you…well, I'm not sure that I would stick around and put up with that kind of hanky-panky either."

Suddenly I wondered if Mrs. Fieldstone knew something about my husband. "So have you seen them together?" I asked, hoping to make my voice sound lighter than I felt. "Geoffrey and Judith, I mean."

"I've seen a woman over there," she admitted. "I knew you were gone, and I knew it wasn't you. I figured it wasn't a good thing."

"No," I agreed. "It's definitely not a good thing. I only just found out myself."

"Really?" she seemed surprised. "Then what made you leave, dear?"

I considered this. "A lot of things, I guess. We were already having problems."

"I'm not surprised," she said. "Knowing a bit about these things, you can be fairly assured that this fling with your husband and his fancy woman didn't just happen because you left."

"No," I said slowly, "I think it was already in the works."

She sighed. "Well, it's an old story, dear. But I hope yours has a happy ending."

I thought about this. How could my story possibly have a happy ending when it looked like a hopeless tragedy right now? "Did yours?" I asked her.

"Have a happy ending?" She held up her hands. "Look at me. Do I look happy to you?"

"Actually, you do. I mean, I know your husband died about ten years ago, but you seem to be getting along just fine. I see your kids over here all the time, and you still work in your yard and—"

"And life goes on." She nodded. "And it will for you, too."

"I hope you're right."

"And in the meantime, your animals are perfectly welcome to stay with me as long as necessary."

"I'll pay for their food," I told her. "And if they need anything, anything at all, like to go to the vet, or if Rufus needs a bath, or whatever, I'll take care of it. Just call me." Then I wrote down my cell-phone number. "Please, call me about anything."

She nodded. "Of course, dear."

"And do you think it would be okay if I took Rufus for a walk sometime?"

"Certainly. I think that's a wonderful idea, dear. And perhaps you'd come for another cup of tea, too."

"And sympathy?"

She reached over and patted my hand. "Of course, dear, I have lots of that to offer."

"It's a deal," I told her, thanking her again and again for everything.

"Keep your chin up," she told me as I went back through the gate toward the house where I once lived.

I decided to go back inside for one last look. I'm not even sure why. Maybe I just wondered if there was anything I'd left behind, like my heart or maybe my mind. But after looking around, I realized that all I really wanted was to get away from this place. It no longer felt like my home. Instead it seemed as if it had been violated, perhaps the way you might feel if someone had broken in and stolen your valuables, or if you'd been invaded by aliens or perhaps just another woman. Whatever it was, it felt terrible and demoralizing.

I was just opening the front door when I heard his voice in the back of the house, calling my name. The sound was like someone dumping a bucket of ice water over my head, and I didn't know whether to stay and face my foe or simply bolt out the door and never look back. Fight or flight, I seemed to remember from some psych class long ago in another life. I felt paralyzed.

"Glennis?" he called again, louder this time.

"Confront him," I remembered Sherry telling me. And hadn't that been my plan when I'd left the apartment? "I'm in here," I answered, but my voice sounded strange. Kind of low and flat and detached from the fear knotting my throat.

"What are you doing here?" he asked when he finally emerged by way of the dining room.

Maybe it was the way he asked this question, but it sounded like a challenge to me. Like he was questioning my right to be in the house. And that made me angry. Very angry. "I *used* to live here," I snapped. "Remember?"

He folded his arms across his chest and carefully eyed me. I could tell he was taking inventory, and I'm sure I wasn't measuring up. When had I last measured up? "But you left," he said in a tightly controlled voice, probably the same one he used in court when questioning the opposition. "Remember?"

I nodded. "That's right. I did leave. And apparently I left just in time."

His left brow lifted ever so slightly, a barely perceivable motion, at least to someone who didn't know him that well. But I'd seen it a lot over the years. It was one of those little signs that he was seriously worried about something. "What do you mean?"

"I mean...I left just in time for you and Judith to come out into the open with your little affair—"

"We are *not* having an affair!"

But I could tell, even as he denied it, that they were. Oh, maybe they weren't actually sleeping together yet, but they were definitely involved. "Don't try to cover it up," I said in what I hoped sounded like a bored voice, like I'd known about this for some time and wasn't highly amused. "Everyone seems to know about it anyway."

"What—who do you mean?" he sputtered. Something the cool and collected city attorney seldom did.

I waved my hand. "Does it really matter? Do you really want me to name names? Let's just say the cat's out of the bag now, Geoffrey." I couldn't believe how calm I was acting when inside I was seething. Maybe watching him lose it made it easier for me to keep myself together.

"I don't know what you're talking about, Glennis." He gave his head a sharp shake and acted like he was looking out the window at something of real interest, but I knew he was just avoiding eye contact with me. "Everyone knows that Judith and I have worked together closely on this case, but that's all there is to it. Simply a working relationship."

"Call it whatever you like, Geoffrey." I stared at him now, seeing him in a whole new way. "Just don't deny it. Okay?" I couldn't believe this was the man I had married and lived with for more than two decades. Was he even in there somewhere? This man before me seemed more like the villain in a bad movie or the devil disguised as the man I once loved. But whatever he was, he was a stranger to me now. My heart didn't recognize him anymore.

"Look, Glennis," he said in a more controlled voice, "you are blowing this way out of proportion. I realize you've been under a lot of stress, and as a result you may be imagining things that aren't really—"

"Are you suggesting that I'm hallucinating?" I demanded, suddenly losing my earlier calm.

He held up his hand. "Not hallucinating, exactly, but perhaps making this into something it's not."

"I am not imagining anything, Geoffrey. I saw the two of you together last night. Mrs. Fieldstone has seen you two together. For Pete's sake, even your own son has seen—"

"It's not like that," he insisted again, talking to me slowly and calmly as if he were addressing a four-year-old child. "I *told* you, Glennis, we are simply working together on this case, and we have to—"

"Just *admit* it, Geoffrey!" I yelled. "Just get it out into the open and admit it!"

"Stop screaming."

"I am not screaming," I said in a quieter but still angry voice. "I'm just telling you, *I know. Everyone knows.* Quit acting like it's not happening, Geoffrey."

He took a deep breath, and for a moment I thought perhaps he was going to come clean. But, no, he only began pouring forth more denials, more platitudes, and finally blamed me for the whole stupid mess. "You're the one who left me, Glennis," he said for about the seventh time. "You chose to walk away from our marriage, not me—"

"No!" I pointed my finger in his face. "You may not have *left* your precious home." I waved my hand around the foyer. "You didn't abandon your expensive furniture and glorious views and perfectly appointed spaces, but you *left* our marriage when you got involved with Judith. You know it, and I know it, and probably half of the town knows it. So why don't you quit lying about it, Geoffrey? Why can't you tell the truth?"

"Judith is a work associate." He sounded like a robot or maybe a message on an answering machine. "She has been working on the case with me."

I rolled my eyes and laughed. "Fine, have it your way, Geoffrey. Tell whatever story suits you."

"It's the truth—"

"Overruled, counselor!" I yelled at his face. Then I leaned forward and stared into his eyes. "Yes, I almost forgot, Geoffrey; you're a lawyer. It's your job to know how to spin any story. You get paid to make crap look good, don't you?"

Then I walked out the front door, got into my car, and squealed my tires on the street as I tore around the corner. I was so outraged that I'm sure I was probably just as dangerous as someone driving under the influence of alcohol or drugs, but fortunately I made it back to the apartment without injuring anything but my pride.

Chapter 11

I was still furious after I got home to my apartment. I paced through the kitchen and into the living room, back and forth, ruminating over all the things I should've said or done while I still had Geoffrey's attention. I wished I had slapped him or spit in his smooth-featured face. Immature perhaps, but I think that something physical would've made me feel better.

I stopped pacing long enough to look at the flower arrangement on my coffee table. I just stood there staring at it and trying to remember why I had thought it so lovely the night before. Then I plucked out the grocery store flowers and shoved them into a juice pitcher. And I picked up the large crystal vase, dumped out the water, walked over to the open window, and pushed the screen aside. I took a moment to peer down, making sure no one was below before I released the vase and watched it plummet to the concrete sidewalk. I stared for a couple of horrified seconds, shocked at what I'd done, but then I looked down in fascination, studying the thousands of shining pieces of sparkling crystal splayed across the sidewalk. Then I got the broom and the dustpan and a brown paper bag and hurried downstairs to clean up my mess.

"What's going on?" demanded the young mother of the two waif children I had been scolded for trying to protect just two days ago.

"I dropped something," I told her, eying her carefully. Did she intend to report me to the manager now? Or maybe the police for endangerment? What if her children had been around? I suddenly felt very ashamed and childish—sheepish even.

She coolly lit a cigarette and watched as I quickly swept up my glittering mess. "It looks like diamonds," she said as she sat down on the steps and continued to watch me.

I paused and looked at the shards of crystal glistening in the sun, then nodded. "It does, doesn't it?"

"What was it?" she asked.

I turned and studied her. She appeared to be in her early twenties but still dressed like she was in high school. She had on a short denim skirt and a little pale pink top that exposed not only a bare midriff but a belly-button ring as well. I suspected she was a single mom since I hadn't seen a guy around. "It was a very expensive Waterford crystal vase," I told her, waiting to see if she would react.

"How did you drop it?" She peered up to the open window of my apartment now.

"Like this." I held out my hand with my fingers together, then opened them wide.

"On purpose?"

I nodded. "Going to report me?"

She got a sly look on her face. "Maybe."

I shrugged. "It was a stupid thing to do."

"Yeah." She took a long drag on her cigarette. "Then why'd you do it?"

I swept the last of the shards into my dustpan, then dumped them into the paper sack. "You really want to know?"

"Yeah, why not?"

I swept the pavement a few more times, pushing the fine remaining glass dust over the curb and into the gutter. "I think I got it all, but you better not let your kids go barefoot down here for a while," I said as I turned back to her.

"So why'd you do it?" she asked me again.

I sat down on the step next to her. "Well, my husband got me that vase for our twenty-fifth anniversary."

She nodded as she blew out a long puff of smoke. "And?"

"And I just found out he's been cheating on me."

"Man, that really sucks, huh?"

I nodded. "Yeah, it really sucks."

"So you left him?"

"Yes. But I confronted him today, and, naturally, he denied everything. And I came home but still felt really, really angry."

"Duh."

"And when I saw that vase in my apartment, well, I just couldn't help myself."

She patted me on the back now. "Well, good for you."

"I guess."

"Do you feel better now?"

I nodded. "A little. I just wish I had smashed the stupid vase in his driveway instead. Then he would've had to clean it up."

"You could always go bash in his car or something," she suggested. "Slash his tires or break his windows—something like that."

I turned and looked at her, curious as to whether she was serious or not. Apparently she was. "I suppose," I said. "But he's an attorney, and his car is a pretty expensive Porsche. It might just make things worse."

"Yeah, maybe." She sighed. "And it wouldn't be fair to make the Porsche suffer, right?"

"Right." I couldn't help thinking of the satisfaction from scarring Judith's car.

Then she smiled and stuck out her hand. "I'm Cammie, and my old man cheated on me too."

I shook her hand. "I'm sorry about that. I'm Glennis. And I'm sorry about the other day, too. I think your children reminded me of mine when they were younger, and I got sort of protective of them."

"Hey, that's okay. I know I'm a pretty crappy mom."

"No," I said, "I'm sure you're a good mom."

She laughed. "Yeah, well, you're the only one then."

"Where are your kids today?"

"With their dad. Don't even ask me why I let them go. We're having this stupid custody battle, and I've told my lawyer that I don't want him to have any custody at all because he's such a total jerk. But then Mike calls up and acts really sweet and says how he wants to take the kids some-place special, and, well, I'm so tired of being a full-time mommy, like 24/7, you know, that I just agree. Great mom, huh?"

"Hey, it's hard when your kids are little," I told her. "Do you have any family around to help out?"

She shook her head. "No, my family's all in the Midwest. I came out here with Mike, and according to my stupid state-appointed lawyer, I can't leave the state until this thing is worked out. And maybe not even then if Mike gets any custody. It really sucks."

"Do you think there's any chance you two can work it out?" I asked. "And get back together?"

"For the sake of the children?" she said in a dramatic voice. "That's what my parents keep telling me. 'Stay together for the sake of the children, Cammie.' Like never mind that Mike is the one who stepped out on me, or that he's the one who messed everything up. No, I'm supposed to stick with this slime bag, *for the sake of the children*. Right!"

"It's hard, isn't it?"

"Yeah! It makes me freaking furious sometimes."

"Me, too." I held up my bag of broken crystal as evidence. "And it's hard even when your kids *aren't* little. My college-aged daughter thinks I should stick it out too, *for the sake of the family*."

Cammie shook her head. "Don't you wish they'd all just butt out?"

I nodded. "I sort of do."

"Was that your son I saw coming out of your apartment today?"

"Yes, that's Jacob."

"He's cute."

I smiled. "Well, he's only nineteen, plus he's got some, uh, problems to work out."

"Drugs?"

I turned and looked at her. How did she know? "What makes you think that?"

"It's just the most obvious guess. I think about half the kids in the country are messing with drugs. I know Mike was."

"Really? Was your husband an addict?"

"An addict? I don't know about that. I guess I'd just describe him as more of a recreational user. But I never went in for that crap. Oh, I smoked a little pot now and then back when we were in high school, but I don't really like how it makes me feel. I don't even like alcohol that much anymore."

"That's probably good," I told her. "Especially for your kids."

"Yeah. I figure I'm sort of all they have right now. And I may not be much, but I probably need to be sober for them. And even though I smoke, I don't do it in the apartment. I know that secondhand smoke is bad, especially for kids."

"Well, see," I told her as I stood up. "You *are* a good mom."

She laughed again. "I wish."

"And if you need a break from your kids sometime, feel free to ask me to watch them for you."

"Really?" She stood up and ground out her cigarette butt beneath the heel of her flip-flop.

"Sure, I love kids."

"Well, that's cool and everything, but I don't want to take advantage, you know."

"Don't worry," I assured her. "I'll feel free to say no if it's not a good time."

"All right then." She nodded. "I appreciate that."

"Take care," I told her as I picked up my broom, dustpan, and heavy paper sack.

"You, too."

I went upstairs to my apartment and started to throw away the broken crystal shards, then stopped. Looking down into the bag, I decided that perhaps I should hang on to this foolish mess for just a while longer—I wasn't even sure why. But I took out a large wooden salad bowl and carefully poured the broken glass into it. Then I set this on the coffee table, and to my surprise it was rather pretty. It was also a good visual reminder of what my marriage had become—broken shards of what had once appeared flawless.

Chapter 12

I decided to take up jogging again. I'm sure I hoped it would be some kind of stress reliever. I hadn't jogged for almost two years, but my old running shoes still fit. On the first day, I could barely keep it up for ten minutes without my sides burning like fire, and that was when I walked part of the time. But by the end of my first week I was almost up to twenty minutes before I could only walk. Of course, my payoff for my efforts was mostly just a great deal of pain. It seemed that every part of me hurt these days. Even so, I kept it up. Physical pain proved a fairly good distraction from the condition of my heart.

And naturally, my emotions were like a moment-by-moment roller-coaster ride. When Jacob was around, I tried to appear upbeat, acting like I was perfectly fine and at peace with my situation. But when he went off to his job at Mama Mia's, I plummeted to the depths, vacillating between feeling enraged and completely crushed. At times I actually thought I had simply dreamed the whole thing up. I'd flash back to happier times, and for brief moments I'd honestly think the recent unhappy events were my own hallucinations. To be honest, I think I even questioned the state of my own sanity. And so I suppose it was somewhat fortuitous that Sherry had gone ahead and made that appointment with Dr. Abrams for me.

"So you're really going to go then?" asked Sherry as we had lunch at the mall on Saturday.

I nodded. "Yes. I think I probably need to."

"Did you mention marriage counseling to Geoffrey yet?"

"No." I stirred my iced tea. "It hardly seemed appropriate when I felt like screaming and kicking and scratching his eyes out."

"No, I suppose not."

I sighed. Suddenly I felt very, very tired.

"How's Jacob doing?"

"Okay," I told her. "He's been going to work every day, coming home afterward."

"So you think he's straightening up?"

I nodded. "Yes, I really do. He had his court date for the MIP—minor in possession—last week, and since it was his first offense, they gave him a break."

"Oh, that's great. It probably didn't hurt anything that his dad's the city attorney."

I frowned. "Don't be so sure. Anyway, all he has to do is forty hours of community service, and he has eight months to get it done."

"That's not too bad."

"Jacob was really relieved. He said it will help him to get on with his life."

Sherry smiled. "Well, that's wonderful."

I forced a weak smile to my lips. "Yes, it really is. I don't even know what I'd be doing right now if Jacob's life was still off track. Sometimes it seems like that's all I really have."

"What about Sarah? Have you talked to her lately?"

"A couple of days ago. I told her about Jacob's coming to live with me, and she told me I was a fool."

"She's young."

"And idealistic. She thinks that her father and I should stay together no matter what."

"It's pretty natural for kids to want their parents to stay together."

"Jacob doesn't seem to care."

"Well, he and Geoffrey hadn't exactly been seeing things eye to eye lately."

"That's true. I just wish that Sarah could try to understand. Do you know what she said to me before she hung up?"

Sherry shook her head.

"She asked me what I thought she was supposed to do when it was time for her to get married. Was she supposed to invite both of us to her wedding?"

Sherry looked surprised. "I didn't even know she was engaged."

"She's not," I told her. "She doesn't even have a boyfriend."

Sherry laughed. "Well, that sounds like Sarah, doesn't it? Always planning ahead."

I frowned. "And thinking of herself. Sometimes I can't believe I raised such a self-centered daughter."

"She's Geoffrey's daughter too."

I nodded. "You hit that nail on the head."

Then we went shopping, and Sherry insisted that I get a new outfit. And even though I protested, she continued dragging me along until she finally found some things that she liked, piling me high with jacket and skirt and blouse and practically shoving me into the dressing room.

"Why?" I demanded as I stood with arms outstretched to show her the DKNY outfit she had picked out for me. "Where on earth am I going to wear this anyway?"

"Doesn't matter." She nodded with approval. "Sometimes you just need a new outfit to make you feel special."

"I don't need a new outfit, Sherry," I told her. "I need a new life."

"Very nice," she said as she fingered the sleeve of the rusty tweed jacket. "And the color suits you."

I examined the tag. "Nice and expensive," I told her. "Remember that Geoffrey canceled my debit card, Sherry."

"Did he cancel *all* your cards?" Her brows lifted hopefully.

I considered this. "I'm not sure."

"When was the last time you charged something here?" she asked with a sly smile.

"I don't know. Maybe last Christmas." I took another look at the outfit and realized that it really was a good style for me, and since I'd lost that weight, it did look fairly nice. But still I didn't see the purpose.

"When was the last time you bought yourself a nice outfit, Glennis?"

"Oh, I don't know…"

"Well, I think you should give your Bradley's charge card a little try."

I shook my head. "Oh, I don't know, Sherry."

"Come on," she urged. "Geoffrey owes you this."

I studied Sherry, my one friend who usually gives me sound advice, and considered this. "Maybe you're right."

She nodded. "Of course I am."

"But what if the card is rejected?"

"Then we just walk."

"Seriously?" I giggled. "We just leave it on the counter and walk out?"

"Yes." She grinned. "Kind of exciting, isn't it?"

So I carried the pieces of my suit up to the cash register and waited anxiously as the salesgirl rang it all up. I held my breath as she ran my card, and to my amazement she handed me a receipt to sign. Sherry winked at me, and without batting an eyelash, I signed my name.

"What about getting some shoes to go with it?" asked Sherry.

And so I purchased boots, of all things, and a matching purse and belt, along with several other nice pieces, which I felt sure must've maxed out the Bradley's charge account, before Sherry and I finally decided to call it a day. Feeling as reckless as Bonnie and Clyde, we stowed my bags and packages in the back of the Range Rover, and then I threw back my head and laughed.

"I can't believe I just did that," I told my accomplice.

"Well," said Sherry as we climbed into the SUV, "I've heard of women who've slit tires or burned clothes or bashed in their husband's little sports cars with sledgehammers. A little shopping therapy seems like a small price to pay compared to that."

"I guess."

"Besides," she said, "you may need that suit when it comes time to look for a job."

"A job." I shook my head as I backed out of the parking space. "Now that's a really overwhelming idea."

"One day at a time, Glennis."

Right. One day at a time, I kept telling myself until the day of my appointment with Dr. Abrams. To bolster my confidence, and since it seemed that fall was really in the air, I decided to wear my new suit. I figured if I had to be a complete mess on the inside, I might at least look like I had it together on the outside.

I liked Dr. Abrams right from the start. She seemed intelligent and compassionate as she asked me questions, then listened with empathetic eyes as I attempted to answer. And although we didn't really solve any major life problems during that first appointment, she did give me some coping mechanisms, including some relaxation techniques and stress-relieving exercises that included a lot of deep breathing. I was relieved that she didn't try to prescribe any medications. Of course, I didn't admit my fear about losing my mind. I decided I'd better save that little prize until later. Even so, she encouraged me to consider what events had brought me to this place in my life. She suggested I begin writing things down. She even gave me a short list of questions, but I wasn't sure I was ready to think about all that yet. One thing she alluded to, but never came right out and said, is that I seemed to focus more on the problems of other members of my family than on my own.

I frowned. "But I honestly don't think I'd have any problems if Jacob hadn't gotten involved with drugs and if Geoffrey hadn't cheated on me."

She just nodded and jotted something down. And for some reason that made me feel nervous. Just the same, I made another appointment with her for next month. I think I'll probably go, but I still have a few weeks to change my mind.

After my appointment with Dr. Abrams, I met Sherry for coffee at Starbucks.

"You look great," she told me as we took our coffees to an empty table by the window.

"Thanks." I attempted a smile.

"So?" she began. "How did it go?"

"Okay," I told her.

"Good."

"She gave me some exercises and an assignment of sorts. I'm supposed to go back next month."

"That's great. Did you ask her about bringing Geoffrey?"

"I mentioned it."

"And?"

"She said that was a good idea if Geoffrey wanted to come, but she didn't think it would do any good to force him."

"Right."

I stirred my coffee. "Do you think I should ask him?"

Sherry nodded, then studied me for a long moment without speaking.

"What?" I asked her, certain she was thinking something.

"Oh, nothing." She waved her hand.

Well, nothing gets to me worse than someone saying "nothing."

"What is it?" I asked her. "I can tell you were about to say something. Is it about Geoffrey?"

"No…" Then she smiled. "It was really pretty silly, Glennis."

"What?" I demanded. "Tell me."

"Oh, I was just wondering why you haven't bothered to cover up that gray hair. You know you would look at least ten years younger without it."

I rolled my eyes at her. "What is this? Make over Glennis month?"

She smiled. "Yeah, maybe."

"What difference does it make if I look younger or hipper or whatever, Sherry? My life will still be a mess."

She glanced at her watch, then suddenly pulled out her cell phone and began dialing. Before I knew what had hit us, we had finished our coffees and gone down the street to a salon called Alta's, and I was standing at the reception desk while Sherry conspired with a short blond woman named Bessie.

"Okay," said Sherry, as if it were all settled. "I've got to go show a house right now, but Bessie can take you in about twenty minutes." She leaned over and picked up a slightly tattered issue of *Vogue* and handed it to me as she led me over to the waiting area.

"I don't know, Sherry," I began.

"Don't you trust me, Glennis?"

"Well, I suppose so, but why are you doing—"

"Look, Bessie knows exactly what to do. Just sit here and wait until she calls you, and then trust me, okay?"

I looked up into her clear blue eyes and realized that very few people are blessed with a friend as loyal and kind as Sherry. I finally nodded, then waved as she whooshed out the door. Then I opened the magazine and tried to think about absolutely nothing as I flipped past page after page of outrageous styles and gauntly thin models who looked about the same age or perhaps even younger than my daughter.

"Glennis Harmon?" called the blonde.

"Bessie?" I said as I laid aside the magazine, picked up my purse, and walked over to her station.

She smiled. "Have a seat."

I sat down in the chair and stared at my reflection in the mirror. I vaguely wondered who that old woman was, but part of me didn't really care. It seemed my drab hair and colorless face suited my spirits just fine. Why bother changing it?

Bessie loosened the barrette that was holding back my hair in a ponytail and let it fall loosely around my shoulders. I gave it a little shake, then forced a laugh. "Great for Halloween," I said. "All I need is a pointed hat and a broom."

Bessie frowned. "Sherry is absolutely right. You are too young to be going around looking like this."

I just shrugged, then followed her like a sheep to the slaughter back to the shampooing station. But I must admit that it felt nice to have someone gently scrubbing and massaging my scalp. I tried to remember the last time Geoffrey had touched me in a gentle or loving way. It seemed like it had been years. Maybe it had. Tears streamed down my cheeks as Bessie started to towel my hair dry.

"Did I get soap in your eyes?" she asked with concern.

"Just a little," I lied as I dabbed my eyes with the edge of the towel.

Then I was back in the chair with the glaring lights and all-too-revealing mirror. I decided not to torture myself, so I shut my eyes as I was subjected to various stages of hair coloring. Throughout the entire ordeal, I didn't allow myself to look at the mirror. What difference did it make? Even if my hair turned bright green or all fell out, who would really care?

Finally I felt a nudge on my shoulder. "Don't you want to see?" she was asking me.

"Sorry," I told her, opening my eyes, attempting to focus. Then I looked up and saw my hair looking very much as it had looked nearly twenty years ago, only without the bangs. She had cut bluntly, just above my shoulders, and the color was auburn again. Perhaps not as intense as it used to be, but it seemed to look more natural like this, more subdued and fitting with my age.

"That's nice," I told her as I reached up to touch it.

She nodded. "A real improvement."

"Glennis!" called Sherry as she came into the salon. "Is that really you?"

I turned and smiled. "I'm not sure."

"Oh, you look absolutely stunning!"

"Oh, I don't know—"

"But we need Linda now." Sherry glanced over to the girl at the receptionist desk. "Is Linda here?"

"She's in the back," said the girl. "You want me to call her out?"

"Yes," said Sherry. Then she took my hand and led me over to a station with cosmetics.

"Oh, I don't know," I said when I realized what Sherry had in mind. "I'm pretty much a minimalist when it comes to makeup."

"Obviously," said Sherry as she practically forced me into the chair.

"But I don't go for much makeup—"

"Don't worry, Glennis," she assured me. "Linda is very tasteful. You won't look like a clown."

Finally it was over, and I emerged from Linda's hands, not looking like a clown exactly, but perhaps a little more dramatic than I would have preferred. However I did like the colors Linda had chosen and even decided to purchase a few items.

"The haircut and color are on me," said Sherry as she pushed my money away.

"No," I insisted. "You can't—"

"I can and I will." She turned and smiled at me. "I just wrote out an offer on a house, and I feel like celebrating."

"Congratulations," I told her. "But you don't need to—"

"No arguing with me, Glennis. It was my idea, and I intend to pay for it. Then I can take all the credit when people start complimenting you on your new look."

So I decided not to argue. Instead I just hugged her when we got outside. "Thanks," I told her.

"I wish I could take you out and show you off," she teased. "But Rod and I are having dinner at the Franklins' tonight."

I waved my hand. "That's okay," I assured her. "It's been a long day for me anyway." So we said good-bye, and I got into the Range Rover just as it began to rain. I couldn't help but pull down the rearview mirror to take a peek at myself again. I blinked in surprise. I really did look different. Then I started the engine and turned on the windshield wipers and just sat there. I considered going home to my apartment but knew that Jacob wouldn't get off work until after nine. Maybe it was hearing that Rod and Sherry had a dinner date, or maybe it was being all dressed up with nowhere to go, but suddenly I felt very, very lonely.

I remembered the deep-breathing exercise that Dr. Abrams had told me about, and sitting there in my SUV with rain pelting down and wipers going, I attempted to calm myself by breathing deeply. To my relief, it seemed to work. Then I remembered something Dr. Abrams had said about taking care of myself first. Now, admittedly, this was a new concept to me. I mean I'd spent the past twenty-five years taking care of everyone else's needs before ever considering my own. I wasn't even sure how to go about it.

"What do *you* need, Glennis?" I asked myself aloud, feeling a bit silly. Then my stomach growled, and I realized I was hungry. And what I felt hungry for was a big plateful of pesto linguini and rock shrimp from Sindalli's.

Why not? I asked myself. I put the Range Rover into gear and drove over to the restaurant. Then thankful that it wasn't quite six, and still early for the dinner rush, I went inside and asked for a "table for one." Okay, it felt very, very strange to do this, and my heart actually began to race with anxiety over sitting by myself at a table and eating all alone. But I took a deep calming breath and told myself it would be okay and I'd better get used to it.

The waiter smiled politely as he escorted me to a lonely little table near the kitchen. But I didn't mind the location so much. It was highly preferable to being right out in the middle where everyone could see that I was dining alone. And I must admit that the noises coming from the kitchen sounded somewhat warm and familiar. Really, I told myself, this isn't so bad.

I watched as other couples and families and groups came in, quickly filling our town's most expensive restaurant. Not so unusual for a Friday night. And slowly but surely, I began to relax, and I started to enjoy a bit of people watching, and I thought perhaps dining alone had its upside after all. Not to mention that the food and service were excellent.

Shortly after the waiter set my entrée before me, and after I'd taken a few delicious bites, I nearly fell out of my chair. My heart seemed to stop beating as I saw Geoffrey being seated at a table on the other side of the dining room, and across the table from him, already seated and beaming up at him, was Judith Ramsey. It appeared obvious by their happy and relaxed expressions that they hadn't noticed me. And perhaps they might not ever look up and see me since the restaurant was dimly lit with only the soft glow of small oil lamps illuminating the tables—and since their eyes seemed to be fixed on each other.

Unreal. I couldn't believe the odds of my seeing them—and in Sindalli's of all places! This is where Geoffrey always took me for our special dates. Perhaps I should've known better. Or perhaps I had done this subconsciously. Is it possible that I came here tonight hoping to see them? Whatever the case, I wished I wasn't here now. And I knew if they saw me, they would assume it was no coincidence. They might even think I was stalking them.

I'm not sure how long I sat there staring at them, wondering how I could escape this predicament, but finally the waiter approached my table and with concern asked if there was anything wrong with my food.

"No," I said quickly. "It's wonderful."

"Oh, good."

"But I'm afraid it's more than I can eat right now. Do you think you could possibly box up what's left?"

"Certainly."

And while the young man was off in the kitchen, dumping my beautifully arranged pasta into a takeout Styrofoam box, I considered how I could slip out of the restaurant without being seen by them. There was an emergency exit just opposite the kitchen, but I felt certain that would sound an alarm and draw everyone's attention. I could try to walk around the far side of the restaurant, but going in and out of tables would probably draw attention as well.

Finally I wondered why I naturally assumed that *I* should be the one to go sneaking around to avoid *them*. It occurred to me that I had as much right as anyone to be eating in this particular restaurant. In fact, I had even more right than my husband, who was barely even separated before he started publicly dating another woman.

And so, after the waiter returned with my box and a bill that was more than I'd expected, I stood up, and with what little confidence I could muster, I began to walk directly through the restaurant. I knew there was no graceful way to avoid their table, at least not without making a spectacle of myself, and besides I had conjured up a plan. Okay, maybe it was a foolish plan, but at the time it felt perfect.

I walked right up to their table and paused there until they finally looked up and realized it was me. I could see the look of horrified surprise in Geoffrey's eyes, not just at seeing me standing there, but also because I looked different. It was almost as if he didn't recognize me at first.

"Glennis," he whispered.

"Geoffrey," I said calmly, "what a surprise."

Judith remained silent, but I could tell by her expression that she was genuinely worried. And perhaps even frightened. I wondered what she thought I might do to her. Make a horrible scene, scream and shout, initiate a catfight with her?

"What are you—"

"Don't worry." I smiled. "I only stopped by to say hello."

He seemed both relieved and yet still agitated. "We came here to celebrate," he said quickly. "The lawsuit is finally over. We won. John and Anton should be joining us any minute." He glanced over his shoulder as if wishing for the other two city councilmen to suddenly appear out of nowhere. However, their table was only set for two, and once again, I knew my husband was lying.

"You must be so happy." I looked evenly at him, then over to her and back to him again. "Congratulations," I said, "to both of you."

He nodded. "Yes, it's a huge relief."

"Well, here then." I handed him my bill. "Since you're celebrating and all."

He nodded. "No problem."

"It's certainly a lot cheaper than taking me on that anniversary trip to the Caribbean."

Then I turned and walked away. All right, a free dinner under those particular circumstances wasn't much of a prize. But I did get a pitiful bit of satisfaction for interrupting them like that and, I hoped, spoiling their dinner.

Chapter 13

By the time Jacob came home, I had removed my new designer suit and donned my old gray sweats again. Even so, he did a double take when he came in the door.

"Wow, Mom, you look different," he said as he put a pizza box on the counter, one of the perks of his job. Sometimes an order was wrong, and if no one wanted it, the employees were allowed to take it home.

I patted my hair. "It was Sherry's idea."

"Looks really cool," he said as he came and flopped down on the couch beside me.

"How was work?"

He sighed and shook his head. "My manager is a jerk."

"Why's that?"

"He fired Daniel today."

"That's too bad. Why?"

"Just because he was late."

"That seems pretty harsh. Had Daniel been late before?"

"Yeah, I guess. But even so, Daniel was a hard worker. Some of the other guys spend all their time trying to get out of work. Daniel would really get in there and get stuff done."

"Too bad. Does Daniel have some idea for another job?"

He shrugged. "I don't know." He looked up at the clock. "I was thinking I might go over and try to cheer him up. Do you mind?"

So far Jacob had been good to come home every night after work. He'd play his music and watch TV and finally go to bed. It had been comforting knowing where he was this past week. Suddenly the idea of his going out made me uneasy. Still, I knew that I couldn't make him stay home against his will.

"Do you work tomorrow?" I asked.

"Yeah, but not until three."

"Oh."

"I just feel worried about Daniel," Jacob said as he stood up. He reached for the pizza box. "Do you want any of this, Mom?"

I shook my head. "No, I've already eaten."

"I thought I'd take it to Daniel." Then he smiled that same dashing smile that had gotten him past me time after time. "You don't mind being alone tonight, do you, Mom?"

"No, I'm fine."

"I won't be out late," he assured me as he headed for the door.

"Drive carefully," I said, not even sure why I bothered. Habit I guess.

"Oh yeah," he said. "I'm almost out of gas, and I don't get paid until next week. Do you think I could borrow some cash, Mom? I promise I'll pay you back."

I pulled my purse over and fished out a twenty and handed it to him. "You don't have to pay me back, Jake," I told him. "I'm just glad that you have a job and are making good choices." I looked into his eyes and hoped that my words were the truth.

"I'm glad too, Mom. It feels really good to be clean and working. I've even been thinking about school."

"Really?" I felt a surge of hope.

"Yeah. I know it's too late for fall term now. But maybe I could look into winter."

"Oh, Jacob!" I smiled broadly. "That would be so great."

"Yeah, I think it'd be cool." He nodded. "Have a good evening."

"You, too," I called as he left.

I suppose I wasn't too surprised when he still hadn't come home by midnight, but I wished I'd thought to ask for a phone number. Still, I reminded myself as I got ready for bed, Jacob was turning his life around. He was working hard, thinking about continuing his education. And tonight he'd even gone out to encourage a friend who was feeling down. Now this was a son a mother could be proud of. Right? Even so, I tossed and turned all night long. I'm not sure if it was over Jacob's absence or the scene at the restaurant, but I know I had dark circles under my eyes the next morning.

Just the same, I was relieved to see that Jacob had come home after all. Sacked out on his futon, he still had his clothes on, but at least he was safe. Feeling somewhat encouraged, I did my regular morning run, which had increased to nearly an hour including a cool-down period. Then after my shower, I peeked into Jacob's room to see that he was still sleeping soundly. I decided to make us both a nice breakfast of blueberry muffins and cheese omelets.

But Jacob's breakfast went untouched as he continued to sleep. About two o'clock I decided to wake him up.

"What's wrong?" he asked as I gently shook him.

I told him the time and reminded him about work, and to my relief he finally pulled himself out of bed, showered, and left. Even so, that same old feeling of worry began gnawing in the pit of my stomach. I wondered if this could be the beginning of trouble again.

But Jacob came home after work and seemed to be doing fine. And for the following week, we continued to live fairly contentedly in our small and slightly cramped home. Oh, sure, he got in pretty late a couple of times, but he was always in good spirits, and his explanation always was that he'd been jamming with Daniel and some friends.

"We might even try to get some gigs this winter," he told me as he poured himself a big bowl of cereal and drowned it with milk.

"That would be great," I said, replacing the milk jug back in the fridge for him.

And, really, I figured music was probably a good distraction for him, something to keep him away from the temptation of drugs. I knew a little about distractions myself, since I spent most of my time trying to keep myself busy these days. It was my way of distracting myself from my own messed-up life—or rather my marriage. I relied on diversions like my daily morning runs. And on Tuesdays and Thursdays, I'd walk Rufus and then have tea with Mrs. Fieldstone.

I also busied myself by keeping the apartment immaculate. For some reason I felt that if I could keep everything perfectly in place and running like clockwork, it would make it easier for Jacob to stay on track. I didn't even mind cleaning his room, a practice I had long since given up when we were living in our old house. But the apartment was small and easy to maintain. Even the menial tasks, like scrubbing the grout between the tiles in the shower until the little room gleamed, didn't bother me. I'm sure the place had never been so clean. Not only would I get my cleaning deposit back in February, but in all fairness the management should thank me for leaving the place in much better condition than I'd found it. In an attempt to remove old pet smells, I'd already steam-cleaned the carpets twice and was even considering painting the walls to freshen them up.

I also distracted myself by shopping for groceries at More-4-Less, and since the store was only eight blocks from the apartments, I would sometimes walk when I only needed a few items. Sylvia had explained the concept of clipping coupons to me. So now I would search through the Sunday paper or old magazines left in the laundry room for useful coupons. These I kept separated by category in an old wallet so they would be ready when I needed them—I knew that Sylvia had little patience for customers who held her up by digging around in search of some missing coupon for fifty cents off. I also knew about "double off" coupons. Sometimes More-4-Less would honor offers made by competing stores by giving you twice the face value of the manufacturer's coupon. Already I had saved more than ten dollars by using these.

Twice a week I busied myself by doing the laundry and had my routine down to a fine science. In my laundry pack, an old backpack I'd confiscated from Jacob's castoffs, I kept a jug of laundry soap, dryer sheets, rolls of quarters, and a magazine or book in case I was inclined to stick around and watch the spin cycle do its thing. I would put on my backpack, then lug an extra-large basket of already separated items downstairs to the laundry room. I'd discovered the best time to find an empty machine was in the morning. And I'd learned the hard way to carefully check the machine before dumping in my load. One time I put a load of delicates into a washer that had just washed a load of what must've been mud-encrusted work clothes. I had to do my delicates twice. A serious waste of quarters.

Today I was doing mostly sheets and towels. I had just filled the washer, loaded my quarters, and was listening to make sure the machine was filling.

"You new around here?"

Surprised, since no one had been in here when I came in, I turned to see a man standing in front of an open dryer. His weathered skin was the color of an old copper penny, and he looked to be about eighty, although I've never been good at guessing ages.

"Sort of," I told him. "I've been here about a month now."

He nodded as he stooped over to pull his laundry from the dryer into a wicker basket. "Thought I seen you before," he said as he slowly stood up straight and extended his hand. "Name's Jack."

I shook his hand. "Nice to meet you, Jack. I'm Glennis."

He dropped his last item into his basket and then cleaned the lint from the filter and closed the dryer door.

I smiled now. "It's refreshing to see that some men actually know how to do their own laundry."

He lifted his basket to the folding table and began to sort and fold his clothes. "Well, I'm very picky about my laundry," he said as he straightened his socks and folded them together. "I like it just so."

"I can see that." To be honest, I felt pretty certain that his laundering skills would put me to shame.

"Reckon it's the result of having been such a slob for so many years."

I surveyed his tidy appearance. Neatly pressed shirt and creased trousers. Even his shoes looked recently polished, and he had a folded handkerchief tucked into his shirt pocket. "You don't look like a slob to me," I told him.

"Maybe not now. But, believe you me, I used to be."

I wasn't sure how to respond to this, so I just nodded.

"That was back in my drinking days." He gave a white sleeveless undershirt a shake, then smoothed it out on the table. "Folks used to call me Jack Daniels back then." He chuckled. "But my last name's really Smart. Thing is, I wasn't too smart back in those days."

"Was that a long time ago?" I asked.

His brow creased as he considered my question. "Well, I got sober on January 17, 1977. I used to keep an exact count of years, months, and days, but after I hit twenty-five years, I figured maybe I didn't need to do that no more."

"That's great," I told him as I turned to fill the second washing machine. The room was quiet as I put in a load of sheets and inserted my quarters. I almost wondered if Jack Smart had already left. But he was just watching me.

"Sorry about that." He ran a wrinkled hand over his short-cropped gray hair. "Don't know what gets me started sometimes. I'm sure you don't want to hear me going on like that."

"Oh, it's okay," I assured him. "I think it's…interesting."

"Really?" he brightened now. "You in recovery too?"

I shook my head. "No…"

"Oh."

"But I have a son with some, uh, problems."

He nodded and frowned. "A drinker?"

"Yeah, and he's had some troubles with drugs, too."

"That's a shame." He gave a white handkerchief a shake. "Alcohol is bad enough, but drugs, well, they can really ruin a young life."

"But he's doing okay now," I reassured him. "He's got a job and is staying clean and everything."

"So he's in recovery."

"Recovery?" I considered this. "Well, sort of."

"Sort of?" Jack looked unconvinced. "That's not exactly how it works. Either you're in recovery or you're not."

"Well, he's not in any program exactly…"

Jack shook his head. "That's too bad."

"You think he should be?"

"I most definitely do." He set his neatly folded handkerchief on the top of his laundry, then turned to look at me. "Maybe your boy would like to come to AA with me."

"Alcoholics Anonymous?"

"We got a couple of fellas who're recovering from drug addiction that come to our meetings too."

"Really?"

"Oh, sure. Sometimes those two kinds of addictions go hand in hand. Why, I wouldn't be surprised if most drug addicts didn't start out by drinking alcohol. Of course, you've got your purists at AA too." He made a little chuckling sound. "There are always those alcoholics who think they're better than drug addicts. Pretty funny if you think about it."

"Yeah."

"Well, I'm in apartment 17A if your son's interested. I don't have a telephone. Don't really see the need for one since I got nobody to call." His smile faded a bit. "But if your boy wants to go with me, just tell him to come knocking on my door. Or maybe he'd just like to talk to someone…someone who's been down some pretty hard roads and lost a lot along the way. I got plenty of stories to tell."

"Thanks, Jack. I'll let him know. Apartment 17A, right?"

"That's the one. And the AA meetings are on Wednesdays at six thirty. I usually just ride the bus unless my buddy Hank decides to stop by and give me a ride in his Caddie."

"Well, Jacob has a car," I said eagerly. "If he decides to go, maybe he could give you a ride." Already my mind was cranking on this possibility. Perhaps I could paint the picture of this sad and lonely old man for Jacob, play upon my son's compassionate side, and encourage him to give Jack a ride to the meeting next week. It might work.

But that evening when I suggested this to Jacob, he was reluctant. "First of all, I have to work next Wednesday," he told me. Then he frowned. "I mean I feel sorry for this old dude, Mom. But, honestly, do you really think I need to go to Alcoholics Anonymous?" He seemed hurt by my suggestion.

"Oh, I don't know," I told him. "I guess I just thought it couldn't hurt, you know. Jack said that anyone who's had a problem with addiction, whether it's alcohol or drugs, needs to be in some kind of recovery program to get better."

"But I *am* better. I mean, don't you think I'm doing just fine on my own?" he asked.

"Of course," I assured him. "You're doing great. But I don't want to—"

"You *know* that I'm a strong person, Mom. I mean I think this is something I can handle on my own, in my *own* way."

"Right." I nodded and told myself that this was probably best. Jacob had always been a strong-willed boy. I'd read that addicts can only recover when they choose to do so. Apparently he was choosing to do so now.

But after a couple of weeks at his job, and after getting his first paycheck, Jacob started staying out all night again. He'd usually come back to the apartment to clean up and change his clothes around noon the next day, and then he'd go in to work like nothing was wrong. But then he'd stay out all night again, and I wouldn't see him again until the next day. Naturally, I wasn't sleeping too well anymore. But when I would question him, he'd simply say, "Mom, I was just at Daniel's again. No big deal. We were just doing music and lost track of the time, so I crashed on the sofa."

At first I tried not to worry too much because Jacob had told me over and over that Daniel was a good influence. I knew that Daniel was a drummer who, according to Jacob, took his music seriously. But when the manager from Mama Mia's called one afternoon, asking where Jacob was since he hadn't shown up at work, I knew we had a problem.

Of course, I had no phone number for Daniel. I didn't have phone numbers for any of Jacob's "friends" anymore. But I knew that Daniel lived in a duplex not far from Mama Mia's. So I decided to drive over to that neighborhood and see if I could spot Jacob's car anywhere nearby.

It wasn't the first time I'd gone out looking for Jacob. I couldn't count how many times I had cruised around in my conspicuous Range Rover, going down one street after another in search of my wayward son. Just like before, I was racked with worries today. What if Jacob was in some kind of trouble? What if he'd been hurt? What if he'd gone back to drugs? Could he have overdosed? Same old questions but with a fresh intensity that always seemed to grab me by the neck and threaten to squeeze the life out of me.

Frightened and numb, I drove around and around until I finally spotted what appeared to be Jacob's car. It was down a deserted alley that had become a kind of panhandle lot. I parked the Range Rover on the street and walked down the drivewaylike street toward a structure that did indeed seem to be a duplex—a very run-down and decrepit duplex with pieces of broken-down cars and old furniture strewn across the tall brown grass that had once been a lawn.

As I got closer, I knew by the distinctive dent in the left-rear fender that it was Jacob's car. I peeked into the Subaru, just in case Jacob was sacked out in the back, but only saw a messy pile of blankets and clothes and general Jacob debris. Taking a breath for courage, I went up and stood before the front door. A broken lawn chair was propped against the porch railing, and the paint on the siding was blistered and peeling. To my left, I noticed what appeared to be a bedroom window, but it was broken and "repaired" with duct tape and a weathered piece of cardboard and appeared to have been like that for some time.

It was broad daylight and about three in the afternoon, so I wasn't feeling concerned for my own welfare, although I was certainly uneasy and apprehensive about knocking on a stranger's door. But, I reassured myself, my son was probably inside. No need to be afraid of my own son. I took another deep breath, remembering Dr. Abrams's exercises for centering myself, as I pressed the doorbell. Then unsure as to whether the bell worked or not, I knocked lightly and waited. It seemed I stood there for about ten minutes, knocking again and again, a little louder each time, but when the door finally swung open, I felt my mouth open right along with it.

Chapter 14

The smell hit me first. A sickly sweet, nauseating mixture of rotten garbage, filthy laundry, and various human body odors. I must've stepped back when it assaulted my nose.

The young woman who stood at the door looked to be anywhere from fourteen to twenty-four, but I couldn't be sure. She wore plaid boxers and a skimpy, stained undershirt that left nothing to my imagination. Her bleached-blond hair fell in greasy tangles around her face, which was extremely pale, and her eyes were glazed as if she wasn't quite focused on me.

"Is Jacob Harmon here?" I asked in a voice that reminded me of an old curmudgeon principal I worked for before Sarah was born.

"Huh?" The girl stared blankly.

"Jacob Harmon," I repeated a bit louder, looking past her bare shoulder to the cavelike interior splayed out behind her. The room was dark and shadowy, the result of blankets that were hanging over the windows. But I could see a couch with what appeared to be a person, not my son, sleeping on it. And in what seemed to be an old recliner was another person, again not my son.

My heart began racing as I stood there witnessing what was obviously some kind of flophouse, a place for people to get high. For all I knew there could be a crystal meth lab percolating away in a back bedroom. Maybe the cops were on their way over to make a big bust even as I stood there gaping.

"I'm, uh, looking for my son," I said and took a tentative step into this den of horrors. "Jacob!" I called loudly enough to echo through the whole house, but the two sleeping bodies didn't even flinch.

I could see the kitchen from where I stood, and it was piled high with filthy dishes, rotting food items, and dozens of empty booze bottles and beer cans. A couple of partially filled garbage bags littered the floor, as if someone had begun cleaning and then given up. Not that I could blame them. It would take days, maybe weeks, to clean up something like that.

"Jacob!" I yelled again.

"Oh, you mean Jake," said the girl as she rubbed her eyes, now waking up.

"Yes!" I nodded. "Is he here?"

She jerked her thumb over her shoulder. "I think he's back there in the bedroom."

I swallowed hard, trying to hold my breath against the stench all around me. "Uh, do you think you could go get him for me?" I asked.

Then she actually smiled, and it was really a rather sweet smile, and it occurred to me that this was someone's daughter. Someone's beloved little girl. And did her parents have any idea where she was at this very moment?

"Sure, I'll get him for you."

I nodded. "Tell him I'll be outside." And then I bolted for the door. One more minute in that place and I think I would've become physically ill. I couldn't get away from the smell quickly enough. It felt like it had adhered itself to me, as if it were clinging to my clothing, seeping into my pores. I wanted to rush home and take a long, hot shower, to scrub and scrub until all traces of this foul place were gone. How could my son stand it? How had he been able to spend so much time here? How could anyone sleep among that kind of filth? Drugs, I reminded myself. The answer is drugs.

I went over and stood next to his car. Even his piles of blankets and junk looked like neatness and order compared to what was inside that horrible duplex. I waited and waited, for nearly thirty minutes, and I was almost ready to go back inside when I finally saw the door open, and Jacob emerged. All he had on were his jeans. His feet and chest were bare, but he was pulling on a sweatshirt as he blinked up at the sunlight. Then he seemed to take a few moments to focus his eyes before he finally spotted me and staggered in my direction.

"What's wrong?" he asked. His eyes looked just as glazed as the girl's had been when she'd first answered the door.

"What's *wrong?*" I parroted back to him.

He leaned his head back and ran his fingers through his unwashed hair, then exhaled loudly. "What are you doing here, Mom?"

"Looking for *you,* Jacob." I pressed my lips together, searching for the right words to say everything that I was feeling. I really wanted to scream at him—to shout and yell and demand to know what on earth he was doing here. Instead I took another deep breath.

"Well, you found me."

"Yes," I said slowly. "But this doesn't seem like a very good place to find you."

He rolled his eyes now. "Maybe not to you."

"Jacob." I pointed toward the duplex. "This is obviously a *drug* house."

"A *drug* house?" He laughed. "Really, Mom, what makes you think that?"

I considered this. "Well, for one thing it's a filthy pigsty."

I could tell by the spark in his eyes that he was sobering up now, and I could sense that I had insulted him. "Not everyone has your high standards for housekeeping, Mom. Not everyone is a neurotic neat freak."

"I am not a neurotic neat freak." But even as I said those words, I knew it was true. Still, it was beside the point.

"Look, Daniel's been a little depressed lately, and I suppose he's let the place go a—"

"Let the place go?" I felt the slightest twinge of hysteria climbing into my voice now. "That place should be condemned by the health department. Not only that, but I'm sure there are drugs in there, Jacob."

He shook his head. "There you go with the drug thing again, Mom. Really, you're acting kind of paranoid."

"*I'm* paranoid?"

"Yeah." He sat down on the hood of his car. "Did you see any drugs in there?"

I thought about this. "Well, not exactly."

"So, maybe you imagined that you did?"

"I didn't *imagine* anything."

"But you're absolutely certain it's a *drug house?*"

I shook my head. "I'm not certain of anything, Jacob, except that it's filthy, nasty squalor and you shouldn't be spending any time here."

"There you go again," said Jacob, "making accusations and judgments. Just because some people aren't rich like you and Dad—"

"That has nothing to do with it—"

"And just because someone's not a total neat freak—"

"A person could pick up a disease in there!"

Jacob frowned. "Look, Mom, just because my friends don't measure up to your high standards doesn't give you the right to dis them. Aren't you the one who's always saying we shouldn't judge others?"

I felt confused now, like I wasn't even sure what we were talking about anymore. But something about this scenario was familiar to me. Painfully familiar. It seemed to happen every time Jacob had gotten involved in drugs. It was as if he suddenly became the expert at throwing confusion everywhere. He could put up smoke screens and get people on the defensive before they even knew what had hit them. And I knew it was happening to me. The trouble was, I didn't know what to do about it.

"These are good people, Mom," he continued in a patient voice, almost as if he were explaining this to a confused child. "They have problems, sure, but they are basically good people."

"Good people?" I repeated, falling right into his trap. "This is a *drug* house, Jacob. I know it. I can feel it. And you say they are good people?"

He shook his head. "See, there you go, judging again. Remember what you used to tell me, Mom? Remember that leather wrist thing you got me with the initials on it—WWJD? What would Jesus do? Well, is this your kind of Jesus, Mom? Is he the kind of person who goes around judging and dissing people just because they're different?" Jacob turned his head and spat on the ground. "Cuz if that's your kind of Jesus, crap, I don't want anything to do with him—or you!" Then he got off the hood of his car and went back into the house and slammed the door behind him.

I just stood there looking at the shabby duplex and trying to figure out what to do next. Did I go back in there and drag him out? Hardly. Did I get on my cell phone and call his dad and insist that he come over here and help me? Right. I could just imagine what Geoffrey would say. Something like "He's made his bed...," or, worse yet, he could blame me for the problem. "What's the matter, Glennis? Isn't your little plan working? Aren't you managing to rescue our son from the demons of drugs?"

I considered calling Sherry, but then I'd never told her everything about Jacob's problems. This would be a lot to spring on her all at once. Instead, I decided to just go home. Defeated, dejected, and depressed, I got into my Range Rover and drove back to the apartment complex.

My apartment, in stark comparison to the duplex, was so spotlessly tidy that it might actually pass a white-glove test. Maybe Jacob was right.

Maybe I was a neurotic neat freak. Maybe if I loosened up a bit, it would be better. Maybe Jacob would feel more at home here if everything wasn't perfectly in its place.

I kicked off my tennis shoes and left them in the living room, then went into the kitchen and poured myself a glass of orange juice. Then I left the used glass and empty orange juice carton on the counter and went to my room where I fell across my neatly made bed and sobbed.

"I can't fix this, God," I prayed in total desperation. "I don't know how. Please, help me."

Then I fell asleep.

When I woke up, I could hear someone in the kitchen. Frightened that it was an intruder, since I felt certain Jacob wouldn't be showing his face around here for some time, I crept around the corner in time to see Jacob tossing my empty orange juice carton into the trash.

"What are you doing?" I demanded as I emerged from my hiding spot.

"Just cleaning up." He turned and grinned.

"Cleaning up?" I leaned against the wall, folding my arms across my front. "But I thought you were against tidiness and neat freaks."

"Look, I'm sorry, Mom," he said as he rinsed out my glass. "You caught me by surprise, and I probably said some stupid things."

"Well…" I studied my son, confused as to whether this was sincere or not.

"But you need to know it's not Daniel's fault. I mean he's cool. It's just some of his friends that are messed up. And he tries to help them out by giving them a place to crash, you know. Like Amber, that girl you met today."

"Amber?"

"Yeah. I mean if you knew what her home was like and the stuff her stepdad does to her, I mean you'd think Daniel was a hero for letting her hide out at his place sometimes."

"Her stepdad abuses her?"

Jacob waved his hand. "It's complicated, Mom. And I shouldn't even have told you that—"

"But she should go to the authorities, Jacob. There are laws to protect—"

"It's not that simple, Mom."

Once again I felt that I was going down the wrong rabbit trail. "But, Jacob," I tried, "what about drugs? Is there any drug use going on at that place? There was obviously a lot of alcohol consumption going on there. I didn't imagine all those bottles. And you're underage, Jacob. Daniel could get into serious trouble just for that."

"It's not Daniel," insisted Jacob. "It's his friends. They bring their crud over and want to party, and they get a little carried away sometimes. But I talked to Daniel, and he said he's going to try to get things under control again."

"Really?"

"Yeah. He doesn't like it either. He wants his life to settle down. And he got a job, too."

"Well, that's something."

"And he thinks he can get me on there too."

"So you got fired?"

"Well, yeah. The manager is such a jerk. If you don't show up for work—just once—that's it."

"But you think Daniel can get you a job?" I could hear the skepticism in my voice.

"Yeah, he said they're short-handed." Jacob poured himself a glass of milk. "I'm supposed to go in tonight to meet the owner."

"What kind of job is it?"

"Just a gas station." He shrugged. "But better than nothing, right? And Daniel said the owner can work it out so I can take classes during winter term. He likes having students working for him."

I sighed, feeling a much-needed sense of relief. I just hoped it was the real thing. "Well, I guess that would be good."

"I'm going to take a shower and clean up before I go over there to talk to him."

I nodded. "Well, good luck."

"Sorry about that scene over at Daniel's, Mom." Jacob smiled that charming smile again, and I had a hard time believing this was the same young man who had crawled out of that filthy pit just a couple of hours ago.

"It's okay," I assured him. "I just want to make sure you're staying on track, Jacob. I want to do everything I can to help you."

"I know that, Mom." He smiled again. "And I appreciate it."

"And I know you don't understand it, but I wish you would stay away from Daniel's place."

"Mom." His voice had the tone of warning in it. "I told you it's not Daniel's fault. He's okay. And we're trying to get the band together."

I considered this. "But I didn't see any music things, Jacob."

"It's in the garage, Mom." He rolled his eyes. "You want me to take you over there and show you?"

"No, that's not necessary. I just want you to be careful, okay?"

"I'm not a baby, Mom. I know how to take care of myself." He rinsed out his glass. "And just so you'll know, I plan to jam again tonight. So don't be worried if I come in late."

"Right." I sighed and wondered exactly how a mother avoids worrying when her pushing-the-limits son comes home late.

It was around ten o'clock when I broke out a new novel that Sherry had given me. "To take your mind off things," she had said. But I was barely through the first lighthearted chapter before I heard sirens blaring outside. I went and looked out the kitchen window to first see several police cars screaming down the street. These were followed by a fire truck and two ambulances, and it looked serious. I wondered where they were headed. Who was in trouble tonight? As I usually do when I hear sirens, I imagined it was Jacob. Perhaps a car wreck or a drug squabble that resulted in a shooting, or maybe someone's meth lab had blown up. Oh, my imagination could go all kinds of places at times like this. I must've paced back and forth for thirty minutes, then I decided to turn on the eleven o'clock news and see if they had anything on it. It turned out to be a three-car pileup on the interstate just a mile away. By the descriptions of the cars I could tell Jacob wasn't in it. That is, unless, he was riding with someone else.

It was after midnight by the time I went to bed, telling myself there was nothing I could do about any of this anyway. But instead of falling asleep, I lay there running all the horrifying possibilities of my son's future through my head. I could still vividly see that horrible duplex and could imagine the awful things that went on in there. And the more I thought about it, the worse it became. After a couple of hours of my self-imposed torture, I finally had to get up and make myself a pot of herbal tea—a calming blend. And there I sat, at the narrow, plastic-topped breakfast bar, sipping my tea and waiting for the sun to come up.

Chapter 15

As luck would have it, Jacob got hired at the Red Devil. It was one of those discount gas stations—the kind that Geoffrey always warned against. "You get what you pay for, Glennis," he'd told me once after I'd filled the Range Rover with cheap gas and it had started thumping and pinging. "Those cut-rate places are known for getting the last dregs off the tanker trucks."

The last dregs, I thought as I drove by the Red Devil just to see if Jacob was really at work like he was supposed to be. To my relief his car was parked around in back, and I spied him talking to an older guy who I had begun to suspect was Daniel. I still didn't know Daniel's last name. According to Jacob, "It doesn't matter." But that only made me more uneasy.

I'd taken to driving around town as part of my daily routine. I would check on Jacob at the gas station. Then later in the evening, if Jacob failed to come home, which he'd started doing again, I would drive by the "duplex dump" to see if Jacob was there. I also kept track of the other cars that came and went from that place. I suspected that the old blue Ford van belonged to Daniel since it appeared at both the duplex dump and the gas station. But there was also a beat-up gold station wagon and a little red Honda parked there frequently. For some reason I felt the Honda belonged to Amber. Don't ask me why.

Jacob had been pumping gas for a couple of weeks. He still stayed out late, sometimes all night, but he seemed to have the uncanny ability of guessing when I was about ready to give up on him. And that's when he'd show up with a smile on his face, sometimes even with flowers, and he'd say all the right words, and, presto, I would feel better. Of course, he was often "between paychecks" at those times and usually needed a "little cash" to get him by, fill his gas tank, things like that. I would tell myself that at least he was still working. Somehow I imagined that if he was working, everything was pretty much okay.

Until the day I found a used syringe. I'd like to say it was quite by accident, but to be perfectly honest, I was snooping. I still cleaned Jacob's room for him. I did his laundry and made his bed. Somehow I believed that this would help him on his road to recovery. Or maybe it was just my penance for being a bad mom. Who can be sure?

Whatever the case, I had taken to looking around a bit as I made Jacob's bed and hung up his clothes. I had discovered some odd things under his futon bed, like a cinnamon candle he had obviously filched from me, although I hadn't noticed it was missing. I didn't see any harm in this, although I wondered why it was under his bed. Worried that he might burn the place down, I got a nice big candle holder and put the rust-colored pillar on it and placed it on his dresser. I figured if he was going for ambiance, he should at least be safe about it.

I'd also found a number of grimy spoons, but why should this seem strange since I'd also found dirty glasses and cereal bowls and the occasional slice of uneaten pizza. But I *was* curious about the mirror at first. It was just a piece of broken mirror, about eight inches in diameter, but I knew it hadn't come from anything in the apartment. Still, I figured that Jacob must've wanted to look at himself in the privacy of his own room. And so I bought him an inexpensive mirror from Wal-Mart and hung it above his dresser. No big deal.

But on this particular day, I noticed what appeared to be a roll of tissue in his wastebasket. Curious as to what it was, I picked it up and examined it. The tissue appeared unused and clean. Somewhat wasteful, I remember thinking, since I now knew the exact cost of a single roll of toilet paper, and this appeared to be at least half a roll. I gave the round wad a gentle squeeze and realized there was something inside that felt like a ballpoint pen. And being a mom, I slowly unwound the ball until I arrived at the center. But it took me a moment to realize what I was looking at.

I carried the object to the kitchen to examine it in better light. And then it became obvious. Of course, it was a hypodermic syringe, probably the kind they used for insulin injections, the sharp-looking needle still intact. It was a wonder I hadn't poked myself with it. As I stared at the bright orange plastic syringe lying there on the kitchen counter, my first response was to wrap it back up and hide it. It felt wrong and illegal and frightening, and I couldn't imagine what I would do if someone walked in here and found me with it. Could I be arrested? Then I told myself to calm down and think clearly. Why was this in Jacob's room?

Suddenly I wondered if Jacob had used this needle. Yes, now it seems silly that it wasn't more obvious to me, but that's exactly what I thought back then. "Has my son used this on himself? Has he really filled it with some horrible substance, actually inserted it into his flesh, pushed the plunger, and"—well, it was just too horrifying to imagine the rest. Somehow I convinced myself that he had only been playing with the idea. Or maybe he had found the syringe somewhere and didn't know how to get rid of it in a safe way. Even so, I felt as if my world was caving in, and I knew I would have to ask him—face to face.

I considered confronting him at work as I did my daily rounds that afternoon. But I felt that wouldn't be right. I waited for him to come home that night, and when he wasn't in by midnight, I thought about making another surprise appearance at Daniel's duplex dump, then reconsidered. Going during the day was one thing; at night was altogether different. Even so, I don't think I slept more than an hour or two that night.

The image of my son sticking a needle into his arm and injecting himself with—well, poison—made me sick to my stomach.

"It's not mine," he told me the next day when I finally had a chance to corner him in the kitchen with my "evidence."

"Really?" I made no effort to hide my skepticism.

He looked me straight in the eyes now. "I found it at work," he told me. "I was cleaning the bathroom, and it was sitting right on the counter."

I made a face. "And you *touched* it?"

"Not with my bare hands," he explained. "I was just starting to wrap it up in tissue so I could put it in the garbage, you know. But then my boss walks up and I got scared, like he might see it and think it was mine, so I slipped it into my pocket."

"Your pocket?"

"Yeah, it was stupid, I know, but the garbage can was already out the door, and I didn't want him to see it and think it was mine."

"You put a *used* syringe in your pocket?"

He nodded. "And I forgot about it until I got home."

"But what if you'd jabbed yourself on the needle?" I demanded. "You could've gotten HIV or hepatitis or who knows what."

He nodded with wide eyes. "I know, Mom. That's what I thought too. That's why I wrapped it up so carefully. I didn't want anyone to get poked by it. Especially you." He looked at me with real concern now. "You didn't, did you?"

"No. But it could happen."

"I'm sorry, Mom. If I had remembered, I would've thrown it away in one of the trash cans outside, but it was really busy that night."

"And that's the truth?" I questioned, still not completely convinced.

"Yeah, Mom." He looked down at the needle and frowned. "You don't really think I'd pump that kind of crap into myself, do you?"

I considered this. "Well, not really." I kind of laughed then, in relief I suppose. "I remember how much you hated getting vaccinations as a kid, Jacob. It was hard to imagine you would inflict that on yourself."

"Want me to throw it away for you?" he asked.

"Be careful," I warned him. Then I grabbed a paper towel. "Here, wrap it in this."

For the next week, Jacob seemed to stay home more, and I felt like maybe, just maybe, we were finally getting somewhere. I thought that perhaps he had finally realized that all those late nights jamming with Daniel hadn't been such a great idea after all.

It was late October, just before Halloween, when I decided to flip the mattress pad on Jacob's futon. He'd been complaining about a backache, and I'd grown concerned that this inexpensive bed might not be very good for his back. I thought I'd try turning it over, just to even out the lumps until we figured out a new sort of bed. But as I lifted the heavy pad, a flash of bright orange caught my eye. With the mattress resting on my head, I knelt down and peered at the now exposed wooden futon frame to see several neat little rows of hypodermic needles lined up on the wooden slats. With a rush of adrenaline, I heaved the heavy mattress pad over and onto the floor, then clasped my hand across my mouth as I stared at maybe a dozen obviously used syringes. I don't know how long I stood there, shock waves jolting through me like bolts of electricity. I knew I needed to do something. But what? I couldn't think straight. I felt angry, betrayed, worried, fearful, hopeless—every negative feeling imaginable coursed through me just then.

I started to leave Jacob's room, then froze in the doorway and stood there. I couldn't leave those nasty things just lying there out in the open and exposed for the entire world to see. As if anyone ever came to visit me in the apartment. Just the same, I couldn't bear to handle those horrid objects. And yet I definitely wanted them gone. I walked back and forth, shaking my head and waving my arms like a crazy woman or perhaps an unfortunate chicken with her head cut off.

Finally I ran to the kitchen to get something to put the syringes in. I opened every cupboard in search of the perfect container. A glass mixing bowl, no. Saucepan with lid, not quite. Tupperware, no, but closer. Finally I reached under the sink and grabbed a recycled paper grocery sack (another money-saving trick I'd learned), then I dashed back to Jacob's bedroom where I used a ballpoint pen to push these detestable objects into my brown paper bag. Then I rolled down the top of the bag, creasing it several times, as if by sealing these things I might forget that picture. But even as I set the sack on the kitchen counter, I could still see all those plastic hypodermic syringes lined up on the wooden futon frame like angry orange soldiers intent upon annihilating my only son. I wanted to throw up.

Instead, I took a deep breath and called Dr. Abrams. After explaining to her thickheaded assistant that it *really* was an emergency, I was connected to the good doctor.

"I don't know what to do." I gasped out the words as if I'd just finished a marathon.

"Take a deep breath," she told me.

I did as she said.

"And now," she continued, "slowly explain what is wrong."

"I found…I found *needles*," I said. "Beneath my son's bed."

"Needles?" Her voice sounded unimpressed.

I hadn't told Dr. Abrams about the severity of my son's drug problems yet, and I immediately imagined her envisioning sewing needles or perhaps knitting needles as if Jacob had suddenly become domestic. "*Hypodermic* needles," I explained. "At least a dozen of them—all used."

"I see." Long pause.

"I don't know what to do, Dr. Abrams. I mean I feel like I can't even breathe, like I'm going to be sick or just give up completely. I've never felt so desperate before. It's as if my husband was right all along; I am only making things worse."

"Do you think it's your fault that your son has hypodermic needles under his bed?"

"No, not like that. But it feels as if I'm just messing everything up. I can't even think anymore." And then I began to sob.

"Glennis," she said in her soothing voice, "listen to me. The only thing you can do about your son's problem is to encourage him to get help. Do you understand? But it's his choice whether he'll do that or not." And then she gave me the phone number of a rehab center in town.

"That's it?" I said in a meek voice. "That's *all* you can offer?"

"Glennis, that's *all* there is. But you need to remember what I told you the other day. Your main job is to take care of yourself right now. It's a job you've neglected for too long."

"I know…" I pressed my closed fist against my forehead, angry at myself for wasting my time by calling her in the first place. Obviously she didn't understand what this was like for me. She had probably never been in this position herself. Of course, I realized, her children were probably perfect. Well, why wouldn't they be?

"I'll see you in a couple of weeks then?" she asked in an obvious hint that it was time to end this conversation.

"Right."

"And you're okay?"

"I'm great."

"Now, Glennis—"

"I'm sorry for bothering you, Dr. Abrams," I said in a tightly controlled voice. "I'll see if Jacob is interested in visiting this rehab center."

"You do have some clout, you know," she said as if suddenly inspired.

"And that would be?"

"You could tell him that he can't continue living with you unless he agrees to seek treatment."

Great, I was thinking. Not only does my son have a very serious drug problem, but my therapist is counseling me to throw him out on the streets. "I…I can't do that."

"Then maybe you *are* part of the problem."

"What?"

"You're enabling him, Glennis. Remember, we've talked about that. When you roll over and allow people to keep making bad choices, walking all over you, you *enable* them to continue in their problems. By letting Jacob live with you when he obviously needs professional help, you're making it easy for him to keep using."

"So it *is* my fault." As I eyed the sack on the counter, I felt a mother lode of guilt burying me.

"If you allow him to keep living with you, Glennis, when you know he needs help…then, yes, you are a part of the problem."

"But it's cold outside. Where will he go? What will he eat?"

"If he gets cold enough or hungry enough, he might decide he'd like things to change." Her voice softened now. "Or he may want to consider rehab when he sees that you are firmly drawing the line."

"Do you think?"

"Draw your boundaries, Glennis. See what happens."

I sighed. "Okay, I think maybe you could be right."

"Good. Let me know how it goes."

"Thanks, Dr. Abrams."

"No problem. And next time you're in, we'll discuss what's a real emergency and what's not."

"Right." I hung up and wondered if Dr. Abrams really understood what constituted an emergency for me. Oh sure, my problems might seem small compared to someone who's standing on the ledge of a high-rise building with emergency crews down below. But that wasn't so unlike how I felt at this moment, like I was teetering on the edge of a cliff with *no* emergency crews anywhere in sight and nothing but a dark abyss below, and it seemed the only way out was down.

Chapter 16

I had done such an excellent job of keeping my problems to myself the past couple of years. Other than Sherry and my immediate family, everyone else was kept safely at arm's length. I had developed a series of pat answers that seemed to work.

"How are you doing?" someone would ask.

"Just great," I would say with a plastic smile.

"How are the kids?"

"Sarah loves college, and Jacob has become quite the musician." More smile. Then I would deflect the attention from my family by asking how they were doing. It worked so well. Admittedly, some of this facade was designed to protect Geoffrey's image. He'd made it clear to me early on that, as city attorney, he didn't want his family's dirty laundry aired publicly. But I must confess these answers became comfortable for me as well. I had enough trouble with guilt and grief without adding anyone's judgments or pity to my pile. Even my mother had remained somewhat in the dark about what was going on in our family since I only gave her bits and pieces, always with a very optimistic spin. I was a bit worried that Sarah might've told her grandmother the whole story during one of her visits, but then I realized that Sarah, as much as Geoffrey, liked keeping up appearances. She never wanted to acknowledge that anything was wrong within our family. Sometimes she even acted as if her brother had ceased to exist.

But on the day I discovered the syringes and called Dr. Abrams, I felt something inside of me snap. As I paced back and forth in my little apartment, waiting for Jacob to come home and trying to decide if and how I should confront him, I knew I could no longer keep this to myself. I realized I wanted to talk to my mother, and before I could stop myself, I had dialed her number. Shocked when I suddenly heard her happy voice answering the phone, I must've stuttered out a questionable greeting.

"Glennis?" she said with alarm. "Is something wrong, dear?"

Now, my mother already knew that Geoffrey and I were separated. "Just for a bit," I had assured her early on. "Just until we can work some things out." And my mother, the perennial optimist, had told me she felt certain we'd figure things out and be back together by Christmas.

"It's about Jacob," I began.

"Oh dear! Has he been hurt? Is it serious?"

"Yes, it's serious, Mom. But it's not like an accident. I'm not quite sure how to tell you this—" My voice broke into a sob.

"Oh dear," she said. "But if it has to do with his sexual orientation, well, dear, you'll just have to take it in stride. These things happen nowadays, and—"

"No, Mother," I said in a sharp voice. "It's not about his sexual orientation. It's that he's involved in drugs."

"Oh, that." She sighed. "Well, now, Glennis, that isn't so unusual. I just saw a show on *Dr. Phil* where these parents and teens were talking about marijuana and—"

"This isn't *Dr. Phil*, Mom," I pleaded. "This is *my* life. And I've just discovered that Jacob is using some very serious drugs."

"What kind of drugs, dear?"

"I, uh…I don't really know."

"Well, now…" The tone of her voice reminded me of when I was little, when I would tell her something I felt was important, but she would simply dismiss it as if it were nothing.

"I found hypodermic needles under his bed, Mom," I said emphatically, wanting my sense of shock to be contagious. "At least a dozen of them. All used."

"Well, that's not good."

"No, it's not good at all." I felt a tinge of relief then, as if maybe she was getting the severity of this after all.

"You know the problem with youth today is that they have too much time on their hands," she began. "Back when I was a kid, we were so busy we didn't have time to think about silly things like drugs. Is Jacob still involved in the church youth group?"

I groaned inwardly. Jacob had quit going to youth group back in middle school. "No, not really," I told her.

"Well, you see, if he was involved in the youth group, he wouldn't have time for that kind of foolishness and such." She paused. "Do you remember when you were his age, Glennis? Why, you went to youth group all the time. Didn't you even work with the youth group after college?"

"Yes." I sighed.

"And wasn't that how you and Geoffrey first met?"

"Yes." I desperately wanted to hang up now. I couldn't see how any of this would help Jacob.

"So how are things going with Geoffrey, dear? Have you been in for your marriage counseling yet? My friend Francis said that her son and daughter-in-law just went to a marriage-enrichment weekend, and it has literally changed their lives. I could probably get the name of the ministry for you. I think it was interdenominational, and they—"

"No, thanks, Mom. I don't think Geoffrey and I are ready for that yet."

"But you are getting counseling?"

"I am."

"What about Geoffrey?"

"I don't think he's interested."

"You don't think…but, honey, have you even asked him?"

"Well, there are other complications, Mom."

"You mean this thing with Jacob? Well, Glennis, you can't let Jacob's problems destroy a perfectly good marriage. That's it, isn't it? Jacob has come between you and Geoffrey. You know Sarah has alluded to this very thing. It must've gone right over my head at the time. But now that I think about it, I know that must be the source of your marital distress. You've allowed Jacob's drug problem to ruin your marriage, haven't you? Am I right?"

"No, Mom, you're not right. I'll admit that Jacob's problem hasn't helped matters. But, trust me, our marriage was already in trouble. In fact it was in a lot more trouble than I realized."

"Oh dear. Does this mean you're not trying to work things out?"

I took a deep breath. "Mom, I think that Geoffrey is having an affair."

Long pause.

"Did you hear me, Mom?"

"Yes, dear, I heard you. I was just thinking about what you said. You know, honey, it's not the end of the world when your husband strays—"

"Mom? What do you mean?"

"I mean this sort of thing happens to a lot of people."

"You mean like you and Daddy?"

"Yes, and many others, too."

"But you guys ended up getting divorced."

"It wasn't my choice, Glennis. I told your father that I could forgive him, but he had to have things his way." She made a *tsk-tsk* sound. "And look where that got him."

"Are you saying that's what killed him?"

"God only knows, Glennis. God only knows."

"Right." I shook my head. "So you're saying the fact that Geoffrey may be having an affair is no big deal. Not grounds for leaving him?"

"I'm saying it's been happening since the beginning of time. Goodness, don't you remember the story of King David and Bathsheba?"

"Mom." I could hear the impatience in my voice growing. I suddenly felt like I was fourteen again.

"Hear me out, Glennis. It's true, men do stray sometimes. But it's the godly woman's role to forgive and forget."

"Oh, please." That was *not* what I needed to hear.

"Well, it's the truth, dear. These things happen in the best of marriages. And God expects us to forgive one another and move on."

"Right." I stared out the window and wished I'd never called.

"I know it's hard to hear the truth sometimes, Glennis. But I'm your mother, and I love you, and I can only tell you what I think the good Lord would tell you."

"That I should go back to Geoffrey?"

"That's right."

"Well, I was almost ready to go back to him," I told her. "I even drove over there, ready to apologize, to tell him I was wrong and wanted to come home…and you know what?"

"No, dear, what?"

"He was having a candlelight dinner with his new love interest."

"Oh my. That must've been hard."

"I'll say. But that's when I knew it was really over between us."

"No, no…it's not over, honey. Don't say that. Where there is life, there is hope. Now, I'll be praying for you and Geoffrey and our poor Jacob. But I have no doubts whatsoever that God is taking you through the fire so you can all be purified and strengthened for his glory."

"Right."

"Will I be seeing you for Christmas?"

"Christmas?" I felt the meekness in my voice. How could this woman talk about Christmas when my life was completely falling apart?

"I thought maybe you'd all like to come out here for the holidays, dear. Get a little sunshine, play some golf. Our church is putting on a wonderful musical this year."

"Right." I bit my lip. "I'll get back to you on that, Mom."

"Okay. But Sarah already said she'd like to come down here."

"Yes, that's not surprising."

"Do you mind if I invite my Bible study ladies to pray for you, dear?"

"Not at all, Mom. Why should I mind?" I took in a sharp breath. Remain in control, I was telling myself. "But I need to go now, Mom. Good talking to you."

"And you, too, dear. And don't worry, honey. It's always the darkest before the dawn."

"Right." And then I hung up the phone and went into the living room where I pushed a chenille pillow into my face and suppressed a primal scream that was coming up from a deep, dark place within me. Why on earth had I called my mother?

I never finished turning Jacob's mattress that day, or even cleaning his room for that matter. In fact, I pretty much let everything go after the conversation with my mother. Why bother, I wondered. What difference did it make anyway? And so I did nothing more than fret and worry all day long, waiting for Jacob to come home so I could confront him. I was almost as angry at him for lying to me about the first needle I'd found as I was about finding his entire collection.

When midnight rolled around and he still hadn't shown, I realized he was probably pulling an all-nighter again. Why should that surprise me? And so I took two Tylenol PMs and went to bed. Sleeping aids were new to me, and I had convinced myself that these little blue pills helped me to rest at night, but I think it was really just another one of my delusions. It seemed I had been wrong about most everything.

However, they must've worked that night because I woke up out of a dead sleep with my heart racing as the overhead light flashed on in my room. I could see someone standing in the doorway, but my eyes, unadjusted to the light, couldn't focus.

"What did you do to my room, Mom?" he demanded in a hard, cold voice that didn't sound like my son.

I sat up in bed, blinking and rubbing my eyes. "Jacob?"

"Why were you snooping in my room?" he snapped.

"Cleaning. I wasn't snooping," I said as I reached for my robe and made my way out of the bed.

"Yeah, sure." He punched his fist into the wall in the hallway, so hard that I saw a hole when I went out to talk to him.

"Jacob," I said. "Look what you did."

"Stay out of my stuff, Mom!"

Now I looked into his eyes and realized that this was a stranger. Oh sure, he was Jacob's height and build, same hair color and facial features, but his eyes were different. His eyes were cold and hard, and I hate to admit it, but they were dark. Clouded and, well, evil looking. I clutched my bathrobe more tightly around me. "Jacob," I said in what I hoped was a calming voice, "I was only trying to flip your mattress so your bed would be more—"

"Don't lie to me, Mom!" He punched the wall again, resulting in another fist-sized hole. "I *know* you were snooping. You and Dad used to do it all the time. You guys have never trusted me. No wonder I'm so screwed up."

"Maybe you should just go to bed," I told him, sensing that it was quite possible my son was under the influence of drugs even at this moment.

"Yeah, that's what I was going to do, Mom. But then I come home and find my bedroom all ripped up into some big freaking mess. Like the KGB's been here. What is wrong with you anyway? Why can't you just stay out of my life and leave my stuff alone?" His fist was raised again.

I blinked and stepped back, afraid that he was aiming at me this time, but *wham.* It went through the hallway wall again. And now I was mad. "Stop putting holes in the wall, Jacob!" I yelled. "Don't you know I'll have to pay to have those fixed?"

"Is that what you're worried about?" He laughed. "*Money?* Why not go back to Mr. Moneybags and ask him for a little handout. In fact, why don't you pick up some for me while you're there?" He smiled, but it was a twisted smile. "I'll take mine in tens and twenties, if you don't mind."

"It's late," I told him. "We need to go to bed. We can talk about this in the morning."

"No," said Jacob. "I want to talk about it now."

I shrugged, knowing I wouldn't be sleeping much tonight anyway. "Fine, Jacob. Let's talk about it now. Are you hungry? I didn't have dinner, and it's been a pretty cruddy day. Maybe if we both ate something and talked this over…"

He seemed to soften. "For you, too?"

"Yeah." I looked at him more carefully. "Was your day bad?"

He nodded. "And now that you mention it, I'm hungry too."

So that's how I found myself in the kitchen fixing French toast for the two of us. And it was weird as I put together our three-o'clock-in-the-morning meal. It was like something in Jacob was unhinged. He began to talk and talk. Some of the things coming out of his mouth were really amazing and slightly profound, but a lot of his words and ideas were confusing and mixed up. Despite my growing suspicion that he was high, I tried to listen, thinking that perhaps it would provide a clue for why he was like this. But by the time he quit talking long enough to eat about a half-dozen slices of French toast smothered in maple syrup and butter, along with about a half gallon of milk, I really had no idea what his conversation had been about. Maybe it was due to my being exhausted or under the effects of Tylenol PM, or perhaps my stressed-out life was getting to me. But when Jacob started talking again, I felt like everything in my world was just spinning around me. Like I couldn't hold on to anything—not my marriage, not my children, not even my own life.

As I bent down to scrape the remnants of my soggy French toast from my plate into the garbage can beneath the sink (since we have no luxuries like garbage disposals), I totally fell apart. I lost it. I started sobbing so hard and uncontrollably that I collapsed onto the kitchen floor. And there I sat, knees pulled up to my chest, hunched over in a heap of flannel pajamas and bathrobe, and I cried.

"Mom?" I heard his voice. It was smaller now, more like the old Jacob or maybe even the little boy who used to pick me surprise bouquets of flowers when I was feeling down. "Are you okay?"

Despite my need to reassure him, to pull myself together so he wouldn't feel bad, I was unable. I just kept crying.

"Mom?" he said again, his hand on my shoulder now. "Should I call someone?"

I continued sobbing.

"Should I call Dad?"

At the sound of that question, which felt more like a threat or a rude awakening, I looked up and shook my head. "No, I…I'm going to…to be o…okay. I'm…just upset."

"Yeah."

I started to stand up, and he reached down to give me a hand. Then I stood and looked him in the eyes. "I can't take it anymore, Jacob," I told him. "I think I'm really losing it."

He nodded. "Yeah, I can see that."

Then I saw my brown paper bag, still sitting under the sink where I'd stashed it earlier. Out of sight, out of mind. I wished. I reached for the bag and pulled it out, setting it on the counter. "I believe these are yours, Jacob."

He looked puzzled but then slowly opened the bag and looked in. I could tell by his expression that he was surprised. And this was a little confusing since he'd obviously seen that I'd looked under his bed. Surely he knew that I'd discovered them.

"Where did you find these?" he asked, still staring at the bag in fascination. Almost as if he liked what he was seeing in there, as if he was proud.

"Underneath your futon mattress." My heart was beginning to pound. I knew I was getting in way too deep right now, but what choice did I have? I couldn't pretend like this was nothing. Still, what if Jacob got angry? What if he was under the effect of some chemical even as we spoke? I'd read stories about people who'd done crazy things under the influence of drugs. How could I be sure he wouldn't do something violent now? I glanced over to the phone, not far from his elbow.

"So you think they're mine?"

I pressed my lips together. "Jacob, they're not mine."

"But someone else might've put them there, Mom."

"Jacob, please, don't lie. I don't think I can take it." I was trying to keep my voice calm, but it was hard to breathe, hard to think, infinitely hard to reason.

"But there are people who're trying to get at me," he continued. "They might've planted them there."

"Jacob," I said slowly. "Please, I need you to be honest with me this time. I can't take any more lies today."

He exhaled loudly. "Okay, you're right, Mom. They're mine."

But here's what took me by surprise. Instead of being relieved that he was finally telling me the truth, I felt my knees growing weak and my stomach knotting. I wondered if there were times in life when the truth was just too much to bear. Would I rather hear lies?

"Let's go sit down," I told him as I made my unsteady way into the living room, then collapsed on the couch. Jacob sat in the old rocker across from me. He looked uneasy, perched on the edge of the chair like a flighty sparrow, as if he was ready to bolt at any given second. I leaned back, picked up a pillow and clutched it to my midsection, and took a deep breath, bracing myself for honesty. "Okay," I said, "tell me what's going on."

He looked down at his feet and said nothing.

"Jacob," I continued, "I need you to talk to me. Tell me why you have hypodermic syringes hidden beneath your bed."

Still nothing.

"Jacob," I tried again, "I know you have a drug problem, okay? There's no point in pretending like everything's okay. I admit that I was pretty shocked to find out that you—that you're using hypodermic needles though. To me that makes everything a whole lot more serious."

He looked up now. "Why?"

"Why?" I was taken aback by his nonchalant response. Wasn't it obvious? We were talking about needles!

"Why do you think using needles makes it more serious?"

"Well, I don't know for sure." I was getting that blurry feeling now, like Jacob was going to muddy the waters again. "It just seems pretty serious to me," I finally said.

"The needles are safe," he assured me.

"The needles are safe?" I studied him, wondering how this messed-up kid could actually be my child. Had aliens kidnapped him, taken him to the mother ship to perform a lobotomy, then returned him when no one was looking?

He nodded. "Yeah, I don't, like, reuse them or anything. And I'm very careful about everything. I sterilize stuff and make sure—"

"Wait," I told him. "Wait a minute. You think that injecting yourself with…with… What do you inject yourself with anyway?"

He sighed.

"Jacob, please, I need you to tell me. It's not as if I'm a policeman. I'm your mother, for heaven's sake. I love and care about you more than anyone else on the planet. If you can't trust me, you can't trust anyone."

He nodded. "Meth," he said in a quiet voice.

"Crystal meth?"

He nodded again.

"As in methamphetamines?"

Again, the nod.

"As in the drug that people manufacture out of fertilizer and chemicals?"

"Yeah, I guess."

"You're shooting *that* into your body?" I tried to suppress the hysteria I felt rising in my voice. I tried not to imagine the little boy I'd worked so hard to care for and protect and how I'd fretted and worried about him when he'd caught the latest flu bug. How could this child of mine have been shooting chemicals and fertilizer substances into his flesh?

"What'd you think I was using?" He laughed then, but it was a sad, hollow laugh. "It's not like I have a lot of money, you know. Pump monkeys don't get paid a whole lot. And Daddy Big Bucks isn't being too generous with me these days. Crystal meth is the poor man's cocaine, you know."

"I didn't know."

"Well, now you do."

Fresh tears slipped down my cheeks.

"Oh, crud, don't start crying again, Mom." He stood up and started pacing. "It doesn't help anything when you get all upset. In fact, it just makes me want to go out and get some more—"

"I'm *not* getting all upset," I said quickly and wiped my wet face. I took a deep breath and sat up straighter. I wasn't about to give him any excuse to go out and get high. Not that I thought he wasn't already high. Whether he was on his way up or down, I had no idea, but I knew something about him was not right.

"Look, Mom." He sat back down on the chair. Then leaning forward, he looked intently at me. "It's not like I'm hurting anyone. It's my own thing. It makes me cope with life better, you know? I mean it's like my medical treatment. I can function when I have it. Without it…" He looked down at his hands. "Well, I'd rather be dead."

I thought about this. In a way it was a somewhat convincing argument. I'd heard about addicts that "self-medicate." Maybe that was what was going on here. Maybe I should just let it go at that, go back to bed, and deal with this crazy thing in the morning. But then, I reminded myself, I wasn't exactly thinking clearly at the moment. "But what if the crystal meth kills you?" I asked.

He laughed. "No one ever dies from meth."

"How do you know that?" I asked. "I read something in the paper almost every week about somebody overdosing or dying as a result of drugs." Okay, maybe that was an exaggeration, but I knew I'd read a few stories. And they had chilled me to my soul.

"Well, it's probably not crystal meth."

"But how do you know that?" My voice was getting loud again.

"Because I would know, that's all."

"Do you even read the newspaper?" I challenged him. "Do you watch the news? What do you really know about this crud you've been shooting into yourself, Jacob? What do you *really* know?"

"I know it makes me feel good."

I sighed. "It's ruining your life, Jacob. Can't you see that? And it's hurting everyone around you. Can't you see it?"

He looked back down at his feet again.

"Jacob," I quieted my voice. "I talked to my counselor today, and she told me I have to give you an ultimatum."

His head jerked up. "An ultimatum?"

"Yes." I steadied myself, and I think I even breathed a little God-help-me kind of prayer. "You can only live here...in this apartment...if you're willing to seek treatment."

"Treatment?" He jumped to his feet now. "What kind of treatment?"

"Drug-rehab therapy. I have the phone number of a place right here in town called Hope's Wings."

"You want me to go into rehab?" He shook his head and walked over to the front door. "No way."

I sighed. "Then, I'm sorry, Jacob, but you can't live here."

"Fine!" He turned and glared at me with angry brown eyes. "I won't miss this crappy place anyway." Then he walked out and slammed the door so hard that a candlestick on the window sill fell over.

I took a deep breath, then went over to pick up the candlestick and look out the window. Dawn was just beginning, but the street still looked grim and gray and cold—bleakly cold. And, of course, Jacob had stormed outside without bothering to get a coat. But, I reminded myself, he had a sleeping bag in his car. He would probably be okay...at least for now.

Chapter 17

As I trudged down to the laundry room, I felt as if I were carrying my entire life on my shoulders. My backpack of laundry items felt like it was filled with heavy stones, stones of guilt, and the laundry basket contained every single mistake I'd ever made. By the time I reached the laundry room, I was out of breath and couldn't even remember what I'd come down here for.

"Hello, Glennis," said a cheerful voice.

It was the old man I'd met down here a couple of weeks ago. But my mind was so weary it took me a moment to remember his name. "Jack," I finally said, as if I were giving the answer on a game show. Perhaps I should've said, "Who is Jack?"

"You feeling all right?" he asked with a creased brow.

I shrugged. "Just tired, I guess."

"How's Jacob doing?"

I was surprised that he remembered the name. "Not so well," I admitted as I set my laundry basket on the washer next to his.

He nodded as if this wasn't too surprising. "Reckon he doesn't want to come to AA with me then."

I shook my head. "He doesn't want help of any kind."

"That's too bad." Jack turned back to his task of moving wet items from the washer into the dryer about ten feet away.

I just stood there watching him, as if I were hypnotized. He moved back and forth between the two machines, carrying just a few items at a time, until the dryer was full, and he, one by one, loaded in his quarters. Finally, his task completed, he turned and looked at me, more closely this time. "Now don't take no offense at this, Glennis, but you really don't look too good."

I sighed. "I don't feel too good either."

"You wanna talk about it?" He scooted a white plastic lawn chair from across the room and set it next to another one, then sat down and patted the empty seat beside it.

I sank into the seat and shook my head. "I had to throw Jacob out last night," I began. "Or rather this morning."

He nodded as if this was a completely normal thing for a mother to do, then waited for me to continue.

"I discovered a lot of hypodermic needles in his room yesterday. And after I confronted him, he admitted that he'd been using crystal meth."

Jack shook his head. "That stuff will kill you."

"Yes," I said. "That's exactly what I told him. But he said that's not true. He said it's perfectly safe."

Jack rubbed his chin. "I reckon this is your first lesson about addiction, Glennis. You can never trust an addict."

"But he's my son, Jack. I told him he could be honest with me."

"Honesty is something an addict just don't get. Take it from me, I used to tell one falsehood after the next. I'd say anything to get folks off my back, anything to get me my next drink. It's just the way the mind of an addict works."

"Then how can you help them?" I demanded.

"Reckon you can't." He leaned back in his chair and folded his arms across his chest. "Not unless they're willing to help themselves."

"Yes, I've heard that."

"But you threw him out?"

"Yes, that's what my counselor recommended. She said if I didn't, I would be an enabler."

He nodded. "Your counselor is right."

"Then why do I feel so horrible now?" I asked him. "Why do I feel so guilty that I'm certain I must be the worst mother in the civilized world? Maybe even the uncivilized world. I can imagine that third world mothers do a much better job than what I've done."

"Can't blame yourself, Glennis. Doesn't do no good. Your Jacob is the only one who can fix this thing."

"But what if he won't? What if he goes out and shoots up so much of that stuff that it kills him?"

"That's the chance we take."

"The chance we take?" I demanded. "Don't you think there's a pretty good chance that my son's life is going to be destroyed by this, Jack? Am I supposed to sit idly by and wait until the police or the hospital calls to inform me that my son has just died of a methamphetamine overdose? Or maybe he'll get in a car wreck while he's under the influence. Maybe he'll kill someone else as well as himself. Or maybe he'll get hit by a train while he's so high he can't even see it coming. Or maybe—"

"Or maybe he'll get so sick of his drugs that he'll wake up one morning and say enough is enough," added Jack.

"I wish it were true."

"In the meantime, you'd better be taking care of yourself, Glennis. When was the last time you had a good night's sleep?"

"I can't even remember."

"Did you know that people who go around driving cars or operating machinery while sleep deprived are as dangerous as drunk drivers?" He nodded as if to accentuate his point. "I saw that on the *Today* show last week."

"Are you suggesting that I shouldn't be operating that washing machine?" I asked, eying my basket of dirty laundry still sitting on the washer.

He chuckled. "S'pect that won't hurt none."

I got up and went over to fill the washer.

"But you need to take care of yourself, Glennis. You need to be eating right and getting enough sleep."

I put the last item in and began digging around in my backpack for my roll of quarters. I knew I had put a brand-new roll in there just days ago. I dug and dug but couldn't find anything. Finally I dumped the contents of the backpack out on the folding table and really searched.

"Whatcha looking for?" asked Jack.

"My roll of quarters," I told him. "I just put it in here."

"Where do you usually keep that backpack?" asked Jack.

"In the coat closet," I told him. "With the extra laundry baskets."

"Is it possible that your son might've—"

"No!" I turned and stared at Jack. "Jacob wouldn't take my laundry quarters. My son may be an addict, but he's certainly not a thief."

Jack nodded, but I could tell he wasn't convinced.

"I probably just misplaced them," I told him as I turned away and began reloading the backpack. "I've been so absent-minded lately. Who knows what I may have done with them." Then I turned back around just in time to see Jack putting the last quarter into my washing machine. He pushed them in and closed the lid.

"What are you doing?" I demanded.

He smiled. "Just my good deed for the day."

"But what about the soap?" I questioned, reaching into my backpack for my laundry soap.

"It's in there."

Now I felt foolish. I'd just jumped all over this kind and generous man for suggesting that Jacob may have taken my quarters, and now he was helping me.

"I'm sorry," I said. "You're probably right. It's possible that Jacob did take that roll of quarters. But he's never done anything like that before."

"Addiction changes you," he told me. "Makes you do things you wouldn't normally do."

"I guess."

"You gotta understand, Glennis, the thing that drives an addict is getting his next drink, his next high. Nothing else matters. Can you understand that?"

"I'm trying." I sighed. "But it just doesn't make much sense."

"Never does," said Jack, "to someone who hasn't been there." He put his hand on my shoulder now. "Why don't you go back to your apartment and have a little rest."

"But my laundry—"

"It's all right," he assured me. "I'm gonna be down here for a while. I'll take care of it. You just promise me that you'll take a nap."

He was guiding me to the door now.

"But I can't—"

"Don't you worry about nothing, Glennis. Just go on up there and lie down and rest a bit. You hear?"

And so, feeling like a zombie or a robot with Jack holding the remote control, I trudged back up the stairs, lay down on the couch, and fell fast asleep.

When I woke up, I remembered Jack and the laundry. Surely it had been done some time ago. But when I opened my door, there sat my basket of meticulously folded laundry, with a folded piece of white paper on top. I took the basket into my apartment and picked up the paper, wondering if perhaps it was a bill for laundry services, but it appeared to be a note.

Written in blue ink and uneven handwriting, the note said, "The Lord giveth and the Lord taketh away. Blessed be the name of the Lord."

Unsure as to the meaning of what I assumed Jack had written, I used a plastic magnet that Sylvia had given me at More-4-Less that said "We Save U More" to adhere this mysterious note to my refrigerator.

Then I put away the laundry, taking time to notice how neatly Jack had folded each piece, with such precision and care. But I did little else that day. It seemed that every ounce of energy I'd ever had was completely spent or lost or maybe even stolen. It was as if I had nothing left for anyone. Not even myself. I slept a bit, then wandered aimlessly around my little apartment. But time after time, I found myself standing in front of the refrigerator, not because I was hungry. I couldn't remember what *that* felt like. But because I couldn't quit staring at those words. Oh, I'd heard them before, but what did they really mean? What did they mean for me? Was it meant to be prophetic? Was Jack saying that God had given me Jacob and now he was taking him away? And that I should thank him for that?

Finally the long day was almost over. Sitting in my sweats, I curled up under a blanket to watch the eleven o'clock news, mostly waiting for the weather predictions since I was concerned about Jacob being homeless just when it was beginning to get really cold. And the forecast didn't look good, with near freezing temperatures tonight, and colder tomorrow. How cold did it have to get before a person got hypothermia? Jacob was probably crashing at Daniel's again. But suddenly I needed to know my son was okay. It wasn't as if I planned on doing much actual sleeping anyway. And if Jacob's car was parked at Daniel's, I would at least know that he was sleeping someplace warm. Of course, there were other issues to worry me about that, but at least my son wouldn't be dying from exposure. Still in my sweats, I hurried down the darkened steps, noticing again that the outdoor light was still out. Then I dashed over to the parking lot and into the Range Rover where I finally felt safe.

I slipped the key in the ignition and remembered how I'd never considered myself much of a night person before. I'd always depended on Geoffrey for any evening excursions. But, of course, that had all changed these past couple of months. Still, I didn't want to think about Geoffrey just now. Maybe I was repressing things, or even in denial, but whenever thoughts of Geoffrey intruded into my otherwise muddled mind, I would push them far away. One has only so much room in one's mind when it comes to madness.

I drove slowly over to Daniel's duplex dump, looking both ways down all the side streets. But I didn't see the Subaru anywhere. I even went by the Red Devil, but it had already closed for the night. I tried a couple of other spots where Jacob used to hang out, but my search seemed futile, and finally I had to give up and return home.

Feeling even more like a crazy woman for running around in the middle of the night like that, I tiptoed up the darkened stairs so as not to disturb my neighbors, but halfway up I realized I didn't have my apartment key with me. I fished around my sweats pockets just to make sure, but it wasn't there. I hadn't brought my purse, so I didn't even have my cell phone. All I had were my car keys and the clothes on my back. I went back down the stairs and sat at the bottom and tried to think. That's when I noticed I didn't even have on real shoes. I was wearing a pair of old slippers that my mother had given me for Christmas years ago. It was getting colder now, and all I had on was my sweats. Not unlike my son, I had taken off without thinking to get a jacket. I suppose madness runs in the family.

I don't know how long I sat there before it occurred to me that if I hadn't taken the apartment key with me, that meant I probably hadn't bothered to lock the apartment door. Feeling hopeful and foolish, I dashed up the stairs to discover it was unlocked.

Not only was it unlocked, but someone was inside. Of course, I didn't realize this until I was safely in and had locked the door and turned the deadbolt. I heard movement in the hallway, and before I could find anything like a baseball bat, which I didn't have anyway, the intruder appeared.

"Jacob?" I said in shocked surprise. "What are you doing here?"

"I came to pick up some things," he said in a quiet and sober voice.

"Oh." I looked at him, trying to discern his condition—was he high or not? But I couldn't really tell.

"The door wasn't locked," he told me. "I was getting kind of worried that something might've happened to you."

Jacob was worried about me? "Really?"

"Yeah. I thought maybe you'd had an emergency or something. I didn't think you'd go off and leave the door unlocked like that."

"I haven't been thinking too clearly today."

He nodded. "Well, I just wanted to pick up some warm clothes and stuff."

"That's fine." I took a deep breath to steady myself. It would be so easy to say, "Oh, just forget everything I said last night. It's okay; you can stay here." But I remembered what Dr. Abrams had said, what Jack had said, and I decided to stand firm. "Get whatever you need, Jacob." Then I turned away so he wouldn't see the tears in my eyes.

I went into the kitchen and pretended to be highly interested in making a pot of tea. Finally he came back out with an old sports duffel bag stuffed full.

"Well, I'm gonna go now," he told me.

"Do you need something to eat?" I asked.

He brightened a little. "Sure, that'd be great."

"What would you like?"

"Oh, that's okay, Mom. I can fix myself something. I know it's late, and you look tired. I'll just make a peanut-butter sandwich to take with me."

"Sure, help yourself."

I took my cup of tea over to the other side of the breakfast bar and watched as my son lathered on a thick layer of peanut butter. He was being very careful and neat, almost how a guest might act in someone else's home. When he was done, he wrapped the sandwich in a paper towel and turned to look at me. "Thanks, Mom."

Again I fought to hold back the tears. Then I thought of something. "I didn't notice your car in the parking lot, Jacob. Or even on the street. Where did you park?"

He sighed. "It's kind of a long story."

I nodded. "Want to give me the sweet and condensed version?"

"Yeah, I guess. It's impounded."

"Impounded?"

"Yeah. I got stopped last night after I left here."

"And?"

"My insurance was expired."

"Your insurance? What do you mean?"

"The card in my glove box was outdated."

"Well, didn't you explain that you had a new one?"

"I don't. Dad hasn't paid it."

"So they took your car because of that?" I stood up now. "That's ridiculous, Jacob. We can have that insurance reinstated tomorrow. I can't believe your father did that. We'll go down to city hall first thing in the morning and straighten this out."

"Well, there's something else, Mom." He looked slightly sheepish.

"Yes?"

"I had an open bottle of vodka in the car."

"Vodka?" I could hear the shrill tone of my voice.

"It wasn't mine, Mom. It was Daniel's. I didn't even know it was there."

"So the police searched your car?"

"Yeah. I guess it was because of the MIP."

"But I thought that was all taken care of. I thought you had six months to do your community service, and that was it."

"Not exactly."

"What do you mean?"

"Well, they don't expunge the MIP from my record until I finish the community service."

"Oh, and I suppose you haven't even started yet."

"I've been busy, Mom." He shook his head. "My life isn't exactly easy, you know. I'm trying to work and make some money, and now I not only don't have a home, but I don't have a car." And then to my total surprise, he began to cry.

"Oh, Jacob," I said.

"I know it's my fault, Mom. I'm a real screwup. And I'm sorry. But I just don't know what to do anymore. It's like things start looking up, and suddenly everything is caving in around me." He sat down on the stool and put his head on the breakfast bar.

I wanted to remind him that the caving-in part was most likely a result of his drug use, but I didn't have the heart to kick him when he was down. Instead I put my hand on his shoulder. "It's true you have blown it, Jacob. But it's not too late to fix things," I told him. "I could call Hope's Wings and—"

"I don't need rehab." He sat up straight and looked at me with a blotchy face and hardened eyes. "I can do this thing myself, Mom."

"You've tried that," I reminded him. "Remember, you told me you were going to straighten up before. But it's not working. You need help, Jacob. There's no shame in that."

He put his head back down on the counter and said nothing.

"What would it hurt to just go in, Jacob? You could talk to a counselor and find out what they have to offer—"

"Yeah, and then they'll lock me up," he muttered.

"Oh, I don't think it's like that."

He sat up straight again. "But you don't know, do you?"

"I can find out."

"Yeah, sure." He shook his head. "But you'd probably say anything just to get me in there."

"Jacob!" I gave him my sternest look. "I have never lied to you."

"Everybody lies, Mom. It's just that some people can pull it off better than others."

I wasn't sure what he meant by that but didn't want to derail our conversation by asking. "What do you say, Jacob?" I continued. "How about if I call and set up an appointment?"

He studied me for a bit, and I could tell he was trying to decide whether to trust me or not.

"When have I ever let you down?" I demanded. "Don't you know that I would give up my life for you, Jacob? You're my son. I wouldn't do anything to hurt you."

"You threw me out."

"It was just because my counselor said it was the only way to help you. Believe me, Jacob, I wouldn't have been able to do it otherwise." And even as I said these words, I felt a tiny ray of hope. Maybe Dr. Abrams had been right after all. Because here we were just twenty-four hours later having a conversation about rehab therapy, and he seemed to be softening. "Let's make a deal, Jacob," I offered. "I'll let you stay here tonight if you'll agree to go in for a counseling session."

"When?"

"I don't know. As soon as we can get one."

"And you'll find out whether they can lock me up against my will or not."

"Really, Jake, I don't think they do that."

"I want to know for sure."

"Okay, I'll ask. No problem."

"Well, I have to work tomorrow."

"That's good," I told him, relieved that he at least still had a job. "What are your hours?"

"Nine to three."

"Fine. Well, I'll see what I can do and get back to you. Okay?"

"I guess."

Then I grabbed him and hugged him. "You do know how much I love you, don't you, Jacob?"

He nodded and appeared to be choking back tears again. "Yeah, I guess. It's just that everything is so messed up right now."

"I know." I held him back and looked into his eyes. And, although I knew I wasn't an expert, I really thought he was sober. "But things are going to get better. I really believe it."

"I hope so, Mom."

And then, unlike the previous night, we both went to bed. And for the first time in weeks I slept for most of the night.

Chapter 18

I felt so hopeful the next morning, even remembered the words from a poster I'd had back the sixties: *Today is the first day of the rest of your life.* That was how I imagined it would be with Jacob. I'd schedule him an appointment at the local rehab center, and he'd finally receive the help he so badly needed. Just like that we'll be on the road to recovery, I assured myself. I thought I could actually see a light at the end of the spiraling tunnel.

After Jacob went to work, I phoned Hope's Wings, the place Dr. Abrams had recommended, and after a short wait I was connected to a helpful man named Marcus Palmer.

I gave him a brief history of my son, concluding with, "But now he's ready to get help. He's agreed to meet with a counselor."

"That's great," he told me. "And you're lucky because I just had a cancellation this afternoon. Will four fifteen work for both of you?"

"That's perfect," I told him. "Jacob gets off work at three."

I made a special point to stop by the Red Devil a little later that morning so I could tell Jacob the good news. I even wrote down the time and place on a card so he wouldn't forget. "I'll pick you up at three," I told him.

"Thanks, Mom." He shoved the card into his pocket and frowned. "You need any gas?"

"Sure. Go ahead and put twenty dollars worth in." I stood and watched as he filled the Range Rover with the kind of gas that would probably make it rattle and ping, and I wondered what I could possibly say to encourage him. "The guy sounded really nice," I said and handed him the twenty.

Jacob actually smiled, and I felt a rush of relief flow through me. "That's cool, Mom." He pulled his ski cap down over his ears. "Hey, do you think you could loan me a few bucks? My lunch break's coming up, and I didn't have much breakfast this morning."

I looked back in my wallet to see a solitary bill, another twenty. "This is all I have," I told him, holding up my twenty.

"Thanks, Mom." He smiled as he took the bill. "I'll pay you back on Friday. I promise."

Not only did he not pay me back, but he was nowhere to be found when I went back to the Red Devil at three. I drove around town looking for him, but I finally had to call Marcus and cancel a little after four.

"I'm sorry to wait until the last minute," I told him through my tears of frustration. "I really thought Jacob was going to cooperate this time."

"Don't feel bad," he said. "Stuff like this happens all the time."

"I know. But he seemed so willing. I gave him a card with the time and everything."

"Do you think there's a chance that he still might show?" asked Marcus.

"I seriously doubt it since he doesn't even have a car right now," I told him. "But I suppose he might have a friend drop him off. Although that seems pretty unlikely."

"Well, hey, I've got that hour available anyway. Why don't you come in, just in case? And if Jacob doesn't show, we can at least discuss some ways for you to cope with your stress in the meantime."

So I got back into my car and drove to the rehab center. It was located on the outskirts of town and was nothing like what I'd expected. I suppose my image of a rehab center came from a scene in an old movie. For some reason I assumed it would be a large sprawling campus with acres of green lawns and gracefully placed trees, perhaps gated with security guards and tall fences to keep the patients confined. Although I had assured Jacob I didn't think that was the case.

But when I turned at the Hope's Wings sign, I was somewhat disappointed to see several rather drab barracks-type buildings compounded next to a large blacktop area. Nothing was fenced or gated. I parked in front of the building that was marked Main Office and went inside to inquire about Marcus Palmer. As I walked past a building marked Rehab Center, I noticed a cluster of people of varying ages. They stood around a doorway smoking and talking. I later learned they were patients and that smoking and eating chocolate were the only vices allowed in this facility. But even the chocolate was rationed. However, the cigarettes were not. I didn't bother to ask why.

"Marcus is just finishing a session," said the girl at the reception desk. She looked to be about Jacob's age and had a pierced lip and spiky hair that had been dyed a bright shade of purple. "But his office is right down that hall. You can wait for him in there if you like."

Near the end of the dimly lit hallway, I reached an office with the right name on the door. The door was open, so I went in and sat down in a straight-backed chair. The office closed in around me with shabby, beige-colored carpeting and a cheap metal desk. Other than the artwork plastered on every available wall, the space would've been quite dismal. Given the amateurish quality of the art, I suspected that these pieces had been created by patients at Hope's Wings. And the more I examined the collages and paintings, the more intrigued I became. One piece was particularly fascinating. It consisted of dozens of cut-out heads of beautiful women, obviously extracted from a fashion magazine. But across each mouth, except for one, was a piece of black tape. And the one head without a taped mouth, tucked down in the left corner, had a handmade blindfold pasted over the eyes. It seemed that, especially in this case, a picture really was worth a thousand words.

"Good morning," said a dark-haired man, extending his hand toward me. "I'm Marcus Palmer." He had on a navy V-neck sweater with worn elbows. But what caught my attention was the tie-dyed T-shirt he wore beneath it.

"I'm Glennis Harmon," I told him. "Jacob's mother."

"Ah, Jacob's mother," he repeated as he leaned against his cluttered desk, folding his arms in front of him. "Is that your official title?"

I wasn't sure if he was making fun of me, but I was definitely feeling more self-conscious by the minute. "Is this how the counseling sessions for mothers usually begin?"

He laughed as he went around to the other side of his desk. I could see now that his dark hair was pulled back into a neat tail, and I guessed he was one of those baby boomers who hadn't quite given up on the sixties yet. Then he pulled out what looked like a fairly decent leather chair, slightly out of place in his otherwise lackluster office.

"Now that you mention it," he said as he sat down, "I suppose there are some similarities in my *mother* sessions." He pushed a pile of papers off to one side of his desk. "The first thing I usually try to get across to family members and spouses of addicts, mothers in particular, is that this is *not* your fault."

"Not my fault?" I echoed.

"That's right." He waited for my reaction.

I wanted to cooperate and hopefully get some answers for Jacob. So I figured I needed to be honest. "Okay, my mind can accept that it's not my fault, but my heart feels differently."

He nodded with a solemn expression as he folded his hands neatly on his desk. It seemed he was waiting for me to say something more. And because I dislike lapses in conversations, I accommodated him.

"I mean I've read a few things...books about addiction, articles on the Internet, and I *know* that I'm not *really* responsible for my son's behavior.

But then I'm a mother." I held up my hands hopelessly. "It feels like everything and anything that goes wrong with my children must be my fault. I wake up in the middle of the night sometimes, and I wonder if I'd breast-fed him, maybe he wouldn't have turned out this way. Or maybe if I hadn't pushed him to potty train by two. Or maybe I took away his binkie too soon."

"Binkie?"

"You know, a pacifier."

"Oh."

"Silly things like that. Of course, that's only on nights when I know he's in his bed, hopefully sleeping. But that seems to be less and less anymore. On the nights when I don't know where he is, I find myself wide awake as I imagine a hundred and one ways he has been killed or injured or arrested. I've even reached the place where the image of his being arrested seems the most favorable."

"You want him to get arrested?" His expression was completely blank now.

"No, of course not. *I'm his mother.* Why would I want to see my son in jail?"

"Because maybe you think he'd be safer there?"

I nodded. "Yes, I suppose that's true. Although I've heard that horrible things can happen in jail, too, and that inmates are still able to get drugs and…" I sighed. "I just feel so completely hopeless sometimes."

"Sometimes?"

"Okay, *all* the time. I feel hopeless *all* the time—24/7."

He smiled now. Not a big smile, but sort of a knowing smile. "Well, you're not alone, Glennis."

"You feel hopeless too?"

He smiled again, slightly bigger this time. "*Sometimes* I do. It isn't easy to deal with addicts day after day, many who don't really want to recover, some who want to but can't. But mostly I'm okay. I was actually referring to other people who have an addict in their life."

"Right."

"Have you ever considered joining a support group like Al-Anon?"

"I went to a meeting."

"Just one?"

"Well." I wanted to blame it all on Geoffrey now, to pour out all my grief and frustration and make it seem like his fault, but I knew that wouldn't be completely true or even fair. "I guess I wasn't sure if it was really worth it."

"Worth it?"

"Oh, at the time I was still with my husband, and we didn't agree on how to handle things, with Jacob I mean."

He nodded. "I've seen that happen a lot."

"He thought Al-Anon was a total waste of time."

"Did he go to a meeting too?"

I firmly shook my head. "I don't think he would've liked being seen somewhere like *that*."

"Not good for his image?"

"Exactly."

"But you went anyway."

I shrugged. "I've long since quit caring about my image. I know I'm a bad mom, and I figure everyone else in Stafford knows it too."

"Oh, come now, Glennis, I'm sure you're not a bad mom. You're here today, even though your son, who really should be here, has bailed on us."

"The fact is, I would do anything to get Jacob away from drugs. *Anything*."

"I'm sure you would." He studied me for a moment. "The problem is, there is nothing you can do."

"Nothing?" I must've looked crushed. "Nothing at all?"

"I'm sorry, but it's the truth. The only one who can help Jacob is Jacob."

"That's what my husband used to say."

"Your husband was right."

With those words came a jagged lump that lodged itself in my throat, making it, I felt sure, impossible to speak. And suddenly I wanted to get far, far away from this hopeless place and never come back. I had come here for answers, for help, and all I got was that.

"Are you all right?"

I nodded.

"Would you like a drink of water?"

I nodded again, looking down at my lap and fiddling with the strap of my purse as he went out, apparently in search of water. I suppressed the urge to dig for my keys and bolt from the stuffy room before he returned. No, I told myself. Knowing I would probably be charged for a full hour of counseling time, I was determined to get my money's worth and, if nothing else, waste this discouraging man's precious time.

He returned and handed me a paper cup of water. I took a slow sip and attempted to gather my wits. "So, if there's nothing I can do, then why am I here? Why am I wasting my time?"

"There's nothing you can do to rescue Jacob," he continued. "But you can do something for yourself."

I wanted to tell him that I wasn't concerned about myself, that when your son is killing himself with drugs, you cease to care about your own life, you almost cease to exist at all. You are only consumed with ways you might be able to help him, things you could do to save him. But I simply sat there and said nothing.

"You need to take care of yourself, Glennis."

I took in a shaky breath, afraid that I was about to completely lose it. "But how can I take care of myself when my son is out there ruining his life with drugs?"

"It's a daily thing, Glennis, a moment-by-moment process. You can only take one step at a time, and sometimes they're just baby steps. It's really not so different from what we teach those who come here to recover. You have to work it out for yourself, one day at a time." He continued to talk for a while, but I'm afraid that most of his words were lost on me. I was probably still stuck on the bit about my husband being right. How could it be that Geoffrey had been right? That must mean I had been wrong.

Finally I couldn't take it anymore. "Excuse me," I said, cutting him off in midsentence. "Do you really believe my husband was right?"

He looked as if I had momentarily lost him. "Oh, you mean about saying that only Jacob could help Jacob."

"I guess so." Actually I meant about *everything*. Had Geoffrey been right about everything?

"Well, I suppose I should be careful with my words. I certainly don't want to devalue the important role that family members can play in a person's recovery. Statistics prove that a good support network of loving family and friends can really improve a person's chances of making a complete recovery."

I sighed. "But what about a parent who is cynical and removed? What about a parent who tells his son, 'This is the bed you made; you sleep in it.'? Or what about a father who ignores his son for days while his son is actually doing pretty well, but then he explodes when he finds out that his son has blown it again?"

"That's not the kind of parenting that encourages a user to recover."

"No, I didn't think so." Yet this news brought me no relief. Only more grief and regret and sadness. It wasn't worth being right if it didn't fix anything.

"Are you suggesting it's your husband's fault that Jacob became involved in drugs?"

"No, no, not exactly. I guess I think it's the fault of both of us." I shook my head now. "No, that's not right, is it?"

"You tell me. Did you introduce your son to smoking grass or abusing alcohol?"

"Of course not."

"Did you help him make connections with the neighborhood dope dealer?"

"No."

"I know you're not a perfect mom, Glennis, because no mother is perfect. But if you walk away from here with only one thing today, I hope you'll remember that *it's not your fault*."

"And there's *nothing* I can do?"

"Well, there are a few things you can do that will help. But it'll be up to Jacob to decide whether or not he wants to change."

That's when Marcus explained to me how their rehab program worked and how there was a waiting list I could put Jacob's name on. "Just in case he wakes up one day and decides he's had enough."

"How long is the wait?"

"Right now it's about four weeks."

"Well, go ahead and put him down. Who knows where he'll be in four weeks." I controlled myself from saying he might be dead or locked up in jail, although I believed those both to be distinct possibilities.

"In the meantime, I encourage you to attend our codependent class."

"Are you suggesting I'm codependent?" I'd read enough to know that is not a good thing.

"I'd be surprised if you weren't codependent. Most mothers are, at least to a certain degree."

"And fathers?"

"A few of them are codependent too."

"But it's mostly a mother problem?"

He smiled. "I'll give you some forms to fill out. For insurance and billing and medical and family history. Basic stuff."

I took the papers and stood, ready to make my exit.

He handed me another brochure. "This will tell you a little more about our codependent class. And you're in luck. We're starting a new session next week. It's on Tuesday evenings."

With no intention of signing up for the session, I nodded and put all the papers into my oversize bag and politely thanked Marcus for his time.

He reached out to shake my hand. "I know it's not easy, Glennis. Being the parent of an addict is probably one of the hardest challenges life deals out. But, believe me, you *can* get through it."

I'm sure I looked unconvinced. I may have even rolled my eyes at this point. Mostly I just wanted to get out of that place.

He cleared his throat. "I always encourage my clients and patients to call upon a Higher Power, something beyond themselves to help them through these difficult times."

"A Higher Power?" I studied this man for a moment. His encouragement seemed sincere, and yet with his tie-dyed T-shirt and ponytail, he didn't strike me as a particularly religious man.

"Do you believe in God?" he asked me.

"Of course," I assured him. "I've been a Christian most of my life."

"And do you pray for Jacob?"

"Of course." Now I was getting a bit irritated. Who was he to question me in the area of faith?

He nodded. "How about when you get those panic attacks in the middle of the night? Do you pray for your son then?"

"Of course."

"But then you continue to worry? Even after you've prayed?"

I considered this. "Yes, I suppose I do."

"Do you *believe* in the Bible?"

"Of course." I wished I could think of some other response, but it was as if my mind was stuck.

"Well, there's a Bible verse…" He pointed to a plaque hanging on the wall behind his desk. It was partially obscured by a collage with dozens of pictures of hands and feet. He took down the plaque and read, "Be anxious for nothing, but in everything by prayer and supplication, with thanksgiving, let your requests be made known to God; and the peace of God, which surpasses all understanding, will guard your hearts and minds through Christ Jesus."

I nodded. "Yes, I'm familiar with that verse."

"I challenge you to become *more* familiar with it." He bent over and wrote down Philippians 4:6-7 on a piece of paper from a prescription pad. "Here."

I looked at the name printed across the top in fine print. Apparently this Marcus fellow was also a licensed psychiatrist, although I hadn't heard anyone referring to him as Dr. Palmer. "Is this my prescription?"

He smiled now. "Yes, as a matter of fact, it is. I think you should memorize that verse as well as practice saying 'It is not my fault that my son has a drug problem' throughout the day."

"And all my troubles will magically disappear?"

"Glennis, there are no magical cures for lives that have been blindsided by addiction."

"I figured as much."

And so I left Hope's Wings feeling utterly hopeless and dismayed. I told myself I didn't ever have to go back, but I had a feeling that I would. Hopefully it would be with Jacob.

Chapter 19

I taped Marcus Palmer's "prescription" of Philippians 4:6-7 to my refrigerator door, right next to Jack's note, which I suspected was also from the Bible.

Naturally, Jacob didn't come home that night. Or the next. After several days I drove by the Red Devil to see if he was around, but one of the workers informed me that he hadn't been into work the last couple of days and was as good as fired now. I drove by Daniel's place, too. But since Jacob no longer had a car, it was impossible to tell if he was there or not. However, I guessed by the number of cars that he might be. I had no doubt that drug activity was going on in the duplex dump. How could it not? I even considered an anonymous phone call to the police, informing them of this address and the likelihood of drug trafficking there. However, I suspected this could get Jacob into as much trouble as anyone. And I just wasn't sure. Most of all I felt desperate, as if I had to do something. Anything!

I dug through my purse until I found the wrinkled brochure that Marcus had given me at Hope's Wings. I knew it had some information about codependent meetings. I had resented the idea at the time, but suddenly I wondered if it might help. Maybe the other parents would have some ideas for ways I could help my son. Or maybe the class would already be full, and I'd have a good excuse to simply forget the whole thing. Perhaps I wasn't so unlike my son when it came to excuses. Even so, I decided to call.

"The codependent class?" said the woman.

"Yes, isn't it on Tuesdays?"

"Yes, a new one starts tonight. I think it's full, but I can put you on a waiting list for the next one."

To my surprise, I was very disappointed and considered just hanging up, but I decided to give her my name anyway.

"Glennis Harmon?" she asked with interest.

"Yes, that's right."

"We already have you down for this session."

"Oh?" I decided not to question how this had happened but simply thanked her and hung up.

As I drove back toward Hope's Wings, I felt mildly surprised to notice that the trees were nearly barren of leaves now. I had noticed the temperature dropping, but when had it become autumn? How had I missed it? It almost seemed as if I'd been trapped in some sort of time warp, as if the past weeks and months had stealthily passed without my even noticing. Yet how could that be when every day seemed longer than the one before? And the nights? Oh the nights could last a lifetime.

I intentionally arrived a few minutes late for the meeting. This allowed me to slip into the back almost unnoticed. I listened to Marcus teaching about the physiological effects of meth use, explaining how addictive the substance was, and assuring the friends and family members that their loved one's addiction was not their fault. Oh, I'm sure he said much more than that, but I felt so uncomfortable being there that it was hard to focus. Mostly I just watched the others, wondering who they were and how they had ended up in this place. To be honest, I felt we were a roomful of losers. Even when the people were invited to share, and some of the stories were very sad, I couldn't help but wonder why we were all there. Was something fundamentally wrong with every one of us? Or were we really just victims of circumstance? When my turn to share came, I said very little. Only that my son had a drug problem and that I was look-ing for answers. I felt Marcus Palmer's eyes on me, probing, as if he could see right through my thin veneer of words, as if he knew I was a being a total phony. Or maybe I was just imagining it.

The funny thing was that I felt a tiny bit better when I left. As I drove back toward town, I tried to understand what made me feel better and finally concluded that it was just the old misery-loves-company thing. As twisted as it seemed, it was comforting to know that other mothers and fathers were going through the same kind of torment I was. I was not alone. Even so, I wasn't sure I'd go back.

In some ways I wanted to crawl into a hole and have everyone just leave me alone at this time. Oh, I knew I was depressed, but then who wouldn't have been? I was unable to sleep at night and napped off and on during the day. I began letting the apartment go, letting myself go. I even quit jogging and hadn't had a shower in days. It felt like my mental health was directly attached to Jacob's. As if some invisible umbilical cord still connected us, and as long as he floundered and suffered, I was forced to endure the pain with him. Did I honestly think this would help anything? Did I think it would make him get better sooner? I'm not sure what I was thinking. Or if I was thinking at all.

Finally I couldn't take it anymore. I'd missed my appointment with Dr. Abrams as well as the second codependency meeting, and I really needed to talk to someone. I knew that my mom wouldn't be any help. And even my two siblings, Edward and Abby, would probably not be terribly sympathetic. Abby, several years younger than I was, was still in the "my children are so perfect" stage since her twins, Lacy and Macy, were only seven and adorable. And I'm sure she would've been appalled to discover what was going on with her nephew. Hopefully my mother hadn't told her yet. And my brother, Edward, had recently gone through a painful divorce—his wife had left him for another man—and he was still in the grieving process. I suspected he would be somewhat sympathetic to my situation with Geoffrey, but since he was childless, I doubted he would understand my dilemma with Jacob. Besides, he was probably at work right now.

I suddenly knew it was time to call Sherry and tell her the complete story. Any last remnants of my pride had long since been crushed. If she was ready to hear it, I was ready to unload it. I wanted to tell her the whole truth, including every sad and gory detail of Jacob's frightening methamphetamine habit.

"Can you meet me for lunch?" she said in her brisk business voice, and I could tell that I'd interrupted something important. I imagined her in a sleek designer suit, every hair in place, perhaps in the middle of some million-dollar transaction, and felt embarrassed as I looked down at my grungy sweats, the same ones I'd been wearing all week.

Even so, the mere idea of showering and dressing seemed totally overwhelming to me. Impossible even. "Uh, Sherry, do you think you could come here?" I asked meekly. "I've been a little, well, depressed, you know, and I just don't think I could get it—"

"No problem," she said quickly. "I'll bring something for us. See you at noon?"

"Thanks," I muttered and hung up the phone. I looked around my messy apartment and wondered where to begin to straighten it. Was it even possible? I picked up a pile of unopened mail that Geoffrey had forwarded to my apartment and moved it from the coffee table over to the breakfast bar that was already cluttered with newspapers and dirty dishes. Then I stood staring in a daze at the kitchen, trying to figure out what to do. I'm not sure how long I stood there, stuck in a hazy fog, but by the time I returned to my senses I looked up at the clock to discover it was already half past eleven. Why had I invited Sherry to come over here? What was I thinking? Feeling like an animal caught in a trap, I paced back and forth, trying to decide what to do. Finally I decided I should call Sherry and cancel. But, of course, I only got her messaging service. She'd probably turned off her phone after my last call had interrupted her morning.

I ran into the bathroom and took a quick shower—the first one all week. But instead of feeling the relief of getting clean, the water from the showerhead felt like hundreds of sharp needles piercing my skin. And the towel felt like sandpaper as I rubbed myself dry. I was surprised I wasn't raw and bleeding by the time I was done. I dug around my tiny closet until I found a less-than-grimy pair of sweatpants and a sweatshirt. I had barely pulled these on when I heard someone knocking at my door.

"Glennis!" exclaimed Sherry when she saw me. "What's happened to you?" As usual, she was impeccably dressed. Today she had on a perfectly cut, cream and camel tweed suit, along with matching camel shoes and purse. Even her jewelry, simple but elegant pearls, was perfect.

"I...I'm sorry this place is such a mess." I put my hand on my still-wet and uncombed hair. "I've been having a...a pretty hard time."

Sherry cleared off a place for us to both sit on the couch, then set a couple of bags on the coffee table. "Here," she said, handing me a deli sandwich. "Let's eat and then talk."

I managed to choke down nearly half of the roast beef sandwich before I felt like I couldn't consume another bite. I sipped my coffee, knowing it was my favorite blend from Starbucks, but it was as if my taste buds had quit functioning. I attempted to calm myself as I waited for Sherry to finish her lunch.

"Okay," she finally said, dabbing her lips with a paper napkin. "What's going on with you, Glennis? Is it Geoffrey again? Has he done something new?"

The last time I had spoken to Sherry about Geoffrey was after I'd seen him at Sindalli's. Naturally, she had been sympathetic and supportive.

"No, it's not Geoffrey this time, Sherry." I took in a breath. "It's Jacob."

"Oh dear, is that poor boy having more problems?"

I nodded, blinking back tears. Then I spilled the whole story, going back and forth until it was a wonder it even made sense. Maybe it didn't.

"Oh, Glennis, why didn't you tell me this sooner?" Sherry leaned over and hugged me. "What a hard burden to be bearing all alone."

Naturally, her compassion only unleashed the rest of my tears. "I wanted to tell you," I sobbed, "but I was embarrassed. It's...it's so hard to admit that you've blown it—not only as a wife, but as a mom."

"That's not true, Glennis. These things aren't your fault."

"How do you know?" I snapped. "It feels like everything I touch gets...gets ruined. I...I'm such a...a complete failure. I can't even stand to look at myself in the mirror anymore. No wonder Geoffrey had to go to another...another woman."

"Glennis." Sherry was using a firm voice now. "You can't keep telling yourself those kinds of things. Those are total lies, Glennis. And I hate having to get all fundamental on you, but I just can't help myself. Those lies are coming straight from the pit of hell. And they're hurting you. Can't you see that? You need to be surrounding yourself with truth more than ever now. Where is your Bible?"

"My Bible?"

"Yes. Where is it?"

"I don't know. Probably in a box in my bedroom."

"In a box?"

"Well..."

"Go and get it."

So I went to my bedroom and dug around in a box of books until I found my Bible. Then I brought it out and handed it to her. Sherry had taught women's Bible studies for years and had only quit when her life got too busy with her realty work. But she knew her way around the Bible. She opened my Bible, took a purple ballpoint pen, and immediately began underlining something. "You don't mind, do you?" She looked up at me.

I shrugged. "Not really."

Then she grabbed an old newspaper and began tearing up markers from it and slipping them into sections that she had marked and obviously expected me to read. Finally she handed it back to me. "And tell me," she said. "Have you been going to church at all?"

"To church?" I echoed.

"Right." She shook her head as if the answer was clear. "So you've not only quit reading your Bible, but you've quit going to church as well."

"But Geoffrey goes to that church," I attempted.

"It was your church too."

"But how can I—"

"I know, I know…" She considered this. "Well, if you can't go to that church, you can certainly come to mine. And I think you'd like it, too."

Sherry and Rod had switched churches a few years ago. At the time I had wanted to switch with them, but Geoffrey had insisted that our church, very old and established within the community, was important for the connections he needed for his work. Naturally, I had agreed.

"I guess I could do that," I told Sherry.

"That's right, you can." Then she looked at her watch. "I'm sorry I have to take off, Glennis, but I have a showing in fifteen minutes. As it is, I'll just barely make it. Mind if I brush my teeth before I go?"

"Of course not."

I sat and waited as Sherry hurried into my bathroom. When she emerged, she was shaking her head. "You need to clean this place up, Glennis. I'd be depressed too if I was living in this kind of mess."

I nodded, feeling like a child who'd just been reprimanded. However, I knew she was right. Sherry was almost always right.

"Thanks," I said and walked her to the door.

"And have you been going to Dr. Abrams?" she asked with one hand on the doorknob.

"I…uh…I missed the last—"

"Glennis," she said sternly, "how do you expect to get through something like this if you sit around and do nothing?"

"Right." I nodded as she blew me a kiss, then whooshed out the door.

"I'll call you tonight," she called over her shoulder. "Hang in there, sweetie."

So, taking Sherry's advice to heart, I began cleaning the apartment. But I found it was hard to think clearly. Sometimes I'd find myself putting something in a totally inappropriate place. Like my running shoes. For some reason I picked them up off the living room floor and carried them into the kitchen, where I put them into the freezer. It was as if I was getting some form of Alzheimer's. I wondered if that was even possible at my age. Still I continued to putter. Two steps forward, one step back. And by the end of the day, I thought things had improved ever so slightly. I kept my phone turned on after six, expectantly waiting for Sherry's call. One thing I knew about Sherry—when she promised to do something, she always followed through.

But by eleven o'clock that night, I realized that for whatever reason, Sherry was not going to call. Maybe she had given up on me too.

I looked at the Bible still sitting on the coffee table with bits of newspaper hanging out like flapping tongues—as if they were taunting me, laughing at my foolishness. Was God laughing too?

Out my window the darkened street looked unfriendly and cold. It was November now, and temperatures were steadily dropping. I wondered where Jacob was and if he was okay. I imagined him sleeping on a park bench, shivering in the cold. Then in a ditch, unconscious from an overdose. Then hit by a car, bleeding in the street. Then in the morgue, covered in a white sheet with a tag that said Unknown attached to his toe.

"Stop it!" I told myself. "Just stop it."

But it was as if my mind had gotten stuck on this track and was not about to be bumped off. Like a slide show gone wild, all I could see was scene after scene of hopelessness and death, and Jacob starred in each frame. Was it possible to bring on your own heart attack simply by getting worked up over something? I tried to take calming breaths, but this time they didn't seem to work. Suddenly I believed that I was experiencing an honest case of mother's intuition and that I was exactly right—Jacob was in some very real danger tonight. Somehow I knew—I knew deep inside my gut—that Jacob might not survive this night.

"Oh, God!" I cried out, falling onto my knees in front of the couch. "I don't know what to do. I desperately need your help right now. Please, please, help me know what to do. How can I help Jacob? How can I spare him from this—this evil thing that is going to destroy him? Please, please, show me what to do…"

I continued praying like this for some time. Crying and praying. Praying and crying. Until finally it seemed there were no words left to pray. "God, help me," I said. "Help Jacob. Spare him, God." And then I crawled onto the couch and fell asleep. I didn't wake up until early the next morning.

Feeling somewhat better, I got up and made a pot of coffee. I turned on the morning news show and began opening my mail. I was just opening an insurance envelope when something the local newscaster was saying stopped me dead in my tracks. I set down the half-opened envelope and listened.

"…earlier this morning the local young man was admitted to the emergency room for alcohol poisoning," she was saying. I turned up the volume, heart pounding and ice water rushing through my veins. I *knew* it was Jacob.

"Sources say friends transported him to the hospital, then left before they could be questioned or identified. According to police reports, the young man's blood-alcohol level was .43 percent, a lethal amount. The young man, whose name cannot be released until family is notified, died shortly after hospital personnel began treating him. In other news…"

I felt my head growing dizzy, and I clung to the breakfast bar to support myself. "Don't jump to conclusions," I told myself. "It doesn't *have* to be Jacob." Even so, I could barely breathe, barely make my way to the phone. But who should I call? The police? The hospital? Geoffrey?

I decided to call the hospital. But my hands were shaking so badly I could barely dial directory assistance for the number. And when the operator came on, my voice was so raspy that I had to repeat myself twice. Finally I was connected to information at the hospital.

"I need to know…" I gasped. "I mean I need to find out if…if the young man who died of an…an alcohol overdose has been identified yet. I mean it's possible that he's my son, and I…uh…I don't know…"

"The young man has been identified," said the woman.

"Have you notified the family yet?" I said in a barely audible voice.

"We were able to locate the young man's father."

I took in a jagged breath. "Can you…can you tell me the young man's name, please? You see, my son's father and I are…are estranged, and I…"

"I can understand your concern," she said. "But I'm not allowed to give out that information."

"But I'm afraid it's my son," I pleaded.

"I'll tell you what," she said. "You tell me the name of your son, and I'll confirm whether or not that's him. After all, I'm a mother too."

"His name is Jacob Harmon."

"Don't worry, ma'am. That's not the young man who was brought in."

I was flooded with relief, as if blood was pumping through my body again and life was returning. "Are you sure? Are you absolutely, positively certain?"

"Yes. It's a positive identification. The young man's father is here, and the mother is on the way."

"Oh, thank you! Thank you!" I said, practically ecstatic as I hung up. Of course, I felt a sharp twinge of guilt over my relief that someone else's child, not mine, had perished today. And, as if in penance, I prayed for the grieving family. I prayed for God to comfort them in their time of darkness. I knew they must be hurting badly.

Still feeling the afterglow of relief, or that I had missed a bullet, I returned to sorting and opening my mail. It had piled up so badly in my little mailbox that the mailman had hand-delivered it to my door a couple of days ago. "Just wanted to make sure these were being forwarded to the right address," he had said as he handed me the stack. "Everything okay?" I had forced a smile and attempted to assure him that I was perfectly fine, holding my door closed behind me to hide my slovenly housekeeping.

I would do my best to heed Sherry's advice today. Thankful that God had spared Jacob one more time, I would respond by cleaning up my act and acting like a seminormal person. Even so, I felt slow and dull, as if I was emotionally impaired and unable to think completely clearly. But I did remove my running shoes from the freezer. I set them by the baseboard heater to thaw, promising myself that I'd put them on and take a run before the day was over.

It was midmorning when the ringing of my phone made me jump and spill a cup of coffee down my sweats and onto the kitchen floor. I used a towel to sop it up as I said hello and discovered it was Marsha Bennett. I'd only met this woman a few times, but I remembered she was a church friend of Sherry's. I suspected she was calling to invite me to some Bible study or women's function at their church. Sherry wouldn't waste any time getting me plugged in.

"I'm sure you've heard the news by now," said Marsha in a sober voice.

"What news?" I asked.

"About Sherry's son."

"What do you mean? Which son?"

"Matthew."

"Oh, that's right," I said, glancing at my calendar. "It's Matthew's twenty-first birthday today. Goodness, I almost forgot." Still, I wondered about the serious tone.

She cleared her throat. "I guess you didn't hear about the accident."

"Accident?"

"Well, maybe accident isn't the right word. Oh, Glennis, it was terrible. Matthew died early this morning of what they are calling alcohol poisoning."

I felt my knees giving way as I sank to the floor in shock. "That young man on the news? *That* was Matthew?" I said.

"Yes. And you're right, it would've been his twenty-first birthday today. He'd come home yesterday to spend the weekend with his family and to celebrate his birthday. Then it seems some old high school buddies invited him to go to a bar to celebrate last night."

"No…"

"Yes. It's so sad. Pastor Allen said that the kids have this game or challenge or something. It seems they buy the one who's having a birthday twenty-one shots of liquor."

"Twenty-one shots?" I repeated in a whisper.

"Unbelievable, isn't it, what kids will do for kicks nowadays?"

"Oh, poor, dear, sweet Matthew." I remembered those big blue eyes, the sweet shy smile. I'd known the boy since diapers. He and Sarah had gone through school together. Tears were pouring down my face.

"Yes, it's incredibly tragic." She sighed. "Anyway, I'm calling you, since I know you're a good friend of Sherry's, to see if you might bring a hot dish over to the family. We're setting up food for them for the next several days—until after the memorial service, which Pastor Allen says will be on Tuesday. Do you think you could help out?"

"Yes, of course."

"How about Sunday then?"

"Sunday is fine."

"Thank you. And sorry to be the bearer of such sad news."

"I appreciate your calling."

I felt numb as I hung up the phone. As if something inside of me was dead. And then I went into my bedroom, climbed into my still-unmade bed, and just sobbed. I wasn't sure if I would ever be able to get up again.

Chapter 20

I must've fallen asleep, but I woke up to a pounding on the door. Shaken and disoriented, I stumbled through my apartment to see who it was. I was hoping it was Jacob, coming home to show me that he was alive and well and ready to go into rehab now. I couldn't have been more surprised when I discovered it was my estranged husband.

"Geoffrey!" I exclaimed when I opened the door. "What are you doing here?"

"I've been trying to reach you on your phone all day, Glennis." He frowned as he looked around my still rather messy abode. "Are you okay?"

I shook my head no, holding back new tears. It seemed unbelievable, but at that very moment all I wanted was for him to take me into his arms, to tell me he loved me and that he was sorry and that we'd start over, to stroke my hair, and then to assure me that everything was going to be okay.

"You heard the news?" he asked.

I swallowed hard, then nodded. "I heard."

He sighed. "It's just unbelievable."

"Poor Sherry and Rod...and Mark. I feel so sad for them."

"I was trying to call you on your cell phone, Glennis," he said, "but all I got was your messaging."

I glanced back to the counter in the kitchen where my cell phone was still sitting. "I think I turned it off," I told him.

"Well, I called Sarah and told her the sad news, and she wanted you to call her."

"Yes, she and Matthew used to be good friends."

"She was very upset, Glennis. She's coming home tomorrow."

Home? I considered this concept. Of course, Sarah still considered her father's house as her home. Lucky girl.

"Where's Jacob?" asked Geoffrey.

I studied him for a moment. Was it possible that he, like me, had been concerned, maybe even worried, about the unidentified young man on the news this morning? "I haven't seen him lately."

He frowned. "I thought he was staying with you."

"He was."

"Well, then where is he?" Geoffrey's voice grew sharp. "How long has it been since you saw him."

"Not quite a week," I said.

"And you don't know where he went?"

I ran my hand through my messy hair and closed my eyes.

"Glennis?" demanded Geoffrey. "What's going on here?"

I opened my eyes and looked at him. "What do you mean?"

"This!" He waved his arm and made a face. "This place is a mess. You're a mess. You have no idea where Jacob is. Your best friend just lost her son, and you're shut up in this little pigsty with your phone turned off. What on earth is the matter with you anyway?"

I felt invaded then. Okay, maybe it was a little pigsty, but it was *my* little pigsty, and I didn't need my cheating husband to come in here and lecture me on how to live. "What is the matter with me?" I repeated in a quiet but seething voice. "You want to know what is the matter with me? Well, for starters my husband of twenty-five years is having an affair—"

"Don't start up about that affair business again, Glennis."

"Call it what you want, Geoffrey. I've *seen* you two together. Half the town has *seen* you two together. Do us all a favor and quit denying it. Okay?"

To my relief, he said nothing.

"Besides that," I continued, "I have a son who is certain his father hates him. But if that's not enough, this same son is using some very dangerous drugs—"

"Dangerous?" His brow creased. "What do you mean?"

"I mean he's been shooting up crystal meth." I waited for him to react.

"Methamphetamines?" He looked truly stunned now.

"Yes."

"You know this for a fact."

"I do."

Geoffrey slowly walked over and seemed to deflate onto my couch, which was still covered with dirty laundry I'd attempted to sort by color but had abandoned. He leaned over with his head in his hands and groaned.

I sat down in the rocker across from him. And, although I don't usually rejoice over other people's pain, I got a strange sense of satisfaction in seeing him suffer like that. Maybe it was my mother-bear instinct, but I guess I hoped that if Geoffrey could really hurt for his son, really suffer a little, then maybe he did love him after all. And despite my mixed-up feelings for this man, I desperately wanted him to love Jacob.

"I can't believe it has gone this far," Geoffrey finally said.

I nodded. "It has. I'm guessing it has been going on for some time. I went to a meeting—"

"*You* went to a meeting?" He frowned. "Why isn't *Jacob* going to a meeting?"

"I had scheduled a meeting for him with a counselor at Hope's Wings—"

"Hope's Wings?" echoed Geoffrey. "You mean that cruddy little rehab joint on the west side of town?"

"It may not look so great on the outside, but it has a good reputation. My therapist recommended—"

"You have a therapist?"

I tried to smile. "Oh, there's so much you don't know, Geoffrey."

"Well, why don't you fill me in?"

So for the next hour I tried to give him an account of both my life and Jacob's since we'd left our home. And to my surprise, he listened. But more than that, he almost seemed sorry.

"You probably think this is my fault, don't you?" he finally said.

I shrugged. "I think we can all share some blame. I know I've been beating myself up quite a bit."

"I never meant for things to end up like this, Glennis. Honestly, I didn't."

Was this it? Was Geoffrey finally going to come clean and apologize and agree to get counseling and put our lives back together again?

"I didn't either," I told him. Then I waited, but since he seemed to be stuck, I thought maybe I could help him out. "My therapist—she's a friend of Sherry's and really quite good—well, anyway, she does marriage counseling, too. And she's been asking me to invite you to come with me, Geoffrey. And Sherry said she's got a really great track record with helping couples…" But even as I said this, sounding like the pitiful little wife who was begging her husband to come back to her, I knew by the expression on Geoffrey's face that it wasn't going to happen. I think I even braced myself for his response.

"Okay, Glennis," he said. "It's time for me to be completely honest with you." He took in a deep breath. "This isn't easy, but I guess you already knew anyway. I can see there's no point in denying it." He leaned forward, losing his courtroom confidence. "You're right. Judith and I *have* been having an affair. And I'm sorry, I'm really sorry, Glennis. I never meant for it to go this far. I never meant to hurt you like this. It's just that it all took me by surprise. And before I knew what was happening, well, it was happening."

"When?" was all I could say. "When did it begin?"

He seemed to be thinking about this. "Well, the actual, uh, the actual physical affair began this summer. But I think we started having an emotional affair sometime last spring."

How many times in a lifetime can a person die, I wondered. In a day even? It seemed that every time I turned around, every time I made the slightest effort to regain my balance, I was dealt another deathblow. Oh, Geoffrey was right. I had known that it was going on—at least at some level. Maybe even last spring, although I'm sure I was in deep, deep denial.

"Why are you telling me this now?" I asked in a weak voice.

"Because I felt so bad when I heard about Matthew. I realized how fragile families are these days. I was thinking about Jacob and you and regretting some things."

I wanted to ask if he was regretting Judith, but knew I couldn't say it in a way that wouldn't sound sarcastic or bitter or mean.

"So, what now?" I asked.

He held up his hands. "I don't know."

"Where do we go from here?" I repeated.

"I'm not sure..."

"To be perfectly honest," I said in an empty voice, just rambling now, "I've been so depressed lately that I'm afraid I'm losing my mind. It could happen, you know..." I waved my hand. "I mean look at this place. It's plain to see that I'm not totally functional. Sherry was just here yesterday—" I choked now, suddenly reminded of her pain today. "She was... she was telling me to get my act together." I leaned over now, clutching my sides, trying to hold it all in. "Sometimes I don't know how I can handle all this pain, Geoffrey. Sometimes I think I'd just be better off dead."

He got up from the couch now and came over to stand by me, putting his hand on my shoulder. "You can't give up, Glennis. Hard things happen in life, but we have to keep going. Sherry has been strong for you when you needed her. I suspect it's your turn to be strong for her now."

"How?" I asked, looking up at him with blurry eyes. "How am I supposed to be strong when it feels like I'm dying inside?"

"I guess you have to ask God to help you."

"You *really* believe that?" I said. "I mean do you honestly believe that for *yourself,* Geoffrey? Are you and God still on speaking terms…I mean after what you've done to…I mean with *Judith?*" Even her name tasted bitter on my tongue.

"I don't know about all that. But I still go to church, Glennis, and I've told Pastor McKinley about everything… In fact, we've talked a couple of times."

"Really?" I was curious. "And what did he say?"

"Oh, you know, the expected things. He wasn't pleased with what I'd done. But he did remind me that no sin is too big for God to forgive."

"Right." I stood up. I no longer wanted his false hand on my shoulder. "So what are you going to do about all this, Geoffrey?"

"About all what?"

"All our messed-up lives."

"I guess there's not much I can do about yours, Glennis, except to say I'm sorry and come to some sort of agreeable settlement."

"Settlement?" I heard my voice getting that high-pitched sound.

"Yes, I want to be fair with you. I realize we didn't have a prenuptial agreement, and most of our holdings came from my side of the family, so a fifty-fifty split wouldn't really be appropriate. But I also know that you've grown accustomed to a certain way of living—"

"You came here to talk to me about a divorce settlement today?" I demanded.

"That wasn't really my intention, Glennis. But I've been thinking about it, and you asked. I'm sorry if this seems premature."

I took a deep breath and quickly counted to ten. "Geoffrey," I said, "even though it hurts, I do appreciate your being honest with me. But your timing isn't the greatest."

"But you must've known it was coming to this. And, don't forget, Glennis, you're the one who left me. That's an important factor in divorce court."

"Well, I could be wrong, but infidelity is an important factor, too."

"Look, Glennis, I think we can handle this in a civilized way. You've always been a sensible woman. Let's just give this some time, and we can discuss it later. I assume you already have a lawyer."

"I'm sure you would assume that." I turned my back to him. I didn't want him to see me seething. A sensible woman, indeed!

"Okay, I can see we're getting nowhere," he said. "But don't forget to give Sarah a call. And if you see Jacob, well…"

"Well, *what?*" I turned around and glared at him.

"Maybe you could let him know that I'm thinking of him. And if I have time, I'll check into some better treatment centers for him. Gary Randolph had a daughter with a drug problem. They sent her off to Colorado—some kind of working ranch. Although it was probably quite expensive, and I expect they'll have a waiting list."

"If you could check," I said, suddenly hopeful. It seemed the first time in ages that Geoffrey had taken a serious interest in his son's welfare. "It wouldn't hurt to get him on a list…just in case."

He nodded and headed for the door, then paused. "And I really am sorry, Glennis."

I took a step toward him. "Which part do you mean?" I asked. "What are you sorry for?"

"Well, everything, I suppose. But I'm sorry that it's come down to this between you and me. It was never my plan, you know."

I sighed, suddenly weary of this whole conversation. "I wasn't *my* plan either, Geoffrey."

He stood there for a moment, just looking at me, and I wondered if he was feeling any serious regrets right now. Was he wondering if there was still hope for us? Then he said, "I just hope we can keep this divorce civilized, Glennis. For the sake of the kids and my career, you know, since I'm the one who'll be paying for their college tuition. No need to turn our little problems into a three-ring circus, right?"

"Right."

And then he left.

So this was about preserving his image again. He was worried that I was going to put up a big fuss over the breakup of our marriage. Maybe he thought I would make a scene down at city hall. I imagined myself going down there in my coffee-stained sweats and bedroom slippers, with my bed-head hair sticking out like a fright wig, and yelling and scream-ing about how their city attorney was a worthless, adulterous jerk of a hus-band. I should've known that's why he'd come. He'd been worried.

Maybe I should give him a little credit. He did seem somewhat con-cerned about Jacob and truly saddened about Matthew. But when it came right down to it, I suspect his biggest concerns were for Geoffrey Tyler Harmon and his impeccable image as he strutted around city hall in his latest Armani suit.

I noticed my Bible still on the coffee table with Sherry's newspaper markers sticking out. Feeling bad that I had ignored it so far, especially in light of Sherry's recent loss, I grabbed it and flipped open to a marker and read the sentence underlined in purple. "I am leaving you with a gift— peace of mind and heart. And the peace I give isn't like the peace the world gives. So don't be troubled or afraid."

I'd heard this verse before. In fact, I think there had been a time when I had even believed it. "Peace of mind and heart," I repeated aloud. That *did* sound wonderful, but impossible, too. Just the same, I copied this verse down on a scrap of paper and taped it to my refrigerator, which now had three messages posted there. The one about not being anxious but praying, from Marcus Palmer, the rehab counselor. And one from Jack in the laundry room. And now one from Sherry. I glanced at Jack's message again and suddenly felt a chill go through me.

"The Lord giveth and the Lord taketh away. Blessed be the name of the Lord." It hadn't made much sense to me before, but now I wondered if it had really been meant for Sherry. Matthew had been one of those sunny children who seemed like a gift. And now he was gone. Gone. And suddenly I realized that Geoffrey might've been a jerk to come like this today, but he had been right about one thing. It *was* time for me to be strong for Sherry. Maybe I couldn't do this for myself, but I thought I could do it for her. "Give me strength, Lord," I prayed as I picked up the phone.

I wasn't really surprised to get their answering machine, and although I hate leaving messages, I braced myself and did the best I could. "Sherry and Rod, I am completely devastated by your news. My heart goes out to you guys, and I am really praying for you. If there is anything—I mean anything—I can do to help out, please feel free to call. Really, I mean it. I may have been a mess yesterday, Sherry, but I am here for you today—"

"Glennis," came a raspy voice as someone picked up.

"Oh, Sherry," I cried. "You're there. Oh, I wish I could just give you a big hug and—"

"Can you come over?" she asked. "Rod had to go take care of some… some things, and I'm alone."

"Of course." I looked down at my hideous sweats. "I'll be there in just a few minutes."

I don't think I've ever moved so fast in my life. I leaped in and out of the shower, managed to put on a somewhat decent outfit, and got down to the parking lot in about seven minutes flat. I combed my hair and then, ignoring the pale gray roots already in need of a touch-up, put on some lip gloss at the stoplight. And I was at Sherry's house in less than twenty minutes. Even so, I felt nervous as I walked up to her door. What could I possibly say to make things better?

Chapter 21

I tapped quietly on the door, then let myself in. The drapes were still drawn, probably just as they had been when the Lexingtons got the horrible news early this morning. Even so, they lent an uncharacteristic somber tone to Sherry's otherwise cheerful country-style home.

"Sherry?" I called tentatively as I tiptoed through their living room. Sherry's house always had a genuine, lived-in feeling. Not messy by any means, but comfortable, as if the occupants really enjoyed being here. I knew this house by heart and suspected Sherry was in the master bedroom. I went down the hallway, keeping my gaze away from the family photos that lined the wall. I knew it would break me into pieces to look into Matthew's sweet nine-year-old face smiling from a Little League photo. I called her name again.

"In here."

I found her on her bed, her face blotchy and eyes swollen. She had on jeans and a sweater, but her hair was uncombed and her face void of makeup. I went straight to her and put my arms around her. "I'm so sorry, Sherry. So, so sorry."

"I know," she sobbed.

And then the two of us just held on to each other and cried. I knew there were no words to soften the pain that had sliced through her heart this morning, nothing I could do to take her suffering away or even lighten her load. I might not have lost a child yet—not physically anyway—but I had lost Jacob time and time again in my heart. And I knew, if things didn't change, I might lose him still. I knew that no amount of sympathetic words would change anything if I were in her shoes. And so we just cried.

Finally it seemed we were both cried out, at least for the moment, and we both just lay back on the bed saying nothing. I could hear the sound of a clock ticking and the occasional sound of a car's tires on the wet street outside. But mostly we were covered in a blanket of silent grief.

"Thank you," she finally whispered as she reached for a tissue.

I rolled over to look at her and nodded.

"Rod hasn't even cried yet. At first he was just really, really angry. He wanted to go out and find the kids who took Matthew out last night. I think he wanted to kill them."

"I can understand that."

"Really?" She seemed shocked.

"Sometimes that's how I feel about some of Jacob's drug friends."

"Oh."

"Sherry…" I knew I had to confess. "When I heard the news on TV this morning, and they weren't releasing the name, I felt absolutely certain it was Jacob."

She nodded.

"And then when it wasn't I was so incredibly relieved." I was starting to choke up again. "But then…then when I heard it was Matthew—" I gasped now, unsure whether I could say this aloud or not. "Well, I just kept thinking about Matthew and what a sweet kid he was and how he's never really done much of anything wrong in his whole life and—well, this is really hard to say—God forgive me, but I…I thought it *should've* been Jacob instead." Now I just totally lost it. I was sobbing and crying hysterically. "I…I thought that Jacob's the one who…who's messed up so badly, and he…he probably should've been the…the one who—"

"Don't even say it." She put her hand up as if to stop me from speaking. "Don't even *think* it, Glennis."

"But it's not fair, Sherry. It's so wrong."

She nodded, then lay back, staring at the ceiling. "I agree, losing my child—especially like that—it does seem totally wrong."

"I just had to tell you that, Sherry. I'm sorry."

"No, I appreciate your honesty. You're a good friend, Glennis."

Then we just lay there in silence again. I couldn't believe I had just confessed that about Jacob. It was a thought that had been haunting me all day, but I'd never dreamed I'd admit it. It seemed to prove that not only was I a terrible mom but a traitor to my son as well. Oh, certainly, it wasn't that I wanted Jacob dead. God knew I would rather be dead myself. But it just seemed so ironic and random and, yes, unfair.

The next couple of days passed in a blur. I tried to make myself as helpful as possible at Sherry's house. I answered the phone, organized the food that was coming in, got the guest room ready for Sherry's parents, and even mopped the hardwood floors. Anything to stay busy.

Then, the night before the memorial service, Jacob came home. I'd spent so much time at the Lexingtons lately that I hadn't caught up on my own housekeeping. Not that Jacob noticed. He smelled so bad and looked so bummed that I suspected he'd been sleeping in Dumpsters. Even so I hugged him, holding him close to me for a few seconds and thanking God that he was still alive.

"I heard about Matthew," he said in a sober voice, dropping his filthy backpack by the front door as if he didn't expect to be here long.

"The service is tomorrow."

He nodded.

"Do you want to come?" I asked.

"I don't know."

"Sarah came home. She's with Dad."

He nodded again, then went over to the kitchen window and looked out for a bit.

"Looking for someone?" I asked as I joined him.

He quickly turned away. "No."

"Are you hungry, Jacob? I made a big lasagna for the Lexingtons, but I made an extra one that's still in the fridge."

"Sounds good."

"Want to take off your coat?" I asked as he sat down on a barstool.

"That's okay."

I nodded. "Okay." I turned toward the refrigerator, unsure of what I should say to my prodigal son. Finally, after I'd heated the lasagna and poured him a glass of juice, I asked how he was doing.

He shrugged. "Not so good."

"What do you mean?" I asked as I set a generous portion of lasagna in front of him. "What's going on?"

He took a big bite, chewed noisily, then answered. "It's not exactly easy living on the streets."

"You're really living on the street?"

"Pretty much."

"Oh." I sat down on the stool in the kitchen. "I thought maybe you were at Daniel's."

He shook his head and shoveled in another bite. "Not welcome there."

"Why's that?"

He was scraping his plate clean now, trying to get every last bite. Then he looked up at me with sad, empty eyes. "It all comes down to the bottom line, Mom."

"You mean money?"

He nodded.

"He wants you to pay rent?"

"Yeah, something like that."

I took in a deep breath. "There's still rehab, Jacob."

He frowned, and his face looked dark and tense, as if he might explode if I said or did the wrong thing just now. I knew that Dr. Abrams would be telling me to throw him out again. But somehow I couldn't do that tonight. Not after having been so frightened to lose him, and not on the day before my best friend was going to bury one of her sons.

"Your dad asked about you."

He made a laughing sound that had no warmth. "Yeah, I'll bet."

"He said he's going to look into some other kinds of rehab places. He heard about something in Colorado."

He rolled his eyes. "Yeah, that sounds like Dad. Ship me off and lock me up someplace far away so I don't embarrass him."

"You don't embarrass—"

"Don't bother, Mom." He shoved the plate away so hard that it went sliding off the counter and crashed onto the floor. I bent down and began picking up the pieces, unsure as to what I should do or say to defuse this conversation. And since I'd taken to praying more lately, I breathed a little "show me what to do, Lord," prayer as I picked up the broken pieces. Finally I stood up and looked at my son.

"Sorry," he mumbled.

"It's okay," I told him. "Those dishes are pretty ugly anyway. Sometimes I feel like breaking them myself."

His eyes seemed to smile at this.

"Do you want to spend the night here?" I asked. Somehow I felt certain this was the right thing to do—for today anyway. I had no idea about what I would do tomorrow.

He looked surprised. "Are you sure?"

"Yeah. Don't get me wrong. I still want you to go in for rehab," I told him. "But why don't you go ahead and stay here tonight if you want."

His face brightened a little. "Thanks, Mom."

I looked at the clock in the kitchen. It was nearly midnight. "The service is at eleven tomorrow morning," I told him. "But I'm going to the church an hour earlier to help get things set up in the kitchen. And I've had a long day."

He nodded. "Me, too."

"Feel free to take a shower," I said, worried that it sounded more like a command than a suggestion. Still I couldn't bear the thought of him sleeping in that condition. Although, judging by his smell, I'm sure he'd slept in filth plenty of nights before. "And put your clothes in the laundry basket in the bathroom," I continued. "Maybe we can get them washed tomorrow." I looked at his hair now. Jacob had always kept his hair cut short in the past, but he hadn't had a haircut since last summer. So besides being greasy and dull looking, it hung limply in his eyes and down over his collar. I wondered if there would be time to get him to a barber before the funeral in the morning.

I was just about to say as much when I, amazingly, remembered something Marcus Palmer had said at the codependent meeting I'd attended a week or so ago. Had it only been that long? "Pick your battles carefully," he had told us. Not that he was encouraging us to fight, but rather to draw the line. He said we had to let the less important things go and focus on the real issues, like reminding the addict in our life that he or she needed to seek treatment. As a result, I decided not to say anything more about Jacob's personal appearance tonight. Besides, I had the distinct feeling that it wouldn't take much to erupt into a totally futile fight, and to be honest, I just didn't have the energy for it. Even if that meant feeling somewhat embarrassed by his appearance at the funeral, I would have to bite my tongue. Eliminating the street stench would be worth a lot.

So I told him good-night and headed for bed, and I know it sounds horrible, and it's difficult to admit, but I suddenly felt very uncomfortable in my own apartment. Unsafe even. Jacob's condition was confusing and frightening to me. And I wasn't thinking only of his lack of personal hygiene, which was bad enough. But that blank look in his eye and the knowledge that he had been using and may have even become addicted to crystal meth were deeply disturbing. I hadn't done much research yet, but I'd seen a TV news show recently that had exposed how meth addicts can often become violent and unpredictable as a result of the drug. And I still remembered how Jacob had been that night when I'd confronted him about the hypodermic needles—like a stranger.

Once in bed, I felt restless and wide awake and suddenly wished I had a deadbolt on my bedroom door. Then I had to almost laugh at myself since the doors in this apartment weren't much heavier than cardboard anyway, and already Jacob had managed to put his fist through the thin walls a number of times. What good would a deadbolt do, really? But as I lay there imagining the kinds of horrors that would lend themselves to a bad scene in a Lifetime movie, I finally had to ask myself why I even cared. What difference would it make? So what if my son murdered me in my sleep. Why would I want to go on living with a son who was such a mess anyway? Perhaps it would be best to simply get it over with. Maybe mothers like me deserved what they got. Besides that, my life wasn't much to fight for these days. Happy thoughts to put me to sleep with, I know, but it was how I felt.

Even so, I did manage to pray again. Despite my hopelessness and apathy, I asked that God would protect both me and my son. And then I managed to fall asleep and eventually woke up the next morning, still alive. At least partially. More and more I was thinking that a large part of me had already died. I couldn't exactly pin down when this had occurred, but perhaps it had been a process. Some of this death was related to Geoffrey, some to Jacob, a little to Sarah and her unwillingness even to speak to me, and some as a result of Sherry's recent loss.

I got up before six and took the basket of Jacob's filthy clothes down to the laundry room. I think I was hoping to find Jack around. But, of course, it was too early for him to be doing laundry. So I put the load in and sat down, and, feeling exhausted even though I had slept relatively well, I put my head in my hands and wondered how I was going to survive all this.

Fortunately or not, depending on how you look at it, I had a funeral to attend today and various responsibilities to fulfill…and as a result I had little time to dwell on my misery just now.

I finished Jacob's laundry, folding each piece just as carefully as I had done when he was my sweet, little, chubby-cheeked baby in diapers. Then I went back upstairs and took a shower and got dressed. I took time to select the perfect outfit, the one Sherry had enticed me to purchase. It wasn't that I particularly cared about my appearance these days but more because I didn't want Sherry to be ashamed of me. I wanted to be strong and dependable for her. In all honesty I'd been living my life for her benefit these past few days. Trying to masquerade myself as a together sort of woman who was fully functional and rational. Perhaps I was even mimicking the way that Sherry had been when she rushed to my rescue as my life crumbled into pieces. But at least my facade was working. For Sherry anyway. It didn't seem to be working for me.

To my surprise, Jacob managed to sort of pull himself together as well. Oh, his hair was still a bit shaggy and limp, and his eyes still contained that lost and vacant look, but his clothes were clean and somewhat appropriate. Sure, it wasn't the sort of outfit that I would've encouraged him to wear to a friend's funeral, but I knew I couldn't be too picky. Then as we got into the car, to my dismay I noticed that Jacob seemed rather agitated and twitchy, and I suspected this was a side effect of the crystal meth. I wondered if he had just injected himself and was experiencing some sort of chemical high. Would it get worse?

As I pulled out of the parking lot, I tried to block the mental image of my son sitting on his futon in my apartment, baring his forearm—or was that only in movies, so much I didn't know—and shooting up that ghastly substance. Even so, I wouldn't have been surprised if that hadn't just happened. And why not? I saw how he clung to his grimy backpack, hauling it around wherever he went, like a security blanket. Was that where he kept his drug supplies? And, if so, wasn't he the least bit worried about getting caught? Getting searched? I felt certain I would never make a good drug addict. The fear of getting caught was more than enough to keep me on the straight and narrow for life.

Chapter 22

It was cold and foggy as we rode silently through town. And by the time I parked at the church, my stomach felt as if it were tied in its usual knots, only more so. I was even beginning to wonder if I might not be developing an ulcer. "Quit thinking of yourself," I silently admonished myself. "You are here to support Sherry and her family."

I'd been surprised that Jacob had agreed to come with me this early. But I had told him I could use some help with setting the tables and getting things ready since a light buffet would be served after the funeral. Of course, this was mostly my way of keeping my eye on him today, because I still hoped we'd have time for another rehab talk before he slipped through my fingers again. But I knew Jacob might attempt his magic vanishing act when Matthew's memorial service ended. "Please, God," I silently prayed as I put another casserole into the oven to warm, "don't let Jacob get away before we can really talk."

As it turned out, Jacob proved quite helpful in the preparations. None of the tables had even been unfolded. So while I was working with Marsha to put together some harvest-inspired table decorations of gourds and Indian corn, Jacob and Marsha's husband, Walter, managed to get the tables and chairs arranged. Walter was being quite the cutup, and I think Jacob was even enjoying being useful for a change. I suppose I entertained brief hopes that doing something as simple as this—especially under these sad circumstances—might remind him of what was really important in life.

We barely finished before it was time for the service to begin, but when we got to the sanctuary, it was packed. Standing room only. Marsha and Walter had been smart enough to have someone save them seats, but I hadn't even thought about it. Feeling somewhat dismayed that we were forced to stand in the back by the entrance, I reminded myself that this was probably exactly where we belonged. After all, Jacob *had* been spared that night. My son had survived, even though he was the kid who continually pushed the envelope, testing his limits, playing with fire. And yet he was still standing. And Matthew, the good boy, was taken. How odd of God.

I sneaked furtive glances at my son during the service, wondering if any of this was getting to him. Did he realize how lucky he was that this funeral was Matthew's and not his? Did he realize that his luck could run out at any given moment? I looked at the backpack now slung loosely over his shoulder and wondered about its contents. A mini meth lab perhaps? No, of course not, I scolded myself. Maybe I was growing delusional. Perhaps as another side effect of my son's troubling addiction. Maybe this was the result of the perennial umbilical cord that never seemed to completely detach itself—at least in my mind. Maybe the drugs were funneling from Jacob to me. Or maybe I was simply losing my mind.

I tried not to feel envious when I spied Sarah and Geoffrey seated comfortably just one row behind the immediate family. Naturally, they hadn't even considered saving spots for Jacob and me. Not surprising. I wondered if they would even speak to us afterward. I wondered why I even cared. Although I do love my daughter dearly. And I realized that I was as much to blame as anyone for her selfishness. I didn't think it would make any difference if she spoke to me or not.

It seemed everyone at the service was in tears by the time it ended. Well, everyone but my son. But I was trying not to look at him. Instead I tried to listen as the pastor reminded us that Matthew had given his heart to God as a teenager and that, although he'd gone through a brief rebellion following high school, he had returned to the fold during his second year in college.

"It's just one of those unexplainable events that we will probably never fully understand," he continued. "Not until we stand face to face before God. But we do know this: God doesn't make mistakes. And even though Matthew and his friends may have made some mistakes that fateful night, the eve of Matthew's twenty-first birthday, we can be assured that God the Father was watching. His hand was on Matthew's shoulder. And even now, Matthew is safe in his heavenly Father's arms and…" He continued to speak, but I had difficulty focusing on the words after that.

My mind felt like a captive bird trapped in a pitch-black box, as if I were fluttering about in the darkness trying to find an escape but banging into walls and falling down and beating myself into oblivion. My head felt light and dizzy as I stood in the doorway, swaying.

"Are you okay, Mom?" whispered Jacob.

"I'm not sure…"

Then he took me by the hand and led me out to the foyer where he found an empty bench by the rest rooms and helped me sit down. "What's wrong?" he asked.

"Just feeling faint," I said. I leaned over and took a deep breath to steady myself.

"You want me to get someone?" he asked as he sat down beside me.

"No, no…I'm fine," I muttered. "You go back in there, Jake." But he stayed by my side, and we listened to the remainder of the service from the bench by the rest rooms.

Finally the speaking stopped, and a woman sang. I was feeling better now, a bit guilty for removing Jacob from the actual service. I turned to encourage him to go back in there but noticed he now had tears running down his cheeks. The first I'd seen today. I reached over and put my arm around his shoulders, pulling him toward me. To my relief, he didn't resist.

"I'll go in, Mom," he whispered.

"I'll wait out here. You go on back into the sanctuary," I said.

"No, I mean I'll go into rehab. I'll go."

My heart leaped with hope, and although I knew it was wrong to feel so elated at the funeral for my best friend's son, I just couldn't help myself. I hugged Jacob and promised him he wouldn't be sorry.

The rest of the funeral passed in a blur for me. As expected, Geoffrey and Sarah were somewhat cool and reserved when we went over to say hello to them after the service ended. And I could feel them both looking at Jacob in that way—as if they were simultaneously thinking what an embarrassing loser he was. Perhaps they felt the same about me, too. Who could be sure? Even so, I wanted to tell them that things were going to change soon, that Jacob had just agreed to go into rehab and would be getting much better. But I kept quiet since I wasn't sure how Jacob would feel. It should be up to him to make this kind of announcement to his family. Most important, he had made the decision for himself. And on the pretense of using the rest room, I went outside and called Hope's Wings on my cell phone, making an appointment for Jacob to be evaluated the next morning.

"We're so glad for you, Mrs. Harmon," said the receptionist named Susan. "Jacob has been on our prayer list ever since you first came in here."

"Thank you," I told her. "I really appreciate it."

"See you two at ten tomorrow," she said.

"Yes." I hung up and wondered if Jacob would be able to make it that long. But I knew that was the earliest they could see him. Still, I remembered what had happened the last time, when I had gone by myself. It was less than twenty-four hours, but I knew that anything could happen between now and then.

I was about to go back inside when I got a whiff of cigarette smoke. I turned and was shocked to see Sherry standing by a fire exit with her back to me, and she was smoking.

"Sherry?" I said as I walked over to her.

Without turning around, she dropped her cigarette, crushed it beneath her shoe, then turned to see me. "Glennis, what are you doing out here?"

I smiled sheepishly at her. I could tell she was embarrassed, but then so was I. "Sorry to interrupt," I said. "I didn't know you smoked."

She squirted some breath spray in her mouth, then tucked it back into her purse. "I used to smoke, back in my college days and up until the boys were born. Don't ask me why, but I took it up again the day after Matthew died." She shook her head. "I know it's totally crazy. I can't even explain it myself. But it's like I needed to do it."

I put my arm around her and gave her a squeeze. "I think I understand."

"Really?" she looked skeptical.

I nodded. "How are you doing?"

She shrugged. "As well as can be expected."

I could see, even beyond the dark glasses, that her eyes were still puffy. "This is so hard," I said.

"Yes, especially when everyone keeps coming up and saying something really sweet about Matthew. It's like I just couldn't take it anymore. I know that's horrible. They're only trying to help. But I really needed a break." She glanced over her shoulder. "I can't believe I sneaked outside the church to smoke. My reputation will be shot."

I smiled. "I don't think anyone saw you."

"What're you doing out here?"

"I was just calling Hope's Wings." I tried to suppress my happiness over Jacob's sudden turn of heart. "He's decided to go in, Sherry," I told her. "I made an appointment for tomorrow morning."

She hugged me. "That's wonderful, Glennis."

"Well, tomorrow's still a ways off. And remember what happened last time."

"I'll be praying especially for him." She sighed. "If God had to take my son, the least he can do is give you back yours."

I felt that familiar stab of guilt again. "Oh, it's not really like that, Sherry."

She waved her hand. "I know. But I guess it's just starting to sink in, Glennis. I mean the way that Matthew died. At first, I couldn't understand how Rod was so focused on the kids who took Matthew to the bar that night and how they bought him those drinks. But now I do. Now I'm really getting angry. Bitter even. Rod is talking about getting a lawyer and seeking some kind of murder charges."

"Really?"

"Yes, and maybe against the bar, too." She made a fist and shook it. "I mean what kind of place allows stupid young kids to buy twenty-one shots for one person to consume? Bartenders are supposed to be trained to know that half that amount can seriously hurt someone. It was irresponsible."

I nodded. "You're right."

"And according to Brent, Matthew's roommate at college, Matthew hadn't been into the party scene at all this year. So his body wouldn't have been accustomed to alcohol. Our family doctor said that Matthew was probably legally drunk after just a few drinks and that as a result he wouldn't have been thinking clearly when he consumed the others. Rod says it must at least be a clear-cut case of manslaughter if not second-degree murder."

"Oh, Sherry, that's so sad."

"Sad and wrong." She was pulling out her package of cigarettes now. "Do you mind?"

"Not at all."

She held the red and white package out to me. "Want to try one?"

I studied the pack of Marlboros and inwardly cringed. Smoking had never appealed to me. But then I decided, I can do this for Sherry. So I took one. And feeling like a delinquent junior high girl, I glanced both ways as I waited for her to first light hers, then mine. I took a tentative puff, then immediately began coughing and sputtering uncontrollably.

"Shh," she warned me, looking over her shoulder to see if anyone was around.

I regained my composure but decided that smoking was probably not going to solve any of my problems. Even so, I pretended to smoke with her. For some reason it seemed the right thing to do.

"Thanks," she told me. Then we both used her breath spray and went back inside.

"I know it seems impossible to believe," I told her as we walked down a hall toward the sounds of voices in the fellowship hall, "but somehow I believe you're going to get through this, Sherry. And that you'll be stronger for it."

She stopped walking and turned and looked at me. "And do you believe that for yourself, too, Glennis?"

I frowned. "I'd like to. But most of the time I don't think I'm as strong as you are."

She grabbed my arm and stared into my eyes. "Yes, you are! If I can survive losing Matthew, you can survive this thing with Jacob too."

I nodded. "Right. Maybe you're right."

The crowd in the fellowship hall had definitely thinned, and I was relieved to see that Jacob was still there. I realized I had taken quite a risk by being gone that long. But fortunately he'd been roped in by Walter to put away chairs. I helped out in the kitchen, but it wasn't long before I noticed Jacob trying to catch my eye, and I knew it was time for us to go.

"You were a good sport," I told him as we headed for the parking lot. "Thanks."

"Well, Walter's pretty funny. In an old-guy kind of way. Did you know he used to be a surfer dude?"

"No, I barely know them. Marsha is a friend of Sherry's."

Then Jacob told me about some of Walter's adventures in surfing, and for a few moments I almost believed that I'd gone back in time. Like when Jacob was still in high school and still doing the normal things. But when we got to the apartment building, instead of going up with me, Jacob announced that he wanted to take a walk.

"Are you sure?" I asked. "It's freezing cold out here, and you don't even have on a coat."

"I've got a sweatshirt in my pack," he assured me.

"Will you be home in time for dinner?" I asked.

"Sure," he promised with a somewhat convincing smile.

Even so, I had a feeling he wouldn't. I had a suspicion that I wouldn't see my son again for a while. If at all. I trudged up the stairs to my apartment as if lead weights were tied around my ankles. I felt almost certain that all my hopes for Jacob had been in vain today. I wondered if I should call Hope's Wings and tell them to give tomorrow's ten o'clock appointment to someone else. Someone who might actually show up.

Just the same, I stayed home all afternoon and evening, hoping against hope that I was completely wrong about Jacob. I even prayed to be wrong, and I begged God to tap Jacob on the shoulder, wherever he was, whatever he was doing, and to tell him that it was time to come home now.

But when I went to bed that night—quite late—I knew Jacob wasn't coming home. I knew I had, once again, been deceived. When would I ever learn? *Never trust an addict.*

Chapter 23

Early the next morning I awoke to someone knocking loudly on my door. I grabbed my robe, and, imagining a state trooper standing with his hat in his hands ready to give me the bad news, I hurried to see who was there. To my complete surprise, it was my own prodigal.

"What are you doing?" I demanded.

"It got pretty late last night," he said as he came in and dropped his backpack on the floor. "I decided to spend the night at a friend's so I wouldn't wake you up."

I didn't mention that his absence had caused me to stay awake most of the night anyway. I was just thankful he'd come back. "Do you think you can make it to Hope's Wings?" I said.

"I guess."

"That's great, Jacob." My life returned to me as I went into the kitchen and started to make coffee. "How about I make us both a nice breakfast."

Jacob sat down on a stool at the counter, but I could tell by his fidgeting and the way his eyes kept darting around the room, almost as if he expected someone to jump out from behind a corner, that it was going to be touch and go with him. It was possible that he could still bolt before it was time to leave for the appointment. As a result I felt I needed to tread carefully, to keep the conversation upbeat and positive, and to focus his attention on everything but the obvious.

"Eggs?" I asked as I surveyed the contents of the refrigerator.

"I guess."

"Did you get to talk to your sister much yesterday?" I asked.

He rolled his eyes. "Barely. I think she was trying to avoid me."

"Join the club," I told him. "I think she was avoiding me, too."

"Why?" he said. "Why should she avoid you?"

I shook my head as I cracked another egg. "Because of what's going on between me and your dad."

"What is going on?" He put his elbows on the counter and leaned forward with interest. "I mean, I know you think he's having an affair. But have you guys talked or anything?"

Relieved that we'd come up with a topic to distract Jacob from the rehab appointment, I decided to be completely honest with him. I told him about my last conversation with Geoffrey and how he was already moving toward a divorce.

"Wow." Jacob sighed as I handed him a plate of eggs and toast. "That's pretty harsh."

I shrugged. "I guess it was inevitable."

"Do you have a lawyer yet?"

I sat down and shook my head. "Things got kind of crazy after that. What with Matthew's death and the service and everything."

"But you're going to get a lawyer, right?"

"I guess."

"You guess?" Jacob pointed his fork at me. "Mom, you have to get a lawyer. Sheesh, dad is a lawyer, and he'll probably hire some sleazebag divorce lawyer and try to get away with everything."

"Everything?"

"I mean all the money."

I attempted a smile. "I don't really care about the money, Jacob. Besides, it was mostly your dad's money. It came from his grandparents."

"But what about us?" demanded Jacob. "Well, me, I guess. I'm sure

Daddy Dearest will give perfect Sarah anything she wants. But what about me? I'm part of the family too. What if Dad just totally writes me off?"

"Oh, Jacob, your father would never—"

"You don't know, Mom. You don't really know how he feels about me. I'm pretty sure he hates me. He probably wishes that was my funeral yester—"

"Jacob!" I firmly shook my head. "Your dad might be upset about some…well, some things. But he really does love you."

"Don't be so sure, Mom."

I didn't know what to say, and I didn't like how this conversation had deteriorated so quickly. "You may be right about getting a lawyer though, Jacob," I said. "But don't worry about finances. Really, we'll be just fine."

"Just fine?" He frowned. "You told me yourself that you're barely scraping by, Mom. And I don't make enough money to support both of us."

I smiled. "You don't even have a job right now, Jacob."

"Yeah, but I can get something," he assured me. "There are always ways to make money."

"Well, don't worry about me, Jacob," I said again. "I've got some money put aside, and I can always go back to teaching or substituting."

"I thought you didn't like substituting."

"Well, it's better than nothing." I picked up our empty plates. "And maybe it would be good for me to get out more anyway."

"But substituting?" He made a face. "Kids treat subs like dirt, Mom."

I rinsed the plates. "I know." And I did know. The last time I had substituted, only to keep my certificate current, was a complete and total disaster. I had subbed for a middle-school English teacher, a friend of mine who had warned me it wouldn't be easy. The one-week assignment had felt more like a year. And when it was done, I had sworn I'd never do it again.

But life had changed a lot since then. And maybe we don't always get to choose what we want. Maybe we just have to take what life dishes out sometimes. And maybe my punishment for failing at both my marriage and motherhood was to spend the rest of my life substituting for a bunch of beastly middle-school kids.

Jacob turned on the TV, and I made a dash for the shower, praying he would still be there when I finished. Thankfully, he was. And to my utter amazement, we made it into the Land Rover and all the way to Hope's Wings before he began to balk.

"I don't think I really need to do this," he said as I turned into the driveway.

"It's just an interview and evaluation," I reminded him.

"This place is a dump," he observed.

I wanted to say that it wasn't as bad as Daniel's duplex but managed to bite my tongue as I turned off the ignition. "Looks aren't everything," I said.

"But really, Mom. This isn't going to do any good."

"How do you know, Jacob?"

"Because this place is totally stupid."

"How do you know it's stupid?"

"I just know." He exhaled loudly. "It's what everyone says."

"Do you know people who've been here?"

He laughed. "Yeah. And they're back on the streets right now, doing the same thing they did before they checked in."

"Well, it doesn't work for everyone, but maybe—"

"It doesn't work for *anyone,* Mom. It's all a crock."

"You have to at least give it a chance, Jacob." I opened the door now. "Just do the evaluation."

"I don't need this," he seethed as he climbed out of the Range Rover.

"Fine," I told him. "If you don't need this, they'll tell you as much after the interview."

"Yeah, sure," he said as we walked across the parking lot. "They don't turn anyone away, Mom. They're here to make money, you know."

"That's not true, Jacob. They only accept people who really want to change." I paused and looked at him as we stood before the door to the office. "You do want to change, don't you?"

He just shrugged.

I reached for the door and prayed for a miracle.

I knew that I wouldn't be included in the evaluation or interview. And that was fine. I felt sure there were things I did not need, or want, to know. Sometimes ignorance really is bliss. Although sometimes it can kill you too.

The whole thing took about two hours, and during that time I paced and flipped through tattered magazines and imagined what an expectant father must feel like while sitting in the waiting room when his wife is in labor. I tried to pray but am afraid my prayers were as befuddled and tattered as my thoughts. Would any of this work? Would they even take him? And if they did agree to take him, would Jacob agree to enroll? And what if he agreed to rehab just to pacify me but really had no intention of cooperating? And what if he cooperated, but it still didn't work? Or what if this place really wasn't any good? What if Geoffrey had been right about sending him someplace expensive and "good"? But what if this experience, here today, soured Jacob on going into any form of rehab? It was all too overwhelming. All I could do was to ask God to help. "Please, help us," I silently prayed. "Help Jacob to get through and beyond this." It was all I knew to pray. I hoped it was enough.

Jacob finally emerged, and it almost looked as if he'd been crying. I wasn't sure if this was a good sign or not. Marcus Palmer was with him.

"This is quite a guy," said Marcus, patting Jacob on the back as if he was proud of him.

"I know. How did it go?"

"Would you like to join us in my office?" asked Marcus.

"Of course."

Soon we were all seated in his little office. Jacob looked uncomfortable and more fidgety than ever.

"Do you mind if I speak candidly in front of your mother, Jacob?" asked Marcus.

"Whatever," Jacob mumbled.

"Well…" Marcus leaned back in his leather chair. "It's my recommendation that Jacob enroll in the thirty-day residential treatment program."

I nodded. "Yes?"

"He meets all the criteria. He was honest with our counselors, and his lab tests were positive for amphetamines. He seems to be in good general health." He paused, looking at Jacob. "There's only one problem."

"What's that?" I asked.

He nodded toward Jacob. "He doesn't think treatment will help him."

"But that's not so unusual, is it?" I said. "I mean don't a lot of, uh, addicts feel like that. Like there's no way to help them?"

"That's true enough," said Marcus. "But we don't enroll patients who aren't at least willing to give this their best effort. Otherwise it's just a waste of everyone's time and money." He was looking at Jacob now. "And we do have a waiting list…"

Jacob looked slightly relieved now. "So I'd have to be on a waiting list?"

"Your mother already put you on the list," explained Marcus. "You could check in today…if you were willing."

Jacob frowned. "I'm just not ready for this."

"Why not?" I pleaded. "Why can't you just try it?"

Marcus cleared his throat. "It's not exactly something you try, Glennis. You have to come here with a willing attitude. You have to want to be healthy."

"But Jacob told me he was tired of living like that. Remember, Jacob?" I reached over and touched his arm, but he pulled away.

"Just because people *say* they want help doesn't mean they do, Glennis."

I nodded. "Yes, I remember that from the codependent class. 'Addicts will say whatever they think you want to hear,'" I quoted.

"Sounds like you were paying attention." Marcus smiled.

"Just because I can say it doesn't mean I believe it."

He chuckled. "Good point."

"So maybe we should quit wasting everyone's time," said Jacob, standing. "You don't want me if I don't want to be here, right?"

"It won't do any good," said Marcus.

Suddenly I felt like screaming. I mean, here I had gone to all this work getting Jacob to come—setting up the appointment, handling him with kid gloves, waiting and worrying. Why couldn't they just go ahead and enroll him now, and sort out the rest of it later? I felt disappointed in Marcus, too. I had expected him to be more helpful. Honestly, it almost seemed as if he didn't want Jacob at all.

"But he's here," I said. "He's here right now. And he's been through the evaluation…and I just don't see…I mean, can't he just…" I was starting to sputter and knew I was very close to tears.

Marcus leaned forward now. "I know you really love your son, Glennis. It's obvious, but you need to accept that you can't change him. He has to want to change himself." He turned to look at Jacob, who was standing by the door, ready to leave. "Right, Jacob?"

"That's right," snapped Jacob, his hand on the doorknob.

"And, clearly, you don't *want* to change," added Marcus.

"Not at the moment," said Jacob glibly. "And not here. I know I can change if I want to. But I don't need this."

"But you've said that before," I insisted. "And it hasn't worked, has it?"

"Sometimes it works," he told me. "Sometimes I go for a week or two without using."

"But you go back to it," I reminded him. "You always go back."

"Like I told Jacob," said Marcus. "Crystal meth is one of the most addictive substances known to man. It's nearly impossible to quit without some form of help. He needs therapy and counseling and—"

"I know, I know," he interrupted. "It's like you're beating it into my brain. I just want to get out of here, Mom. Can we go now?"

I felt torn. I glanced over at Marcus, begging him with my eyes to do something.

"I wish I could help," said Marcus. "I think Jacob has a lot to offer this world, but only in a life of sobriety. Without that, he'll have nothing."

"That's not true," said Jacob. "I have my music."

"How's that going?" asked Marcus with a knowing look. "Is your band getting lots of gigs? Any recording contracts?"

Jacob swore at Marcus, then went out, slamming the door behind him.

"I'm really sorry," I said.

"It's not your fault, Glennis."

I shook my head. "You can say that, but it sure doesn't feel that way."

He stood up now. "You need to keep coming to the codependent classes, you know. Even if Jacob refuses treatment, you still need to take care of yourself. Perhaps even more so if Jacob continues doing meth."

I nodded. "I'll think about it."

He put his hand on my shoulder. "Believe it or not, I know how you feel right now."

I frowned. "I don't think anyone knows how I feel right now."

"You feel like a failure. You feel like giving up...like God has turned his back on you."

I studied him closely. "And...I feel like I've lost my son."

"You haven't lost him yet."

"Meaning, *I could.*"

"It's always a possibility."

"I'd better go," I said. "I'd better go find him."

"He can still change his mind, Glennis."

"Right." I'm sure my doubt was obvious.

Jacob was standing by the Range Rover, smoking. It was the first time I'd seen him smoke, but even so I was slightly shocked.

"You smoke?"

He shrugged.

I wanted to grab him and shake him and say, "What's wrong with you?" But instead I unlocked the Range Rover and climbed in and waited as he finished his cigarette.

Finally he got in. "There are worse things, Mom."

I nodded. "Yes, you've made me well aware of that."

He turned and faced me. "Look, Mom, I don't need this place. The people in there are a bunch of losers. Did you see them?"

"Who?"

"The patients."

"But they're in there for help," I tried.

"But you should see them, Mom. They're a mess. This one woman… she was like about forty and totally out of her head. She was in the detox area barfing her guts out. It was sick."

"But she's trying to get help," I said.

"Yeah." He shook his head. "She needs it."

"But, Jacob—"

"I'm not like them, Mom. I'm not that messed up."

"But you're using—"

"I can stop anytime I want." He nodded his head. "I can stop right now. In fact, I think I will. What day is it today?"

I considered this. "I think it's November 8."

"Okay, then, on November 8 Jacob Harmon has officially quit using crystal meth. There, are you happy now?"

I didn't know what to say. "I wish it could be that easy, Jacob."

"It is that easy, Mom. Don't you get it? I just quit. I kicked the habit. End of story. Watch me and you'll see."

"But, Jacob—"

"Don't you believe in me, Mom? Don't you think I have the will power to kick this thing on my own?"

"I don't know…"

"Crud, Mom. I would think that you of all people would believe in me."

"I *do* believe in you, Jacob. It's just that I think you need some additional help. At least you could go to some meetings and—"

"That's for losers. Look, I had a bad habit. I'll admit to that. But it was just for fun. Recreational, you know. I'm done with it now. Really, you gotta trust me on this, Mom."

I just shook my head. I didn't know what to say, what to do. I wanted to believe him. And I certainly didn't want my lack of confidence to trip him up. Finally I nodded. "Okay, Jacob, I do believe you can do this. But are you sure you don't want any help? What about Jack Smart downstairs? He's such a nice guy. Maybe you could go to AA with him."

Jacob actually seemed to consider this. "Yeah, I suppose I could do that, Mom. Would it make you feel better if I did?"

I smiled. "I think it really would. And it couldn't hurt, could it?"

He shrugged. "Probably not."

"And Jack does seem kind of lonely. I'm sure he'd like to get to know you. I think he said the AA meetings are on Wednesday nights, but maybe you could stop by and ask him for the specifics. I wrote down his apartment number somewhere."

I was rambling now, probably a result of stress and nerves as well as disappointment mixed with hope. But I realized there wasn't much I could do besides move on. So I started the engine and began driving toward town. By now I knew enough to realize that this plan with Jack and AA probably wouldn't work. But what else did I have? And, I asked myself, what if Jacob's plan could work? What if Jacob and Jack formed a real friendship, and what if Jacob really opened up to the old guy and managed to work some things out? And what if AA meetings really helped Jacob? Maybe he'd come to accept that recovery groups weren't so bad after all. Okay, it was a long shot, and someone like Marcus would probably think I was a fool to nurture such feeble hopes. But what can a mother do?

Chapter 24

I have been wrong about so many things in life. Why was I surprised to find out I was wrong about Jacob? Again. Not only did he completely avoid every attempt made by Jack Smart to get him to attend an AA meeting, but he continued to deceive me over and over about what was really going on in his life. First, he told me he'd gotten a job at another gas station. False. Then he told me that he had to give up the job so Daniel's band could perform at a local restaurant on weekends. Untrue.

But the worst lie of all was when he would look me straight in the eyes and swear that he was clean. He was convincing, too. And, of course, I wanted to believe him. Jacob put a great deal of effort into appearing credible. He was the master of cover-up and double-talk and smoke screens. And I fell for it. Again and again and again. As a result, I allowed him to stay in my apartment for nearly two weeks during November.

But the day came when I discovered three more used hypodermic syringes wrapped in tissue and discreetly wedged behind the tank of the toilet. Almost unnoticeable. Almost.

"I just don't know what to do anymore," I confessed to Marcus after a codependent session. I think it was about my fifth session by then, and it didn't seem that I'd progressed at all. I felt certain I was either the most gullible woman on the planet or a born enabler. Or perhaps I was simply stupid.

"You *do* know what to do," he reassured me.

"Throw him out?" It was as much statement as question. My head knew this was the correct answer. But my heart was still unsure.

Marcus said nothing.

"But he hasn't even been home in three days." I held up my hands in frustration. "How do you throw someone out who isn't even there?"

"Maybe you box up his things and—"

"What?" I demanded. "Throw them out the front door? Maybe toss them down on the sidewalk and ignite them?"

He laughed. "Just pack them up and get them out of his room so it won't be so easy to allow him back in."

"Seriously?" I considered this. "But really, what am I supposed to do with his stuff once it's boxed up? Just set it by the door so I have to look at it every day—a reminder that I am throwing my only son out in the middle of November?"

He smiled. "That might not be such a bad thing. Kind of a visual aid, you know? Or maybe you could put his stuff into storage."

I sighed. "Why does life have to be so complicated?"

Marcus glanced around the nearly empty classroom. "You want to grab a cup of coffee?"

I was caught off guard by this invitation. Was he asking me out? No, of course not, I told myself. He was probably just trying to get me out of the center so they could close up for the night.

"I'm sorry," I said. "I'm taking up too much of your time. I should just get—"

"No. That's not what I mean, Glennis. I'm not trying to get rid of you. I only wondered if you'd like to get a cup of coffee and just talk as friends."

"Just talk?" I queried. "As friends?"

He shrugged. "If you'd like to."

I considered this. I hadn't really "just talked" to anyone during the past couple of weeks. Sherry, still grieving over Matthew, had taken some time off work and gone to stay with her mother in the mountains. Other than seeing Jack in the laundry room occasionally, I'd lived the life of a hermit these past few weeks.

"How about it?" Marcus asked.

"That actually sounds kind of good," I admitted.

We agreed to meet at Starbucks, but as soon as I began driving over, I started to feel nervous. Was I making a mistake? Could this be perceived as a date? And what if someone saw us together? What would they think?

Then I had to remind myself that Geoffrey had served me with divorce papers just last week, and everyone in town seemed to accept that he and Judith were a couple now. I'm sure the story circulating the community was that I had left him. And perhaps that was true. But I knew he had left me long ago.

Then, as if my life wasn't miserable enough, Geoffrey had decided to sell the Range Rover. He didn't even ask me about it. And, of course, since he'd purchased it without me, only his name appeared on the title, so it was legally his property, to do with as he liked. He had "generously" given me a small portion from the sale, which was why I suddenly found myself driving across town in a seven-year-old Taurus. Quite a step down from the Range Rover, I'll admit. But at least this car was paid for and registered in my name alone. Now if it would only get me through the winter.

I parked on the street by Starbucks and asked myself what I was doing meeting a man for coffee at nearly nine o'clock at night. Was I totally crazy? Perhaps, I thought as I pushed open the door, but then why shouldn't I be?

We ordered our coffees and sat down. I knew I was glancing around, still nervous that someone might see me here.

"Are you okay?" he asked.

"I'm sorry," I told him. "I just feel a little awkward."

"Having coffee with a man who's not your husband?"

"I guess so."

"But didn't you just tell the group that you were served divorce papers last week?"

"I know…"

"But it's still uncomfortable."

I nodded.

"Well, don't worry, Glennis. I'm not out to get you." He tossed me a mischievous grin. "I'm only offering my friendship."

"Thanks." I felt some of the tension draining away.

"So, how's it going?"

"How's it going?" I echoed, almost wanting to throw my head back and laugh hysterically. "Well, my life is a lot like a roller-coaster ride, Marcus. Up and down, and just when I begin to relax a little, it turns on me and goes sideways. I get so tired of it."

He nodded. "Unfortunately, that's life with an addict."

"The divorce doesn't help either."

"No, I'm sure it doesn't." He stirred his coffee. "But that's what makes it so important for you to get control of your life."

"Control?" I rolled my eyes. "That sounds more and more like the impossible dream to me. I honestly don't believe I'll ever have control of anything again."

"That's where you're wrong, Glennis. You *can* get control, but you can only get it over *your* life and *your* decisions. You have to know by now that you can't control anyone else." Then he laughed. "Sorry, I didn't mean to start lecturing you. Sometimes I forget to turn it off."

"That's okay. I probably need some extra lectures." I set my cup down. "I do keep telling myself that—I mean that I can't control anyone else's life. Not Jacob's or Sarah's or Geoffrey's. I've even got the AA prayer taped to my refrigerator. My neighbor Jack gave it to me. He's the old guy who's been trying to get Jacob to go to AA with him. I've read it so many times that I'm sure I must have it memorized by now." Then I recited it, albeit somewhat sloppily. "Give me the grace to accept what I can't change…the strength to change what I can…and the wisdom to know the difference." I smiled like a schoolgirl. "How's that?"

"Very good. I wish I had a gold star to give you."

"But saying it and living it are two different things."

"It takes time, Glennis. Just like with an addict in recovery, it's a daily thing that takes a lifetime to live out." He took a sip of coffee. "So, tell me, what are your daily routines? What are you doing to keep yourself healthy and on track these days?"

"Well, I've really been trying to get back to some kind of schedule since Sherry's son died." I'd already told the codependent group about Matthew's death. I knew they would understand. "I think his death was sort of a wake-up call for me. Or maybe I was just being codependent again, you know, doing it for Sherry."

"Well, I suppose it's not so bad when you're the one who benefits from it."

"That's sort of what I've been telling myself. Anyway, I'm back to jogging every morning, but I'm not quite as obsessed as I used to be. I try to keep it around thirty to forty minutes. Then I take a shower and clean my apartment, which takes about five minutes. Of course, I do regular things like the laundry and buying groceries." I paused, trying to think of something else, something not quite so mundane.

"And that's enough to fill your day?"

I shrugged, then looked down at my coffee, studying the reflection of the overhead lights on its dark liquid surface.

"What do you do with the rest of your time, Glennis?"

I sighed and looked up. "Not much. To be perfectly honest, I probably spend a lot of time just looking out the window, hoping that Jacob is going to show up and tell me he's ready for recovery. Or if he does pop in or call me with some little emergency, like last week when he needed a tetanus shot for stepping on a nail, well, I stop whatever I'm doing and let my little routines just tumble to the side while I try to fix things for him, hoping he'll realize how much I love him and want him to get help."

Marcus laughed. "You are such a natural codependent, Glennis. You could be our poster girl."

I frowned.

"Sorry. And, just for the record, a lot of people with codependent traits are very loving and caring people. They don't mean to enable or cripple their loved ones. It's just that they think their love is going to fix everything."

"How can you stand to spend time with me, Marcus?" I told him. "I mean you work with addicts and codependents all day long. Why would you even offer to have coffee with me during your free time?"

"Maybe it's because I'm a bit codependent myself."

"You?" I found this hard to believe.

He chuckled. "The truth is, it's almost impossible to be in my line of work without being a little that way."

"So you want to fix everyone too?"

"Well, I know without a doubt that I can't fix *anyone*. But I don't mind using what I know to help people find their own answers—as long as they're willing to take the steps themselves."

"Right." I tried not to think about Jacob now. Tried not to imagine some way I could trick him into entering rehab, some way I could help him put his life back together again with someone like Marcus holding his hand. I knew I should know better.

"You mentioned that you have a teaching certificate," he continued. "Do you think you'll take that up again?"

"I'm not sure." I frowned. "I doubt I'd be any good at it now."

"It's not surprising for you to feel that way. After everything you've gone through in the past year or so, well, it just stands to reason that you'd feel less capable than before."

"Less capable?" I forced a laugh. "I feel like a complete and utter failure, Marcus. I feel like everything and everyone I touch falls apart. And if it doesn't fall apart, then it's probably my turn to fall apart. Honestly, I can't even imagine myself standing in front of a classroom and teaching again."

"Did you enjoy it before?"

"Oh, I don't know. It seems so long ago since I got my degree in education. At the time it felt like the right thing to do, and I really do like children. But now I wonder why I didn't pursue something, well, something more creative." I couldn't believe I'd just admitted that.

"Creative?"

I shrugged. "I know it probably sounds silly. Like I don't even know who I am or what I'm capable of doing. But I suppose that's how I feel right now."

"That's not silly. Under the circumstances, it's totally understandable."

"So I'm really not sure what I'll do."

"What kind of creativity interests you?"

"Oh, I don't know." Then I paused to consider his question. "I used to love gardening and arranging flowers. It seemed like the only creative outlet I had, back in my old life. But besides that, I've always been interested in interior decorating, and my friend Sherry thinks I'm good at it. I also like antiques." I shrugged. "I guess I don't really know what I'd like to be when I grow up."

"But it sounds like you're heading in a direction, Glennis. You should give yourself some time to really consider what you love doing and what you're really good at. Think about what kind of options there might be in that field, and then allow yourself to dream a little."

"Dream?" I felt skeptical now. Couldn't he see that my life was too messed up to dream?

"Yes, the older I get, the more I believe we all need to dream more."

"I don't think I even know how," I admitted. "The only dream I have is to see Jacob get clean, and even that gets wearisome."

"Of course you want him to get clean. But that's not the dream for *your* life, Glennis," he continued. "I believe that God plants dreams in everyone."

"Well, if that's true, then mine is probably dead."

"Maybe it's not dead as much as it is buried by the circumstances of your life. I can't tell you how many times I've seen God use trials and challenges to dig into our hearts and shake us up until the dreams finally rise to the surface."

"Are you suggesting that God ordained Jacob's drug problem and my divorce just so he could shake up my dreams?"

"No. Not at all. You have to know by now that the people we love make their own choices, both good and bad. We can't control their choices, but their choices can affect our lives. Right?"

I nodded.

"But we still get to choose for ourselves, Glennis. And if we choose to trust God, things can turn completely around for us. God can turn bad into good."

"I'd really like to believe that." I looked down at my now empty cup. "But it's so hard."

"Glennis." His voice softened. "I…uh…I don't usually tell people my own story, but I think I'd like to tell you."

"You have a story?" Suddenly I wondered if he had been an addict himself. I remembered my first impression of him, with his long ponytail and tie-dyed shirts, and how I'd assumed he was an old hippie. Maybe I'd been right.

"Everyone has a story," he continued. "Mine is about Hope's Wings and how I became a rehab counselor." He looked intently into my eyes. "I'll tell you if you're interested."

"Of course I'm interested." I leaned forward to listen.

"Well, in some ways my story's not unlike yours. I was married too, I thought happily, although I realize now that I wasn't being a very good or attentive husband back then. I worked long hours and put all my best energy into my growing psychiatric practice. My wife and I had only one child, a daughter. She would've been twenty-nine now."

I swallowed hard when he said "would've."

"You're probably guessing right. Yes, she got involved in drugs. And just as the shoemaker's children go without shoes, I, the trained psychiatrist, was oblivious to my child's cries for help. Looking back, I can see that all the signs were there. But at the time I was either in denial, or I simply failed to notice. Or maybe both. I've heard you talk about your husband's attitude toward Jacob's problem, and in some ways I have to admit that I wasn't much different. I think I actually believed that Hope was simply going through a rebellious stage and she'd soon outgrow it and move on. I knew she was a very bright girl, and I guess I really believed she'd figure out that drugs weren't the answer and get on with her life." He set his spoon in the empty cup.

"But she didn't?"

He shook his head. "I didn't even know that she was hooked on crystal meth. To be honest, I really didn't know much about that specific drug or its addictive properties, which aren't much different than cocaine's. I'd been out of med school for nearly fifteen years by then, and I rarely treated patients with chemical dependencies. Plus, this was about twelve years ago, and I was convinced that the drug generation was over and done with. Karen, my wife, felt differently, and she kept nagging me to do something about Hope. As if she thought I could fix things."

"I used to do the same thing with Geoffrey."

He nodded. "Finally, when it became clear that Hope had a very serious problem, I jumped in. She was only seventeen and still in high school, and I thought the answer was for me to play police dad. I started enforcing tight curfews and demanded to know where she was and whom she was with. I even followed her sometimes. In many ways I turned into the classic codependent. Not unlike you. And my daughter, not unlike Jacob, could play me like a fiddle. But what I didn't fully realize was that the drug had gotten a real hold on her, and, naturally, she became very adept at hiding this from me. I even thought that she'd kicked the habit and gotten clean at the end of her junior year. And maybe she had. I guess we'll never know for sure…but late in August, just before her senior year, she died of an overdose."

"I'm so sorry." I could see his eyes glistening, and I knew that I was close to tears myself.

He cleared his throat and scratched his head as if he was trying to remember something. "I know I was going somewhere with this whole thing…"

I searched my memory, retracing our conversation. "Oh yes," I finally said. "You'd been telling me how God uses hard things to give us dreams."

"Right." He sighed. "I guess this is why I don't usually share this story at the rehab center. It sort of messes with my mind."

"I appreciate your sharing it with me."

"Well, the point I was trying to make was that Hope's death really rocked my world. I honestly didn't think I would ever get over it. Not only did my practice fall completely apart, but Karen left me shortly after Hope's death. She met a guy within the same year, and they got married and even had another child. He's about ten now."

"That must've been so painful."

"I honestly didn't think I'd survive it. But it did break something in me. I suppose it was my pride." He ran his finger around the handle of his coffee cup. "And at my lowest point, right when I was about to give up, I somehow had the sense to cry out to God."

I nodded.

"And slowly, very slowly, I began to recover. But during that time I realized that more than anything I wanted to start a rehab clinic. There had been nothing available—not locally anyway—when Hope really needed help. Not that she would've gone in necessarily. But even so, I felt driven to create a place where people with addiction problems could go for help. That's when I started Hope's Wings."

"Hope's Wings..." I used my napkin to stop a stray tear. "For your daughter."

"It seemed right."

"I had no idea you were the founder."

"That was my dream that sort of came out of the ashes."

"Wow. That's an amazing story, Marcus. Why you don't share it more often?"

"I don't really like telling it for several reasons." He folded his paper napkin into a neat triangle. "For one thing I can never be sure that I won't completely lose it during the telling. Also I don't really like people knowing that *I'm* the founder of Hope's Wings." He sort of laughed. "Who knows, they might complain about how shoddy the place is, and I don't know if I could take that." Then he grew more serious. "But mostly I don't like talking about Hope because I know it might make parents fear the worst—that their own child might die of an overdose too." He studied me closely. I could tell he was worried that this might be the case with me, too.

"Don't worry," I assured him. "I already fear the worst."

"I know."

"But you told me anyway. Why?"

His brow furrowed. "I guess I hoped it would encourage you to dream again, to remind you that good can rise out of something hopeless." He paused, looking slightly uncomfortable. "Or maybe there was more to it than that..."

"What do you mean?"

"Maybe I wanted to make a deeper connection with you."

I considered this. And while I couldn't help but feel flattered, I also felt a bit uneasy.

"I value your friendship, Glennis."

"Thanks, Marcus. I value yours, too."

He looked at his watch. "Well, I have an early meeting in the morning. I guess I should call it a night."

After Marcus walked me back to my car and said good night, I felt as though something had occurred that night. Something unexpected and somewhat confusing, but a gift nonetheless. I got into my car and turned on the ignition, then wondered what was going on. More than that, I wondered if I was ready for anything to be happening at all.

Chapter 25

Shortly after Sherry returned from the mountains, I invited her to have lunch at my apartment. "But this time I don't want you to bring anything," I'd told her the night before.

It was the Monday before Thanksgiving, and I hadn't seen Jacob in days. I'd been trying to function in a normal fashion, bearing in mind what Marcus had said as well as Sherry's encouragement before Matthew's death. I wanted to at least *look* like I had my act together. I suppose in some ways I was as much a liar as my son.

"Your place looks great," Sherry said, forcing a sad little smile to her face. "Much better than last time."

I hugged her. "And you look better than the last time I saw you too," I said. "How are you feeling?"

"Feeling?" She set her expensive designer purse on the counter and sighed. "I'm not sure if I have any feelings left, Glennis. Most days I feel like I've been completely drained, wrung out, and hung up to dry."

"I think I know what you mean." I handed her a hot cup of cinnamon spice tea. "Well, I may not know *exactly* what you mean, but I understand."

She looked into my eyes and nodded. "Yes, I think you do."

"And we don't need to talk about it," I assured her as I put the finishing touches on the salad, a Cobb, Sherry's favorite.

She sat down on a stool across from me and watched as I chopped the turkey into small pieces. "It's okay. I don't mind talking about it so much. It's probably good therapy."

"I'm sure Dr. Abrams would agree. She's always encouraging me to process my pain. She says that I repress too much."

"That sounds about right."

"But I'm not as bad as I used to be. When I think of how much I repressed when I was with Geoffrey, it's a wonder I didn't blow up or have a complete breakdown." I smiled. "Although I suppose I have experienced some *partial* breakdowns over the years."

"How do you measure a breakdown?"

"I'm not sure. Too bad there's not some sort of seismic meter for it. Like a nervous-breakdown Richter scale. That way people would know when to watch out or back off."

She smiled, a little bigger this time. "So, tell me, just how does Dr. Abrams suggest you process your pain?"

"Mostly by not burying it. She keeps encouraging me to start writing about it in a journal."

"And are you?"

"Not so much. For some reason I can't make myself write this kind of stuff down. It feels too painful to see it in bold black and white. As if that makes it more real somehow. Isn't that weird?"

"No. I totally understand. I don't think I could write anything about Matthew just yet. I mean it's hard enough even to speak about it." She turned and looked away, and I wondered if that was a hint to change the conversation.

"How are Rod and Mark?"

"They're both doing better, I think. Although they seem to be stuck in this crazy vengeance mode right now. Mark got the names of some of the kids who were involved that night, and Rod is set on suing those boys."

"Well, what they did was sort of like murder, Sherry. Something should be done. Don't you think?"

"Of course, but I just wish Rod would leave it for the D.A. to work out. It's so stressful when he talks about it all the time, as if he's obsessed by it. And it won't bring Matthew back."

"I know, but it might spare someone else's son."

She nodded. "Yes, you're probably right. Speaking of sons, how's Jacob doing?"

I paused from slicing the aromatic loaf of rosemary bread that I had splurged on at Delicato's Bakery—just for Sherry. "I haven't seen him since last week," I confessed. "And he wasn't doing too well then."

"I'm sorry." She shook her head. "I hoped that things had changed for him. He seemed better at Matthew's funeral."

"It comes and goes," I told her as I put several slices of bread in the napkin-lined basket. "Crystal meth is like that. Kind of up and down. Sometimes he seems like he's doing really great." I paused to rinse the bread knife. "And ironically enough, he probably seems like he's doing better when he's high. It's when he's coming down that he gets really agitated and difficult. At least that's what Marcus says."

"Marcus?"

"He's the rehab counselor who teaches the codependent classes at Hope's Wings."

"Any chance of getting Jacob to go in?"

"I keep hoping. And he's been evaluated, and they're willing to take him—but only if he's willing to go."

"And he's not?"

"No. According to him, he can fix this thing himself."

As we ate our lunch, I filled her in on all the other sordid details of the past few weeks of my life—about the divorce papers and losing the

Range Rover, as well as Sarah's continued standoff against me. I suppose I thought that all the dismal gloom in my life might somehow make hers look a bit better.

"Any plans for Thanksgiving?" she asked.

"No. I feel like I need to stick around for Jacob's sake, in case he shows up."

"I haven't even decided what we'll do this year. All I know is that I don't want to be home. I don't want us all sitting around the table, looking at the chair where Matthew used to sit, and feeling bad."

"I can understand that."

"I suppose we'll visit my parents."

"My mother tried to get me to join her and Sarah in Phoenix." I sighed. "To be honest, the sunshine sounds tempting. And I wouldn't mind getting a chance to talk to Sarah—"

"Oh, you should go out there, Glennis."

"I would, but I'd feel so guilty about Jacob. What if he wanted to come home or needed help, and I wasn't here for him?"

She frowned. "I can see your point. But then you can't keep doing that forever, you know. I mean putting your life on hold for Jacob. Isn't that what being a codependent is about?"

I nodded. "Unfortunately, it's a hard habit to break. Sometimes I don't think the classes or even the books I read do me a speck of good. It's so hard to step completely out of his life, Sherry. I mean he doesn't really have anyone else to fall back on right now."

"What's going on with Geoffrey these days? Can't he help out?"

"Oh, he's perfectly willing to pay the big bucks to get Jacob into some fancy rehab place in Colorado. And, believe me, *that* would be wonderful. I'd be the first one to jump up and down with joy. The only problem is that Jacob totally refuses to have anything to do with his father, including his *generous* offer. Jacob is certain that Geoffrey simply wants to get rid of him—an embarrassment, you know. And I suppose he may be right."

"Well, I'm sure it'll all work out…in time." Sherry looked tired now, and I suspected this conversation had drained her even more.

"I've really missed you," I told her as I began clearing the table. "And I've been reading the Bible verses you gave me, and I think it's helping some."

"Good for you." She refilled her teacup. "Maybe I should start reading them myself. Practice what I preach, you know."

I smiled. "I'm sure it wouldn't hurt."

"I heard that you've been going to my church."

"See," I told her, "I've been following your orders."

"Good girl."

"And you were right. It does help."

She sighed. "God seems so far away from me now, Glennis. It's as if there's this wall between us."

I placed a small plate of Delicato's famous white-chocolate-and-macadamia-nut cookies on the table, then sat back down. "That's how I felt too," I confessed. "Back when everything in my life was falling apart."

"But you're over it now?"

"Over it? Yeah, I wish. Let's just say that it's slowly getting better. But, believe me, I have good days and bad days. I'm beginning to think it's a matter of faith. Of choosing, you know."

"Choosing what?" Her brow was creased with interest.

"Like to believe that God is really good despite everything."

"And you're able to do that?"

"I'm trying. That's why I say it's a matter of faith."

She nodded. "I guess that makes sense."

"I still have a hard time getting to sleep at night," I admitted. "Or if

I actually go to sleep, then I wake up in the wee hours of the morning feeling certain that Jacob is dead or dying."

"I do that too." She shook her head. "Only I realize it's true. Matthew *is* dead."

"But what about heaven, Sherry? Don't you believe that Matthew is in heaven?"

"I try to believe it. But there are times—probably when my old fundamentalist upbringing raises its ugly head—when I worry about the way that he died, you know, out in a bar and drinking. And then I'm not so sure."

"But you know as well as anyone that Matthew had recommitted his heart—"

"Then why was he there that night, Glennis? Why was he getting so drunk that he wasn't even thinking straight?"

"We all make mistakes," I told her. "Surely you don't think a loving God was up there shaking his finger at Matthew that night, saying, 'Sorry, son, you blew it tonight. Can't let you in'?"

She sort of smiled now. "No, I can't imagine a loving God saying that. Still, I can wish it had never happened."

"Me, too."

We talked some more, and then Sherry announced that it was time to go. "I promised to attend an annual sales meeting this afternoon. I'm really trying to get back into the swing of things," she told me as she gathered up her coat and purse.

"That's probably good."

"This was really nice." She smiled. "And I did notice that you fixed all of my favorite things." She reached out and hugged me. "And I really appreciate all your encouragement today."

"Well, I learned from the best," I told her.

"And it seems like you're really coming along," she said as she walked to the door. "I think you're going to make it after all, Glennis." Then she said good-bye and left.

I wished I felt as certain as she did about my making it. Mostly I felt as though I'd put on a pretty good show for my best friend. Oh, not that the things I said weren't true. I mean I really was trying to have faith and to trust God. But it wasn't coming nearly as easily as I had made it sound today. Still, if it helped Sherry to believe that I was "coming along," well, maybe it was worth it.

Jacob made a quick appearance the following day. To my surprise he looked like he was doing okay. He told me that he'd just gotten a job at a video store and was staying with friends until he could afford a place of his own. "Sorry I didn't call or anything," he said.

"Is there a number where I can reach you?" I asked.

"No, there's not a phone."

"How about your work number?"

"Look, Mom, you don't have to keep checking up on me. I can take care of myself."

"But what if—"

"Really, I just stopped by to let you know I was okay. And I'm doing fine. So don't worry, okay?"

I nodded but still felt unsure. I also remembered what Marcus had said as I realized that Jacob's upbeat appearance might have more to do with being high than being healthy. "Do you have any plans for Thanksgiving?" I asked.

"Is it Thanksgiving this week?"

"Yes. If you like, I could fix us a small turkey or something."

He smiled. "Sure, Mom, that'd be nice. Maybe I could bring the guys from the band. I don't think they have anything planned."

"Yes," I said eagerly. "I'd love to meet them. How many should I plan for?"

"There are six of us, counting me. But then Barry probably won't come. I think he's going to his girlfriend's."

"Great," I told him. "What time do you think would be good?"

"Maybe in the afternoon," he suggested. "Like around two or so."

"That sounds perfect."

Then he reached out and hugged me. "Thanks, Mom. That'll be really cool."

Already calculating where I could seat everyone in the tiny apartment, I knew it would be a squeeze. But I knew I could make it work. "This will be fun, Jacob," I said.

"Well, I gotta go, Mom. I just wanted to let you know I was okay."

"I appreciate it, Jacob. I really wish you'd stay in touch more."

"I'll try to do better, Mom," he promised. "Life is looking good for me right now."

I nodded.

"By the way, do you think I could borrow a couple of bucks?" he asked casually. "I'm kind of broke at the moment, and I promised Justin that I'd pay him back, but I don't get paid until Friday."

"I'm a little low," I told him, which was only partially true. I actually had a fair amount of cash since I'd just been to the bank. But I was worried about giving him very much. Marcus had told us how anything more than ten dollars was enough for an addict to go out and get a hit of crystal meth. If the addict knew the right people, that is, and I had a feeling Jacob did. Marcus had explained how it was better to give food or clothes than actual cash. And also to avoid giving anything that could be sold or returned to a store for cash. I went into the bedroom and dug out a five and a couple of ones, plus some loose change. "Sorry," I lied to my only son. "This is all I can spare right now."

He looked disappointed but didn't say as much. I felt certain he'd been expecting at least a twenty. Still, I reminded myself, I might not be able to get him to go to rehab, but I didn't need to support his habit.

"I love you," I said as he headed out the door.

"I love you too, Mom."

After the door closed, I wondered if I should've asked him about rehab again. But then why bother? He knew that I desperately wanted him to go, that I was willing to drop everything to take him over, that I'd probably even sell my vital organs just to get him in. What good did it do to continually nag him? Perhaps it was better if I backed off a little. Maybe it would help him to see this need for himself.

All the various warnings I'd heard and read about codependency and enabling during these past few weeks seemed to be echoing through my brain. Naturally, that only made me feel totally inadequate as well as quite certain that some experts, including Marcus, might say I was a complete fool to give Jacob a single penny, not to mention my offer to fix Thanksgiving dinner for him and his, most likely, junkie friends.

But books and lectures don't always speak to a mother's heart. And perhaps some of the best lessons in life are, after all, learned the hard way. Fortunately, I was able to distract myself during the next couple of days as I forced my tiny kitchen to produce the Thanksgiving dishes that I'd so easily prepared in the past. I felt like a Pilgrim commando as I shoved the large turkey into the small oven, hoping that there'd still be room for rolls. And, feeling festive, I even arranged some Indian corn and brightly colored gourds among the candles I'd set out on the coffee table.

So why was I shattered and shocked when my turkey and dressing and mashed potatoes and pumpkin pies were all done, and the table was all set, but nobody showed? I mean, really, why was I surprised? The warm aromas of favorite dishes had comforted me temporarily, but my fuzzy feelings vanished when I realized it was four o'clock, and once again I had been duped by my son.

Oh, it was entirely possible that Jacob had had every intention of coming for dinner and bringing his music buddies. But he'd probably simply forgotten. Most likely a result of his addiction and substance abuse. I knew that addicts had difficulty keeping appointments. I just hoped he was okay and not strung out or lying unconscious on the freezing street somewhere. This was another one of those times I wished I'd gotten that boy a dog-tag ID to wear around his neck. That way if he wound up in the emergency room or worse, he could at least be identified.

I paced back and forth in my little apartment, still hoping that Jacob and his friends might show up apologetic and hungry. But I knew this wasn't going to happen. The sky was growing dusky as I peered out the window and down the street, hoping beyond hope to see a small band of renegades making their way toward the apartment complex. But the street remained surprisingly quiet. Everyone was probably tucked away in warm houses, sleeping off the effects of too much turkey and dressing.

I turned and looked at my feast, now cold and unappealing. My appetite had faded with my hopes, and for a moment I considered simply throwing the whole mess out. But that would be such a waste, and I had used nearly two weeks of my grocery budget for this dinner. Suddenly I remembered the story that Jesus had told about the man who had prepared a feast but no one had come. That man had sent his servants out to the streets to invite all the poor people. Of course, I had no servants to send out. And, as it was, I had already invited the poor people. After all, who was poorer than my son at the moment?

Then I remembered Jack Smart and Cammie and her two kids downstairs. Was it possible they might be interested in a Thanksgiving dinner this evening? Was the dinner even fit to serve? Without giving myself time to rethink or question myself, I pulled on a jacket and ran downstairs.

"What's wrong?" asked Cammie as she opened the door. She looked haggard and tired, and I could hear the kids arguing back in a bedroom.

"I know this sounds crazy," I began, "but I have this big Thanksgiving dinner upstairs. And, well, my guests never came, and I was, well, wondering if—"

"I would love to come!" she exclaimed, grabbing my hand. "I'd do anything to get out of this place today. The kids are driving me bonkers, and I was going to make macaroni and cheese. What time can we come?"

I smiled. "Give me about thirty minutes to warm things up."

"Cool!" She turned and yelled, "Avery! Warren! Get ready. We're going out tonight."

I waved and took off for Jack Smart's apartment, certain that I couldn't get lucky twice in a row. But there was Jack in his slippers and cardigan.

"Are you hungry for turkey?" I asked.

He grinned. "Well, I did have a turkey TV dinner for my lunch, Glennis. But it sure wasn't anything to write home about."

"Well, I have turkey and dressing and pumpkin pie," I explained. "And my guests never came, so I thought I'd invite some neighbors."

"Sounds delicious." He smacked his lips. "Can I bring anything?"

"Just your sweet self," I told him. "Give me about thirty minutes to get it together."

"Hello, Jack," called a woman's voice down the hall.

"That's Mrs. Gardner," said Jack in a quiet voice. "Widow lady, been here for years." Then he called out a greeting to her and quickly introduced us.

"Would you like to join us for turkey dinner?" I asked her without even thinking it might sound strange.

She seemed surprised but pleased. "Why, that'd be very nice, dear. Are you sure?"

"I'm positive. I made enough to feed a small army, or a rock band." I smiled. "Anyway, no one showed up, and I'd hate to let it go to waste."

So it was settled. Jack and Mrs. Gardner and Cammie and her two little ones would be my guests tonight.

I was just turning on the oven to warm the food when the phone rang. I dashed for it, imagining it was Jacob saying that he and his friends were on their way. Well, even if that was so, they'd have to make do with a little less food. I certainly wasn't about to turn my neighbors away now. But it was Marcus.

"I just thought I'd see how you were doing," he said. "I still remember how hard it was on the holidays in the beginning."

Touched by his thoughtfulness, I told him about fixing dinner for my no-shows.

"That's too bad, Glennis, but not too surprising. I hope you didn't go to too much trouble."

"I did the works," I told him, describing the menu in detail.

"Wow, that sounds good."

"Why don't you come join us?"

"Us? I thought you said no one showed up."

Then I explained my plan B to him, and he laughed. "I'd love to come."

"Great," I said. "Hopefully the turkey won't be too dry."

"I happen to like dry turkey."

"Then come on over."

So, what could've been a totally disastrous and depressing day turned out to be something of an adventure. The turkey wasn't terribly dry, and the gravy was some of my best. Everyone seemed to enjoy themselves, and to my relief, all the leftovers fit in the refrigerator.

Then, after dessert was finished, Cammie decided to lead our somewhat diverse group in a rousing game of charades. But eventually we realized that the generation gap was a serious challenge. ("Britney who?" asked a bewildered Jack Smart.) Plus, it was almost nine o'clock, and Avery and Warren were getting cranky, so the party began to break up.

"I should probably get the rug rats to bed," said Cammie as she balanced a fussing Warren on one hip. "But thanks for having us over. I really do like your apartment. I wish you'd help me fix mine up cute like this."

"I'd love to," I told her as I handed her a paper plate of leftovers.

"And thank you so much for including me, dear," said Mrs. Gardner, giving my hand a squeeze. "I feel that I've made a new friend today."

"It's been great getting to know you," I said and handed her a plate of leftovers too.

"You're a good cook, Glennis," said Jack as he shook hands with Marcus. "And it's been a pleasure meeting your friend Marcus here."

"Thanks, Jack." I handed him yet another plate. "I'm so glad you could come."

"How about I give you a hand with the cleanup," offered Marcus after my apartment emptied.

"Oh, you don't have to—"

"I *want* to, Glennis. And you might be surprised to learn that I know how to wash dishes." He reached for my chef apron, then put it on and grinned.

As it turned out, Marcus proved to be quite adept in the kitchen. But first he insisted that I sit at the counter and simply watch. "You've already put in a long day," he told me as he filled the sink with hot soapy water.

"But I feel guilty not—"

"No arguing." He pushed up the sleeves of his sweater and turned back to the sink. "Now, tell me, how's it going?"

"What do you mean?" I studied him as he wiped down the counter next to the sink before he set the drain rack on it. I hadn't failed to notice that Marcus was a nice-looking man, but seeing him wearing my apron with his sleeves rolled up and making himself quite useful in my kitchen, I actually thought he was rather handsome.

I wondered what Geoffrey would think of someone like Marcus. He'd probably assume by his ponytail and unpretentious manner that Marcus was an "old hippie" or even a loser. Geoffrey was quick to sum up people based on appearances. He claimed that he could pick the perfect jurors purely by their looks. I also knew that Geoffrey would be equally unimpressed by Marcus's career change from a private practice in psychiatry to running Hope's Wings, a place Geoffrey had already judged as an eyesore. But for some reason these things made me appreciate Marcus even more.

"I mean, how's it going in regard to figuring out what you want to be when you grow up," continued Marcus as he set a sparkling glass in the drain rack.

"Oh." I brought my thoughts back to reality and considered this. "Well, I've been thinking about it and trying to be really honest with myself. I've never told anyone this before, but I think I'd like to run some sort of shop."

"A shop?" His brows raised with interest. "Hmm. I hadn't really pictured you as a businesswoman."

I shook my head. "No, neither had I particularly. But this would be a shop where I could express my creativity."

"A creative shop?"

I smiled. "I imagine it as kind of a gift and decorating shop. It would have antiques along with decorating accents, maybe even flowers. Does that sound crazy?"

"No, not at all."

"I've been in shops like that in other towns. But we don't have anything quite like that in Stafford."

"There's the Decorating Den, but it doesn't have antiques."

"And I know we have a number of antique and secondhand stores, but they don't really do much with them. I mean, to show off the antiques and how they could be used to beautify a home."

"And you definitely have a knack for that." He turned and nodded to the apartment. "You've made this place into something special."

"Thanks." I leaned my elbows on the counter and continued to watch him. "It's funny though. I mean, I always wanted to decorate my home in a unique way, but I never really got the chance...before..."

He frowned as he scrubbed a plate. "Why not?"

"My husband." I paused. "I guess I'll have to start calling him my ex-husband before long. It sounds strange though."

"Your husband wouldn't let you decorate your home?"

I explained about Geoffrey's grandparents giving us a home and furnishings and how the die had been cast after that. "Geoffrey has very strong tastes. He likes what he likes, and since he was the one who brought home the paycheck, well, it didn't seem right for me to argue with him."

"Wow." Marcus shook his head. "You were quite the little woman."

"I know...it's pathetic, isn't it? Sometimes I felt as if I'd gone back in time, as if I were stuck in a fifties family sitcom like *Ozzie and Harriet* or *Father Knows Best.* I even wore sweater sets and pearls."

He laughed. "That doesn't sound like you."

"I suppose not, since most of the time now I wear sweats and jeans. But that's probably more a sign of depression than personal expression. Or maybe I'm just rebelling."

He picked up a dirty saucepan. "Don't worry, Glennis. I'm sure it's all part of your journey to find yourself."

"Find myself," I echoed. "Do you think it's even possible?"

"I know it is."

When the dishes were done and the kitchen was sparkling, I offered to make us a pot of coffee. "Unless you need to go," I said.

"Do you think I could have another piece of pumpkin pie with it?"

"Of course."

And so we sat down in the living room with our pie and coffee and continued to talk. And to my amazement, I found myself relaxing even more. I was laughing and feeling as if someone had miraculously turned back the clock, and I was suddenly a carefree college girl again. And then someone knocked on the door, and, presto chango, the magical moment came to an end.

Chapter 26

"Who can that be at this hour?" I set down my coffee cup and stared at the door. Already my chest was tightening, and, as usual, I feared something was wrong. Could it be the police? Had something happened to Jacob?

"Want me to get it?" offered Marcus.

"No, that's all right." I stood up and headed for the door. Bracing myself for bad news, I opened it, and there stood Jacob.

"Hey, Mom," he said as if it were perfectly normal for him to show up on my doorstep this late at night. And to be honest, I suppose it was. Just the same, his unexpected visits always took me by surprise.

"Jacob." I opened the door wider. "Come in."

He stepped inside, and I suspected by the jitters and twitches that he was on something. "Hey, it's you," he said, pointing at Marcus. "I remember you. You're the counselor dude from the loony bin. What're you doing here at my mom's place anyway?" He glanced at me with suspicion. "What? Is this some kind of intervention or something?" He looked over my shoulder as if he expected someone else to come down the hallway.

"No, Jacob," I said, trying to keep my voice even. "Marcus was here for Thanksgiving dinner."

Jacob slapped his forehead. "Oh yeah, I totally forgot, huh? Sorry, Mom. But seriously, are you pulling something on me here?" He returned his focus to Marcus, then scratched his head.

"No one's pulling anything, Jacob," said Marcus.

"I don't know." Jacob still had his backpack securely in one hand. "This doesn't feel right to me." He turned and narrowed his eyes at me. "Mom?"

I held up my hands. "Honestly, Jacob, Marcus was simply here for dinner, along with some other friends that I managed to round up when you didn't show."

"Is anyone else here?" asked Jacob, peering toward the hallway again.

"No. My neighbors just left. Do you want some leftovers?"

"I, uh, I don't know." He looked at Marcus again.

"Maybe I should go," said Marcus, standing.

I wasn't sure what to do or say now. On one hand, it would simplify things if Marcus left. But at the same time, I was feeling a little uncertain about Jacob's behavior tonight. Something about the look in his eye wasn't only unsettling but also a bit frightening. Still, I reminded myself, he's my son. Jacob would never do anything to hurt me. And yet I wasn't sure.

"Or I can stay," offered Marcus, carefully studying me as if he were reading my thoughts. I think he understood that I was uneasy.

I nodded at Marcus, then turned my attention back to Jacob. "I'm glad you're okay, Jacob," I began, "but I wish you had called me about not coming today. I was getting worried about you."

"Like I said, Mom, I just totally forgot. Don't you believe me?"

"Right." I went into the kitchen now. "Are you hungry? There are still some leftovers."

"I...uh...I don't think so."

"Want me to fix you a plate to take with you?" I asked. I couldn't believe that I was hinting to Jacob that he would have to leave, that he wouldn't be spending the night here. But I knew that he was still using, and I'd been trying to remain firm with him about not living here without getting help and getting clean. Still, I felt like the world's worst excuse for a mother as I realized I would be throwing my very own son out on Thanksgiving.

"Huh?" He looked back and forth from me to Marcus and back again, as if he was trying to keep an eye on both of us, as if he thought we were really up to something.

"In case you get hungry later?" I said to get his attention back. "You could take some turkey and things with you."

"No, that's okay. I don't want anything." He turned back to Marcus, but his expression seemed to be turning hostile now. "Really, man," he said in an agitated voice, "I want to know what you're doing here in my mom's apartment. Why'd you come? Are you trying to get me into your loony bin again? Cuz I'm not going. I'm not into that kind of crap. I mean that place is for psychos and losers, you know. And I don't care what you guys think. You're not forcing me to go there."

"That's right, we're not." Marcus sat back down on the couch and looked evenly back at him. "No one gets forced into rehab, Jacob. It's a personal choice that only you can make for your—"

"And don't think you can sit there and talk me into it either." Jacob shook his fist. "I don't need your crap, man."

"I'm not trying to talk you into anything, Jacob. And I realize that you're high right now." Marcus was speaking in a soothing but personable voice, probably the same tone he used in working with patients. "And that naturally makes you feel a lot more edgy and suspicious about people. I know what that's like. But, honestly, Jacob, I only came for turkey tonight."

Jacob walked over to the front door now. "Yeah, *right*."

"Your mom's a great cook, Jacob. You missed out on a really good dinner."

"Yeah, you bet." He slung his backpack over a shoulder as he reached for the doorknob.

"I wish you'd take something with you," I said returning to the living room area.

"I'll just bet you do, *Mom!*" But the way he said "Mom" sounded like he really meant "Traitor." And as ridiculous as it seemed, I knew that's just what he thought—that I had invited Marcus over here in order to corner him and drag him, kicking and screaming, into Hope's Wings for imprisonment and subsequent treatment.

Jacob just shook his head in disgust, as if he was seriously disappointed in me, as if I was the enemy. Then he walked out of the apartment, slamming the door behind him.

My hands were shaking as I sat down in the rocker across from Marcus. "What just happened?" I finally managed to ask.

"Paranoia is one of the many side effects of crystal meth use, Glennis. It doesn't take much to set it off either. But in Jacob's defense, it probably seemed perfectly obvious to him that I was here to take him away tonight."

I nodded. "That's what I thought he was thinking."

"The best thing you can do in that situation is to remain calm and be honest."

"Calm." I took in a deep breath. "I was frightened of my own son just now, Marcus. I'm not sure what I would've done if you hadn't been here."

"I think the problem was that I was here, Glennis. In Jacob's mind, right now, I am a threat to his freedom. He sees me as the enforcer who will take away his fun."

"Fun? I just don't get it, Marcus. How can anyone think it's fun to be so messed up? Why on earth does he keep going back to it?"

"Because it makes him feel good."

"But how can that be? Honestly, I don't understand."

"Meth is like cocaine, Glennis. Most addicts say that the high is incredible."

"I know," I admitted. "I've read that it's totally euphoric, that it makes you feel powerful and creative and all sorts of stuff. Sometimes I even think I should try it myself." I made a face, and Marcus laughed.

"Unfortunately that high never lasts. Almost everyone I've treated says that it's never as good as that first time."

"Then why do they continue?"

"They think they can recreate that big high again."

"But they can't."

"Not really. But they still get a brief feeling of euphoria. Unfortunately, they have to use more and more meth to feel any effect. And that's when it gets dangerous."

"Because of overdose."

He nodded. "But we don't need to think about that now." He glanced at his watch. "Besides it's getting pretty late."

I thanked him for coming and walked him across the small room. "I'm glad you were still here when Jacob showed up," I admitted as he opened the door.

"So am I," he said, smiling down at me. "And he really is a good kid, Glennis. He just needs to get clean."

I nodded. "I know." Then I closed the door and listened as Marcus went down the steps. Still feeling a bit worried about Jacob and what he might be capable of doing while under the influence of crystal meth, I secured the deadbolt and left the outside light on. Then I got down on my knees and begged God to do something.

"Please," I cried out in desperation. "You've got to help Jacob. Somehow you've got to get through to him, God. Can't you make him see that his life is worth so much more than this? Can't you do something? Anything?" I continued like that for quite a while. Then feeling completely exhausted and not any more hopeful than when I'd started praying, I headed for bed.

But once in bed, all I could think about was Jacob. Where was he tonight? Did he really have anyone to stay with? Was he out on the streets? I knew that temperatures were supposed to drop again that night. "In the teens," the weatherman had said that morning. What if Jacob was so strung out that he didn't realize how cold it was out there? What if he fell asleep on a park bench and died of exposure, hypothermia? How would I ever be able to live with myself knowing that it was my fault? That I had turned my own son, my own flesh and blood, out into the cold? And on Thanksgiving, too.

After an hour of such questions, I couldn't take it anymore and got up and began pacing around the darkened apartment. I kept looking out the window, wishing that Jacob would come back. Wishing that I had handled things differently. So what if I'd been scared? Which was more scary—my son high on drugs sleeping it off in this apartment or my son lying dead in a gutter? And perhaps none of this would've happened, I considered, if I hadn't had Marcus over here. What was I thinking to invite him anyway? I should've known this could present a problem for Jacob. In his eyes, it probably seemed I was linking myself with the enemy and subsequently making myself into the enemy. That's how I'd felt tonight—as if I'd suddenly become Jacob's enemy. Poor Jacob. In his twisted, drug-inflicted mind it must've felt like the final blow. His very own mother consorting with someone from Hope's Wings. What had I been thinking?

By now I had myself so agitated that I knew I would never go to sleep. I continued pacing and fretting until I felt my sanity was in serious peril. Was I completely losing my mind? And how had I wound up in this unstable condition after enjoying a relatively nice evening? What was wrong with me?

I paused in front of my refrigerator and read all the notes I'd posted there. While the words were of some comfort, I knew that something was missing. In front of my shabby slipcovered sofa, I got back down on my knees again. And this time I didn't cry out for Jacob as much as I cried out for myself. It seemed that my own soul was hanging precariously by a thread. How could I possibly ask God to help someone else when I was floundering like this?

"Help *me,* God," I prayed out loud. "I am such a complete mess, and I don't even know what to do about anything anymore. Please, I'm begging you, help *me* to survive this. Help *me* to trust you more. To believe what your Word says and to have the faith to function without having these meltdowns all the time. Please, God, I need you." Then I went back to bed and lay down again. To my surprise, I did feel a little better, a little calmer. And as I lay there, still thinking about Jacob but trying very hard not to imagine the worst-case scenario, I began to see something I'd never seen before.

With crystal-clear clarity, I began to see Jacob as God's child. Not that he wasn't my child, because I knew that indeed he was and always would be, but I began to understand that if God had truly been the one to create my son—and I think I believed this—then God must bear some responsibility for the way Jacob's life seemed to be heading. Not only that, but if God was the loving God I had once believed him to be—even if I had questioned this lately—then wouldn't he want to take care of Jacob, his own child?

And so I imagined myself handing my only son over to God and saying, "Here he is, God, the child that you created. I trust you to take care of him now. I know that I cannot. I give him over to you, God. Please watch over him and protect him, for he is, after all, your son." And then believing that God was far more able to handle this heavy responsibility than I was, I closed my eyes and went to sleep.

Chapter 27

I wish I could say it was *that* easy. *That* simple. That I handed Jacob over to God that Thanksgiving night and that, once and for all, I quit worrying about my wayward son and resumed life as normal. Good grief, I didn't even know what normal was anymore. Perhaps there is no such thing as normal. But like a toddler learning to walk, I continued moving through my new life one hesitant step at a time. And like a toddler I still fell down.

The AA prayer became my mantra. I prayed it at least a dozen times a day. During the next couple of weeks, I continued going to Dr. Abrams and to the codependency meetings, and I tried to imagine that life was getting better and that I was becoming healthier. And perhaps it was true. But I couldn't deny that I was still haunted by my son's perilous lifestyle. Oh, yes, I prayed more. And I practiced the codependency recovery phrase of "letting go and letting God" more. But I could never completely escape that dull, aching knowledge that Jacob's life was in danger. Perhaps this is the price a mother must pay for loving.

I did receive one consolation during that time, albeit a bittersweet one. Sarah called me during her finals week—to apologize.

"I'm sorry, Mom," she told me almost immediately after I said hello.

"For what, honey?" I asked. "Are you okay?"

"Yeah, I'm okay. I just wanted to say I was sorry for giving you such a bad time about Dad. I can't believe what he did."

"What he did?" I echoed, bracing myself for fresh pain.

"Yes. I thought he went on a business trip the week after Thanksgiving."

"But I think you're right, Sarah. That's what I heard too."

"Well, I called his secretary at work to get the number for the place where he was staying since I kept getting his message on the cell phone. I'm trying to get moved into an apartment on campus before Christmas break, and I needed him to cosign and give me a check. But it turns out that he was off on a Caribbean cruise. Betty gave me the ship's number, and I called and left a message."

"Oh. Did he call you back?"

"Yes. But he made up this stupid story about it being a working vacation."

"Right."

"So I called city hall again and asked for Judith Ramsey this time. And guess what?"

"She was gone too?"

"You got it. I asked her secretary when she'd be back and was told she was on vacation. So guess what I did?"

"I have no idea."

"I called the same cruise ship number and asked for her and was able to leave a message."

"Did you?" I asked. "Leave a message, I mean?"

"Yes. But I just made something up and gave a phony name."

"I'm sorry, honey."

"Well, I'm sorry too, Mom. I can't believe I was blaming you for everything, and here it turns out that Dad really was messing around."

It sounded like she was crying now. "Are you okay, honey?"

She sniffed. "Yeah, but it makes me so furious that my whole family is falling apart like this. It's just not fair."

I sighed, unsure what I could say to make her feel better. Maybe nothing. "Well, life doesn't always go smoothly, Sarah, but sometimes the bumps make us stronger."

"How's Jacob?"

"I don't really know. I haven't seen him since Thanksgiving."

"I wish he'd straighten up."

"You and me both, Sarah."

"I just wish the whole freaking world would straighten up," she said in an irritated voice. "I wish everyone would just grow up and life could go back to what it was before."

I considered this. What *had* life been before? The unblemished image of the happy little family living the perfect little life? But hadn't it all been an illusion? A carefully constructed cover-up?

"Well, I hope we can all grow up too," I finally told her. "But I don't think life will ever go back to what it was before." I paused. "But, who knows, maybe it will get better."

She groaned. "I don't possibly see how."

Then we talked about plans for Christmas, and she told me that her dad had already given her money for a ski trip with friends. "I thought maybe I could stop in and see Grandma for a couple of days. Do you think you could come too?"

"I don't know, Sarah…"

"Still trying to fix Jacob?"

"No…not really. I'll tell you what, I'll call your grandma and give it some serious thought. Okay?"

"Okay."

"I love you, sweetie."

"I love you, too, Mom. And I'm sorry I put all the blame on you before."

"As I said, Sarah, we're all a little to blame."

"You mean me, too?"

"No, not in regard to our marriage. But you're not perfect either, honey. I'm sure you get to take the blame for *something*." I laughed lightly, hoping I hadn't hurt her feelings.

"Maybe. But I guess that's between me and God."

I felt a clash of feelings as I hung up the phone. I was hugely relieved that this thing between Sarah and me was finally improving. But it really stung that Geoffrey had taken Judith on the Caribbean cruise. This fall was supposed to have been our time to celebrate our anniversary by going to the Caribbean.

"Move on," I told myself as I went over to the window to look out on the street below. I peered up and down the street and knew I was, once again, searching for my son, hoping I'd see him walking this way, ready to come home, ready to get help. "Get a life!" I yelled at myself, forcing my eyes away from the window.

And that's when I finally took Dr. Abrams's advice and began journaling my thoughts about Jacob and my upcoming divorce and all the other elements of my life that had unraveled during the past six months. It was hard putting these painful thoughts into written words at first, but the more I pressed on, the easier it became. After three days I discovered an entire spiral notebook was filled with sentences and paragraphs describing my recent ordeal. There was a significant amount of venting and self-pity, but it was becoming clearer that I was progressing, too. I was just about to go out for a cup of Starbucks coffee, to celebrate, when the phone rang.

As usual, I thought it might be Jacob. That was always my first assumption. And I hadn't heard from him for more than a week now. Instead it was Geoffrey, and he sounded very agitated.

"Where's Jacob?" he demanded without even saying hello.

"How was your cruise?" I asked without answering.

"None of your business," he snapped. "Now, tell me, Glennis, *where* is Jacob?"

"Why?" I countered. "Why are you suddenly so concerned about your son?"

"Because I am going to kill him!"

"Geoffrey!" I gasped. "What on earth is wrong with you?"

"What is wrong with me?" he yelled so loudly that I had to hold the phone away from my ear. "My son has broken into my house and stolen and vandalized and..." He sputtered and swore and then continued, "and I'm about to call the police and have him arrested, and I want to know where the—"

"How do you know it was Jacob?"

"I *know*, Glennis! Believe me, I *know!* Now where the—"

"But how can you be so sure? You were gone for more than a week, Geoffrey. Anyone could've broken—"

"Where *is* he, Glennis? And don't cover for him! I'm warning you, if you—"

"I haven't seen Jacob since Thanksgiving. And only barely then. I have absolutely no idea where he is."

"Well, he *was* here. He must've been flipped out on his psycho drugs. This place is a disaster area." And then he began swearing again.

"Calm down, Geoffrey," I told him.

"Calm down? You should see the place, Glennis. You should see what your dear little boy has done. Why don't you come over here and look around? See for yourself that it was Jacob's work."

"Fine," I told him. "Maybe I'll do that." Then I hung up and hurried over there, hoping that Geoffrey was wrong, hoping that this was the work of someone else. Not Jacob.

But when I arrived, it seemed obvious that Jacob had been the culprit after all. Apparently he had no concern about being caught either since he'd left several incriminating notes to his dad, as if he was proud of his senseless destruction. The navy blue leather couches had been slashed, several windows were broken, furniture was overturned and moved, debris from food and drink was everywhere. And some of Geoffrey's valuables were missing. He pointed out where various pieces of expensive electronics used to be. And despite my negative feelings toward Geoffrey, I did feel sorry for what had happened during his absence. It wasn't anything that anyone should have to come home to. I'd already noticed his luggage dumped in a heap by the back door and suspected that he'd just gotten home.

"Have you called the police yet?" I asked.

He slumped down into a club chair in the living room, and putting his head in his hands, he moaned. "No…"

I sat down on a sofa across from him. "Why not?"

He looked up at me, and despite the unseasonable golden tan on his face, he looked worn out and tired and old. "What am I going to tell them, Glennis?" He shook his head. "That my son has robbed and vandalized my home? And how's that going to go over down at city hall? Can you imagine what people will think and say?"

I shrugged. Who cares? I wanted to ask, but remained silent.

"Why did he do this to me?"

I picked up one of the notes. The words scrawled in black felt-tip pen seemed etched in anger and pain. I read it aloud, wanting Geoffrey to really hear it. "Sorry to be such a disappointment to you, Dad. But here's what I think of your precious house. Maybe it's time you learned that stuff is just stuff, but people feel the pain. Your lame excuse for a son, Jacob."

The other notes were similar. All raging and angry and symptomatic of deep anguish. Didn't Geoffrey get it? I held up another note. This one was unfinished and sounded almost suicidal. "Can't you see that he needs you, Geoffrey?" I demanded. "Don't you know that this is a cry for help?"

"It's insanity, Glennis. Jacob needs to be locked up until he can get over this drug habit. It's making him crazy."

"You've said it yourself," I reminded him. "And it's taken me a while to accept this, but you were right: only Jacob can fix Jacob. And until he's willing to get rehab treatment, there's nothing you can do to fix him." I sighed. "Well, other than to love him, that is."

"Love him?" Geoffrey stood up now, his hands in tight fists and his face twisted with bitter rage. "I think I might actually kill him if I saw him today. Look at this place, Glennis. Look at what he's done to me. I'm supposed to *love* this?"

"Not this, Geoffrey. Your son. You're supposed to love your son." I started walking toward the door now. It was clear that my presence wasn't helping anything. I paused halfway to the door, turning to look at the man who had once been my husband, at the house that had once been impeccable, everything perfectly in place. I figured it would probably be put back together again before long. And maybe even better than before if Geoffrey was as adept at insurance claims as he was at breaking hearts.

"You can't blame this all on Jacob," I told him in an even voice now.

"I don't, Glennis." He folded his arms across his chest and glared at me. "I blame *you,* too."

I blinked. "Fine. I'm willing to take *some* of the blame. But you need to take some of it yourself, Geoffrey."

He didn't respond.

"I know I'm not perfect," I continued. "And I made some mistakes in this marriage and as a mom, too. But you have hurt *all* of us—Sarah and Jacob and me. You broke promises, Geoffrey. Important lifetime promises! And it's ironic. You're so angry at Jacob right now, but think about it, Geoffrey. You're no better than he is. You lied to us, you cheated us, you stole from us. And if you think you can just calmly walk away from your family as if nothing whatsoever is wrong…if you think you can run off and take a cruise with your new girlfriend and that life will go on just the same as usual, well, then you're going to be in for a few disappointments."

"Is that a threat?"

I shook my head. "No, no, not at all. I just want you to know that what goes around comes around, and even though it was wrong for Jacob to do"—I waved my hand at the mess that surrounded us—"*this,* I think maybe you had it coming." Then I walked out.

Okay, I wasn't *glad* that Jacob had done what he'd done. In fact, I was seriously worried, not only about his mental state, which seemed frightening enough, but also that he could end up in jail because of this. Of course, there was nothing I could do about it one way or another. And I tried to convince myself that maybe, just maybe, this might finally force Jacob to face up to the seriousness of his addiction problem. But what I'd said to Geoffrey was true; I *did* feel that he should bear some of the responsibility for Jacob's problems. No, it wasn't Geoffrey's fault that Jacob had started messing with drugs. But he had let Jacob down. A lot. And Jacob had often complained that his dad didn't love him or that he loved Sarah more.

So maybe this whole mess could be a good reminder to Geoffrey that, like Jacob had said in his note, "stuff is just stuff, but people feel pain." Maybe this was a lesson that Geoffrey needed to learn.

My biggest concern, as usual, was where Jacob was. What was he doing? And how long would it be before his whole world caved in on him? It seemed it could only be a matter of time.

Chapter 28

December

Then I get the phone call, which brings me back to the present and my drive toward Ambrose Park to meet my son. And despite all I've been through with him already, I am still worried about what I'll find there.

From my parking spot near the playground, through the mist I spot a hunched-over figure that I recognize as my son. He's sitting on a picnic table with his back to me. His olive drab coat, one that he got at the army surplus store, drapes over him like a small tent. If I didn't know better, I would think he was a bum. I suppose he is.

"Jacob?" I call from where I remain standing in the parking lot. I pull my jacket tighter around me and wait. It's a foggy kind of day where the freezing cold air crawls beneath your clothes with long, damp fingers. After what seems an unreasonable amount of time, he turns and looks at me, then slowly stands and meanders my way. His knit cap is encrusted with grime and pulled so low on his brow that it's hard to see his face, but he appears not to have shaved for days, and I can tell by the blank, dark look in his eyes that he's been using again. No surprises here.

Jacob's pattern seems to be to "binge on crystal meth." Or at least that's the way Marcus puts it. This terminology about drugs, addiction, and treatment is still something of a foreign language to me. But I am learning.

Without speaking, he gets into the car, and soon we are driving. I glance from the corner of my eye to see his head leaned against the window of the passenger side. He is already asleep. Probably coming down from his meth high. I can see that he's tired and sick and probably needs a good long rest, but I'm tempted to drive him straight over to Hope's Wings and simply drop him on their doorstep. However, I know that it will do no good. They will refuse to admit him unless he is willing to stay.

At a red light, I resist the urge to reach across the front seat and push a strand of greasy blond hair away from his face. It's obvious he could care less. Worried that he might be cold, although he appears to have several layers of clothing on beneath his oversize coat, I turn up the heater. I'm sure this layering of clothes is a trick he learned after his car was impounded and he was no longer able to spend nights sleeping in the back of it. I wonder if his "friend" Daniel kicked him out, but I don't think I will ask.

I wait for the light and watch as a young mom and two small boys cross the street. She's walking between them, securely holding on to their little hands. Bundled up against the cold, the boys both have flushed cheeks and happy smiles, and judging by the candy canes in their free hands, it looks as if they've just been to see Santa Claus at the minimall across the street. I vaguely recall a time when life was simple and sweet like that. Too bad I didn't fully realize or appreciate it then. I remember how I could hold on to my son's hand as we crossed the street and how he would cling tightly to mine. I never worried that he wouldn't make it to the other side. Now I'm not so sure.

It's hard to believe it's only two weeks until Christmas. I suppose I've been pretending that Christmas doesn't really exist this year. And it's too painful to imagine how it will feel to spend it with our family split up like this with Sarah in Arizona, me in my crummy little apartment, and Jacob…well, only God knows where Jacob will be by then.

The light turns green, and I get on the freeway for home, or what I have learned to call "home" during these past several months. But lately I've decided that little apartment is not my real home. It's not a place I'd care to live permanently. Despite the improvements I've made, I know I need to move on when my lease is up. If not sooner. Still, I am hesitant to look for another place. I worry my money will run out if I don't stick to my strictly regimented budget. I know I should probably get a job, and I've already checked into substitute teaching, but it seems to take all my energy to simply make it through one day and then face the next. Even so, I am plagued by the nagging fear that I will be completely broke someday. I wonder what will happen after my savings account is finally depleted. What will Jacob and I do then? Where will we live? It's not that my savings account was so small, but even so, it is steadily dwindling. I am slightly surprised that these are the thoughts trailing through my head right now. I am actually thinking about myself, my own welfare. Could it be that my codependency training is finally sinking in?

I glance back over at my son, or rather the remnants of my son. Besides being unshaven, his face is dirty, and several open sores look slightly infected. I recently read that this is another symptom of meth use. The sores resemble bad acne, something Jacob never had, but these nasty-looking lesions are caused by the toxic chemicals that have been injected into his bloodstream. Perhaps it's the tortured body's attempt to excrete the corrosive substance that is slowly killing it. But it makes this mother's heart sick.

The heater in my old Taurus has finally come to life, and the car is getting warmer now. I turn my attention back to my driving, but I can't help but wonder if life will ever change for Jacob. Will it ever get better? Or is my son one of the lonely ones—one of those unfortunate people destined for a life of addiction, failure, and finally and unavoidably an untimely death?

These thoughts pierce me like well-aimed arrows, but at least I am trying to be realistic now. I am trying to face facts and come to grips with this horrifying life my son has chosen. Oh, I still pray for him. How could

I not? But my prayers have slowly changed from begging and pleading tantrums to calmer petitions where I remind myself (and God, too?) that he is Jacob's Creator, Jacob's heavenly Father, and I believe that his love for Jacob is greater than mine. As difficult as it is, I know it's the only way I will survive this thing. I am entrusting my son to God.

Jacob moves slightly, and I glance over and wonder where he's been these past two weeks. What has he been doing? How long did the goods stolen from his father finance his habit? Was he sleeping in Dumpsters once his money was gone and he was too high to notice? Selling his plasma? Or perhaps he peddles his poor emaciated body to strangers? I know such things happen in Seattle. Even so, I can't bear to think about it.

I want to ask him about the break-in at his father's house, but I know he's in no condition to answer me right now. Perhaps that will come later. If there is a later. It's just as likely that he will sleep this off, eat some food, then disappear before I have a chance to question him. Besides, I know the answer. I know that he's responsible for the theft and vandalism at Geoffrey's. In the whole scheme of things, in the shadows of life and death, it seems a small thing now anyway.

Hot silent tears streak down my cheeks as I exit the freeway and head toward town. But as I wait at the light, before I turn down the street to the apartment complex, I hesitate. What am I doing right now? Haven't I been trying to remain firm on my boundaries? Haven't I made it clear that Jacob is not allowed to stay at my apartment unless he is willing to get help? Meaning residential rehab therapy like Marcus has recommended. But here I am, driving him home again—whatever is wrong with me?

Even as I drive toward the apartment, I don't know what to do. Despite my recent steps of faith—of giving Jacob to God—he is still my son. And I still desperately want him to get the help he needs. I pray silently as I approach the apartment, begging God to give me some direction, some help, some answers, something. And then I simply continue driving past.

Jacob *called* me, I remind myself, and he's the one who said he needed help. And it's true; he does need help. Well, maybe that's just what I will give him today—*help*. I continue driving with a resolve I've never felt before. It's as if some kind of force is pulling me down the road. I am going to Hope's Wings, and I hope I get there before he wakes up.

I don't know what else I can do. Of course, I realize that Jacob will probably get angry and defensive, and he may just storm away and perhaps never call me again. But, really, what else can I do? For all I know his life might be in danger from an overdose right now. I convince myself that I'm doing the right thing, and I pray for God to help me this time. Help *us*. Help this to work and help Jacob to see that he needs this.

Jacob abruptly sits up as the car comes to a stop and I turn off the engine. Looking around as if he's not sure where he is, he turns and stares at me. "What's going on?" he asks.

"You called me for help today, Jacob," I remind him.

He nods. "Yeah?"

"And I can't help you." I take a breath. "But this place can."

He looks across the parking lot to the drab buildings on the other side, frowning as full realization sets in. "Oh, Mom," he moans.

"You *need* treatment." I use the firmest voice I can muster. "If you continue using crystal meth, *you are going to die,* Jacob." I reach over and touch the shoulder of his filthy coat. "Can you hear me, Jacob? *You are going to die. Do you want to die?*"

He shakes his head. "No…"

"Then just try this," I tell him. "If it doesn't work, it doesn't work." Even as I say these words, I have absolutely no idea whether they can even take him right now. It's only a couple of weeks before Christmas, and I don't even know if there's a bed available. But I don't know what else to do, where else to go. I continue to pray silently now. Hoping for a miracle, I guess.

"I don't need this, Mom," he says, and I sense that his strength and resistance are returning to him.

"You *do* need this, Jacob. Without *this* you are going to die."

He closes his eyes tightly, as if trying to shut out my words.

"I don't want to lose you, Jacob," I tell him, choking back a sob. "I've seen Sherry after losing Matthew… I don't want that to happen to—"

"I'm *not* going to die, Mom." He sounds seriously agitated now. I know that I am pressing too hard.

I take a deep breath. I want to be strong, to play this out the best I can. "Okay, maybe you *won't* die, Jacob. At least not physically. But your soul is dying every single day that you continue using meth. Your spirit is dying."

"You don't know that."

"I *do* know that, Jacob. When I look in your eyes, I see emptiness, hopelessness. Death. How can you stand it? Don't you want to be alive again?"

"I *want* to get out of here," he says in a tight voice. "Let's go, Mom. *Now!*"

I know this is my last chance, and I feel desperate. Very desperate. I consider the one thing I've been holding back, my final possibility to persuade Jacob to rethink this thing. I know that it could either work or blow up in my face. And if history repeats itself, I should be prepared for an explosion.

"Okay," I finally say. "You say you're not going to die, Jacob. And maybe that's true. I certainly hope it's true. But how do you feel about going to prison?"

"Prison?" he looks at me and shakes his head. "Yeah, sure."

"It could happen, Jacob. In fact, it's quite likely."

"What are you talking about?"

"You made it very obvious that you broke into your dad's house, Jacob."

He looks surprised now, confused even. As if he barely remembers the incident, as if he never expected to be found out. *"What?"*

"You broke the law, Jacob. You vandalized and stole expensive items, I assume to be pawned for more drug money."

"Huh?"

"Maybe you don't remember it clearly, Jacob. I'm guessing you were high at the time. But, believe me, you left plenty of evidence behind. Notes, fingerprints, you name it. Not very smart unless you wanted to get caught. Did you want to get caught?"

He shrugs and looks away. I can tell he is getting very uncomfortable.

"Your father could press charges against you, Jacob. Maybe he already has. I don't know for sure, but he was very angry. Has it occurred to you that you could be picked up by the police at any time? That you could end up in jail and eventually prison? Is that what you want?"

"Do you think Dad would really do that to me?" He turns and looks at me with slightly frightened eyes, as if this is somehow penetrating the tough exterior that he has created to protect his addiction.

"What do you think, Jacob?"

He looks down at his lap now.

I reach over and put my hand on his hand. "But what if you were in treatment?" I ask in a gentle voice. "What if you were really seeking help, Jacob?"

He looks at me again. "You mean you're going to use this to pressure me into rehab?"

I shake my head. "Obviously, it's your choice, Jacob. You know as well as I do that they won't even admit you if you don't go in willingly. To be honest, I don't know if they even have room right now."

He frowns and sighs. "I don't know what to do, Mom."

"Jacob," I say. "Look at me."

He looks at me again.

"I am your mom, Jacob. I'm sure that I love you more than anyone on earth loves you. Do you honestly believe I would try to get you to do something that would hurt you? Have I ever tried to hurt you?"

He shakes his head.

"Have I ever lied to you?"

He shrugs now.

"When?" I demand. "When have I ever lied to you?"

His chapped lips curve into what is almost a smile. "The Easter bunny, tooth fairy, Santa Claus…"

I laugh and squeeze his hand. "Seriously, Jake. I would never deceive you. I would never do anything to hurt you. You can trust me."

"Was Dad really mad about the break-in?"

I nod. "I wouldn't lie to you, Jacob. He was furious."

"Do you think he called the police?"

"I honestly don't know, Jacob. He did say he was going to. But it's hard to tell with your dad. It could be pretty embarrassing, you know, that his own son burglarized his house. On the other hand, he was really angry. I don't know what he did."

Jacob looks toward the buildings now. "I guess it wouldn't be as bad as jail here. Do you think?"

"I wouldn't think so."

"But what if they can't take me today, Mom?"

I think he sounds honestly worried now, as if he's finally made up his mind to get treatment and will be devastated if he can't get in.

"All we can do is ask." I feel myself choking up again. "Do you want to go see?"

He nods and reaches for the door handle. Together we get out of the car and walk through the fog toward the main office building. I pray with each step. I pray for a miracle.

"Is Marcus here?" I ask the receptionist. This is a new girl I haven't met before, and I decide not to waste time trying to explain anything.

"Do you have an appointment?" she asks.

"No. Is he busy?" I glance up at the clock and see that it's twelve thirty, so it's entirely possible that he has left for lunch. I know he likes to go to a deli not far from here. Maybe I can find him there. Still, the idea of getting Jacob back into the car and away from Hope's Wings worries me. What if he suddenly changes his mind?

"Glennis!" calls a familiar voice, and I turn to see Marcus walking toward us.

"Hi," I say, trying to sound calm although I feel certain my eyes are giving me away. "Do you have a few minutes?"

He smiles. "Of course. Come on back to my office." He extends his hand to Jacob, waiting to shake. "How's it going, Jacob?"

"Okay." Jacob tentatively shakes Marcus's hand, then glances over his shoulder as if he's considering a fast break.

But Marcus puts his other hand on Jacob's shoulder and guides him back down the hallway. "How's your music coming along?"

"All right," mumbles Jacob as we go into the office.

Once we're seated I quickly tell Marcus that Jacob is interested in treatment now. Marcus, being the professional that he is, turns his attention to Jacob, ascertaining that this is really true.

"You really want to be here?" he asks, studying Jacob's face closely.

Jacob swallows, then nods.

"This is a decision you're making of your own free will?"

Jacob nods again.

"You really want help? You want to change?"

Then Jacob begins to tear up, and I grow worried that the emotion will make him change his mind. I know how he hates crying in front of anyone.

"All right then," says Marcus quickly. "You're in luck, Jacob. We just got a vacancy this morning."

Jacob looks back up at Marcus, and his face actually looks relieved. I wonder if I might faint. "What do we do?" I ask, afraid this is all just a dream that will blow up in my face again.

"You don't need to do anything, Glennis," he tells me.

I feel confused now. What does this mean?

"You're free to go." He nods to the door.

"Just like that?" I ask, standing.

He smiles at me, probably to reassure me that everything is fine. "You've already done the paperwork, Glennis. Of course, Jacob will have to sign some things himself. Then we'll take him over to detox and get him a room and maybe some lunch if he's hungry." He looks at Jacob now. "I think it's meat loaf today, but don't let that discourage you. It's really pretty good. I thought I'd have some myself."

"So I just leave then?" I repeat.

Marcus nods.

"Okay." Then I pause by Jacob, and leaning down, I tell him I love him and that I'm proud of him. "Everything's going to be okay," I assure him as I move toward the door. "I know you're in good hands now."

He sort of nods but doesn't look completely convinced. I can tell he's starting to get the jitters now. I suspect it's not so much out of anxiety as a side effect of the meth. And then I walk out of Marcus's office, down the hall, out of the building, and across the parking lot to my car.

I feel like a war veteran as I slowly drive home from Hope's Wings. I remember this old guy who used to live next door to my parents when I was a kid. He'd survived World War II but had lost a leg. I remember how he used to say he could still feel the pain of that missing leg sometimes. I think he called it "phantom pain." And that's how I feel right now. Like Jacob is still in the car with me. Still hunched over and hurting and hopeless. And I am still hurting for him. Phantom pain. I wonder if it will ever go away.

Chapter 29

Feeling slightly stunned after I get back to the apartment, I walk around in a daze for nearly an hour and even begin to wonder if I simply imagined my entire morning. I pick up the phone, then set it down again, fighting the urge to call Hope's Wings and ask if Jacob Harmon is really there, really enrolled, and getting treatment. Then I realize it's entirely possible that he may have gotten cold feet after I left. He might have refused to sign the papers and be admitted. He could be walking back toward town this very minute. Even so, I don't allow myself to call. Not yet.

Instead I gather up my things and go downstairs to do the laundry.

"Glennis," says Jack as he sees me turning toward the laundry room, "how're you doing?"

"I'm not sure, Jack."

He opens the door for me. "Something wrong?"

"Not exactly." I set down my laundry basket and remove my backpack. "I took Jacob to Hope's Wings this morning."

He slaps me on the back. "That's great news."

I nod. "I know it is. But I think I'm still in shock." Then I tell him the whole story, still questioning whether it really happened or not.

"You need to take a deep breath," he tells me, "and just relax."

"I'm not sure if I even know how," I admit.

"It takes time," he tells me as he opens the lid of the washer for me.

I put my dirty laundry into the washer, pour in the soap, insert my quarters, and wait for the water to start coming in. Then I turn and look at Jack. "It's so amazing," I tell him, finally allowing myself to smile. "I think it's a real miracle, Jack."

He nods. "But it's only just beginning, Glennis. It's up to Jacob to make the miracle work."

"Right." I feel myself deflating again.

"But it's a great start, Glennis." He smiles broadly. "And the Bible says not to despise small beginnings."

"Yes. I'm sure you're right, Jack. But in some ways I'm almost afraid to believe the whole thing. It seems so unreal."

"Well, take it easy on yourself. Give it a few days to sink in."

I pick up my laundry backpack as Jack opens the door for me again. "Thanks," I tell him, "for everything."

"I'm not done praying for your boy yet," he says as we walk outside together. "He's got a long road ahead of him, and old Jack here is going to be praying every day that Jacob gets there in one piece."

"I appreciate it." Then I go back upstairs and sit down on the sofa and wonder what to do. But I am so tired and drained that all I can do is lie down and fall asleep. But it is a good sleep. Perhaps the best sleep I have ever had.

I'm surprised to wake at the sound of the phone's loud ring, and just the same as before—as if nothing has changed at all—I rush for the phone, worried that it's bad news.

"Hello?" I say breathlessly.

"Glennis," Marcus says in a calm voice. "How are you doing?"

"Oh…" My relief is overcome by fear. "Is he still there?" I ask quickly. "Did Jacob stay?"

Marcus chuckles. "Yes. I thought you might be worried. He's still here. He's signed all of the appropriate forms and agreed to stay with us until he is well."

I sigh now, deeply. I feel like maybe I can breathe again. "Thank you so much for calling," I tell him. "Can you tell me how he's doing?"

"Well, as you can imagine, it's pretty rough at first. But the staff is used to this sort of thing. Don't worry, Glennis. He's getting the best treatment."

"Good." Still, I'm not sure. I feel personally responsible if anything goes wrong.

"I may even stick around here myself tonight," he continues. "To keep an eye on things."

"Really? Does that mean it's serious? Is Jacob in any danger?"

"No, not really. But the first couple of days are always the hardest. And he's got a lot of crud in his system. He must've really had some binge. Poor guy."

"I'm so glad he agreed to stay." I sit down in the rocking chair and feel my shoulders relax a bit. "I can hardly believe this is finally happening."

"It usually takes a while for it to really sink in," he says.

"It's like I don't know what to do with myself."

"It's time for you to take care of yourself, Glennis."

"I know…" And I *think* I do know, but then I'm not sure.

"No, I mean *really.* You've been under an incredible amount of stress. And you've made some progress. But it's time for you to get serious about your own welfare."

"What do you suggest?"

"Whatever makes you feel good. Just take it easy, relax, unwind, let it soak in that Jacob is in recovery. *Just breathe,* Glennis."

I almost laugh. "Do you know you're the second person to say that to me today?"

"Who was the first?"

"Jack. He met me doing laundry."

"Well, Jack is right."

"Which reminds me," I say. "My laundry is still in the washer downstairs."

"Why don't you just leave it?"

"The management doesn't like it when you do that."

"Well, remember what I said. Just enjoy this time, Glennis. Take it easy and don't forget to breathe."

"Thanks."

I hang up the phone and put on my jacket and prepare to go down to the laundry room. But there in front of my door, just like before, is my basket with my dry and neatly folded laundry and a little note pinned on the top. "He who dwells in the secret place of the Most High shall abide under the shadow of the Almighty. I will say of the Lord, 'He is my refuge and my fortress; My God, in Him I will trust.' Psalm 91:1-2."

I'm beginning to believe that there are, and have been, angels watching over me these past several months. I bring in my clean laundry and close the door, then sit down and contemplate some way I can show my appreciation to Jack.

When I was a little girl, growing up in my conservative and fundamentalist Christian home, I adhered to the belief that if I did everything just right, if I did my very best...then life would go well for me. Now I realize that may not be true. Oh, it's not that I think I should throw in the towel and just give up. But I no longer see my life as predictable. I've given up on the expectation that my "good behavior" controls the outcome of my life. In fact, I think the only thing I really control (and I'm not even sure about this) is my own choices. And that's it. But maybe that's the way God wants it to be. Maybe this feeling of vulnerability and helplessness is what makes us keep running back to him. It works for me.

Tomorrow is Christmas. But you wouldn't know this to look around my apartment. Other than the few Christmas cards on my coffee table, there are no signs of the holiday here. This is unusual for me, since I've always been one of those women who decorate every available surface. But this year is different. It's not that I'm depressed so much as that I am trying to be thoughtful and intentional. I don't need stuffed Santas or snowmen or jolly sprigs of holly to remind me of the gift God has given.

I felt a little bad when Sarah begged me to join her at my mother's house, but I knew this was more than I could do. I simply told her that I needed to be here for Jacob.

"I don't mean to sound jealous," she told me, "but it seems you've given enough to him."

"I know," I assured her. "And if he wasn't in rehab right now, I think I would've considered leaving town."

"But if he's in rehab, he should be okay."

"Yeah, that's sort of true, Sarah. But for rehab to really be successful, they encourage the support of family members. I go once a week for the family meetings, and they'll have this special program on Christmas Eve that they really want family to attend. It's my way of showing Jacob that I haven't given up on him."

"Do you think I should come home for it?" she asked suddenly.

"Oh, honey, it's so sweet that you'd even consider doing this."

"Well, should I come or not?"

"I think you should come if you really want to come, Sarah. It's your decision. And if you can't do this, I don't think you should feel bad about it."

There was a long pause. "I guess I don't really want to come," she finally admitted. "But if you thought it would help him—"

"Don't worry about it," I assured her. "But if you have time to write Jake a note or a card, I think that might help him as much as a visit."

"I'll do that, Mom," she promised.

And she kept her word and did it. And now I have this card along with a few other things all bagged up and ready to take over to Hope's Wings tonight.

Is this really how I wanted to spend Christmas Eve? I ask myself as I scrape a thin layer of ice from my windshield. Hanging out with a bunch of addicts and their sad-eyed families in the drab rehab-center activities room? Then I remind myself of how life felt just a few weeks ago, and I am surprised that I can even question this, but I suppose I'm just a little emotionally drained.

Still, I know this is far better than being home alone in my apartment and wondering whether Jacob is dead or alive. Count your blessings, I tell myself as the engine in my car finally turns over. Besides, I remember as I pull out into the street, Marcus will be there tonight. I turn on the radio, and it's not long before I am smiling and humming to the Christmas music as I drive across town. To be honest, I am warmed at the thought of not only seeing Jacob clean and sober but also spending some time with Marcus as well. Really, life is not so bad.

"Merry Christmas, Mom!" calls Jacob as soon as I enter the room. He is instantly by my side, taking my coat and smiling just as he used to smile back in the old days.

"Merry Christmas," I tell him as we hug. Then I hand him the bag. The "gifts" I brought for him are only practical items like shaving cream and socks and boxers, and all remain unwrapped (as specified in the party invitation), and no edibles are allowed since there is always the concern that drugs might be sneaked in through food. Although why a loved one would smuggle contraband into this place is way beyond me. I can't imagine emerging from all I've been through to get Jacob into this place just so I could sneak him in a stocking full of needles and crystal meth.

Just the same, I had to pass through the "detox" entrance where Molly (tonight's "guard") inspected everything to make sure it was acceptable. They even go through your purse and pockets when you come to visit.

Marcus told me that I'd be amazed at the lengths some recovery patients will go to in order to get a friend or family member to smuggle something past the "guards."

"Then why are they here?" I asked him.

"Some are trying to get out of being sentenced for a drug-related crime," he told me. "They say the right things and act like they're here for the right reasons, but later we find out it was really a scam to avoid the rap."

Of course, that only reminded me of the pressure I'd put on Jacob to agree to treatment. I hadn't actually told Marcus about that yet. Hadn't told anyone. Not even Geoffrey when I called to tell him the good news about Jacob's recovery, just in case he wanted to visit his son, which didn't seem likely.

"Well, I suppose it's better than nothing," Geoffrey had said, clearly unimpressed.

"Yes," I'd agreed, ready to end the conversation quickly. Then to my surprise my ex-husband admitted that he hadn't told the police that the break-in was Jacob's doing.

"But I thought you said that you *called* them?" I asked, feeling confused. "Didn't you have the police come up to the house?"

"Yes."

"But couldn't they tell by the notes and the fingerprints that—"

"I took care of all that." He loudly cleared his throat. "And if you want to help keep your son out of trouble, you'd better keep that little bit of information to yourself."

"What do you mean, Geoffrey?" I demanded. "You took care of *what?*"

"The incriminating evidence."

"You tampered with evidence?" I felt stunned now. Geoffrey was a lawyer; he knew better than to do something like this.

"Look, Glennis," he said in a gentle voice. "Jacob doesn't need me to add to his problems."

"Yes," I agreed, still shocked. "I…uh…I suppose that's generous of you."

"And the less we say about any of this, the better."

"That's fine with me."

So we said good-bye and hung up in a very civilized way, and I even wondered if this divorce might actually proceed in the controlled and dignified fashion that Geoffrey Harmon hoped for.

Of course, I later learned through Sarah that Geoffrey was getting a very nice insurance settlement for the damaged and stolen items. Naturally, I didn't mention her brother's involvement in the break-in. Nor did I mention her father's unethical behavior in covering it up. Perhaps some things really are better left unsaid. I'm still not sure.

"Merry Christmas, Glennis," says Marcus as he comes up from behind. I turn around to see him wearing a rather garish red and green Christmas sweater. I try not to wince at the clashing colors.

"It's a gift," he explains, nodding over to where an overweight young woman is seated on the sofa. She seems intently focused on a knitting project, and the yarn is a bright orange shade that would probably be welcomed by a highway worker. "Janice made this for me," he tells me in a slightly louder voice. "For Christmas."

"It's very festive," I say, smiling at Janice. She looks up and smiles back. "It looks like you're a fast knitter," I tell her.

She nods. "I do this to keep my mind off of other things."

"Yeah," says Jacob, "and we all know what those other things are, don't we, Janice?"

Several others make comments, and I am amazed, once again, at the openness of these people to discuss their addiction problems with such candor. I've heard them admit to all sorts of things and even joke about them. Marcus says that's just part of their recovery, and I must admit that it's helped me to lighten up a bit about the whole thing. Not that I take addiction lightly. I still don't. But more and more I am realizing that addiction is just another element of the human condition. Whether it's chocolate, coffee, or sugar, I suppose we're all addicted to something.

The patients (or clients as Marcus calls them; Jacob still calls them inmates) perform a little Christmas play for us. A quiet young man named Oliver wrote it, and it's really not bad, although their acting abilities range from stuttering stage fright to a thirty-something woman who later tells me that she's destined for Broadway. "Once I'm clean and sober," she admits as she pours herself some red punch.

The highlight of the evening (for the patients) is when they get to go outside for a cigarette break. "It's their only legal vice," Marcus reminds me as we stand out in the icy cold and wait. The patients huddle together like an elite little club, puffing and joking among themselves, impervious to the cold night air.

"Does everyone in the program smoke?" I ask Marcus.

"They usually do by the time they leave." He laughs. "But, hey, it's better than some things. And some of them are just social smokers."

This reminds me of the time I smoked in the church parking lot with Sherry. I suppose smoking's not so bad, although I wonder how hard it will be for them to break this habit once they're on the outside. However, I also know from my classes here that it will be even harder for them to stay clean and sober. That's the real challenge. The counselors here make no secret of the fact that most of the patients will blow it within the first month of being back on the outside.

"You almost have to expect it," Marcus told me after I questioned him about this statistic last week.

"But what do you do?"

"*You* don't do anything, Glennis. It will be Jacob's problem to solve."

"But how will he know—"

"Don't worry. This is what he's learning right now. He'll know exactly what to do, what steps to take to get back on track. The question will be whether or not he is willing to do it."

I sighed in frustration. "Then we're right back—"

"No," he assured me. "Just remember it's a process. A day-by-day process."

I consider this as I watch these people bunched together with a white cloud of smoke forming over their heads. I wonder how many of them will make it all the way through this process. How many of them will make it clear to the other side? And how many will be clean and sober one year or two from now?

"Hey, it's snowing!" yells Jacob, pointing up to the flakes that are illuminated in the overhead light. And soon they are all out in the parking lot dancing like children among the falling flakes. They are laughing and whooping and getting totally silly about the change in weather. And it occurs to me that they are having a really good time...*without* drugs. And suddenly I feel surprisingly hopeful and happy too.

After the cigarette break we go back inside, and with Jacob's accompaniment on guitar, we sing Christmas carols for a while. Then we visit and eat the treats that were prepared by the patients, and finally it's nearly eleven, and the party begins breaking up. But first Marcus invites the visiting friends and family members to attend the midnight candlelight service at his church.

"We're all going over there in the bus," he explains. "But you're welcome to follow in your cars if you like."

So my old Taurus joins the peculiar pilgrimage as we parade across town toward Marcus's church. I vaguely wonder what Geoffrey would think if he could see Jacob and me tonight. Jacob, as one of the motley crew of inmates riding on the decrepit bus with "Hope's Wings" painted in bold purple letters across both sides. Or me in my Taurus, trailing a bunch of other equally old and beat-up cars. I'm sure he'd want to pretend he didn't know either of us, like we'd never been a part of his immaculate little family. But maybe that doesn't matter so much anymore. Maybe it's time that we all learn to stand on our own feet.

The candlelight service turns out to be the best I've ever attended. And when it's over, I have tears in my eyes as Jacob turns and thanks me for pushing him to get treatment.

"Things are really going to be different," he promises. "I don't ever want to go back to my old life, Mom."

Well, that's the best Christmas present anyone could've given me this year. And despite all the changes in my life, the heartbreaks, the disappointments, the challenges, I feel like maybe it's worth it to have my son back again.

Chapter 30

I wish I could say that we all lived happily ever after, that my worries were over, and that Jacob never stumbled again once he "graduated" from his inpatient rehab treatment, but it wouldn't be honest, or even fair.

Naturally, I was pleased and proud to attend Jacob's graduation ceremony at Hope's Wings in mid-January. All of the patients made a little speech, but I felt Jacob's was totally amazing. Oh, I realize he's my son, and I see things through a mother's eyes. But in my opinion, he was truly a new man. His big brown eyes were clear and bright. His smile was genuine. And best of all, he was truly happy. I have no doubt about that.

The little graduation was held in the activity room at Hope's Wings. Sarah came home from school in order to attend the ceremony with me. And to everyone's surprise, Geoffrey showed up as well. I didn't even notice him at first. Like me on my first visit at Hope's Wings, he, too, lingered near the back of the room, clearly uncomfortable with these unfamiliar surroundings that have come to feel like a second home to me. But I have to give him this, he did come up and shake Jacob's hand afterward. He even said a few kind words. And for a brief time, even Geoffrey was a believer in the rehab program at Hope's Wings.

But our relief was short-lived. For, as we all know by now, there is no *sure thing* in rehab treatment. It's all up to the addict to live out his plan, to make that daily decision to remain clean, to attend his meetings, to meet with his mentor, to succeed at his recovery. And to be perfectly fair, circumstances do play a small role as well. But this role is highly overrated by the addict himself. Especially if he's still in denial.

Jacob got a job with a janitorial service within a week of his graduation. I was surprised that he was willing to clean toilets to earn money, but he assured me that he was perfectly fine with this sort of menial labor.

"I feel like I have to pay my dues," he told me as he showed me his gray uniform. "Kind of work my way back up through the system, you know."

"I'm really proud of you," I said.

"And I'll be able to take classes and still work," he told me. "I think I'll try to start going to SSCC during spring term."

"That's great."

And it was great. For one whole month it was absolutely great. I felt like life had really returned to normal by then. Of course, anyone involved with a drug addict should realize that normal doesn't exist anymore.

Then one day when I'm not looking, it all falls apart. In one evening, in early February, it all just seems to go to pieces.

Of course, Jacob tells me that it's not his fault. That he was just minding his own business last night, scrubbing a hallway floor in a local business, when some jerk shoved him and made the bucket of dirty mop water go everywhere.

"It just kept getting worse and worse," he explains the next day after I've been called to come to the emergency room to help pick up the pieces of my son's recently shattered life.

"My boss showed up and really tore into me," he tells me as the nurse rechecks his blood pressure. "And I was so sick of it, sick of everything—cleaning up other people's messes, never being appreciated for anything." He shakes his head and quietly lets out a curse. "Well, that was it. I just walked out. And then I was on my way home, and I ran into an old friend…" And on his story goes until he is telling me how his friend offered to hook him up with some "good stuff." Before the night was over, Jacob had binged on an undisclosed amount of crystal meth and somehow made it to the emergency room before it was too late.

"I guess being clean made it easier for me to overdose," he tells me with some embarrassment, as if his previous ability to use a lot of meth to get high was some sort of an accomplishment.

Jacob doesn't even know who called 911, which resulted in a trip to the hospital, where it was impossible to hide his substance abuse. Of course, Marcus later assures me that this was really a blessing in disguise.

"You might not have found out about it otherwise," he reminds me after I pour out the whole overdose story. "Or, even worse, he might've died."

"I know," I say as the tears finally start to gather. Jacob has gone to bed now, and after keeping up a cool, calm exterior all day, I feel like it's finally my turn to experience some emotion. "I just don't understand why…"

"This is just the way it goes sometimes, Glennis."

"But he was doing so well," I tell him between sobs. I am not ready to go down this road again, feeling so hopeless and discouraged.

"He *was*," Marcus says. "But you have to understand that this happens. The addict is doing just fine, and then something happens that acts like a trigger. Usually it's something stressful, although I've heard all sorts of excuses. I remember this woman who had been clean for nearly a year. She told me how she was out shopping for a pair of shoes for her sister's wedding when she *just happened to find* a bag of meth sitting on a bench in the mall. And, well, she was feeling so stressed about not finding the right shoes that she just decided to get high. Does that make any sense to you?"

"No." It's almost funny. "She found a bag of meth?"

He laughs. "That's what she said. And, you're right, it makes absolutely no sense to us. But to an addict, especially early on during rehab, it's always a daily thing. They're constantly asking themselves, will I get high today or will I stay clean? And, believe me, any excuse is a good excuse if they have decided that they're going to get high. Really, I've heard them all."

"But what do we do now?"

"*We* don't do anything. It's up to Jacob."

"I know, I know..." Sometimes I get so sick of all this codependent talk. "But he's staying here in my apartment," I remind Marcus. "I feel I have some responsibility or authority. Shouldn't I say anything?"

"You can remind him to call his mentor. Or he can talk to me if he wants."

"What if he doesn't want to?"

I hear him sigh and know exactly what he is thinking.

"I'm sorry, Marcus," I say. "I already know the answers to these questions, don't I?"

"Yeah, but it doesn't make it any easier, does it?"

The kindness in his voice only brings more tears to the surface. "Thanks," I tell him. "I don't know how I would've survived all this without you."

Jacob does call his mentor the next day. And he attends an NA meeting that night and three more the following week. But then he blows it again. Of course, he is very contrite and sorry afterward and promises me that it's the last time he'll mess up like that. But it's not. And back and forth he goes until I must finally tell him he has to either stay clean or move out of my apartment, which I've already given notice on anyway. This is despite the fact that I have no place to move to. But Jacob seems to flounder like this for about a month until he finally comes to me and tells me that he thinks he needs to go back to Hope's Wings for inpatient treatment again.

"This time I want to do it for me," he tells me. "I think I did it to avoid that whole thing with Dad last time. And even though I appreciated getting clean, I was kind of resentful about a lot of stuff."

Well, I honestly don't care what his reason for succeeding or not succeeding is; I only want him to get whatever kind of help he needs and quickly. Jake calls Marcus that same day and is accepted back into the inpatient program starting in early March. In the meantime, it seems that he is staying clean and working his program. But I can't be certain. Mostly I am relieved when March 5 rolls around and it's time to take him back in. He seems quiet and sad as we drive over, but it's not like the last time, not like he is unhappy to be going into rehab. It's more as if he regrets blowing it.

As I get back into my car, I try to assure myself that this is a normal step in Jake's recovery, that it's a good thing he wants more help. Even so, I feel anything but hopeful as I drive away. And after a few minutes my eyes are so blurry from tears that I am forced to pull over.

I get out of my car and slam the door. I want to yell at God, to shake my fist at the sky and to blame him for what seems to be this continual and never-ending mess in my life. But suddenly I am aware of the unexpected spring sunshine that's warming my head. And I see the bright green of fresh grass and notice that tulips and daffodils are blooming and the delicate pink buds on the plum trees are just starting to open. And I realize that no one can be angry with God on a day like this.

Instead, I begin to walk, and that's when I notice that I have stopped next to a small neighborhood park. I've probably driven past it before, but I honestly don't remember seeing it. I'm sure that's because I have always had other things on my mind as I travel back and forth from Hope's Wings. But the park is old and quaint with metal swings and an ancient-looking merry-go-round. Other than an elderly woman walking a small dog on the other side, the park is deserted. But all the lovely blooming trees and flowers seem to beg to be enjoyed. And so I slowly walk through it, and as I walk, I begin to pray. And, once again, I surrender Jacob to God.

"You'd think I'd know this by now," I admit. "That you created and designed Jacob. That he's as much, or probably more, yours than he is mine. And I believe you know what you're doing in his life." I stop and take a deep breath. "And so I give him back to you, God. Do as you like with him."

I continue to walk until I come to a quiet little neighborhood that borders the other side of the park. The houses are small and old-fashioned, but something about them draws me, and as strange as it seems, I almost feel at home here.

And then I see it—a For Sale by Owner sign pounded into the dirt in front of a rather forlorn little house that's painted the color of a dirty old sock. I pause and look at the sad little house and its neglected yard, and I know I must have it.

Of course, I've never purchased a house before and don't even know if I can afford one now, although I have offered to sign a divorce settlement with Geoffrey that I think, along with my savings, might just cover the price of a modest home. But how does one go about something like this? What are the proper steps? And is this crazy?

Suddenly I know who to call, and by four o'clock that same afternoon, Sherry is leading me through the vacant house and pointing out all of its weaknesses as well as its strengths. Unfortunately, according to Sherry, the weaknesses seem to outweigh the strengths. Although she does admit that the house has potential.

"It's a good neighborhood," she says.

"And how about that guesthouse in back?" I remind her. "Wouldn't that be great for Jacob?"

"But it'll be a lot of work," she tells me as she locks the front door.

"Work is good," I say with determination.

"And it'll take money to make the repairs."

This gives me pause. "Don't you think I can do a lot of it myself?"

"Maybe…"

"Well, I want it," I finally tell her.

"Now, Glennis, you need to realize that some people make decisions to buy houses with their heads, and others make decisions with their hearts."

I nod. "Then this is definitely a heart decision. But, really, I have a strong feeling that it's the right decision. Just call it a God thing."

"Well, I can't deny that it's a good location, Glennis." She glances over to the little park. "I can't believe someone hasn't snapped it up by now."

"Well, let's not waste another minute."

She smiles now. "Okay, let's go to my office and write up an offer."

We meet at her office, and after the paperwork is finished, we go out for coffee to celebrate, although she reminds me this is premature. Naturally, I have to give her the latest news on Jacob, and she is understandably disappointed. But I take the high road, and, sounding a lot like Marcus, I explain that it's just part of the recovery process.

"The good thing is that it was totally his choice to check into treatment this time," I finally tell her.

"Well, I hope that it works." She sighs. "I'm still praying for that boy."

"Thanks." I want to ask how she's doing. It's been several months since losing Matthew. But I'm afraid I'll only make her sad if I bring it up.

"Mark's getting excited about graduation," she tells me.

"He's graduating this year?" I shake my head. "How did that happen so soon?"

"Yes, but now he's decided to go for his master's."

"You must be so proud of him, Glennis."

She smiles. "I am."

We chat some more, and it occurs to me how perfectly normal and happy we must appear to a casual observer. Just two middle-aged women meeting for coffee and chatting about their children. Oh, if only they knew. If only they knew...

——

Time graciously passes, and it's late August now, and my garden looks better than I ever imagined possible. Especially after getting a late start on planting, since the divorce settlement didn't come until April, and I didn't actually take possession until early May. By then I knew it was too late to grow anything from seed, and so I got some wonderful seedlings from the little nursery that's only four blocks away. But everything just took off. Even my neighbors are impressed with my green thumb, and I've been giving away tomatoes and cucumbers and zucchini by the wheelbarrow load.

Besides cleaning up the yard and putting in the garden, the first thing I did to my little house was to paint its exterior, transforming it from dirty-sock beige to buttery yellow. If I do say so myself, it was quite an improvement. But that was only the beginning. I'm pretty certain that my hands have gone over every square inch of my little house by now. Well, not the roof; I left that to the professionals. But I have refinished the hardwood floors, repainted the walls and cabinets, and even replaced some of the broken windowpanes. It's amazing what they can teach you to do at Home Depot these days. I've also sewn curtains and decorated it in "shabby chic," causing some of my friends and neighbors to think I should attempt to make a living doing this sort of thing. And I might just do that.

Having and fixing up my own little house has probably been the best form of therapy I've found so far. And it's good to have Winnie and Rufus back too. Mrs. Fieldstone insisted on delivering them to me herself so she could have a tour of my new place.

"It's perfectly lovely," she told me, although it was still pretty torn up at the time. "I can imagine a divine garden party in this backyard."

Jacob graduated again from Hope's Wings in early April, and he has been surprisingly helpful in restoring my house. I let him do as he liked with the guesthouse, his quarters for the time being and for as long as he remains clean and sober. I was somewhat surprised when he painted the interior walls an odd shade of aqua blue, but it looked quite nice once his things were in place. So far, Jacob has worked his recovery program and stayed clean. He's even held the same job since May. He's also enrolled for classes at the local college, and I am feeling hopeful.

Do I think we're out of the woods yet? Not at all. I didn't get this far in the recovery process for nothing. I know as well as anyone that it's still a day-by-day thing, and I suppose I won't rest completely easy until Jacob has been clean for a couple of years or more. Just the same, I sleep much better at nights when I remind myself to put my son back into God's hands. I've come to accept that only God's hands are big enough to hold something as overwhelming and daunting as a loved one who's an addict.

But today is a happy day, because I am finally having that garden party that Mrs. Fieldstone recommended. And besides her, I am inviting Jack and my other friends from the apartments as well as Sherry and some of my new church friends and even Sylvia from the grocery outlet store. And, of course, Marcus will be here too. I'm not sure whether Jacob will make it home on time or not, but I did tell him that even though it's mostly older people, he's more than welcome to join us. Even so, I won't be worried or fretful if he doesn't show up. I know he's got friends and things to do too.

My life's certainly not perfect by any means. I still have my ups and downs and doubts that come knocking in the middle of the night. In some ways I'm as much in the recovery process as my son—it's definitely a daily thing for me, too. But I have come to accept something. Or almost.

I guess I'd better be careful lest I fall flat on my face tomorrow. But I have decided that God never meant for life to be perfect or easy or even what we might consider normal. I mean, just look around this crazy old world at all the hardships to be found along the way, and you'll have to agree that this must be true. Bad things happen to everyone. And I believe that God fully intended for us to struggle along, sometimes wading right through the middle of waist-high crud. But even so, he still wants us to trust him; he wants us to hold on to him as we muck our way through these unfortunate life messes. And I believe our reward is to become stronger in the end.

Not only that, but we get to make some wonderful friends as we journey along—the kind of friends who know how to stick by each other even when life isn't tidy or neat or easy. Those are *real* friends, and I have learned to appreciate them. Because I don't believe that God ever meant for us to do this thing called Life alone.

1. The Harmon family seems somewhat blindsided by Jacob's drug problems. What signs were perhaps missed? Do you think anything would've played out differently if they'd been more aware of Jacob's susceptibility to chemical addiction? If so, what?

2. Early in the story Glennis portrays her family as rather "picture perfect." Do you think she really believed this? Why or why not? Why do we sometimes believe what we want to believe?

3. Glennis didn't seem to know that her marriage was in trouble when she left Geoffrey. When do you think their marital problems began? What could they have done differently?

4. Glennis had a classic codependent personality. Why do you think she was like this? What do you see as the negative and/or positive traits of someone who is codependent? Do you see any of these traits in yourself?

5. Glennis had difficulty discerning the difference between loving and enabling. How would you distinguish between them? What guidelines do you use to determine this in your own life?

6. Sarah had almost completely disengaged herself from her brother and his problems. Do you think this was selfish or self-preserving or both? Explain.

7. What factors do you think were most critical to Glennis's discovery that she was part of the problem? Where did she find her best sources of help? If you were in her situation, where would you go for help?

8. Glennis's marriage was in worse shape than she had originally thought. Do you think she should have done something differently? What would you have done in a similar situation?

9. Were you surprised when Sherry's son Matthew died? Some may view this as a departure from the story line about Glennis and Jacob. In your opinion, what was its role and significance in this story?

10. *Crystal Lies* is as much about codependency as addiction. Did this story change any of your attitudes toward people who become caught in these traps? Do you know anyone who's dealing with these issues? Do you view addicts and codependents differently now that you've read this book? Explain.

BOOKS

Beyond Codependency: And Getting Better All the Time by Melody
Beattie

*Codependent No More: How to Stop Controlling Others and Start
Caring for Yourself* by Melody Beattie

Cracked: Putting Broken Lives Together Again: A Doctor's Story by
Drew Pinsky

WEB SITES

Do It Now! Foundation—www.doitnow.org/pages/101.html

Crystal Meth—www.crystal-meth.us/

Crystal Meth Anonymous (CMA)—www.crystalmeth.org/

About the Author

Over the years Melody Carlson has worn many hats, from preschool teacher to youth counselor to political activist to senior editor. But most of all, she loves to write! Currently she freelances from her home. In the past nine years, she has published more than 100 books for children, teens, and adults—with sales totaling more than two million and many titles appearing on the ECPA Bestsellers List. Several of her books have been finalists for, and winners of, various writing awards, including the ECPA Gold Medallion Award and the Rita Award. She has two grown sons and lives in Central Oregon with her husband and chocolate Lab retriever. They enjoy skiing, hiking, gardening, camping, and biking in the beautiful Cascade Mountains.

Faced with her son's crystal meth addiction and her husband's affair, Glennis Harmon searches for the ways she can best reach and help those she deeply loves.

Real-life struggles. A family's pain.
A hope for healing.

Bright and ambitious, college student Alice Laxton is diagnosed with schizophrenia—and embarks on a painful and eye-opening journey toward recovery and healing.

Available in bookstores everywhere.

WATERBROOK PRESS
www.waterbrookpress.com